THE ... STARDOM

When the door had closed on their guests, Dana looked at Don uncertainly. She hated having him disapprove of anything she did. "I'm sorry, darling. I was listening to them talk about their jobs, and it just slipped out. But I meant it. I have to go back to work."

Don went to the coffee table, picked up his brandy glass, emptied it. "You really think you have talent, hmm?"

"Yes, I do. That's part of the problem. When you think you can do something, then you want to try. If you don't, there's an important part of you that isn't being used."

He walked to the window, and she stared at the solid set of his shoulders, wondering what he was thinking. "All right," he said at last. "I'll make a bargain with you. You can try it for a year. If you really have talent, you should have some recognition by then. If not, you have to promise me you'll give it up completely and concentrate on being my wife again."

She went and put her arms around him and leaned her cheek against the white crispness of his shirt. For a moment she was silent, savoring the strength, the authority, the unequivocal maleness of him. She wanted so much to please him, always. "All right. I accept the bargain."

"Good." He kissed to top of her head. "Come to bed."

(Cover photograph posed by professional model)

Wives and Lovers

T. A. GABRIEL

LEISURE BOOKS   NEW YORK CITY

For
Shirley, Jackie, Dorothy, Linda,
Jeremy, and Michael

A LEISURE BOOK

Published by

Dorchester Publishing Co., Inc.
6 East 39th Street
New York, NY 10016

Copyright©1986 by T.A. Gabriel

All rights reserved. No part of this book may be reproduced or transmitted in any form or by any electronic or mechanical means, including photocopying, recording, or by any information storage and retrieval system, without the written permission of the Publisher, except where permitted by law.

Printed in the United States of America

Wives and Lovers

Prologue

After the creation of Adam, God fashioned from the same clay a woman called Lilith. But Lilith would not obey Adam on the pretext that being formed from the same clay she was his equal. God was then constrained to create a new woman named Eve, whom he took from Adam's side that she might have no cause to boast of her origin.

This is Dana's story, whose real name is Lilith, although she does not know it yet. She sits in front of a television set with her arms around her small son, watching, listening with a strange absorption. Beyond the glass wall at the end of the living room, Los Angeles lies baking in the afternoon sun of a day in early September. The Santa Ana, the hot wind from the desert inland, has been blowing for two days, and there is no smog. In the clear air the view is magnificent, but she has not pulled open the draperies to admire it. Instead, she sits and watches the screen in utter concentration, and her eyes, the deep-set eyes of a saint or a witch, are troubled, not amused . . .

One

Jeremy turned suddenly and thrust his head, which was boulder-hard and too big for his body, against the crook of her elbow. "Why can't I watch cartoons, Mama?"

"I told you. Because this afternoon I have a program I want to see," Dana said. She did not take her eyes off the set. "That lady on the screen is my friend."

"I don't like this program."

"Then go to your room and play." Her voice was low, but it had such arresting vibrancy that she never needed to raise it to command attention. She pushed him gently off the large footstool they had been sharing. "Go on."

"I don't want to."

"Jeremy."

He sighed, recognizing finality, and left the room slowly, scuffing the toes of his blunt, smudgy-white tennis shoes along the carpet, which was white, too.

His mother's eyes had never left the screen.

Ann. Ann Hayes. She's better than she used to be. But then she never stopped. Five more years of experience. She's better looking, too. Not really pretty, but striking. She's learned how to make the most of herself. Poise. That she never had before. And something else. Authority. It's as though she really knows who she is.

Dana's stomach contracted slightly. She did not move until the program was over. When the production credits began to unroll, she switched the set off and sat staring at the screen while the light it contained drew itself down to a pinpoint and then vanished. After a moment, she got up and went to the window wall, pulling the cord that separated the draperies. Beyond the little balcony outside which hung cantilevered into space above the brush-covered hillside, the city lay stripped of smog, brilliantly in focus. To the east she could see the cluster of tall, white buildings which marked the civic center. To the south, the Baldwin Hills bordered the opposite side of the city from where she stood on a hill above Hollywood. Westward the Pacific lay along the horizon, a bright streak of dazzle in the late sun. Within the vast, flat basin which held the metropolis, every house, every street stood out clear and sharply defined, tinier than usual without the magnifying blur of damp, dirty air, exquisite as a toy community. It all looked nearer than it ordinarily did, but it was still much too far away, Dana thought, rubbing her forehead distractedly.

When she and Don had first looked at the house two years ago, she had fallen in love with the view, but ever since they had actually lived there, she had found it vaguely disturbing without knowing why. Now it came to her quite suddenly. *I don't want to be looking down on it. I want to be in the midst of it.*

Impulsively she pushed back the sliding glass partition. A breeze, hot and dry as furnace air, struck her and with it came the faint, busy rumble of homebound traffic. She could see the cars flowing in a thick, multicolored stream along Hollywood Boulevard and along Fairfax, slowmoving, clotted, as the city left its shops and offices and stores and fought its way home to dinner. The honking of a horn floated up to her, the squeal of tires making a sudden stop. There they went, all the people who were doing something in the world. *I can see it, I can hear it, but I'm not part of it. Oh, I cannot live this way any longer! I must be part of it again!*

An emotion long growing unrecognized within her burst out at last, demanding acknowledgment. Her throat ached, and she closed her eyes and leaned her forehead against the glass, still hot from the day's sun.

The sound of a key opening the front door made her

turn. Don was home.

"Are you melted?" She gave him an appraising look as he walked into the room and noted with a certain pride that except for a slight flush, he looked as cool and well groomed as he had when he left that morning.

"Not exactly, but that drive through the Valley is no treat in this weather." He set down his briefcase and kissed her, and they looked at each other fondly.

They had been married five years, and they resembled each other so much that people often took them for brother and sister. They were blond and blue-eyed and fair, and they looked as if they belonged together, as though they were the masculine-feminine counterparts of each other. Don Hurst was stocky and squarely built, with an air of immutability. His face had a stolid look, but it was not stupid. Dana was smaller, more fragile, with a sensitive face that only the perceptive recognized as beautiful at first glance. People were not inclined to turn and watch her pass unless by chance they had heard her speak or noticed her eyes, which spoke, too, in an extraordinary and subtle way.

"Gin and tonic?" Dana asked. "I'll make you one while you shower. We have an hour before they get here."

"What a night for company. You've put the wine to chill, haven't you? On the bottom shelf, away from the freezer?" Don was very particular about wines.

"Yes, darling," she said, feeling dutiful. "Two bottles."

"Who's coming again?" He was loosening his tie and unbuttoning his white shirt which still, surprisingly, looked immaculate. "The Connors?"

"The Connors and Vivian. She's bringing John. As usual."

"Fine." He sounded ironic, but tolerant. "Bob Connors, who'll undoubtedly try to sell me another policy, and that jerk who does nothing but talk about himself. A great night for me while you gossip with the girls."

"I know. But after all, you like my girlfriends, too. And what about the evenings I spend making PTA chitchat with the wives of your NASA buddies while you talk shop? Turnabout, Don, turnabout."

"All right. Don't look so serious about it."

"That's not what I'm looking serious about," Dana murmured.

"What, then?" He was already heading down the hall toward the bedroom.

"Wait till I get your drink."

She sat on the edge of the bed watching him as he dressed. His body, still deeply tanned from the summer, was well muscled and strong with a faint gilding of fine, blond hairs. Don liked sports, and at thirty-three with tennis and golf, skiing and surfing, he was in superb condition. The Greek ideal, Dana thought, as she often did. The cultivated mind in the cultivated body. She admired him as much now as she had when they met. She adored being his wife, and hoped that what she was going to say would not upset him.

"I saw an old friend of mine in a TV soap opera this afternoon—Ann Hayes. She was at Drama Arts with me."

"Drama Arts?"

"You know. The little theater where I was working when you met me. I don't suppose you'd remember her."

"No, I don't. How was she?"

"Not bad. I would have been better. It was a part I really could have played."

Don laughed. "Brought out the ham in you again, did it?"

She frowned. "I was good, Don. Anyway, sometimes I thought I was. And so did other people."

"And you gave it all up. Your budding career. To be my wife." His hair, darkly wet from the shower, gleamed in the late orange light from the window as he combed it carefully, looking in the mirror.

"Sometimes I think I'd like to do a little acting again," Dana said hestantly.

"Come on, Dana. You know my views on that subject.

One career per family is enough."

"I don't mean a career, exactly. But if I could just do a show once in awhile I wouldn't feel so . . ."

"So what?"

"I don't know. So out of things. So confined."

He looked at her in the mirror. "What do you mean, confined? Now that Jeremy's in nursery school, you can get out of the house whenever you want to."

"I need to do more than get out of the house. I need to play a part again, I . . ."

"You've got a part, Dana." He was putting on his tie now, and he looked at her levelly as he tightened the knot. "You're my wife. You're Jeremy's mother."

"I know. And that's the most important thing in the world to me, but . . ." She stopped helplessly. How would it sound if she said it was not enough?

"I'm going to have to get you pregnant again. If I wasn't so damned tired, I'd do it right now! Dad always maintained a pregnant woman is a happy woman."

"Not necessarily. Anyway, as your father should know, being a doctor, it's only a trick of metabolism. Like the post-maternal blues."

"Is that what you've got, Dana? The post-maternal blues? Jeremy's four. For an actress you're a very slow study." He had put on his trousers, and as he fastened the belt he came over to her. "Stand up."

When she obeyed, he led her to the mirror over her dressing table. It was large; it returned their images generously framed, a handsome young couple, a man and a woman who anyone could see belonged together.

"Who's that?" he demanded. "Who's that girl?"

Dana stared at herself. Her eyes, as she saw them reflected, looked baffled and uncertain. "I don't know," she said at last.

"You don't know? I'll tell you who it is. Its Mrs. Don Hurst, that's who it is. Keep it in mind. And fix me another drink, will you, while I go turn the water on outside."

They dined by candlelight on the minute balcony overlooking the city. The air was quiet and still hot, and the vast, intricate pattern of light below them twinkled and vibrated, audibly it seemed, as the distant, far-flung murmur of traffic came up to them like a sound made by the lights themselves. Overhead, high-flying strays from the city below, the running lights of an invisible plane hummed steadily southwest toward International Airport through the impersonal, faintly starred blackness of the night sky. How lucky I am, Dana thought guiltily, cooling her fingers against the moisture-beaded globe of her wineglass. How can I not be satisfied when I have this view, this house, Jeremy, and Don . . . She looked down the table at her husband. He was talking politics to Vivian, talking quickly, authoritatively, with an occasional thrust of his head for emphasis, and Vivian was listening attentively, as was Beverly Connors on his other side. My friends respect him, she thought with pride, and they are intelligent women.

"Look at the girl mooning at her husband," she was suddenly aware of Bob Connors saying. "She hasn't heard a word I said. If my wife ever looked at me like that, I'd . . ."

"I'm sorry, Bob. Can I give you some more wine?"

"Just a drop. Ju-u-ust a drop." His fair, inconsequential face was flushed, and as he reached for the filled glass, he knocked it with his hand and spilled some. "Oops." He took his napkin and mopped clumsily, catching the empty lobster shell on his plate and making it rattle.

"Don't bother," Dana told him. "It's all right."

"You'r a good kid, Dana. You know what?" As Dana smiled at him, he looked down toward the other end of the table. "Nebraska was never like this, hey, Vivian?" he said loudly, pulling her attention away from Don.

Vivian Hunt looked at him blandly. She was a tall, sophisticated-looking woman with black hair cut short and rather straight. "No. Nebraska was never like this."

"If the hicks back there could only see you now, they'd

never believe it." He laughed immoderately.

"If you mean because she looks more like New York than Elkhorn, you're quite right," Dana said smoothly.

"Is that where you're from? Elkhorn?" Bob asked.

"That's right. I'm sure you've heard of it," Vivian said.

John Majors, potentially the next Paul Newman, a cologne ad come to life, gave her a proprietary look. "Jesus. Can you see Vivian doing the rural bit?"

"I bet she was combing the hay out of her hair all the time," Bob said, snickering.

"Beverly, how's your job these days?" Dana said hastily.

"Oh, fine," Beverly said. The glare she was directing at her husband broke off, and she gave Dana a grateful smile. She had a pleasant, determined face, undistinguished brown hair, and a more matronly look than either Vivian or Dana although they were all the same age. "We're working like mad on the back-to-school ads."

"Is your boss still sick?"

"She's not well. I've had a lot more responsibility lately because of it."

"Miss Bigelow? Is she ill?" Vivian asked. "I'm not surprised. I thought she looked it that day I interviewed her for the series."

"What series is that?" Don asked.

"I've been doing some features on outstanding local businesswomen. You mean you don't read the *Times*?" Vivian said banteringly.

"We should," Dana said. "We really should subscribe just so I could see what you're doing." She sounded wistful.

"You should also come downtown and have lunch with us more often now that Jeremy's in school," Beverly said. "In fact, come next week. Mayfield's is having a sale in Better Dresses you could look at, then come upstairs and pick me up, and we'll go over to the paper and get Vivian."

"Yes," Vivian said. "Come to Smogville and see how

the other half lives. One afternoon downtown on a day like this, and you'll really appreciate your beautiful hilltop."

"Can I come, too?" Bob Connors asked. "Maybe you could do a feature on me, Vivian. Hell, I'd like that. Come to think of it, why aren't you doing features on men, anyway, instead of wasting valuable time with women?"

There was an awkward silence.

"Bob, why do you always needle Vivian?" Beverly's face was red with embarrassment.

"Because she gives him an inferiority complex, that's why," Don said. He gave Bob a look of mild loathing.

Bob jerked around. "Not an inferiority complex, chum. A pain. That's what all these liberated women give me. A pain. I won't tell you where."

"I'm thinking of going back to work myself," Dana said. The words came out almost without her volition, and she was startled to hear them.

"Oh, no! Not another one," Bob Connors said.

"Dana! How marvelous!" Beverly said. "When did you decide?"

"Just today." She avoided Don's eyes. "I've been feeling restless for a long time, especially now that Jeremy's gone all day. Then this afternoon I saw an old friend of mine on TV, and that did it."

"Good girl," said John. "You never quite came off as a housewife. You're not the type."

"That's a matter of opinion." Don's voice had the edge that meant he was angry.

"Got an agent?" John went on, unperturbed. "I'll get you an appointment with mine. Not that the bastard ever does a damn thing for me."

"That would be wonderful." Dana's heart was beginning to pound. She felt disturbed and frightened and excited.

"You, too," Vivian said. She was looking at Dana with a strange little smile. "I thought you had it licked. Well, welcome to the club, Lilith."

"Lilith?"

"It's just a theory of mine." Vivian hesitated, and her face had a diffident expression Dana remembered from their college days. It meant she was about to say some thoughtful thing that meant a great deal to her, and she hoped nobody would hate her for it.

"Come on, give," Dana said, smiling at her.

"Well, all right then. There are two kinds of women—the Eves and the Liliths. Lilith—well, it's a strange story. A myth, really. It isn't in the Bible. Lilith was Adam's first wife. God made her out of the same clay, so she felt she was Adam's equal and behaved accordingly, and they had all kinds of trouble." Vivian bit her lip. "So then God created another woman, Eve, to be Adam's wife instead, and He made her out of Adams rib so she'd have nothing to brag about. Well, you can see how it works out. Eve, of course, is the woman who's perfectly happy being an appendage to a man, cooking his food, washing his socks, bearing his children. And Lilith—well, Lilith has other goals she thinks are important."

"Then you're a Lilith, too," Dana said. "Aren't you? And what about Beverly? She has a job."

"It's more than just having a job," Vivian said. "Yes, I think Beverly is, too."

"Then we all are?" Beverly laughed. "That's funny, since we're such good friends."

"Oh no, that's the way it always is," Vivian said quickly. "Liliths stick together, and so do Eves. I think it's because each of them finds the other's way of life kind of disturbing."

"Why should that be?" Dana asked.

Vivian shrugged. "No matter which a woman chooses, marriage or a career, she's afraid she's missing out on something. And of course, the ones who try to combine the two have their own problems. Anyway, that's what I've gathered from these interviews I've been doing."

"That doesn't surprise me in the least," Don said pointedly. In the silence that followed, Dana could feel him staring at her down the length of the table.

"Whatever happened to Lilith, anyway?" Beverly asked.

"I don't know," Vivian said hesitantly. She twisted her wineglass, rolling the stem between her fingers. "I think maybe God destroyed her because she did't work out."

"It's nine-thirty," Don said abruptly. "There's a rerun of the Space Shuttle launching at the Cape I want to see on TV. Anybody care to join me?"

"Oh, Christ," Bob muttered.

"Sounds exciting," Beverly said, giving him a look. "I'll buy it."

"Okay by me," John said. "And while the set's on, I'm doing something at ten."

"A show?" Dana asked.

"Hair spray commercial."

The Hursts' living room was furnished with slim, modern furniture of European design. The TV set was encased in a teak cabinet which also held the stereo system.

They took seats as Don quickly found the channel. On the screen, men were moving intently around a control room. There was an electric air of concentration, of held-in tension. Orders and information crackled between these men and the astronauts in the shuttle. At last the countdown began. The space shuttle stood erect and waiting in its scaffolding. *Four, three, two, one*—slowly it rose with an immense determination. The scaffolding fell away in slow motion as it lifted its blunt, ominous head into the atmosphere.

"These shuttles kill me," Vivian said. "Airplanes are positively alive by comparison. At least you can see moving parts on them. This thing looks as though it's propelling itself by an act of will."

"It is, Vivian, it is," Don said. His face, usually so stolid, was tense with excitement. "The will of man."

Vivian smiled at Dana. "Well, just listen! The scientist turns poetic."

The scene shifted to the control room. Tension

released, the men were laughing, pounding each other on the back. As a jumble of excited voices came over the speaker, Don turned back to watch, sharing their elation.

"Look at him," Dana said to Vivian in a low voice. "He loves his work so. NASA is his whole life. And you know something? I could get the same way about acting."

The conversation went on for another hour. Outside the air remained desertlike, and crickets chirped so loudly they seemed to be in the room.

"I hate to break the party up so early, but I have a terrible day tomorrow," Beverly said at last. "Dozens of layouts to check."

"Don, have you thought any more about that accident policy I told you about?" Bob said. "Cover you for surfing, all that skiing you and Dana do . . ."

"I'll call you about it, Bob. I'll call you," Don said.

When the door had closed on their guests, Dana looked at Don uncertainly. She hated having him disapprove of anything she did. "I'm sorry, darling. I was listening to them talk about their jobs, and it just slipped out. But I meant it. I have to go back to work."

Don went to the coffee table, picked up his brandy glass, emptied it. "You really think you have talent, hmm?"

"Yes, I do. That's part of the problem. When you think you can do something, then you want to try. If you don't, there's an important part of you that isn't being used."

He walked to the window, and she stared at the solid set of his shoulders, wondering what he was thinking. "All right," he said at last. "I'll make a bargain with you. You can try it for a year. If you really have talent, you should have some recognition by then. If not, you have to promise me you'll give it up completely and concentrate on being my wife again."

"A year? Only a year? Don, acting is the hardest field in the world to get established in!"

"It should be enough if you're as good as you say you are."

"You saw me," she said softly. "The night we met. Didn't you think I was good?"

"Frankly, I don't remember. I wasn't interested in that aspect of you."

She stared at him curiously. "What *were* you interested in?"

"You really want to know?" He hesitated, looking a little self-conscious. "I looked at you in that crazy costume you were wearing, medieval or whatever it was, and I could see you holding a child in your arms. My child."

She went and put her arms around him and leaned her cheek against the white crispness of his shirt. "That's a lovely thing to say." For a moment she was silent, savoring the strength, the authority, the unequivocal maleness of him. She wanted so much to please him, always. "All right. I accept the bargain."

"Good." He kissed the top of her head. "Come on to bed."

After that he made love to her. She gloried in the things he did to her and the knowledge, later, when she lay with her head on his shoulder, that she had pleased him.

Don fell asleep quickly, head flung back as if to catch any breeze that might come from the wide-open windows. Dana lay awake, feeling the perspiration dry on her body, thinking over the evening. Beverly and Vivian seemed to her more three dimensional than she herself was. Their lives were more richly textured, deeper in scope and purpose. She had envied them a long time without actually realizing it. Now that she was about to seek her own challenges in the world they inhabited, she could admit this to herself. Whatever the need was that drove them, she had it, too. She stirred restlessly on the hot bed, finally tossing even the sheet back so that they lay naked. Darkness seemed to make the air more stifling than ever, but the stifled feeling within her had abated since she had made and announced her decision.

Just before she went to sleep, a faint, unexpected wave

of annoyance at Don swept over her. Had he really any right to exact a bargain like that from her? She turned and looked at him. He was dead asleep, his breathing, regular and deep, making a faint whisper in his throat.

"How dare you?" she murmured. Then she jabbed him lightly in the ribs with her forefinger, a tiny gesture of defiance.

Don stirred a little, and slept on.

"Why do you have to be so obnoxious? Why do you always have to drink too much and be obnoxious?" Beverly Connors asked. She hadn't meant to bring the subject up until they got home. Arguments always had an adverse effect on Bob's driving.

"Because she gives me a pain in the ass, that's why." They were in Laurel Canyon, heading home to the Valley, and already he was driving a little too fast for the narrow, winding mountain road. "Always giving herself airs. Who the hell does she think she is, anyway? Some little hick from Nebraska who's making out in the big city with her great journalistic talent and sleeping with every guy she can lay her hands on. Big deal."

"What makes you think she sleeps with everybody?" Beverly said indignantly. "She's a perfect lady as far as I can see, and I know her better than you do."

"You're naive. And Don Hurst. The big NASA scientist. Conceited son of a bitch!"

"He's not conceited. He's just self-confident, that's all."

"Self-confident? Boy, you know it! He makes that ham actor of Vivian's look shy and retiring, he's so self-confident." He took a curve viciously, and the car lurched across the double line and then swung back. "Who the hell does he think he is?"

"I don't know. Who does anybody think they are? Who do you think *you* are, for instance, being rude to everybody and embarrassing me in front of my closest friends?"

"Don't ask me that."

"Well, I just wonder sometimes. It all seems so unnecessary." She gasped as the car near-missed another curve, tires squealing. "Bob! Will you please stop going so fast! Do you want to kill us both?"

He swerved abruptly to the side of the road and jerked on the brakes. "Do you want to drive?" He waited. "After all, you do everything so much better than I do, don't you, baby-cakes?"

There was a silence.

"Oh, let's not start that again," Beverly said in a tired voice. "Honestly. Every time you drink."

"Don't you? Don't you do everything better than I do?"

"Please, Bob. Let's get home. I'm tired, and I have a big day tomorrow."

"You have a big day tomorrow. Well, well. Do *I* have a big day tomorrow? No, I just have an ordinary day tomorrow. No Summit Meetings with Russia. No big decisions. Just a few people to see about a few policies. Hell, if I stayed home in bed for a week the world would still go round. But it wouldn't without you, now would it?"

"Please, Bob. Let's get home."

Eventually he laughed quietly, unpleasantly, sliding down in the seat and stretching his arms over his head. "Okay, baby-cakes, if you want to go home, you drive, okay? I'm beat. I could stand a little nap."

"All right. Get out."

He looked sidelong at her. "Dangerous to open the door on this side."

"Oh, honestly!" She felt her pantyhose snag as she climbed over him and slid under the wheel.

They said nothing the rest of the way. It was always like this lately, Beverly thought wearily. Bob always seemed to resent anyone successful—male or female, it didn't matter which. Well, if he'd work a little harder himself instead of relying on charm to get by . . . She turned her head a little so she could see his profile out of the corner of her eye, the straight blond hair, the small, neat features. Evenings like this it was hard to remember he had any charm at all. What made him so eternally defensive?

As they were getting ready for bed, she remembered something. "Did you put the trash out?"

"I'll do it in the morning."

"You forgot it last week, and there's a ton. You won't forget again, will you? You're always in a hurry in the morning."

"Naw. I won't forget." He yawned, already in bed. "Hurry up and turn off the light, will you?"

For several minutes after she had slipped into bed, she lay staring into the dark, debating with herself. Finally she got up, felt in the closet for her robe, and putting it on, moved cautiously through the quiet house to the back door.

The rubbish cans were not so much heavy as bulky. She tugged each of them out to the street in turn, the toe of her slipper under the rim to keep the metal from scraping on the concrete driveway and waking the neighbors. By the time she had finished, she was perspiring.

Well, that was done. She could dismiss it from her mind. Bob would forget in the morning. He always did. It just wasn't in him to accept a responsibility of any kind, major or minor, and see it through. It's lucky one of us is efficient, she thought. And I guess one's enough.

Nevertheless, on the way back to the house her mind went briefly, enviously, to Vivian, who had only the responsibilities of her job and not those of a home, husband, and child as well. The men she went out with looked after her, at least while they were on a date. She didn't have to look after them. It must be a nice feeling. Well, she was no Vivian Hunt and never would be. Unconsciously she straightened up and pulled in her stomach. She'd have to go on another crash diet one of these days.

The air outside the house was stifling. If it was this hot in the middle of the night, tomorrow would be deadly. Every year that she could remember, the back-to-school ad campaign had coincided with a heat wave. So Vivian had noticed how ill Miss Bigelow looked. What would happen to her job as Miss Bigelow's assistant if Miss Bigelow had to retire? Don't borrow trouble, she told herself. Take each day as it comes. Tomorrow night there was the midweek marketing and then a PTA meeting, so she couldn't just come home and collapse. Life was full, all right, if you didn't weaken. Resolutely she shut her eyes and courted sleep.

Speeding down the hill, John Major's 1983 red unpaid-for Ferrari turned and twisted and clung to the road as if magnetized, never skidding. Automatically, Vivian braced her legs and held one hand firmly against the dashboard to steady herself, while the hot night air whipped the ends of her chiffon scarf against her cheeks. The after-dinner brandy had left her with a nice glow, and she felt relaxed and calm.

"So Dana's an actress," John said, raising his voice against the wind. "You never told me that. Is she any good?"

"Yes, I think so. And I've seen quite a lot of her work. She was a theater arts major when we were at USC together. Then after we graduated and began looking for jobs, she started doing shows at Drama Arts, one of those little theater groups. She was very serious about it. She had a job as a receptionist in the daytime, and every night she'd go to the theater and rehearse. And paint scenery and sell tickets and sew costumes and clean the dressing rooms and heaven knows what else. You know how those outfits work their kids to death. They know they can get away with it with all the people in this town dying for a chance to perform in public."

"Yeah, I've heard. Actually, I never did the bit myself. I was parking cars when I was discovered. Discovered! Jesus, what a joke."

"Little theaters are good experience," Vivian said thoughtfully. "Maybe you should try it. Dana did everything there. 'West Side Story.' 'Who's Afraid of Virginia

Woolf?' 'Barefoot in the Park.' "

John laughed. "No kidding. Will you tell me something, doll? How the hell did an educated type like yourself ever get mixed up with a character like me who never finished high school?"

"You're not stupid, John."

"I'm not stupid, but I'm sure as hell no great brain. You know, you oughta be running around with some bright guy. Like a college professor or something."

Vivian slitted her eyes against the wind and looked at him sideways. "I'm not complaining."

"Yeah. I see what you mean. It wasn't exactly our minds brought us together, was it?"

"Not exactly." She laid her hand on his thigh and kept it there as he drove.

They were on the Sunset Strip now, and the late traffic was heavy and erratic. Cars full of cruising teen-agers passed them, yelling; crowds stood around the entrances of the big cafes and clubs; parking lot boys swung expensive cars recklessly into the stream of traffic. A black Mercedes pulled abruptly in front of them from a driveway, and a woman's hand, white-gloved, tossed a bottle from the window so that it slid across the pavement before smashing against the curb.

John hit the brakes. "Damn tourists! Jesus, I'm glad I'm not jockeying those bastards' high-priced crates around any more. Although the way things are going, I may wind up doing it again."

"What does your agent say?"

"Say? Who can talk to him? The son of a bitch never returns my calls."

"Maybe you need somebody else."

"Yeah. Maybe I do, maybe I do. Christ, I love this town! When you really need an agent, you can't even get 'em to talk to you on the phone. Then when you've got everything going for you, you're combing the bastards out of your hair."

"That's show biz," Vivian said sweetly.

John made a disagreeable sound. "Please. I just ate."

"I'm glad she's going back to it," Vivian said suddenly. "Dana, that is. Acting. I was really kind of surprised when she gave it up, but she was so much in love with Don, it was as though he'd hynotized her in some way. They were so gone they hardly talked for the first six months. Then when Dana found out she was pregnant, she was radiant. Absolutely radiant. It didn't seem to wear off for a long time after Jeremy was born, but the last couple of years—I don't know. She's seemed restless."

"What was all this Lilith jazz you were giving out with at the dinner table? How do you come up with ideas like that?"

"It's just a theory. I've been thinking a lot about those women who feel trapped by marriage and children."

"There's nothing wrong with any woman," John said, "that can't be cured by a good lay."

They turned south off the Strip, and now the car halted outside the fieldstone and glass front of Vivian's apartment building, the Carriage House. When they reached the door, John unlocked it with a key from his own chain.

Inside, the air was hot and stale. "I should have opened the place up before I left," Vivian murmured, going to the windows. She had not finished cranking them open when she felt John's hands on her bare shoulders, pulling down the straps of her dress.

"Let's get the show on the road, doll. I've got an early golf date tomorrow . . ."

Vivian reached out for him eagerly, pulling his mouth to hers, holding his head between her hands and kissing him again and again. John matched her frenzy, pulling her body closer to his. After a while they stopped, breathless, and he guided her unprotesting to the bed.

He laid her down gently and began kissing her once more, more softly now. She lay with her eyes closed, one hand caressing his cheek, the other looped around his neck, as if she feared he might pull away. She moved her body to make it easier when he began undressing her, then lay naked before him almost proudly, one arm behind her head so that her breasts were lifted for his view. He bent, trapping a nipple between his teeth, and she mewed and circled her hand around his neck, pressing him down upon her. He snailed his tongue lower and she opened her legs: her hand was firmer on his neck, guiding him to where she wanted him to go. It wasn't a mewing sound any longer. She was groaning, emotion shuddering from her. Her body began to thrust into him, in urgent, arching movements. Her nails were biting into his neck, holding him there. Then she gave a tiny scream and the thrusting gradually subsided. Vivian's face was flushed and her hair lank with sweat.

"You've still got your clothes on," she complained. Her voice was thick.

"You didn't give me time."

"I'm giving you time now."

John hurried his clothes off, easing onto the bed beside her. She felt out for him, her fingers and mouth butter-flying over his body.

"Now it's your turn," she said, the words blurred against his stomach. She seemed to get as much enjoyment giving as receiving pleasure. He started to move very quickly and she straddled him, bearing down and groaning afresh when he entered her. She controlled their pace, hands pressed down against his shoulder, saying, "No, no," when he tried to go too fast. They exploded together, clutching each other, and she kept moving, not wanting him to stop.

"My God!" he said. It was a disbelieving sound.

She pulled herself from his shoulder, holding her head just above his so that they were nose to nose. "Was that a note of criticism, sir?" she said, lightly.

"That was definitely *not* criticism," he said. She seemed very pleased with herself.

Afterwards she lay propped on one elbow admiring his profile in the dim light from the window, which glowed all night with the yellow floodlights illuminating the front of the building. A year had passed, but she still had not tired of looking at the carved mouth, the straight nose which continued the line of his forehead like a classical statue. No one had a face like that any more. No one but John. And the body matched. She lifted her hand and ran a finger from the base of his throat downward, feeling a pleasurable thrill of possession.

"Hey," he said. "I've got something to tell you."

"What?" She began the soothing, voluptuous journey again, this time using all her fingers.

"Cut it out." He seized her hand and held it against his stomach. "Listen to me, will you? This is important."

"All right." She leaned forward and kissed him on the ear. "I'm listening."

"I'm gonna marry Janet Redman."

She was too stunned at first to feel anything but incomprehension. "You're *what?*"

"I'm gonna marry Janet Redman. Now don't get excited. It's nothing to get excited about."

"But you said those dates you were having were just for publicity!"

"They were, doll, they were. And so is the marriage bit, in a way. It'll be good for both of us, but especially for me. Janet's got everything going for her now. She's really on her way, she can do me a lot of good . . . Well, what are you staring at?" he said indignantly. "I'm lucky she goes for me. It's a helluva lot better than sleeping with guys. You know I don't go for that jazz."

"What do you mean, it's nothing to get excited about?" Vivian said. Her heart was beginning to thump irregularly as it always did when she was upset.

"Well, look." He sat up and fumbled on the nightstand for a pack of cigarettes, found it, lit one. His face in the brief glare from the lighter looked angry and uncomfortable. "Look Vivian. I'm thirty. I've been knocking around this town six years now. I've gotta get moving, or pretty soon it'll be Charactersville, and I'm not the type, know what I mean? The reason I said don't get excited is, it doesn't need to make any difference to us. We can't make the scene in public any more, but that doesn't mean we can't see each other. You know how this business is. Janet'll be out of town a lot on tours and one thing and another. As a matter of fact, she's up for a picture right now that starts in London the end of November. Hell, if I can't take care of two women at a time . . ."

"Thanks," Vivian said faintly. "Thank you very much. Now will you please go and not come back?"

"For Christ sake!" He snapped on the light. "What's eating you, anyway? Did we ever talk about marriage?"

"No, we didn't."

"Did I ever say I was in love with you? Did you ever say you were in love with me?"

"No. We never said that."

"You're damn right we didn't! It was strictly fun and games right from the beginning, and you wanted it that way yourself. You said so. Jesus, Vivian. What's with you? We make beautiful music in bed, right? All I'm saying is we can go on doing it in spite of this other arrangement I have to make, and you get mad! Christ, you'd think I was giving you the brush or something."

"I don't want to . . ." Vivian said. She was having difficulty breathing. "I don't want to . . . to share you with anybody."

There was a frustrated silence. He ran his hand through his hair. Her eyes followed the gesture, and her hand ached to make it.

"Christ, Vivian. I don't know what to say. I just don't know what to say." He looked at her helplessly. "Look. Why don't you sleep on it, and give me a call tomorrow? Why don't you do that, doll?"

"No," she said.

After he had gone, she lay awake and stared dazedly at ceiling. I can't be in love with him, can I? Not John, whom I picked for a lover because he was so unlikely, because I knew I could never be serious about him? She considered the possibility carefully and logically for quite a long time. It was, she decided finally, simply that John had become a habit with her. She had come to consider that he was hers, and losing him was distressing in the way that you might become upset over losing a raincoat or a pet canary. It wasn't that the item was irreplaceable. You simply had got used to the idea of possession. Still, it was painful. Next time she would have to be more careful about getting emotionally involved.

The problem now was to become *un*involved as quickly as possible. This was simply a matter of will, and she had the greatest confidence in her ability to meet the demands she made on herself. I shall forget him, she told herself, in one month. After all, I have my job, and it's the most interesting one I can imagine. I shall work hard and in time, probably not much time, there will be someone else.

Nevertheless, she did not fall asleep until after the lights outside had winked out, leaving only a blue wash of dawn above her head.

Two

It was stupid not to be able to decide. Dana Fitzgerald. Dana Hurst. Which was she going to use professionally, her maiden name or her married name? A little decision like that, and she was having so much trouble making it that she was beginning to feel panicky.

Dana looked at herself appraisingly in the full-length mirror on the bedroom door. It had not been difficult deciding how she wanted to look for the interview. Her dress was a narrow streak of blue silk which matched her eyes and made her look cool and taller than she was. Her fair hair, wholly natural, was swept back from her slender shoulders and fell like a pure silken waterfall from her classical face, and there were pearls at her throat and ears. The effect was dignified, ladylike, chic. She caught her own gaze and was startled. It was as though she were being sized up by a stranger, a possible rival. Involuntarily, she shivered a little. She had drawn a band of pale blue shadow along her eyelids, and it made her eyes seem more hooded and withdrawn than ever. Their expression baffled her. There was no clue there as to whether she should be Dana Fitzgerald or Dana Hurst in her new professional life. Leaving that decision for a simpler one, she chose a handbag. Then she looked at her watch. A quarter to three. Time to leave. She picked up the bag, a pair of white gloves, the manila envelope with her pictures in it, and started out.

She had an appointment with John's agent. Driving down the hill, she felt her stomach begin to contract with a cold, prickling urgency. The sensation was vaguely familiar, but it had been so long since she had experienced it that at first she could not place it. Then she remembered. It was the fear of rejection. Direct, personal rejection. Not of something she had done, a poem or a painting, something outside herself, but of what she was, her face, her body, her voice, her personality. Her very self was what she was selling. What if no one wanted it?

Her breath came back rapidly, and she gripped the steering wheel with damp palms. She did not know this man, this Mr. Meyers. He would look at her with the same coldly appraising stare she had surprised on herself in the mirror. She would tell him she was an actress, a dramatic actress. Would he believe her? All at once she was far from convinced of it herself. It had been so long since she had stood on a stage and spoken lines into the hollow, peopled blackness. How did it feel? What was it like? What happened? She could remember only that it was like nothing else.

Then it came to her. There seemed to be a power over her sometimes in the old days, a secret feeling she could not explain, as though she were a witch with the certainty of magic in her. It did not always happen, but when it did, she was very, very good. That much she knew. But perhaps, after so long away, it had deserted her. Perhaps she would never feel that way again. And if not, what did she have to sell? And how could she explain that feeling to this man she did not know?

Mr. Meyers's office was on the third floor and overlooked the Sunset Strip. His receptionist was a glossy-looking girl whose face had been lacquered as expressionless as her nails.

"Dana Hurst," Dana said. She was horrified to discover that her voice was shaking.

"Sit down, please. Mr. Meyers will be with you in just a moment."

The shaggy gold sofa smelled of a cheap, flower-sweet perfume. The last potential client, no doubt. Or a bona fide client. Dana shut her eyes and breathed deeply to calm herself, although the odor made her slightly nauseated. This was ridiculous. If she couldn't talk to an agent, even an agent's receptionist, without getting upset, how did she ever expect to perform in public to a whole theater filled with people? How had she ever done it before?

"Mr. Meyers will see you now."

The receptionist's voice made her jump, and she felt the girl watching her curiously as she walked past into Mr. Meyers's office. Does she want to be an actress, too? Dana wondered irrelevantly. If she does, God help her.

"Sit down, Mrs. Hurst," Mr. Meyers said from behind his desk. He was squat and dark, and he waved her to a chair without rising.

Dana sat down hastily. It seemed to take the last remaining strength from her knees to lower herself into the seat. As she crossed her ankles, an alarming thought presented itself. Would he ask to see her legs? Oh, surely nobody did that any more.

"So you're an actress. Cigar?" He was smoking one himself, and now he pushed the box toward her across the shiny black glass top of his desk.

"No, thank you," she said, baffled.

He shrugged. "Just thought I'd ask. A girl came in here last week, and I'm talking to her, and all of a sudden she says, Mind if I join you? What did you have in mind? I ask her. The cigar, she says. May I? And I'll be damned if she didn't light up and smoke it. Like she enjoyed it, too. So when she left, I gave her one to take with her, and she sticks it in her handbag and walks out. What a business. I'm glad you don't smoke 'em, though."

"I'm for pipes myself," Dana said and laughed shakily.

"That's better," Mr. Meyers said. "Just relax. Nobody's going to eat you. I can never figure why all you shy types want to act. I should think it would scare the hell out of you, getting up in front of hundreds of people when you can't even walk into somebody's office without looking like you might faint."

"Maybe it's the challenge," Dana said.

"Yeah. Like going over Niagara Falls in a barrel when you're scared of the shower. Well, honey, it's your business. Now suppose you tell me about your experience."

"I was a drama major in college and I had four years of acting there. Then another three years of little theater here when I got out of school."

"Ever done a professional show?"

"No."

"Movies, TV?"

"No."

"Then you haven't got any film on yourself."

"No. Just these stills." She handed him the brown envelope, and he set it down on the desk without opening it.

"What's the last thing you did?"

"A play by Neil Simon. 'Barefoot in the Park.' That was four years ago at Drama Arts."

Mr. Meyers looked at her meditatively.

"Then I retired and got married and had a baby," Dana said hastily, seeing his expression. "And now I want to start acting again."

Mr. Meyers sighed. "Well, look, honey. I'll tell you what I'll do. I'll call you, okay? You give me your number. I'll look around. There may be something. I don't know what, but there may be something. You're not the new Marilyn Monroe, but I suppose you know that."

"That isn't what I do. I'm a dramatic actress."

"Yeah," said Mr. Meyers. "Simon, huh?" He stood up and held out his hand. "Okay, honey. Thanks for coming in. I'll call you."

"Thank you very much," Dana said. She forced herself to give him a bright smile and a firm handshake, and then she left.

The receptionist did not look up as she walked out the door and down the steps to the street.

The windows of the smart Strip shops glittered in the afternoon sun. She walked past them, moving automatically, the travel agencies and the antique stores and the coffeehouses and the decorators' showrooms. Occasionally she paused and looked into one of them, carefully avoiding her own reflection. She felt small and empty and without identity, rather as if she were invisible. She felt crushed, as though Mr. Meyers had been diabolically cruel instead of merely indifferent. She wondered if a psychiatrist, armed with the most powerful of psychic microscopes, would be able to detect a trace of ego if he examined her right now.

After a while, she noticed that it was very hot, and that her mouth felt cottony. Ahead was an ice cream parlor, an elegant establishment with candy-striped decor and unimaginably flavored goodies. She looked in. No one was there but the counter boys. Gratefully she sat down and ordered a chocolate soda. The counter boys continued their afternoon as though in solitude. While one of them scooped up her ice cream, the other ticked his ear with a bent straw. Then they both giggled. Dana looked out the window and concentrated on the passing traffic.

And what a failure, thinkest thou, my maid? Has't not a vile and bitter taste? It was a habit she had formed in college, this addressing of herself in pseudo-Elizabethan English. It dated back to the times when she, drama major, and Vivian, the English major, had read Shakespeare aloud by the hour for the good of their grades. She still reverted to it occasionally in times of stress. Dost think this sweet will o'ercome it? she went on wryly, as the chocolate soda arrived. Nay, nor all the perfumes of Araby . . . Anyway, it was a pretty color.

A white Rolls Royce, the kind of car that advertises its owner's importance, swooped to the curb outside. The man who got out and came in was gray-haired and handsome, with a tan and the lean muscularity that suggests a lifelong cultivation by personal masseurs in private gyms, and Dana knew him at once. He had been famous in the film world for twenty-five years, and a native of Rome or Paris or London might have recognized him as easily as she. Lounging elegantly at the counter while he waited for ice cream to go, he saw her staring at him and smiled, acknowledging her recognition. Is that what I want? she thought, as the counter boys swooned. To be famous, to be rich? To be able to walk into an ice cream parlor and have everybody know instantly who I am? No, what she wanted was something more basic, but as yet she could not give it a name.

Guiltily, she looked at her watch. It was past the time to pick up Jeremy at nursery school. She had not thought of him once in the past three hours, probably as long as he had been out of her mind since the day he was born. She paid the check hastily and left.

"So he didn't think you were the greatest thing he'd ever seen?" Don said as they were finishing their steaks at dinner.

"He offered me a cigar."

"He what?"

"He offered me a cigar. He did it to make me laugh. Because I was nervous. He was really very nice." Her smile faded, and she looked thoughtful. "I can't say he wasn't nice."

"Well, anyway, you gave it a try."

"Yes. Tomorrow I'm giving it another try. I have an appointment with Ann's agent. I got in touch with her this morning through the TV network."

"Aren't you the eager beaver."

"I've wasted enough time already," she said and stopped short, but it was too late.

"You mean like five years?"

"Oh, Don, I didn't mean it that way. I . . ." There didn't seem to be any satisfactory explanation, so she let the sentence trail off.

They looked at each other in consternation.

"I'm sorry if you feel our marriage has been a waste of time," he said coldly.

"Oh, Don," she said helplessly again. There was a silence. "You know how you feel about NASA?" she said at last. "That's how I feel about acting. It's what I do."

"I thought women were supposed to feel that way about their homes and families. Isn't Jeremy enough of a vocation for you? I don't know why I ask. Obviously he isn't."

"It only takes up a part of me," she said slowly. "A big part, but not all. There's something left over, something that I have to use just as I need to use my capacity to love. Would just having Jeremy and me be enough to fill your life?"

"That's different. I'm a man. It's completely different."

Dana shook her head. "It's not that different. I wish I could make you understand."

"So do I." He looked at her stolidly. "So do I."

She got up from her place and went to him. "Please try." As she held him, she tried desperately to think of something to say that would please him. "I'm going to use Hurst for my professional name," she said finally. "I just decided today. Dana Hurst. So people will always know I'm your wife."

He looked at her quickly. "What do you mean, you decided? That's your name. What other choice was there?"

"Well, I was Dana Fitzgerald when I acted before," she said, disconcerted. "A lot of women go on using their maiden names for their professional careers."

"Career? I thought you said you just wanted an occasional job. Now it's a damn career."

"I mean I have to use some name when I work, whether it's once a year or all the time. Goodness, Don, don't be so touchy! I was only trying to please you."

"Please me?" He looked at her steadily. "No, you weren't. You were just offering me a little consolation prize. If you wanted to please me, you'd give this whole thing up before it comes between us."

"Comes between us! You agreed I could try it for a

year!"

"It will come between us the moment it begins taking your mind off me, my home, and my son," Don said. His jaw, when he set it like that, reminded her of some kind of trap.

"You know," she said softly after a moment, "you sound just a little bit selfish when you talk like that."

"Maybe I am. I know how I want my life, and that's how I intend to have it."

"What about me? What about my life?"

"That, Dana, is your problem. And don't expect me to help you with it."

Three

At the end of a month, the memory of John was only an unpleasant stain somewhere at the back of Vivian's memory. She drank a little more than usual, but only in order to sleep. For several years now, insomnia had been a problem. Ordinarily she did not mind. She liked to read, so she simply turned on the light and picked a book from her nightstand, anything from romance to mystery. Eventually, in the trafficless dead silence between two and four, the book would drop from her hands. Lately, however, the sleeplessness had begun to affect her work, and that worried her. This particular Monday morning, she sat at her desk in the city room of the *Times* staring unhappily at the blank piece of copy paper rolled into her typewriter. She had work to do, but concentration seemed to have deserted her. Fortunately, she thought, no one could tell. You could be planning a murder, figuring out your income tax, or deciding where to go for dinner, and as long as you looked as though you were working on a story, nobody accused you of procrastinating. It was one of the minor advantages of newspaper work.

All around her, typewriters rattled, phones rang, people talked, and none too quietly. The unearthly clatter of more machines augmented the uproar whenever the door to the composing room was opened. She was used to it. She heard nothing. That was not what disturbed her. When she had first gone to work for the paper, she had thought she would never learn to concentrate in the electric atmosphere of many people working under pressure in one big room. Now she could not have worked in a quiet place.

Vivian was a feature writer for the *Times*. At one time she might have been called a sob sister, but this was another era. Hers were the special assignments where the city editor felt a woman's touch might be valuable. She covered love-triangle murder trials and the weddings of prominent movie and TV stars. She wrote about children who were having their visit from Santa Claus early because they were dying of leukemia, and old people who were victims of crime. She interviewed wives of visiting foreign dignitaries to learn what a woman's life was like in Peking or Tokyo, and accompanied them to Disneyland to note their reactions. Occasionally she wrote a series for the women's section. The current one, "Career Woman," describing the lives and jobs of various women prominent in the Los Angeles business world, was being enthusiastically received by the feminine readers of the *Times*. They not only wrote to Vivian, they wrote to the editors, which was even nicer. Vivian appreciated it. Generally people only wrote to the editors when they were furious with a story and wanted to get you fired.

"Vivian, are you busy?" The growly voice of Lou Adams, the city editor, interrupted her reverie. He was a big, good-looking bear of a man, shaggy-headed, good-natured, and tough.

"Not especially. Why?"

"Would you interview an eagle for me?"

"What does he do for a living?"

"Not a damn thing. That's the point. Some guy up in Simi Valley found him with a broken wing and mended it and fed him, and now the damn bird won't go away. He's tame, he doesn't want his freedom, he wants to keep on getting that free meal every night. The guy's got him in the hall. He wants to get a story in the paper, so he can maybe get him on a TV show. I'd throw him out on his ass, but it's a dull morning and we could use some filler."

"Okay," Vivian said with a sigh. "Wait'll I get my bird

seed."

In the hall was a young man painfully dressed in his Sunday best. The eagle sat on his shoulder, moving its head in nervous jerks as it looked around.

"Is he heavy?" Vivian said, going up to them. "Does he bite?"

"Yes, ma'am," said the young man, his throat working nervously. "No, ma'am, he don't bite. He's tame as a canary."

"Why don't you set him on the floor if he's heavy?"

"Well, ma'am, he-ah-he needs a perch."

She brought a chair and turned it over, and the young man lifted the bird off his shoulder and set it on a rung where it sidled tensely back and forth.

"Now, then," Vivian said. "What's your name? And what's his name?"

The bird's name was Rex. "That means king," he said shyly, with pride. With a little prompting, he told her all about finding the bird and taming him.

When the interview was over, Vivian asked, "May I pet him? I've never petted an eagle."

"Go right ahead."

Gently she touched the top of its head with the tips of two fingers. The bird's head jerked sideways, and a fierce eye glared unwinkingly up at her. The formidable beak remained closed. She felt a surge of delight. "I love birds," she said. "Where I come from, back in Nebraska, we have so many kinds—hawks and bobolinks and meadowlarks and robins and bluebirds. I used to know them all when I was a little girl. I could recognize them just from the way they flew."

"We've got a lot of birds up in Simi, too. Lots of eagles. But I always know old Rex even when he's just a little bitty speck way up there," the young man said.

They smiled at each other. She was still smiling when she walked back into the city room.

Writing the story took until coffee-break time. The employees' cafeteria was on the top floor of the *Times* building. She took the elevator up alone and sat by herself with her coffee and doughnut, looking out over the city. The smog was thick, staining the air the color of spoiled oranges. There was no blue anywhere in the sky, and buildings more than a block away disappeared in the murk. The smog problem had been going on for years, and there were years more of it to come.

Part of the employees' cafeteria was an outdoor terrace, not used much because of the smog. On it, a lone pigeon walked about, searching for remembered crumbs. Vivian crumbled a piece of doughnut into a paper napkin and went out to him. As she opened the door, the hot, acrid air struck her, clamorous with the din of cars and construction, smelling like the exhaust fumes of a million buses. The pigeon walked over to her boldly, and as she knelt to give him the crumbs, she remembered fleetingly the air of a Nebraska morning, sweet with planted fields. Impossible to think what it was like now. Her eyes began to smart almost immediately, and she turned and went quickly back into the air-conditioned protection of the building.

The rest of the morning, she worked on her next series feature. It did not go well.

"God, Vivian, you're gonna kill yourself if you don't cut down," said Tim, the copy boy, emptying her full ashtray into the wastebasket. He was a tall, blond kid, so skinny that his Adam's apple seemed to be the most prominent feature of his silhouette.

"That would be a loss?"

The phone rang, and she picked it up quickly, grateful for any interruption.

"Miss Hunt? One moment, please. Mr. Williamson calling."

After the impersonal, secretarial voice, there was a momentary pause before a man's voice came over the wire, raspy but with a certain warmth. "Hello, Miss Hunt, Sid Williamson calling. I'm with Syndicated TV Productions. We're interested on these articles on career women you've been writing. We think they might be the basis for a syndicated daytime TV series. I'd like to talk to you about it."

"Well, fine," said Vivian. "Thank you."

"Are you free for lunch tomorrow?"

"Yes."

"Then come out to the studio and meet me in my office at one. We're in the Valley. Here's the address."

Syndicated Productions operated out of a former film studio. Grosses had been down for some time before the former bosses had decided to lease the major portion of the lot to an all-purpose TV studio. Cars were parked everywhere, and people hurried back and forth between the offices and sound stages. A small jeeplike truck chugged by, dragging an enormous piece of scenery which rested on its own wheels. Four or five men walked alongside, steadying it. Outside a sound-stage door, over which a red light flashed steadily, two improbably tall men in frontier clothes with holsters strapped low on their hips stood smoking. When the light stopped, they ground out their cigarettes beneath the high heels of their boots, swung the heavy doors open, and went in.

The gate policeman pointed out Mr. Williamson's office, a bungalow set with several others like it in a small, parklike area with green lawns and shrubs and winding paths. Inside, the effect was equally homelike with early American furniture, chintz curtains, and flower prints on the walls. There was a worn path in the brown carpet between the anteroom where Mr. Williamson's secretary sat and his private office.

"Miss Hunt, how are you?" Sid Williamson stood up and held out his hand. He was short, and his head was set formidably low on thick shoulders, but he had an agreeable face.

"How do you do?" His handshake was as warm and enveloping as the look he gave her.

"Let's get over to the commissary. I've got a table reserved."

They walked briskly across the lot. "Ever been out here before?" he asked. He seemed to have no trouble keeping up with her, although she, in her high heels, was much taller.

"No," she said slowly, shaking her head.

"I don't suppose you've had any experience writing for television."

"I've written a few scripts in my spare time. Like everybody else. So far nothing has sold."

"Well, I'm not offering you a job as a writer." Sid Williamson said. "But you're a good reporter, and we might be able to use you on the research end if the show gets going. And if you're interested."

The commissary was a big, noisy room packed with variously arrayed humanity—some in costume, plus an equal number of civilians. Vivian stared around with interest. It reminded her of a masquerade party that hadn't quite come off. Sid Williamson steered her to another, smaller dining room at the side, and they sat down.

"The food's not bad," he said, scanning the menu. "It used to be better but it's not as bad as the NBS commissary. Usually I go off the lot to eat."

"You stayed today on my account?"

"I thought you might like to see the studio." He glanced briefly at her. "Now I'm sorry. If I'd taken you out, we could have had a drink first."

Talking business proved to be agreeable. He obviously knew what he was doing, but he had a sense of humor about it, and he did not seem to be always "on" like most of the Hollywood people she had met with John. From business, they went on to what Vivian's mother had called "topics of general interest."

"Sid!" They were down to dessert when a redhead stopped at the table.

"Nancy! For Christ's sake! What are you doing out here?"

After introductions, Nancy sat at the table with them.

"I thought you gave up the rat race and got married," Sid said.

Nancy shrugged. "I did. Now the marriage has had it, so I'm back."

"Damn, I'm sorry to hear that. What happened?"

"Oh, I don't know. It's my fault, I guess." She lit a cigarette and smiled at Vivian, and the corners of her eyes wrinkled deeply under the heavy makeup. "I can't make up my mind. When I'm working, I think I want a vine-covered cottage and kids, and when I'm doing the housewife bit, I can't wait to get back in harness. It just got on Pat's nerves, finally. He was out of town on location half the time anyway with that TV series of his. And when he wasn't, I was."

"Damn, I'm sorry to hear that," Sid said again. He sounded genuinely concerned.

"Oh, well. Never mind about me. How've you been? How's Joan and the kids?"

"I was coming to that. I've joined the club too. Joan's gone back to New York. Took the kids with her."

"Oh, no," Nancy said. "You too?"

Sid's lips twisted into a smile, but it was merely a movement of physical muscles and not a real smile at all. "So I'll find another broad. The town's full of 'em." His tone was light, but Vivian noticed that his eyes did not join in the fun.

"Well, lots of luck," Nancy said slowly, shaking her head. She looked at her watch. "God, the time. I have to get back to the set. Pleased to've met you, Miss Hunt."

When she had gone, Vivian said, "I have to get back to work myself."

"All right. Just one more thing. Will you have dinner with me sometime?"

"Let me get one thing straight. You said you were separated. But are you divorced?"

"No. No, I'm not. Not yet."

She hesitated. He was a nice person, and she liked him immensely.

"I hate to sound stuffy," she said at last, "but I have

old-fashioned prejudices against dating married men."

"Married?" Suddenly he looked quite tired. "Look, I haven't seen my wife or heard from her for two months. As far as I'm concerned, married I'm not. Lonely I am. Does it break any laws if we have a steak together?"

"I guess not," Vivian said, weakening. Her own loneliness the past month had sensitized her to the same feeling in others.

"Look." He spread his hands. "I'm a perfect gentleman. You been married twenty years, you forget how to chase dames around the furniture. Besides, at my age I'm afraid I might break a leg. No passes, okay? Does that make you feel any better?"

The pleading beneath the kidding reached her. "All right," she said at last. "I won't even wear my track shoes."

They smiled at each other.

"I'm tied up tonight," Sid said. "How about tomorrow?"

Back at the paper, the afternoon went beautifully. She finished her feature, humming to herself. Driving home on the freeway, she sang along with Lionel Richie's "Hello" on the radio. Tonight she would not mind being alone because she had things to do. She would wash her hair and manicure her nails and pick the dress she was going to wear tomorrow. Maybe the white linen with lace lapels. It was October now, but still hot. Just before she got home, she stopped and bought a late edition of the *Tribune*, the other Los Angeles evening paper, and a copy of Cosmopolitan.

When she opened the paper to read while she ate dinner, John's picture confronted her. He was kissing Janet Redman and cheating slightly, so that his face was turned toward the camera. Janet was wearing a low-necked dress with a tight bodice and a hat that seemed to be mostly flowers.

HOLLYWOOD COUPLE
ELOPES TO VEGAS

was the head on the story that went with the pictures. It was a good head, she noted automatically. The two lines balanced nicely. She couldn't have written a better one herself. She read the brief story rather carefully, then read it again. A vague feeling of panic seized her. She went to the bathroom and, turning on the bright overhead light, studied her face in the mirror.

A woman was supposed to start getting wrinkles when she was around thirty, and she was getting them. So far they were only the kind that are always described as adding character to the face. She put the tips of her forefingers at the outer corners of her eyes and pressed gently. Then she assumed a serene expression, the kind that is supposed to keep the skin unlined and smooth. As she regarded it critically, it cracked suddenly, to her horror, and became a face of anguish. Quickly she switched off the light and went into the bedroom.

The glow from her bedside lamp was warm and diffused. In it, she took off her clothes and stood before the mirror. Firm and young, and why not? She ate sensibly and had borne no children. Her stomach was flat, her breasts held their shape without a brassiere. Reassured, she slipped on a robe and went back to her dinner.

Sid Williamson. A nice man. A nice, safe man. He wasn't young, and wasn't good-looking, thank God. Not like John. It would be easy to date him without getting involved.

She went to bed early, thinking it would be easy to get to sleep, but it was not. An inexplicable resentment gnawed at her, something she could not define or put down. Eventually she went to the kitchen and fixed herself a glass of hot milk and brandy which she sipped slowly, sitting up in the darkened bedroom, until sleep began to fuzz the edges of her consciousness. With it, some last defense dissolved as well, and she felt infinitely sad and abandoned.

Reaching into the drawer of her nightstand, she groped around until she found a small flat piece of metal. "Hello," she whispered to it forlornly. It felt cold in her palm. "Hello, there." *I am drunk or lonely or both. Only drunks and lonely people talk to inanimate objects.*

Holding it in her hand like a talisman, she fell asleep at last.

Four

At 7:30 a.m. Beverly Connors, wearing a gray linen and cotton two-piece dress, walked briskly through the door marked EMPLOYEES ONLY into the cavernous interior of Mayfield's Downtown. The store was deserted at this hour. The counters and tables were still sheet-draped, the aisles were empty, the escalators stood motionless, and the light which illuminated the first floor was dim and uncertain. The cool, dead air smelled faintly of merchandise—of leather and fabric, cosmetics, mothballs, perfume, and paper—overlaid with a stronger odor of whatever the janitor had used during the night to clean and polish the tile floors. Beverly glanced briefly at the scene, which always reminded her of a dark stage before the performance, as she walked toward the employees' self-service elevator, her high heels echoing. The elevator awaited her; apparently she was the first one in. She had it to herself as it moved, up to the twelfth floor where the executive officers were.

The director of advertising and publicity for the Mayfield stores, Carol Bigelow, had a corner office with windows on two sides overlooking a clamorous intersection in downtown Los Angeles. Her secretary worked in a small cubicle adjoining it on the right. Beverly, who was Miss Bigelow's assistant, had an office of her own on the other side of the secretary's cubicle. It had one window looking out across an alley far below to an office building which effectively blocked the view of the city she might otherwise have had. Beverly did not mind. Her office had less daylight than Miss Bigelow's, but it was also quieter. She unlocked the door, turned on the light, put her white gloves and her handbag into the bottom drawer of a filing cabinet, and sat down at her desk.

Office personnel of Mayfield's were not due until 8:30, but Beverly had work to do. Miss Bigelow had not been feeling well lately, and she had delegated certain of her usual responsibilities to Beverly. The job of publicity-advertising director was a big one. There were four Mayfield stores in Southern California—the Downtown, the Valley, the Hollywood, and the Westchester. Soon there would be two more, one serving East Los Angeles and the other Long Beach. Their combined advertising budgets totaled several million annually. Advertising for all of the stores was handled by Miss Bigelow's office.

A stack of eight ad layouts lay on Beverly's desk. They were due at the printer's at 11:30. Beverly laid them out, side by side, over the top of her desk and typewriter table. Standing up to get a better view, she studied them, frowning in concentration.

"Hi, Beverly. Damn, you been here all night?" Lynn, Miss Bigelow's secretary and hers too, theoretically, stood in the doorway. She was a cute, watery-eyed girl with short brown hair that usually suffered from an overdose of home permanent.

"Hi. No," Beverly said, smiling. "Just half an hour or so."

"Want some coffee?"

"I'd love some. I haven't had breakfast yet."

Lynn walked into her own office, picked the glass carafe off the automatic coffee maker which stood on a little table in the corner behind her desk, and went to the ladies' room to fill it with water. When she returned, she filled the brew basket with coffee and took three white china cups out of a drawer in her desk. The cups had initials, LS, BC, and CB, painted on their sides with red nail polish.

"Old Bigelow will want some, too, won't she?" she called to Beverly.

"Undoubtedly," Beverly said, unwinding paper from the neck of a red grease pencil.

At nine Miss Bigelow arrived. She was short, square, and bowlegged, with stiff gray hair cropped almost as close as a man's. Angular of body and mind, she had lost the last vestiges of whatever femininity she had once possessed with the coming of middle age. Now, from the bony jaw to the arch-supported shoes, there was only a rigid determination left.

"Beverly, have you checked those layouts yet?" she rasped, marching into the office. Miss Bigelow never walked; her bearing was too military for that. "Good morning, kids."

"Good morning, Miss Bigelow. Yes, they're right here."

Miss Bigelow inspected them, rummaging in her black leather shoulder bag for a cigarette. She found one, and Beverly lit it for her. "That's got to go," she said gruffly, stabbing at one of layouts with a blunt finger. She yanked open the center drawer of Beverly's desk, snatched up the grease pencil, and slashed a red X across it. "Were you going to let that go through? Where's your head? I told you yesterday those robes have been delayed in transit. Now we can't advertise merchandise we haven't got in the store yet, can we?"

Beverly opened her mouth to speak, then changed her mind and shut it. Miss Bigelow had not told her about the robes being delayed, but why argue? The older woman was touchy enough as it was these days. "I'm sorry, Miss Bigelow," she said. "I must not have heard you. What do you want to run in place of it?"

"Where's this week's ad schedule?" Miss Bigelow strode off to her own office, and Beverly followed her. On her desk was a roll of four or five large sheets of paper. She separated the top sheet from the roll and studied it. It was marked off in seven boxes, one for each day of the week. "Move up the Aries shoe ad from Friday. That's ready. I saw the paste-up yesterday. Go talk to Sam about it."

Sam was art and advertising manager for soft goods, which meant ready-to-wear, as opposed to hard goods, which meant furniture and appliances. His desk was in an area set off by railing from the big room where the artists and copywriters worked.

"The Aries ad's not ready," he said when Beverly told him the problem. Small and ferret-faced, he was the kind of man who always looked pleased when he had an opportunity to deliver unwelcome news.

"Yes, it is. Miss Bigelow said she saw the paste-up yesterday."

He looked around. "All these last-minute changes. It's no way to run a department."

"We just this minute got word the merchandise wasn't arriving," Beverly lied calmly. She would protect her boss from his man any day of the week.

"All right," Sam said, pursing his lips. "I'll see if I can rush it through."

"You do that," Beverly said smoothly. She did not like Sam, but she considered it part of her job to avoid personality conflicts.

He looked away from her, behind her, and his expression changed to one approximating amiability. "Good morning, Mr. Ladd."

"Good morning, Sam. Mrs. Connors?"

"Yes?" Beverly turned. "Good morning, Mr. Ladd."

The man who had come up was big and handsome, with thick white hair and pink skin, and looked as though he should be posing, with a marble mantle and Irish setters, for bonded whiskey advertisements. In actuality, he was a Mayfield's vice-president.

"Mrs. Connors. Were you working late here last night?"

"Yes, I was." Beverly's heart contracted slightly. What could be coming next? Ladd was always out to harass the female executives.

"The lights were left on again in this department. You know the last one to leave is to turn them out."

"Oh," said Beverly. "Yes, I know, but—"

"These things cost the store money, Mrs. Connors. We have to watch ourselves."

There is a fussy housekeeper in every office, not necessarily female, and Mr. Ladd, in spite of his imposing appearance, was Mayfield's.

"I wasn't the last to leave, though," Beverly said firmly.

"Oh?" Mr. Ladd looked faintly irritated. "Then who was?"

Beverly looked at Sam. There was a pause.

"I was," Sam said at last. He gave Beverly a furious glance.

"Oh," said Mr. Ladd. "Well, Sam. Try to be more careful in the future, will you?"

At 9:30 there was a meeting with Miss Bigelow, the hard and soft goods advertising managers, the copy chiefs, and the production manager. In the past Beverly had not always attended these meetings, but lately Miss Bigelow had insisted on her being there. Together the staff reviewed fifteen or twenty ads before they were sent to the printer. The photographs and drawings were checked for overall effect, the copy read to see if it could be strengthened in any way; if so, it went back to the copywriters for reworking. This meeting lasted about an hour. Afterward, it was time for coffee break.

Usually Beverly took hers in the employee cafeteria, but today, since she had not had breakfast, she decided to go out. The store was open and alive with people now. The show was on. She dodged among the shoppers on the main floor, not looking at the counters, and walked out onto the street.

Downtown Los Angeles is not chic, not elegant. The Fifth Avenue, the Rue St. Honoré of the city was Rodeo Drive in Beverly Hills, a long way from the metropolitan shopping district. The shoppers on the street as Beverly walked along were slightly rundown, bargain hunters rather than big spenders. The women wore sweaters and jeans and had done their hair themselves. Mingling with them on the broad, dirty sidewalks were the regular citizens of this part of town, the middle-aged, seedy-looking men with a limp or a cast in one eye or an arm missing who lived in the nearby cheap hotels; the swaggering young boys with their long hair; the old ladies in house dresses with a brown paper parcel under one arm and a cracked imitation-leather handbag over the other. Merging into the flow of these people, who seemed to spend their days endlessly going somewhere else, Beverly walked north past the wholesalers' outlet shoe stores, the cheap movie theaters, the stands selling tacos and fruit juice and hot dogs until in half a block or so she came to a small diner with a counter going back along one wall and a row of booths opposite.

"Hiya, honey," the counterman said, slapping spilled coffee off her section of the counter with a rag as she sat down. "Aren't you kinda early?"

"Late," Beverly said. "I haven't had breakfast yet. Let me have some bacon, one egg, toast, and coffee."

"Sure." He gave her a smile from which a tooth was conspicuously missing. He had a pale, greasy face and hair to match, and when Beverly had first begun eating an occasional quick lunch here, she had found him rather repulsive. Now she no longer really saw him, any more than she saw the rag or the cripples on the street outside or smelled the stale air of the diner itself.

She ate quickly and returned to the store. It was time to take the layouts to the printer. Miss Bigelow was hard at work on the monthly budget. The ashtray on her desk was already clogged with half a dozen cigarette butts.

"Can I do anything for you while I'm out?" Beverly asked.

"Yes. You can stop at a drugstore and get me some cough medicine," Miss Bigelow said.

"Do I need a prescription?"

"Get that red stuff, whatever it is. You don't need a prescription for that. I can't remember the name. Ask the druggist."

"You smoke too much."

"Aaaaah, it's the smog," Miss Bigelow said gruffly.

"How do they expect people to have healthy lungs, breathing that junk all day long?"

She began coughing as Beverly left, a short, harsh sound like a bark. In spite of her concern, Beverly had to smile. Miss Bigelow always seemed to her to have a canine quality. Rather like a bulldog, she was.

The printer was ten blocks away. Beverly got her car from the executive parking lot and eased into the bumper-to-bumper stream of traffic. Technically she was not an executive, but she was allotted a parking space because she often used her car during the day for errands like this one. She drove slowly, resigned to the traffic, taking a familiar, circuitous route through the network of one-way streets.

At the printer's, Shorty came to help her, and she felt a twinge of pleasure. Shorty was middle-aged and not particularly handsome, but he thought Beverly was pretty, and she appreciated it. Not many men found her attractive enough to flirt with.

"How's my girl?" he said, beaming. "Putting on a little weight these days, aren't you?"

From another source, this would not have been a compliment, but Beverly knew her admirer. "Well, maybe a little around the hips," she acknowledged gracefully.

Shorty winked. "I'm an old-fashioned boy myself. I like to see a well-padded woman."

"I'm afraid it's not very fashionable."

He flapped his hand deprecatingly. "Never mind that stuff. You leave the diets alone. A little meat on the bones, that's what a man likes to see."

"You're a great source of encouragement to me, Shorty. My husband prefers the thin type."

"He does?" Shorty registered amazement. "Well, you just send him around to me. I'll tell him what's what."

Beverly departed, smiling. She remembered to hold her stomach in all the way to the parking lot, so her waist would look as small as possible. Hips were all right if you had a small waist.

Back at the store, she lunched abstemiously on a combination salad plate and iced tea. Then the lemon chiffon pie caught her eye, and she had a slice of that, too. Afterward, feeling guilty, she went down to lingerie and bought herself a new girdle, flesh-colored elastic overlaid with black lace.

All afternoon she talked to the buyers of various departments about which items to plug through direct-mail advertising, which was sent out with customers' bills. This took her away from the floor where the personnel offices were and down into the store proper. When she thought about it, and she still did occasionally, Beverly liked the feeling of being able to go back into the stockrooms and through doors marked PRIVATE and into all the secret, behind-the-scenes nooks and crannies where customers were not allowed. It gave her a feeling of importance.

At 5:30 the store closed for the day. On the twelfth floor, the office personnel and executives worked until six o'clock.

Just before six, Miss Bigelow walked into Beverly's office with a stack of layouts under her arm.

"Beverly. I'm sorry to stick you with these at the last minute, but I couldn't get to them today, and they've got to go out first thing in the morning." She paused, and her breath seemed to come rapidly. "I won't be in tomorrow till around eleven."

"I'll be happy to take care of them, Miss Bigelow." Beverly rose and took the layouts. "However, I think I'll do them at home instead of staying here. I don't like to make my family wait for dinner too often."

"That's all right," Miss Bigelow said softly. "Thanks, Beverly."

She got home around 7:15, having stopped at the market on the way. When she reached the front door, loaded with groceries, her daughter Belinda opened it for her.

Belinda was seven, pigtailed and self-assured, with a

determined mouth. People always said she looked like Beverly, but it was her personality rather than her appearance that was reminiscent of her mother. While Beverly was pleasingly plump, Belinda was wiry, and her hair was fine and blond and straight like her father's.

"Hello, Mother," she said primly. "You're late."

"I stopped at the market." Maternally, Beverly's eye fell at once on a fresh bandage on Belinda's left knee. "Now what's happened to you?"

"Touch football," Belinda said matter-of-factly. "Only I got tackled."

"Marvelous," said her mother. "So ladylike. Who put the bandage on for you?"

"Billy's mother. It was Billy tackled me."

"You know you're going to be permanently scarred, like a veteran of the wars, if you don't stop being such a tomboy?"

"I didn't even cry," Belinda said irrelevantly. She followed her mother into the kitchen and watched Beverly set two large paper bags down on the sink. "Let me put the groceries away. You go wash up."

"Thank you sweetie. Incidentally, where's Daddy?"

"Out in back. Watering."

Beverly went to the bedroom, kicked off her shoes, and dropped her dress on the floor. Limp and wrinkled, it was due for the cleaner's. Sighing, she opened the sliding door of the wardrobe, took a cotton housedress off its hanger and a pair of sandals off the floor, and put them on. Her back ached, as it always did after a busy day. To relieve it, she stretched her arms over her head and then flopped forward like a rag doll, letting her fingers brush the carpet.

When she got back to the kitchen Belinda had the groceries put away and was sitting on the floor trailing a piece of string back and forth for the cat to play with. She got up when her mother came in. "Can I peel the potatoes?" she said eagerly. "Can I give Morris his dinner?"

"Morris, yes. Potatoes, no," Beverly said. "You cut

yourself last time, remember? That's his food in the orange dish."

Belinda opened the refrigerator door. Purring, the cat wound itself lovingly in and out between her legs. Beverly began peeling potatoes. She would fry them, she decided, since it was so late. It would be quicker.

"Hi," Bob said, coming in the back door with a glass in his hand, empty except for melting ice cubes. "How's my beautiful wife?" He bent over, smelling faintly of bourbon, and kissed the back of her neck.

"Fine," said Beverly, smiling. The epithet, which was a tradition with them, never failed to please her.

"Rough day?"

"Oh, the usual."

"I did a little work myself. Sold three policies. Including one to Don Hurst."

"Bob, that's wonderful!"

"It was a good day," Bob admitted modestly. "I thought maybe we'd go out and celebrate tonight. See a movie or something."

"Oh, I can't," Beverly said, frowning. "I'd love to, but I brought home some work. Something Miss Bigelow asked me to do at the last minute."

"Dammit, not again! Beverly, what do you do that for?"

"Because it's part of my job."

"Part of your job! Do you get paid overtime for it?"

"No," Beverly admitted. "But it's—well, it's part of being an executive. You don't necessarily get paid overtime."

"Part of being an executive! Part of being a sucker, you mean."

"I am not a sucker!" Beverly said hotly. "I want to do it. I'm interested in my work, and even if I weren't, I'd feel obligated to help Miss Bigelow out when she asks me to."

"What's that matter with the old bat?" Bob said sullenly. "Why can't she do her own work? She's got nothing else to do."

"Bob, you know she isn't well."

"Yeah? Well, she's still collecting the top salary around there, isn't she? You're not getting any extra for doing half her work for her."

"Bob, you can't always treat a job that way. Not if you want to get ahead. Sometimes you have to give more than you're getting paid for."

"Yeah. Okay. Never mind. Spare me the lecture on getting ahead. If you don't want to go to a movie with me, I'll go by myself." He poured himself another drink, splashing in the whiskey ostentatiously.

"Mother," Belinda said, "what does getting ahead mean?"

Beverly looked at her, trying to think how to explain.

"Trouble," Bob said unexpectedly. "Just trouble, honey. And some of us think it's worth it, and some of us don't."

Five

At least twice a month Vivian, Beverly, and Dana had lunch together at one of the better restaurants around town. On a Tuesday in late November, their meeting place was Columbo's. Posh, expensive, discreetly elegant, it was a rendezvous for society women rather than career girls, but they were celebrating Vivian's thirtieth birthday.

Dana arrived first. She slid into the booth, which received her luxuriously, and glanced around. The other tables, except for an occasional all-male gathering which had the air of a business conference, were occupied by groups of women who seemed to have had a previous, intuitive understanding about what they were going to wear. Almost without exception, they wore the same costume—a black dress, one to three rows of pearls at the throat, a small, frivolous hat, a mink stole. The major variation came in the stole. It was silver-blue, silver-gray, or pale beige, but never brown. Dana, who was wearing a green wool suit and no hat, smiled to herself.

"Hi," said Vivian, coming up behind the maitre d'. "What's so funny?"

"Nothing. Just planning a style revolution. Someday I'm going to come in here wearing a mink-colored mink."

"You wouldn't dare." Vivian sat down, and they smiled at each other companionably.

"Have a drink on me, birthday girl," Dana said. "Remember when Poochie Cole and I smuggled the iced champagne into the dorm, and we all got sloshed in the

WIVES AND LOVERS 61

pitch dark? That was the most hilarious night I ever spent in my life, your twentieth birthday."

"Please," Vivian said, wincing. "No girlish reminiscences. I feel old enough as it is."

"Well, you look marvelous. How's your new man? Sid, is it?"

"I'm having a wonderful time with him. He's exactly what I need right now. Nice and funny and no complications."

"I don't suppose you've heard anything from John."

Vivian laughed. "Poor idiot John. No, I haven't. But then I wasn't expecting to after I told him I wasn't interested in his polygamous little plan."

"Actually, he never struck me as your type."

"No. Well, he was good for a few laughs. I like variety, you know, and as long as I'm single I might as well experiment with all the kooks there are in this town."

"Hi, everybody. I'm sorry I'm late." It was Beverly, looking breathless and annoyed. "I hate being unpunctual, but just let me have a lunch date, and something always comes up just as I'm walking out the door. Happy birthday, Vivian. Lordy, I need a drink."

"How's everything at Mayfield's?" Dana asked.

"Frantic. Absolutely frantic. How's your job-hunting coming along?"

"Ugh."

"No luck. Well. Tell old Aunt Bev all about it."

Dana sighed. "It's simple. The product isn't selling."

"Damn, that's discouraging."

"Yes. Particularly when the product is you."

"Well, dear, there are two things I've learned to do in the merchandising business when an item isn't moving," Beverly said briskly. "Number one, put it on sale. Number two, advertise. The first is impractical, I would say, in your case, but what about the second?"

"Take an ad in the trades with my picture?" Dana said doubtfully. "Oh Beverly, I don't know if that would do any good. It isn't my face I'm selling. It's my—I hope—talent."

"Come now, you're not so repulsive as all that," Beverly said. "You've got wonderful eyes. You look spiritual. If I wanted somebody to play Saint Joan, for instance, or Florence Nightingale, I'd hire you in a minute just from seeing your face."

"Thanks. I only wish you were a casting director."

"What about little theaters?" Vivian asked. "Did you go back to Drama Arts?"

"Yes. Naturally. Only it's under new management, and they couldn't care less about me. I answered a couple of casting calls I heard about, but no luck. The amount of competition is simply incredible. You wouldn't believe, would you, that every other person in this great big city is out for an acting career? Well, that's my estimate."

"I think your voice is your main selling point," Vivian said. "If only there were some way you could be heard. You know, Dana? If you could even get a job doing a TV commercial."

"I can't, because I haven't got a union card. No union card, no job. On the other hand, no job, no union card. You have to be working before they'll take you in."

"Have you got an agent yet?" Beverly asked.

"Nobody wants me. You have to be either young, meaning eighteen, or gorgeous. Preferably both. And they just glaze over when they hear how long it's been since I worked last. Oh, they're all very nice. They say they've already got a client the same type as me, so there'd be a conflict. Or they don't handle my type to begin with. Or something."

"Haven't you even had a nibble?"

"Well, yes. A nibble. One of them actually took me on an interview. I was in his office, and he was giving me the brush when all of a sudden he stopped and said, 'Honey, I just got an idea. There's a part in a series casting right now that I think you might be right for.' So he picked up the phone, and we went over to the studio that same afternoon. Of course, nobody there thought I was right for it. So that's the last I heard from him."

"Maybe Sid," Vivian said. "He's got connections. And

I know him well enough now to ask for a favor. You've got to meet Sid."

"All right," Dana said. "Oh, God. I hate to use my friends, but I'm getting desperate."

"Don't be silly," Vivian said. "I'd love to help."

They lunched on crab Louis and champagne. At dessert time, the waiter appeared bearing a small, chic cake with chocolate curls. "Come on, the hell with decorum," Beverly said. "Let's sing 'Happy Birthday.' Happy birthday to you-u-u, happy birthday to you-u-u . . ."

Vivian looked at them in alarm. Her eyes filled with tears, and she got up hastily and ran toward the powder room.

"Did I do something?" Beverly asked, shocked. "What's wrong with her?"

Dana frowned. "I don't know."

"Man trouble again? She sure got a raw deal from the last one."

"I don't think so. She says this one's nice. I don't know what's happening to her any more, really. I wish we saw more of each other, but we haven't been as close as we used to be since I had Jeremy. She's certainly changed a lot since I knew her in school. Sometimes I can hardly believe she's the same girl."

"Was she popular in school? With men, I mean?"

"That's what's so strange. She never went out at all. And I mean never. She was terribly smart and terribly shy, sort of withdrawn and intense. Once in a while somebody she met would get up the nerve to ask her for a date, which wasn't easy, but she always turned them down. She was afraid of men, we all thought, but she never admitted it. She always maintained she had better things to do. It wasn't until she got the job on the paper that—Hi, Vivian. Are you all right?"

"I'm fine." She sat down and gave them a bright, unauthentic smile. "It was just the birthday bit. Thirty and all that, you know. I suppose I'm feeling sorry for myself because I'm getting old."

"Oh, come on," Dana said. "I've known you since you were eighteen, and you never looked better."

"Bob says you're the most sophisticated-looking friend I have, and he can't see why I don't lose a little weight," Beverly said.

Vivian smiled at them tremulously. "Anyway, I have nice friends."

"Neither of whom are exactly debutantes themselves," Dana insisted. "Now have a piece of your cake."

They ate quietly for a few minutes.

"Vivian," Dana said at last. "Do you think you'd be happier if you got married?"

"Somebody has to ask me first, I believe."

Dana and Beverly looked at each other. "Well, surely somebody's asked you," Beverly said hesitantly. "All the boyfriends you've had."

"No, that's right," Vivian replied. "No man has ever asked me to marry him." She said it slowly and distinctly, as if she were listening to the words.

"But that's just not possible," Beverly said, bewildered. "Somebody asked me, and I'm not half as pretty as you are. And besides that, you're smart and talented and—"

"I don't want to get married," Vivian said. "I don't want to belong to a man, be his chattel, his possession. I won't be used by a man. They always use you if they can."

"What do you mean—they use you?" Beverly asked.

"You know what I mean. Well, they don't use me. I use them. When and where I please."

"If you're talking about sex," Dana said, "then it's a mutual thing, isn't it? Each uses the other, if you want to put it in those terms."

"The difference is in who's running things," Vivian said. "In my case I do. It's simple if you don't get emotionally involved. I hope I'm not shocking you. It's the champagne."

"You're not shocking me," Dana said. "At least, not in the way you think. You and I are going to have a talk sometime soon."

"Don't think you're going to sell me marriage," Vivian said. "I like what I've got. Not that I necessarily recommend it for everybody, you understand. Not every woman can take sex like a man."

"Is that what you call it?" Beverly asked. "Taking sex like a man?"

"That's what I call it," Vivian said flatly. "And I like it."

The following day Vivian called Dana. "Hi. I just talked to Sid. He said to bring you over to NBS tomorrow for lunch, and he'll introduce you to a friend of his who produces one of the court shows. Are you free?"

"Very."

"Good. I'll pick you up on my way out from town. It's only a little out of the way. Around quarter to twelve?"

"I'll be ready," Dana said. "You're a doll."

As they drove to the studio the next day, Vivian seemed to be in a happier mood, Dana thought. "This is fun," she said as Dana got into the car. "I've been wanting you to meet Sid."

"Incidentally, what's happening with the television show based on your series?"

"Oh, that fell through. But at least I got Sid out of the deal." Vivian smiled. "He's a doll."

"What's he like?"

"Well, he's not young, and he's not handsome, but he's —oh, I guess I like him because he has warmth. He gives."

"Is this rare?"

"Oh, come on, dear. Have you been married so long you've forgotten what dating young men is like? If they've got anything at all to offer in the way of externals, a sports car or a good job, they're so choked up with their own importance it's disgusting. You're supposed to curtsy low and kiss the hem of their trousers in gratitude for being taken out. Frankly, I'm a little sick of that."

"I knew that was true of actors," Dana said. "That's what I dated mostly until I met Don. Of course, most of mine were lucky if they had either a job or a car. Don had both, but he wasn't so much wrapped up in himself as in his work."

"That's not so bad. You were lucky. If all you have to do is bone up on the space program or something, at least it's instructive."

"I didn't have to do that, even. I found out right away that he loved music and sports the way I did, and we started going to concerts and skiing, and things proceeded from there."

"Right to the altar. Well, like I said, you were lucky. You got married at the right age, too. After twenty-five the men get more impossible every year. Of course, I was practically that old before I started dating."

"What was it with you in school, anyway? You never would go out."

"Oh, scared to death. Scared I wouldn't know what to do, how to behave. No, it was more than that. I was afraid of caring. I had some kind of idea that it led to disaster."

"You mean like having a baby?"

"I was afraid of my feelings." She paused. "You don't know what kind of feelings I have, Dana."

"What kind do you have?"

"Strong. Strong. It's like having a tiger on a leash. I was afraid that if I let myself go, there I'd be, walking down the street or trying to, and the beast pitching and roaring and dragging me all over the place. And all the normal people who were out walking their dogs would look at me condescendingly and say, 'Heavens, what's wrong with you? Why can't you control yours like I do mine?' It's hard to keep a tiger in hand, Dana. I knew I had one, and I thought it would just be simpler to leave it in the cage."

Sid was waiting for them at the auto gate, the main entrance to the huge NBS Television complex of buildings which housed sound stages, offices, film storage vaults, and a small army of employees.

"We're going over to Sullivan's office right now," Sid

said. "He can't make lunch, but he's going to talk to Dana and introduce her to the casting director."

"What does he produce?" Dana asked.

" 'The Judge's Court.' It's a weekly series. Different cast every week, so they use a lot of people. You ever worked TV before?"

"No."

"You belong to the union?"

"No."

"Well, Sullivan or I will have to get you a thirty-day waiver."

"What's that?" Vivian asked.

"Non-union actors can apply for a thirty-day work permit. After it expires, they have to join the union before they can work anymore."

As they walked across the lot, Dana felt the by-now familiar contraction of her stomach begin. After nearly two months of looking for work, she should be used to the strain, but it never seemed to get any better. Today was even worse. Now that she was dragging her friends into the struggle, she felt more desperately than ever the need to make good, to prove herself. Sid was nice, but what would Sullivan be like? How many times in the past few months she had asked that question about a stranger who might be going to help her, asked it in panic or fear born of her unbearable, unconquerable shyness. Oh, God, let me get through it without making a fool of myself, she prayed as always, walking through the door of yet another unfamiliar office.

Sullivan was an oldish-looking young man with tired eyelids and a limp handshake.

"How are you, dear?" he said to her. His skin looked as though it had been pickled slowly in expensive Scotch. "Now what is it we're going to do for you?"

"Little lady's trying to get her foot in the door," Sid said. "Hasn't done any TV before."

Sullivan eyed her appraisingly. "I think we can make an unhappy housewife out of her. Would you like to be an unhappy housewife, dear?"

"Anything," Dana said.

"Do you have a card?"

"No."

"She'll have to get a thirty-day waiver," Sid said.

"Let's have Leo take a look at her," Sullivan said. He picked up the phone.

"Leo's the casting director for the show," Sid told Dana in an undertone while Sullivan was talking. "Treat him easy. He's a frustrated actor. Couldn't get work, so now he's a casting director and doing okay. Only, he's still bitter. Know what I mean?"

"I read you," Dana said.

Leo, when he arrived, proved to be the collegiate type, short hair and a tweed sports coat. "Sid," he said. "How are you, boy?"

"What about it? Can we use her?" Sullivan asked, waving a limp hand in Dana's direction. "I think we can use her."

Leo looked Dana over through his horn-rimmed glasses. "Any TV experience?"

"No."

"What have you done?"

"Mostly little theater."

"Any improvisation?"

"Yes. A lot when I was taking drama in college."

"The show is taped before a live audience, you know. The cast is all professional except the attorneys and the judge. They're real. We think it lends an authentic touch."

"I think I could handle it," Dana said.

Leo looked at her quizzically. "Are you just loaded with talent, dear?" he asked softly.

"I don't know," Dana said calmly. "I haven't set the world on fire yet, but I don't know if that means anything. A lot of no-talent types I've known are working, while people of real ability can't get a job. But that's the way this business is."

"God, how true," Leo said. "How true." He placed a brotherly hand on her shoulder. "Come in for an audition

Monday. Don't prepare anything. It'll be improvisation."

"Well, that seemed to go all right," Vivian said after they had left Sullivan's office. "Do you think they'll really call her, Sid?"

He shrugged. "Why not? What the hell, someday he may want to get some young chick he's on the make for on my show."

"What is it you produce?" Dana asked.

" 'The Late Show' with Alex Lovell."

"You know, Dana. The one who thinks he's a comedian," Vivian explained. "All the kids are crazy about him."

"And vice versa," Sid said. "Jesus. Alex Lovell, boy sex fiend. Don't mention the little bastard to me. I've got him out of my hair for two weeks doing P.A.s in New York, I don't even want to hear his name."

"Yes, I saw in the paper," Dana said. "Didn't he almost get arrested for soliciting a prostitute?"

"Almost, but not quite. That lucky I'm not."

Vivian giggled. "As a friend, I wouldn't want to work his show, Dana. From what Sid tells me, you'd need a chastity belt."

"Don't you think I'd be a little old for him?"

Sid shook his head. "I wish I could count on it, but you never know. Old ones, young ones. The kid has a wide variety of interests."

The commissary was nearly full.

"I'm glad to see somebody's working," Dana said.

"How long has it been?" Sid asked.

"Four years. I retired. Got married and had a baby."

"You've got a family? What do you want to get back in the squirrel cage for?"

"I don't know that I want to," Dana said slowly. "It's more like I have to."

Sid shook his head. "You're gonna have trouble."

"I know. I am already."

"You ever thought about changing your type? No offense, but you could be sexier."

"Uh-uh." She gave him a level look. "I know what I'm selling. And sooner or later, I think somebody will buy."

Sid shrugged. "Lots of luck. Now, what do you want to eat? And while we're talking about food, how about dinner, Vivian? You feel like being fed again tonight?"

Vivian smiled at him. "I feel like it."

"Pick you up around seven." He looked at Dana. "What do you think about your friend here, with her Phi Beta Kappa key, running around with a dirty old man like me?"

"She could do worse," Dana told him. And has, she added silently to herself.

The pattern of their dates was established by now. After cocktails and dinner at one of the big, expensive restaurants on Wilshire, they went to a club or drove down to Malibu Beach or watched television in Vivian's apartment. Occasionally they held hands, but it had never gone any further than that. When Sid had looked as though he might kiss her, Vivian had subtly withdrawn herself, and he had understood the message. So they stayed friends, and laughed a lot, and even learned to sit in silence together comfortably and without strain.

By evening, it was raining. On an impulse, Vivian stopped at a market on her way home from work and bought two thick steaks, a head of romaine, and a bottle of California burgundy. When Sid arrived, she was wearing a velvet blouse and pants, and the record player was pouring out Julio Iglesias.

"Christ," he said, blinking. "What is this? A party?"

"I've gone soft in the head. I'm getting dinner at home when I could have been taken out."

"So don't apologize. A great idea. I didn't even know you could cook."

"Well, the rudiments. Don't expect souffles or anything. Simple, wholesome fare is about all I can manage."

"That's fine with me. With my stomach the way it is lately, I'm gonna be on bread and milk soon."

"Sid! You're not getting an ulcer!"

"I'm not? Good. I was thinking maybe I was, with the pains when I get hungry and all."

She looked at him with concern. "You never told me that before. I've just mixed cocktails, and now I'm going to give you one. That's the worst thing you could possibly have if you're getting an ulcer."

"Baby, give me the drink already. I was only kidding. Jesus, don't start mothering me."

When she brought the glasses from the kitchen, he had taken off his coat and tie and unbuttoned his shirt at the neck. "What an afternoon. You know I was on the phone to New York for one solid hour after you left? The kid's in trouble again. Sleeping with some sixteen-year-old, for Christ's sake. In his dressing room at the studio. She was hiding under the couch when he walked in, and the next thing she knew she was on it. The couch, that is. Somebody got wind of it, and it's gonna cost plenty to keep it out of the papers."

"Can you? Buy people off, I mean?"

"Probably. If she doesn't get pregnant, so her folks decide to sue."

"What a nice, clean business."

"Come on, baby. You work for a paper. You know how the world operates."

"Yes. But I never get used to it."

They sat down on the sofa, and Sid groaned in comfort.

"Incidentally," Vivian asked, "what did you think of Dana?"

"Another ladylike type. Like you. Frankly, I thought she was a rabbit, no guts at all, until the way she reacted to what I said about changing her type. All of a sudden I got the impression she knows what she's doing. In which case, she may make it."

"Dana has a lot of character," Vivian said slowly. "I've always known that. But somehow she's always allowed herself to be overshadowed by other people. I don't really know why."

They ate looking out the window at the rain-washed street. The swish of passing cars blended pleasantly with the sound of Julio Iglesias's romantic Spanish voice.

"That's nice," Sid said. "Who is it?"

"Julio Iglesias. He does have a nice voice, doesn't he?"

"Music to come unstuck by," Sid said soberly.

She looked at him in the candlelight. His dark eyes had a far-off gentle look, and the unbuttoned shirt made him seem younger than usual. She had never seen him so relaxed. He held the bowl of his wine-glass between his hands and rolled it slowly as he listened to the music. The movement had a caressing quality, as though he enjoyed feeling the smooth curve between his fingers.

"More wine?" she asked. Quite suddenly she wanted to touch him.

He looked up. "Got any brandy?"

She brought the bottle and two glasses. "Let's move to where it's comfortable."

"This is better than TV," he said when they were settled on the sofa again. "We should do this more often. I like your records."

"I have lots more," she said absently.

"Records and books," he said looking around. "Funny how they make even a furnished place look homey. Have you really read all those books?"

Vivian nodded. "I've been a compulsive reader all my life." She looked at him intently. The conversation had become quite unimportant. Now that she knew what she wanted, she was amazed she had not wanted it sooner. She poured the brandy with a hand that shook slightly.

"How old is Dana's kid?" he asked.

"Four."

"Just Mike's age. He'll be five next month. Christ, how the time goes."

"What are you going to send him for his birthday?"

"I'm gonna get him a tricycle. He wanted one last year, but Joan thought he was too young. He's old enough now, though, don't you think?"

"I should think."

"Where in hell he's going to ride it in New York is the next question. Cooped up in an apartment. You can't let a kid that age out on the streets, and Joan's miles from a park. New York is a lousy place to bring up kids. I know. That's where I grew up. If he was home, he'd have the whole backyard with grass, and he could ride up and down the driveway yelling his brains out like Chris used to do . . ." His voice trailed off.

"You miss them," she said softly.

He shook his head. His eyes shone with tears.

"Sid." She put her glass down and laid her hand on his shirt just above the belt buckle.

"Vivian. Oh, Christ, Vivian." He turned and caught her with a ferocity of pent-up longing that stopped her breath. For a moment, he only held her, and she had time to think. Everything is going to be all right, it's going to be nice, it's going to be wonderful. Then he kissed her. The taste of his mouth pleased her; that meant their chemistry was good. He was ardent, but he was not rough, he was too sensual for that. He touched her the way he had touched the wineglass, gently, experiencing the quality of her flesh. His own skin, when she pulled his shirt out and laid her hands against his back, was soft. Not flabby, but soft, soft.

In the bedroom, she could hear the quick sound of his breathing matching her own as they undressed. His body was good, better than she would have thought for a man of his age. Desire made his face almost beautiful, not ugly as it did some men. The last thing she noticed before turning out the light was his eyes, dark with longing, warmer and gentler than she had ever seen them. She would not have believed that this fluent, cynical man could be so quickly transformed.

The first contact of naked flesh made them both gasp. Almost immediately, with a violent surge of pleasure, she felt her body begin to move convulsively, rhythmically, with an urgency that was beyond the control of her conscious will. Liberated, uncaged, she abandoned her self blindly to movement, to feeling.

"Christ, why did we wait so long?" Sid whispered, his mouth hot, ravenous, against her ear.

She gave a fierce, quiet little laugh. "To make it better," she said.

Six

Bob Connors put down the Sunday paper and yawned noisily, stretching his arms above his head. "Beverly? What's taking so long?"

"Waffles. I thought we'd have waffles this morning."

"Hurry up, will you? I'm starving."

"In a minute. Plug in the iron, will you?"

Beverly stood by the stove in her housecoat, frying bacon. It was a chilly morning, and the heat from the two electric burners, one for the bacon, one for the coffee, felt good. The windows with their flowered curtains were slightly steamy, and the metal hardward on the natural wood cupboards was cold to the touch.

Beverly and Bob lived in the Rio Ranchos tract in the San Fernando Valley. The flat rectangle of land on which it stood had once been a pecan grove, and there was a pecan tree or two still on each lot. This feature made it slightly more expensive than most of the neighboring tracts on which the raw new houses rose out of the bare dirt without a single blade of vegetation to soften their outlines.

Their house, like those around it, had a shingled, gable roof, a living room with a dining area at the end near the kitchen, two bedrooms and and den, two baths, and a two-car garage. The stucco portions of the exterior were painted gray. This, plus the fact that it was placed differently on its lot, was the major feature distinguishing it from its neighbors on either side, which were painted yellow and white, respectively.

The tract lay, as it were, between two rivers of asphalt. Five houses above the Connors, the street came to a dead end at the edge of an arroyo, one of the tributaries of the Los Angeles River. Only a trickle of water customarily flowed through this arroyo, which was enclosed in high chain link fencing and lined with concrete for flood control. When it rained hard, which was seldom, the trickle quickly became a torrent two or three feet deep and thirty feet wide. A mile to the south, the concrete bed of the Freeway carried a flood of traffic from the West Valley to downtown Los Angeles and back. The flow of this river of automobiles was daily, swelling to a crescendo during the morning and evening rush hours and dwindling to a trickle in the small hours of the morning. It was this freeway which Beverly took to work every day.

The cat jumped into Bob's lap and began rubbing its ear lovingly against his chest. He chuckled and pulled its whiskers. The cat purred louder.

"Hey, Beverly. How about this crazy Morris? Why do you suppose he likes to have his whiskers pulled?"

"I haven't the faintest. Maybe he's a masochist."

Beverly came into the dining area, carrying a bowlful of batter. "Haven't you plugged the iron in yet?"

"Okay, okay." He got up, pouring the cat off his lap, and bent over to pick up the cord.

Sitting down to wait for the waffle iron to heat, Beverly regarded her husband. He had not yet shaved, and the faint stubble on his boyish face made him look, not older, but slightly seedy. There was always an air of inconsequence about him which could not be attributed either to his coloring, which was fair, or his features, although they lacked boldness, or his build, which was not as slight as it appeared. Nor was it his present attire, pajamas, slippers, and a plaid wool bathrobe, which made him so distinctly unimpressive.

It would have been the same if he had worn tails and a ribbon across his chest.

"If you're going to do any work in your shop today," Beverly said, "would you fix the kitchen stool? The leg's wobbly."

"I thought I already fixed that."

"You did, but it's loose again."

"I don't know," Bob said. "I don't feel much like it." He rattled the sports pages. "There's a good pro game today. Want to go?"

She considered it. "I should really finish cleaning house."

"Aw, come on."

"No, really. There's too much to do around here. When the Gibsons dropped in yesterday, it threw my whole schedule off."

"Beverly, why in hell don't you hire a maid?"

"I'm not going to have some strange woman messing around my home. If a woman can't work and run her house too, then she shouldn't work. That's what my mother always said."

"Well, it would be better than having you run around all the time like a chicken with its head cut off."

"A chicken with its head off! Well, that's nice, I must say. Are you implying I'm inefficient?"

"Inefficient." Bob snorted. "Boy, that's really a dirty word with you, isn't it?"

"Mama," said Belinda from the floor where she was reading the comic section, "isn't the iron hot yet? I'm starving."

After the batter was poured, there was a silence.

"I suppose I could go," Beverly said at last, "if you'd vacuum the rugs for me."

"Oh no, you don't. You don't turn me into the maid. Like I said, hire somebody."

"It's expensive. Do you know what it would cost to have somebody come in here one day a week? One hundred dollars a month."

"So what? Are we poor or something?"

"We're trying to save money. You know what we're trying to save money for."

"Oh, hell," Bob said. "The waffle must be done by now." He picked up his knife.

"No, it isn't. It's still steaming."

"It's been in there for five minutes. How long can it take?"

"It's not done yet."

"Well, we'll just see about that." He inserted his knife in the crack, raising the lid a little. "It's done," he said triumphantly. He lifted the lid all the way up. The waffle parted doughily in the center, half of it sticking to each section of the iron.

"Oh, no," Beverly said.

Bob stared at it in consternation. "The edges were down," he said lamely.

Belinda giggled. "Daddy's not very efficient, is he?"

"That's enough out of you!" Bob snapped.

"There's no point in getting mad," Beverly said. She stood up and unplugged the iron.

"All right. So I was wrong." He followed her to the kitchen.

"Never mind." She got out a knife and began scraping the half-done batter out of the iron.

"You don't have to act so damn superior."

"I'm not acting superior. I'm just cleaning the iron."

He lounged sulkily against the sink, watching her. "Christ. Now we'll never eat."

"Well, I'm sorry, Bob, I told you it wasn't done."

"Yeah. You told me. I knew you'd get it said sooner or later. You were right, and I was wrong."

Beverly said nothing.

"I'm always wrong," Bob said moodily. There was resentment in the look he gave her, a resentment which invovled, in some indefinable way, more than the situation of the moment. "I'm sick and tired of always being wrong."

There was a long silence. They didn't look at each

other. Then Beverly put down the knife and said abruptly, "Then why don't you try being right once in a while?"

He stood erect immediately in a kind of angry triumph. "Come on, Belinda," he said abruptly. "Let's get dressed. You and I are going out to breakfast. Then we're going to the ball game."

Resigned, she let them go. Once the day was off to a bad start, she knew from experience it was no use trying to salvage it. Bob did not get over a bad mood easily. Well, she had plenty to do. First she would get the curtains ironed and rehung, she decided, and then finish the dusting and vacuum. Work was a refuge, always, when she and Bob had trouble. The pattern of effort and achievement seemed so sane, so logical, compared to the unpredictable emotional changes of marriage. She had tried with Bob, she really had, but her results in this sphere, she was beginning to realize more and more, were far from the glowing success she was accustomed to in her other projects. Troubled, she tried once more to think it all through, to discover just where things had started to go wrong, as she set up the ironing board and began the curtains.

They had met at college when Beverly, an advertising art major, was about to graduate, and Bob, just discharged from the Army, was beginning his senior year in business administration. Principles of Advertising was name of the course in which they had found each other.

He was blond, he was impressively casual, he was terribly cute, Beverly reported to her girlfriends, delighted at the accident of fate which had placed her side by side with such a desirable male. On days when he did not sit next to her, she looked around the room for him in alarm. He was never anywhere to be seen.

Until the first exam was announced, they hardly exchanged a word beyond hello. After the lecture that day, Bob turned to her with a winning smile.

"I-ah-haven't been around too much," he offered. "You know. Having a beer with the boys. Could I borrow your notes?"

"I don't know," she said doubtfully. "I need them to study with myself."

He looked disappointed. "You take great notes. I've been watching you."

"I am quite methodical," Beverly admitted, flattered. She looked at him with mixed emotions. It was dreadful to refuse him, but on the other hand . . .

"Maybe we could study together," Bob suggested. "You know. It helps to go over the stuff with somebody. When do you have a free hour?"

They made a date for three o'clock the next afternoon.

"What are you doing in a business ad course when you're an art major?" Bob asked. They were sitting under a eucalyptus tree on a grassy bank overlooking the college.

"My field is Advertising Art, so it just seemed logical to find out something about advertising."

"What are you going to do when you graduate?"

"Look for a job with a department store. They have big advertising departments, and I think there'd be a future there. All the local stores are expanding like mad the way the population of Southern California's growing."

He was impressed. "You've really got it all figured out, haven't you?"

"I better have. I'm graduating in June. What are you going to do when you graduate?"

He shrugged and gave her the winning smile. "I wish I knew. I can't seem to settle on anything."

He had, it seemed dabbled in marketing, real estate, insurance, and personnel management after switching to business administration from economics. None of them, in the final analysis, appealed to him as being his life's work.

"How can you tell?" he said, running a hand

bewilderedly through his shiny, straight blond hair. "I mean, how are you supposed to know?"

"Well, in my case, I just did."

He looked at her respectfully. "You must be a very decisive type."

Inevitably the study sessions turned into dates, and the dates became regular. Beverly had never been so happy. Most boys were put off by her efficiency, her self-possession, but Bob seemed to value these qualities in her. Proudly she introduced him to her mother and her twin sisters, Shirley and Sherry, who already at fifteen had more dates than Beverly had ever dreamed of.

"Aren't they pretty?" she said to Bob.

"Oh, I don't know. I don't think they're any prettier than you are."

She blushed. He had never said anything complimentary before about the way she looked. "You're kidding."

"No, I'm not. Sure, they're good-looking kids, but so are you, Beverly. Don't underestimate yourself."

After that, of course, she became prettier. She lost weight. She had her hair restyled, so that her face looked oval instead of moon-shaped. Her expression became less determined, more eager and alive. Two other boys she had known only in class asked her out that spring, but she did not go. She was too absorbed in Bob.

Eventually he took her home, which was an apartment in the Wilshire district, to meet his mother. "Might as well get it over with," he said gloomily, and Beverly gathered they were not on the best of terms. Mrs. Connors, who had been a widow for ten years, worked in a bank to support herself and help put her only child through college. She was a spare, dark woman with a thin mouth in which a cigarette burned almost incessantly. Her manner was cool, and for a reason she wasted no time in making clear.

"Bob is too young to marry," she told Beverly

bluntly when he left the room momentarily soon after their arrival. "He hasn't found himself yet. I've made him promise me he'll finish school and work for two years before he settles down with a wife." She exhaled a cloud of smoke through her nostrils and took a sip of her Martini, regarding her guest with maternal hostility.

"What a good idea," Beverly said coolly. "I think that's terribly wise."

Mrs. Connors looked at her thoughtfully and changed the subject. During the pot roast, the two of them behaved toward each other with a polite distaste which escaped Bob's notice entirely. Beverly was not alarmed, although she recognized in Mrs. Connors something of herself. She was the younger, she had stronger weapons, she knew she would win.

In June, Beverly graduated, and by mid-July she had a job as advertising artist for Mayfield's department stores. Toward the end of August, she and Bob were married.

At first it had been exciting, the simultaneous challenge of the new job and the new marriage. She worked at them with equal enthusiasm, reveling in the demands on her capabilities. She did everything she could to relieve Bob of the responsibilities of marriage so that he could concentrate on his studies. Since she was the wage earner, it was only natural that she should be the one to set up the family budget, write the checks, pay the bills. Bob did not object. He admired her sense of organization.

He had settled on a field at last; Beverly had seen to that. He had balked at first when she insisted on a decision.

"But I don't really know what I want to do."

"It doesn't matter," Beverly said firmly. "It's time you made up your mind. Any decision is better than none at all."

He looked at her helplessly, running his hand through his hair. "But what basis do I make it on?"

"Well, use the same one I did. Los Angeles is a big city, and it's still growing. What's the best way to take advantage of the population increase?"

Eventually they decided that insurance, the selling end, would be his field. Bob would make a good salesman, Beverly thought. His easy way with people would help him work, and as long as he was so fond of having a beer with the boys, he might as well combine business with pleasure.

It seemed to work out splendidly at first. He got a job without much trouble and sold a thoroughly adequate number of policies the first few months, winning a tribute of "Nice going, kid" from his boss. Elated, Beverly got pregnant.

"God, what about your job?" was Bob's first comment when she told him about it.

"I've already told them, and they're giving me a two-month leave of absence," Beverly said triumphantly. "They like me down there, you know."

He hugged her. "My smart wife," he said admiringly. "My smart, beautiful wife."

As usual, she giggled happily at the compliment, which already had become a family tradition.

After the usual number of months, Belinda was born. Bob was the proudest of new fathers. During this time he sold very little insurance. There were beers with the boys in celebration, and more golf than usual to help him adjust to the unfamiliar status of parenthood. Unexpectedly, he got fired three weeks after Beverly came home with the baby.

"I can't understand it." He paced the bedroom floor in panic. "He knew about the baby. What'll we do?"

"We'll manage," Beverly said bravely. "It won't take you long to find another job. And I still have mine, remember."

Finding another job took an endless two months. During that time their meager savings dwindled away to less than a hundred dollars. Worse still, something in their relationship dwindled away and disappeared.

When he came home at night after another fruitless day of searching, Beverly would know immediately by his face that he had found nothing. "Any luck?" she would say, trying to sound cheerful.

"No luck," he would say. Then he would go into the kitchen and pour himself a stiff drink.

One night when she made the usual inquiry, he turned on her. "Damn you! If I find anything you'll be the first to know," he burst out.

New mothers are notoriously sensitive. Beverly burst into tears and rushed into the bathroom, locking the door behind her. Bob was appalled; crying was so unlike her. "Beverly?" he said timidly, knocking on the door. "Beverly?"

"Leave me alone," she sobbed. "I'm sick of the whole mess."

The truth was, she was becoming frightened for the first time at the kind of man she had married. He was ineffectual; there was no other word for it. During the weeks he had come home night after night after night still jobless, she had slowly begun to understand that Bob was simply not a man who impressed people very much. Jobs were not that hard to find. She knew, if it were up to her, that she could find one within a week. It simply took drive, initiative, self-assurance . . . These were not qualities, she was finally forced to acknowledge, that Bob possessed. It had never bothered her before, but now, with motherhood newly upon her, she felt a sudden, deep need to rely on him, to lean on him, to have him take over and manage their lives. Clearly, he was not capable of this. The knowledge, in her sensitive emotional state, aroused a kind of terror and an even deeper resentment.

After that, he drank quite a lot every night. More and more often he started on the day's round of interviews with a headache and bleary eyes. Beverly watched him with growing contempt.

"I really don't think we can afford this much

expense for liquor under the present circumstances," she said icily at last.

"If it wasn't for the present circumstances, I wouldn't need the liquor," he observed with some dignity. He drained his glass with a clinking of ice cubes.

"Furthermore, I doubt that a chronic headache is the best possible condition for a man when he's looking for a job," she went on, raising her voice.

"Oh, you do, do you? You doubt that it is, do you?" he said nastily, mimicking her lofty air.

She went hot all over with anger. "You're a disgusting bastard," she hissed. "Why don't you pull yourself together? Why don't you behave like a man for once in your life?"

There was a short silence, during which they stared at each other with loathing. Slowly his face reddened. "Bitch! Why don't you behave like a woman?" he said thickly. "Show a person a little—sympathy."

"I have other things to do," Beverly said, her voice shaking. "For example, I have a baby to look after. That's my first duty as a woman."

"Damn the baby!" he shouted so abruptly that she jumped. His face was transformed with anger. "Damn the baby! What about me? What about me?" He slammed the highball glass to the floor, and then he was shaking her, shaking her until she fled screaming and locked herself in the bedroom with Belinda who wept too, loudly and bitterly, as though she had heard and understood everything beyond a doubt.

Remembering, Beverly felt her eyes fill with tears. Seven years had passed, but this episode above all others in her married life had the power to upset her anew every time she thought of it. Had things, she wondered, ever been the same after that? She asked herself if Bob ever thought about that night, and if so, how often.

The phone rang, and she went to answer it.

"Beverly?" said her sister's voice.

"Hi, Sherry. How are you?" Not many people could tell Sherry and Shirley apart over the phone, but Beverly always knew.

"Okay, I guess." She sounded uncertain. "What are you doing?"

"Cleaning house. Bob took Belinda to the ball game."

"Could I come over and talk to you?"

"Sure. I'll put some coffee on."

When Sherry arrived, Beverly experienced the usual esthetic thrill that most people felt when her beautiful sister walked into a room. There was no point in being jealous of a girl like Sherry. She was simply to be appreciated like any other work of art. Great natural gifts had been enhanced to an awesome degree of perfection by subtle technical skill, and the result was a masterpiece that it seemed doubtful even age could destroy entirely.

"Hi, sweetie," Beverly said. "You look gorgeous."

"I'll bet. The top's down, and I forgot to take a scarf." Sherry ran a slender hand over her short, silver-blond hair, which the wind had merely restyled into an enchantingly casual disarray, and sank into a chair.

"What's new in the modeling business?" Beverly asked. "How did the Las Vegas layout go?"

"Oh, fine. Had a ball."

"When did you get back?"

"Yesterday."

"What a life you lead. I wish I could spend a week or so lounging around a resort in expensive clothes and getting paid for it."

"The place is a disaster. The night life just doesn't stop. You know? I never remembered to go to bed until it started getting light. I'm an absolute wreck."

Beverly looked at her. The only shadows on Sherry's lids were pale blue and artfully matched to the cashmere sweater and pants she wore. She smiled. "Oh, you'll get by. Want some coffee?"

"Love some."

When Beverly returned, setting the tray on the French Provincial coffee table in front of the sofa, Sherry was humming a vague tune and staring restlessly around the room. It was a mood Beverly recognized.

"Got a problem?" she asked lightly, pouring coffee.

"I guess so." Sherry paused uneasily. "I've got an admirer."

"This is bad?"

"Well, yes, really." The blue lids fluttered nervously. "He's sort of—insistent."

"Why don't you tell old Bev all about it," Beverly suggested after a moment.

Sherry sighed, a delicate sound like a breeze in a birch tree. "I met him the very first night we were there. He stood next to me at the crap table and showed me how to bet. He even gave me the money to bet with. Two hundred dollars. At first I lost, but then I started winning, and before I quit I won almost three thousand dollars. Think of it, Beverly. Three thousand dollars! And he made me keep it, even though it was really his because he gave me the original two hundred. Of course, he'd made a lot, too, betting along with me. Well, after that we celebrated. We went around to the other hotels, and he bought champagne, and we saw the shows and drank and lived it up until morning. Everybody seemed to know him, and we got ringside tables with no trouble at all. We absolutely had a ball."

"What business is he in?" Beverly asked. "I presume you found out."

"Oh, yes. He's an importer."

"All right. Then what happened?"

"Well, he made a big play for me. The next day he sent up tons of roses, and I had cocktails and dinner with him that night after I got through posing, and then we went around to the shows and did the whole bit again. On Wednesday he proposed. But I didn't accept till Friday. That was the day he bought me the bracelet."

"Diamonds?" Beverly asked facetiously.

"And sapphires. To go with my eyes."

"Sherry, you didn't marry him!"

"No. But I almost did. We were supposed to get married yesterday. He reserved the bridal suite, and we were going to have a champagne reception and everything, just like movie stars. Only, then I got scared."

"What happened?"

"Oh, he started saying such peculiar things. About what he'd do—after we were married and everything. This was Friday night, late. After we got engaged. We'd been drinking, and I guess he was feeling pretty good. I was, too, but I still got nervous when he started talking about—" She broke off and glanced, embarrassed, at Beverly. "So Saturday morning when I woke up and remembered, I just packed my bags and sneaked out of the hotel and got the first plane back."

"Well, thank the Lord for that," Beverly said. "What in the world came over you? After all, men have been chasing you since you were fourteen."

"I know. But he's not like American men. He's—"

"He's not American?"

"No. He's Sicilian or Greek or something like that. He told me, but I forgot. His name is Andreas. Andreas Kollias. He was so charming. I see what they mean about European men. He made me feel so—wanted."

"And you were going to marry him, just like that, without a word to your family?"

Sherry hesitated, picking at a bit of fuzz on her sweater with delicate fingers. "I thought about it. I even mentioned it, but he thought it would be more romantic to just do it by ourselves."

"I'll bet. Well, you're of age."

Sherry looked at her uncomfortably. "Don't be hurt, Beverly. I wouldn't hurt you for the world. I

WIVES AND LOVERS 89

don't know what came over me. I don't think I would have considered such a thing if I'd met him here. It's just that crazy town. Everything seems so unreal. It's just one big, long party, and nothing's really happening. Like a dream."

"Only you woke up in time."

"I don't know," Sherry said slowly. For the first time, Beverly noticed a faint blueness below her eyes as well, the veins that showed through her porcelain skin only when she was very tired or ill. "Last night when I went out to dinner, a man followed me. Then this morning when I went outside for the paper, the same man was sitting in a parked car across the street. He sat there all morning. About noon I got scared and packed a bag and went over to Shirley's."

"Why didn't you come here? We could put you up."

"I didn't want to get you mixed up in any mess. What with Belinda and all. I would rather have come here."

"What did Shirley say?"

"She told me I was an idiot." Sherry sighed. "I guess I am."

"Have you still got the bracelet?"

"Yes. And the three thousand dollars. I thought about leaving them at the hotel for him, but I was afraid if I made a production out of leaving, somebody would tip him off, and he'd try to stop me."

"So now he's got detectives on your trail," Beverly said, frowning.

"That's not the only reason. He doesn't just want them back. He wants me back. The phone rang practically all last night, and finally I answered it, and it was him, and he was furious. He said if I didn't come back to him, he'd make trouble."

"What kind of trouble?"

"He didn't say." Sherry looked at her pleadingly. "Beverly, what am I going to do?"

"Nothing," Beverly said slowly. "Nothing at all. Let me handle it. I'll go up to Las Vegas tomorrow after work and see him. Where's the bracelet and the money? At Shirley's?"

Sherry nodded. "In my makeup case."

I'll stop and get them on my way to work in the morning. Tomorrow night, I'll take them back and make him leave you alone."

"Would you? Oh, Beverly," Sherry said gratefully. "I'm sorry to cause so much trouble. I don't know why I'm so stupid."

"Nonsense! You're not stupid." Beverly said briskly. "You're just impulsive, and you always were. Remember the time you washed Dad's pipe out with soap and water? And then got so nervous you just stood there and giggled when he blew up?"

"He was so furious. He would have whipped me if you hadn't stood up for me and explained I was just trying to be a good housekeeper. Dear old Bev." She gave her sister a rueful smile. "You've always fished my chestnuts out of the fire for me, haven't you?"

"That's what big sisters are for," Beverly said comfortably. "Now which hotel is this man in?"

After Sherry had left, Beverly went about her housework humming. She was worried about Sherry's situation, but she was confident she could handle it. And it was nice to be needed, pleasant to have someone she loved coming to her for help and advice. Once she had felt that way about Bob, too. Why, she wondered with an uneasy pang, could she feel that way about him no longer?

Seven

"Be a pussycat, Mama," said Jeremy. "Be a pussycat."

"All right," Dana said. "A pussycat doing what?"

Jeremy concentrated, chewing his lip after the manner of his father. "A pussycat drinking milk."

"What kind of a pussycat? A happy one or a sad one?"

"A sad pussycat. What got no home."

Obediently Dana crouched on the living room floor. She put her hands together, folding the fingers under so that they became paws. Lonely, she thought. Lonely, alone, got no home. She extended her head, making the gesture both meek and humble, and began lapping milk from an imaginary saucer. Jeremy screamed with glee and, squatting beside her, began to pat her on the head.

Don surveyed his wife indulgently. "How can you do that hour after hour?"

"It's fun," Dana said, sitting up. "And it's the only acting practice I get."

"You think it'll be useful? Are there a lot of parts for pussycats?"

She made a face at him. "That's not the point. Being a cat or a tree is just an exercise to develop one's empathy."

"Maybe I should do it. Maybe I should spend five minutes every morning imagining I'm a space shuttle."

"Don't laugh. A little more empathy wouldn't hurt you."

"Oh? And what does that mean?"

"Nothing," she said lightly. "Anyway, it's an important tool for actors." She reached for her son and pulled him, laughing, into her lap by the seat of his pants. "And Jeremy's a wonderful audience. It's a pleasure playing to him."

It was Saturday morning, and it was raining. Beyond the big windows, the city had disappeared into misty grayness in which only the top of a giant eucalyptus, growing on the hillside below the house, was visible. The long, green leaves glistened and shook as the raindrops battered them.

"What did they tell you when you did the audition?" Don asked. "About a job, I mean?"

"Nothing. Just thank you, and we'll call you when we have something for you."

"So now they've done their duty, and that's the last you'll hear from them."

Dana frowned. "He liked my improvisation. I'm sure he did. And he even said I'd be good for the show because I'm not too pretty. I look more like a real person than an actress, he said."

"Aren't you too pretty? I always thought you were too pretty."

"Oh, you know what that means. Like the agent said, I'm no Monroe. That's a poem. Or a lyric. I'm no-o-o Monro-o-oe. That's why I'm in the sho-o-ow!" She got to her feet and improvised a few dance steps. "Maybe they could use me in one of those terribly successful little revues that play the Performing Arts Center and then go to Broadway."

Don grinned and stretched, throwing back his head, and Dana paused and looked with approval at his neck, framed in the open white shirt collar and V-neck of his yellow pullover. It was a masculine neck, sturdy without being thick. She went over and kissed him just below the jawline, feeling faintly privileged.

"What are we doing this afternoon?" he said, pulling her into his lap.

"Writing Christmas cards."

"Oh, no. All afternoon?"

"Most of it. And we should take Jeremy shopping. He's outgrown everything, and he needs a new suit for the holidays."

"It's raining. It's a terrible day for shopping. Couldn't he get the new suit next week?"

"Well, possibly. Possibly you might talk me into it."

They kissed each other rather more thoroughly than they usually did when Jeremy was in the room. Rain is an aphrodisiac, all right, Dana thought. Perhaps because it was such a dark day, Jeremy had slept later than usual that morning, and they had enjoyed the infinite luxury of making love right after awakening. Now, only a few hours later, she was in the mood again. She would have seduced him right there and then if it weren't for Jeremy. Sighing, she pulled away and looked at Don, moving her head in the direction of their son, who was sitting on the floor pushing his toy fire engine back and forth and making siren noises.

Don laughed.

"It's funny?" She eyed him reproachfully.

"It's tragic. The sacrifices parents have to make."

"We might as well go shopping. Get our minds on something else."

Don chuckled contentedly, looking pleased with himself.

"Why so smug?"

"Nothing. It just crossed my mind that you don't act like a woman who's being eating alive by ambition."

It was the wrong thing to say. The desire, the contentment of the moment died out of Dana with chilling suddenness. She *was* being eaten alive by ambition, although she was just as happy to have him think she was not. She was keeping her frustrations to herself these days, but they were with her constantly, gnawing obsessively at everything she did. Driving, for instance. Traffic had never bothered her until lately, but now she found herself getting annoyed every time she took the car out. Everywhere there were too many people. They were always in the way, holding her back. She could never get where she wanted to go fast enough through the crowded, clotted streets. Once, when a succession of left-turners made her miss two green lights in a row, she had erupted into a rage that was utterly foreign to her nature. "Idiots!" she had muttered through clenched teeth. "You damned idiots!" Choking with frustration, she had pounded the steering wheel with her fists until they hurt. The outburst amazed her so much that afterward she had examined herself until she found the reason. Unrealized ambition, that was what it was. It made her impatient, irritable at every minor delay and inconvenience that city living entailed, ready to snap at everyone who got first to where she wanted to be, an audition, the teller's window at the bank, the meat counter at the market. Somebody else was always there first, and she was sick to death of waiting and waiting and waiting for her turn.

"Why so quiet all of a sudden?" Don asked, puzzled.

Depressed, she did not answer. Then the phone rang. As she got up from his lap to answer it, pulling her sweater down, she thought ironically, This will be it. This will be "The Judge's Court" calling me about a job. Are you available, Mrs. Hurst? Oh, sure I am. I'm so available I could yell and scream and shake strangers on the street. I'm so available—

"Mrs. Hurst? This is Leo Harris of 'The Judge's Court.' Are you available to do a show for us on Monday?"

Shocked speechless, she thought, It's a joke. Somebody's been reading my mind. The idea flashed through her head and was gone before she had a chance to realize the preposterousness of it.

"Mrs. Hurst? Are you there?"

"Yes," she said. "I'm available."

"Good. The actress we had has just come down with the flu, and we're in a bind. We rehearse Monday

WIVES AND LOVERS

morning and tape in the afternoon. Can you come over here right away and pick up the script? Before noon?"

He went on for several minutes more, describing the story to her. Her mind took the information down automatically, like a tape recorder, without her actually hearing what he said. When he hung up, she put the phone down dazedly and walked back into the living room.

"Who was that?" Don asked.

"It was the court show. They want me for an episode Monday."

"Really? That's great, honey." He seemed to be looking at her with unnecessary intentness.

"It's about a child custody case. I play a woman who's been unhappily married to a man older than I am. I start to drink because of my marital problems, and then we get a divorce, and he wants custody of the child, claiming I'm an unfit mother, and I'm fighting it." Repeating what Leo Harris had said to her on the phone seemed to give his words substance for the first time.

"Sounds like a good part," Don said.

"Yes. It sounds like a wonderful part. I have to go over right now and pick up the script," she said dreamily. "Before noon." The thought of time brought her back to earth. She looked at her watch in alarm. "It's after eleven now!"

Galvanized into action, she rushed to the bedroom, flung open the wardrobe door, yanked down her coat, not pausing to pick up the hanger as it rattled on the floor. Halfway to the front door, she thought, Makeup. Somebody might see me. Back to the dressing table. Her hands shook as she ran a comb through her hair, freshened her kiss-smeared lipstick, and powdered her nose. It was more than excitement; it was as though a powerful force within her had been released. She felt vigorous, dynamic, as though she could sing for hours, or run for miles without tiring. Yes, she could run all the way to the studio, in the rain, to pick up that script.

Running out of the bedroom a second time, she bumped into Don.

"Sorry, darling. Back in forty-five minutes or so."

He caught her arm. "Don't you need a scarf or an umbrella? It's raining pretty hard."

"It doesn't matter," she said, impatiently pulling away from him. She had to go. Right now. This minute. Until she had the script in her hands, she could not believe that it was true, that she had a job at last after all the months of waiting and looking and hoping.

"Honey . . ." He was looking at her strangely.

She was wild with haste. "What is it?"

"Nothing." His face set in its usual stolid expression. "Go ahead."

As she ran from the front door to the carport, the rain hit her like a shower turned on full force. For some reason, getting wet seemed terribly funny, and she laughed as she flung herself into the car and backed out into the steep little street, where the water ran as swiftly as a mountain stream.

At five minutes to eleven on Monday morning, she drove through the auto gate at NBS once more and parked her car in one of the unreserved spaces in the huge parking lot. It was a beautiful day. The weekend storm had cleared before a brisk wind which scoured away the smog and sent clouds so white they hurt the eyes scudding across a sky of unfamiliar blueness. Script in hand, she walked across the parking lot and into the building the policeman at the gate had indicated.

Rehearsal Room 1 had a big table in the center with people seated around it, apparently in conference.

"Mrs. Hurst?" A man with salt-and-pepper hair and a thin, not unfriendly face came toward her. "I'm Frank Arnold. I direct the show." He introduced her to the rest of the cast. Pete Hicks, who was to play the husband, was ruddy-faced and tall with amused, intelligent eyes. As he acknowledged the introduction, he bowed slightly and winked at the same time, as though they shared some pleasant joke.

"Ready to go?" Arnold asked.

"Right," Dana said. She sat down at the table, crossed her legs, and placed her script before her in a businesslike way, feeling cool and organized and thoroughly able to cope with the situation.

Two hours later, she was not so sure. Her script was full of penciled corrections, all of which she had to memorize during the lunch break. She surveyed it in utter dismay.

"Never worked a court show before?" Pete Hicks looked at her in sympathetic amusement as they walked out of the rehearsal room.

"No, I haven't. Is it always like this? Why so many last-minute changes?"

"The shows are based on actual cases, and they're taken from court transcripts, but sometimes the writer gets carried away and makes alterations he thinks will improve the story. These sometimes make the verdict come out differently. And then the lawyers find things wrong with the way the testimony sounds in the script, as you saw this morning."

"Why do they use real lawyers instead of actors?"

"I rather suspect they do it to get free technical advice on the script."

"I see. That makes it a little rough on the rest of us, though, doesn't it?"

"There aren't always this many changes," he said, and wandered off with a casual wave of the hand.

With a ham sandwich and a glass of milk in front of her, Dana sat in the commissary and began rememorizing the script. It was 1:30. In just two hours, she would be taping the show. Before that, there would be another run-through. Less than two hours to be letter-perfect in her part again, the way she had been that morning when she arrived at the studio. Lips moving, frowning with effort, she tried to concentrate in spite of the bustle around her.

"Mind if I sit here?" Two girls, trays in hand, stood beside the table.

"Not at all," Dana said, trying to smile.

"It's the greatest shade I've ever seen. Absolutely the greatest. What is it?"

"Darling, I'll tell you my secret. I mixed two. You know Jade Green? That's what I used to use, but Bill thought it was a little dark. So then I tried Gold Mist, and that came out the color of a canary, know what I mean? So I was going absolutely mad, and then this idea came to me, why don't I mix the two of them? Just mix them. So I did."

"The greatest. Absolutely the greatest. What are the names again?"

"Jade Green and Gold Mist. Are we bothering you, darling?"

"It's all right," Dana said. She gulped the rest of her milk, picked up the other half of her sandwich, and left the commissary.

Outside, she looked around for a place to sit. There didn't seem to be any benches, so she settled for the lip of a large fountain. "Davey needs a mother," she began again, "and if you think . . ." The splashing of the fountain seemed to drown out the words on the page. She got up and started walking. The sun shone in an idiotically cheerful way, and the people who passed her seemed maddeningly happy and carefree, people for whom the afternoon held no crisis. Eventually she sat down again, this time on the bottom tread of an iron staircase leading into one of the buildings. "Davey needs a mother . . ."

"How's it going?" It was her leading man. He was smoking a cigarette, and he looked as relaxed as though he were about to play golf.

"Not so well. I'm having trouble concentrating. This is the first TV show I've done, and I guess I'm a little nervous."

"No TV? What have you been doing?"

"Nothing for several years. I retired and had a baby."

"Find it boring being a housewife?"

"Yes. Only right now I'd be delighted if all I had on my mind was washing clothes."

"How old is your child?"

"Four," Dana said. "Look, I hate to be rude, but I really have to work on this."

"Quite so." He waved his hand airily and started to leave. Then he came back. "Look. Would it help any if I cued you?"

"Would you? That would be wonderful. How nice of you."

"Not really. It's better for me if you know your lines. Otherwise you may blow up and get us all in trouble. Now, where were you?"

"It's where I say, 'Davey needs a mother . . .'"

At 2:15 he stopped her. "If you're going to get made up, you'd better go now."

"Makeup? Nobody said anything to me about makeup."

"You don't get it unless you ask. They'd just as soon you'd wear your regular street makeup. It looks more natural."

"Fine. Then I'll skip it. That will give us more time to rehearse."

"Good Lord, but you're eager." He shook his head. "Just like any starving young actress. Only I gather from the way you're dressed you've not precisely been starving."

"Well, not for food, anyway," Dana said grimly.

Just before three they walked to the studio where the show was to be taped.

"What happens if somebody makes a mistake?" she asked nervously.

"Somebody else covers it."

"And if it's a real disaster? Something that can't be

covered?"

"Then the whole show has to be taped over."

"You mean they can't do over just that one little section?"

"Costs too much. Cheaper to do the whole show over. After all, it's only half an hour."

"Do they have to do it over very often?"

"No." Pete Hicks squeezed her elbow comfortingly. "And they won't have to do it over today. Now pull yourself together. You're going to be very good."

The courtroom set, an artificial chamber with no ceiling and only two and a half walls, took up only a small section of the vast sound stage. The judge's bench, the table for the attorneys, and the rows of seats for the spectators stood out in a blaze of lights anchored to the catwalks overhead. Besides the people who had been at the rehearsal that morning, there were now three cameramen, a sound man, and a floor manager on the set. The stage had the unnatural quietness of heavily soundproofed rooms, and their voices as they moved about were swallowed up without echo or resonance to amplify them. The cameras, one in front, one in back, and one to the right, moved soundlessly on their thick rubber wheels.

"I don't know which direction to play in," Dana said, whispering automatically in the dead, muffled atmosphere. She had intended the comment to sound like a joke, but it came out worried.

"One thing less to fret about," Hicks said reassuringly.

The camera rehearsal went better than Dana anticipated. She remembered her lines, and it seemed to her that she spoke them with conviction.

"Well done," Pete told her in the break before they went on to the taping. "You're going to be fine."

"Thank you," she said gratefully. "You've been a great help."

"While we're taping, don't worry about which camera is on you. A little red light goes on in the one that's operating, but just ignore it. Play as you did, without thinking about them at all."

"To tell you the truth, I forgot about them," Dana said. "They're so quiet. And then I knew they weren't working," she added with a sudden, small misgiving.

She walked over and examined one of the cameras. It was small, not nearly as big as the movie cameras in the pictures she had seen. The glass eye where the red light went on was rather like the light in a glove compartment. However, that was not the camera's real eye, she thought. Now she examined the hooded lens with interest. A big, blank eye. A mechanical eye. That's my audience, she said inwardly. Through that I will be watched by all the people who watch daytime television. I wonder how many of them there are. Millions. How many millions of people would see her through that staring, thickly glassed, inhuman eye? She would never know, just as she would never know how they felt as they watched her. She would not hear them laugh or cry, and she could not count them. What's the most people I've ever played to before? she wondered. Twenty-five hundred, maybe, in the USC auditorium?

"Places, everyone," the floor manager called. He, like the cameramen, wore an earphone and mouthpiece to communicate with the director in the control booth.

"One minute. Stand by, all position."

All at once she was alarmingly frightened. Unable to stop herself, she looked in turn at each of the three cameras watching her, the concentrated eyes which stood for the uncounted millions in her unknown audience. She felt a hand on her arm. Pete Hicks shook his head at her. She managed to pull her face, which has become peculiarly stiff, into a smile.

"Number thirty for air, number thirty . . ."

"Fifteen seconds . . ."

Why was the stage, which had seemed so abnormally still before, so much quieter now? The microphone, which hung high in the air on a long boom over their heads, would surely pick up the thunder of her heartbeat.

"Five seconds . . ."

Now.

"All right, I drank, your honor," she heard herself say in a voice that trembled all too convincingly. "But I drank because of him. If he'll leave me and Davey alone, I'll be a good mother. I promise you I will. Not another drop if he'll just leave us alone. But don't let him take Davey away. Please don't."

"The Judge's Court," the announcer said in rich tones into a microphone somewhere behind the set, "based on actual cases from California court records, is brought to you today by the makers of Natural, the hair shampoo made for today's active woman, and Mariano, the new frozen pizza that says Italian with every bite—"

The red light. Which camera had its red light on? She tried to see out of the corner of her eye without turning her head. Which one? She absolutely had to know which one.

"Charges and countercharges, and the court wishes to establish which of you is a fit parent to bring up this boy," the judge was saying.

If I just knew which one it was, Dana thought in a panic. She was too terrified to analyze why this was important, but all her security seemed to depend on knowing. She turned her head, pretending to look at Pete Hicks. Beyond him the side camera moved in toward them swiftly, silently. The red light was on. There, she thought triumphantly. Around her was dead silence. Pete was looking at her now. I've missed a cue, she thought, horrified. At that moment, every line of the script vanished from her head as completely as if she had never seen it. Pete, his head turned away from the camera and toward her, silently mouthed her opening words.

"It all started about five years ago," she began quaveringly.

From then on, the show proceeded in a nightmare distortion of reality. It seemed like an eternity. She spoke her lines mechanically, hardly aware of what she was doing. The interspersed commericals slid by without giving her time to organize her thoughts, locate her misplaced self-confidence. She heard the others dimly, aware of what they were saying only when the familiar words of her cues penetrated the numbness of her terror. Twice, for agonizing, eternal seconds, she could not remember what came next. Then the blankness passed, and she was back on the track. Eventually, it was over. Surprised, she felt they had just begun. On the other hand, she was ten years older.

"There now. That wasn't so bad, was it?" Smiling, Pete held out a package of cigarettes.

Dana shook her head. Her body was leaden, and she felt that quite some time would have to elapse before she would be light enough to get up from her chair. "It's a good thing it was a dramatic part," she managed to say. "Maybe they'll think my shaky voice was part of the act."

"You started thinking about the cameras," he said reprovingly. "I told you not to do that."

"I know you did. That's what made me think about them."

"Oh no. I'm sorry. But you did beautifully. Really you did. You had me worried for a moment or two, but you recovered nicely. And that's all anyone can ask."

"You don't think they'll have to do it over?"

"Good Lord, no. Certainly not. You'll see. They'll tell us in a few minutes."

When word came that the tape was a wrap, they walked out of the studio together.

"You know, I've forgotten how to concentrate,"

Dana said soberly. "That's the trouble. The first thing they taught us, and I can't do it anymore."

"Had you thought any about joining a class?"

"An acting class? No, I haven't. I guess I thought I was past that stage."

"You haven't acted in a long time. It's a technique, a discipline one can forget. Joining a class might get you back into the right habits of mind. And give you some experience while you're waiting for jobs."

"I don't know where I'd find one," Dana said doubtfully.

"Have you heard of Ryan Parker?"

"Of course. He's one of my favorites."

"He has a small, private class of a few people he thinks have talent. If you'd like to join it, I may be able to help you. He's a friend of mine."

"Mr. Hicks, that would be wonderful. How very kind of you."

"Not at all. It would be a pleasure." He looked at her. "You know, you really have a quite remarkable voice. It registers emotion with extraordinary sensitivity. In high fidelity, one might say."

"Why, thank you."

Unaccountably, he looked abashed. "Well. Should you like to give me your telephone number, or would you prefer to call me up in a few days after I've talked to Ryan?"

Dana opened her handbag. "I'll give you my number."

As she walked back to the parking lot, it seemed as though several days had elapsed since she had arrived that morning. It had been a difficult day, and she was far from feeling triumphant about it. It was, however, a beginning. At least it was a beginning.

Eight

On Monday evening, Beverly went directly from work to the airport to catch a plane for Las Vegas. She had told Bob that morning where she was going and why. "I should go," he had said, sounding uncomfortable. "This guys sounds like he might be tough."

"Nonsense," Beverly had said. "I can handle him. Besides, it's *my* sister who's involved." Bob had protested a little further, but in the end, looking relieved, he had allowed himself to be persuaded that she was the one to go.

As the plane flew north, Beverly considered plans of action. Clearly the man, whoever he was, was an undesirable character. Would he threaten her? She thought not. She might, on the other hand, theaten him. The question was how? Perhaps womanly persuasion might be a better course. She might be able to offend his pride by implying it was unmanly to pursue a woman against her will. In the end, she decided that she must meet her adversary first and then decide how to attack him.

The plane banked suddenly, leaning on one wing tip to reveal a violent blaze of lights below stretched longitudinally across the blackness of the desert. That must be the strip, Beverly thought, where all the big hotels are. It looked bizarre, an oasis of neon in the midst of nothingness, Times Square transplanted to the desert.

"The Ambassador," she told the taxi driver at the

airport. She leaned back in the seat and set her jaw determinedly.

The hotel was sleek tropical-modern, chilled to the temperature of a walk-in refrigerator. As soon as she had taken off her coat, she picked up the telephone.

"Mr. Kollias? This is Mrs. Connors, Sherry's sister. I wonder if I could talk to you."

There was a brief pause. "You are in Las Vegas?" His voice, with only the barest trace of accent perceptible, sounded mildy incredulous.

"I am in this hotel. Room 139. Can you come here?"

"Please, no. I am waiting for a long-distance call. Perhaps you could come here. Room 147?"

"I'll be right there," Beverly said, and hung up quickly.

As she lifted her hand to knock on 147, the door opened and a waiter came out with an empty bar tray. He glanced at her curiously. Apparently she was not the type of woman visitor Mr. Kollias usually entertained.

"Come in," said Mr. Kollias, rising from the sofa. As he came to meet her, Beverly felt a slight shock. Unconsciously she had been expecting someone large, greasy, and sinister, rather like a gangster. Mr. Kollias was small, bland, and well kept, and the hand he extended to her smelled discreetly of expensive cologne. He wore a dark gray business suit of conservative cut, and he looked newly shaven. "I have taken the liberty of ordering us a cocktail." A silver shaker, beaded with moisture, and two glasses stood on the table before the sofa.

"Thank you," Beverly said, abashed. She had formulated no method for coping with civility.

"She has run away," Kollias said immediately when they were seated. "My lovely little Sherry has run away."

"I notice you didn't follow her."

He shrugged delicately. "One hires people for that. They will bring her back."

"You mean they'll kidnap her?"

"Please, madame." Clearly he deplored the word. "They will persuade her to come of her own accord."

"I doubt that. I talked to her yesterday. She told me everything."

The implication of her words did not disturb him. He sat quietly for a moment, tapping with well-manicured fingertips on the sofa cushion. He was dark and round and sleek as an otter, Beverly thought. Round, brown eyes, round, smooth face, sleek, dark hair. She could imagine him living elegantly in some limpid river having fish brought to him by . . . whom?

He leaned forward abruptly and poured the martinis. "Just what is it you want, madame?"

"I want you to stop annoying my sister," Beverly said levelly.

"My dear lady. If I do not grant her that request, how do you think I will grant it to you?"

"If you don't I shall have to go to the police."

He took a sip of his drink. "They will do nothing. No crime has been committed."

"You are having her followed."

"And so? She should be flattered."

"She is frightened, not flattered. What do you propose to do?"

"I propose to persuade her to return to me."

"And if she doesn't?"

"Then, madame, her life will become quite unpleasant." He smiled, and his round dark eyes sparkled gaily, as though he were planning a picnic.

"Mr. Kollias, what do you do for a living?" Beverly said, to change the subject.

"Madame, I cannot feel that is any concern of yours."

"On the contrary. You intend to marry my sister. I have a right to know if you are able to support her."

"In the style to which she is accustomed, I believe the phrase is." He was still smiling, but his eyes had gone a little flat.

"She says you seem to have a great deal of money. Are you in business for yourself?"

"Madame, I find your questions tiresome," he said swiftly. "It was very stupid of you to come here. Your sister is of age, no? What happens between us is no concern of yours. Let us bring this fruitless conversation to an end at once." He stood up.

Beverly stood up too. "Do you know what I think? I think your behavior is most unmanly," she said steadily. "No American would stoop to doing these things."

"That, madame, is of no interest whatsoever to me." His eyes were totally black and impenetrable now, and he was no longer smiling as he showed her the door.

She was too angry to go back to her room; besides, she had not yet had dinner. The main dining room was jammed for the first floor show, but she found a table in the coffee shop where she sat, hot all over with frustration and annoyance, and considered what to do next. The most sensible course was probably to consult an attorney. She mulled this conclusion over, frowning, while she ate her salad. There was only one thing wrong with it. It involved getting outside help, and she had promised herself she would handle this situation alone. That was what she had made the flight up here to do, but this bland little man had defeated her and made her feel faintly like a fool.

After dinner, she sat in the bar adjoining the casino and had a bourbon and water. On a raised platform above the bar, a four-man band played contemporary jazz, paced intricately by drums. When the music stopped, she could hear the subdued, insistent rumble of the casino, the clank of slot machines, the ritual chant of the pitmen, the whir of roulette wheels. Fascinated, she turned to watch the gambling crowd over the back of the booth. Different was the word. Mink and sport coats, tank tops and tennis shorts, jeans and diamonds elbowed each other for positions at the crap table. "Pay the line," chanted the pitmen, matter-of-fact, infinitely bored, impervious to the avid excitement all around them. As the soundproofed ceiling absorbed the uproarious clatter below, making it bearable, so the frigidity of the air-conditioned atmosphere seemed to chill the fevered emotions of the people around the tables, keeping them below the boiling point of faintings and hysteria. Only later, when they got outside in the fresh air, would they realize what had happened to them, Beverly thought. Sherry was right. There was something unreal about all this.

All at once she saw Kollias shouldering unobtrusively through the crowd. He was in evening clothes, suave as a maitre d'hotel or a foreign prince amid the tourist vulgarity. As he took up a stand at one of the crap tables, he nodded to the pitmen, and they returned the greeting. Beverly watched him play with interest. He handled the dice with casual familiarity, his round dark eyes studying the table like a stockbroker watching the board. It's more like business than pleasure with him, she thought, and suddenly clapped her hand to her mouth. In an instant, she summoned the waiter.

"Who is that man in evening clothes over there?"

"The dark one? That's the Greek. Kollias is his name. He's one of our best customers."

"What do you mean?"

The waiter lowered his voice discreetly. "He's a professional gambler. One of the biggest."

"You mean gambling is his profession?"

"Who knows? Like they say, he's got no other visible means of support."

"How interesting," Beverly said thoughtfully. "Thank you very much." She watched Kollias a few minutes more, studying the way he played, calmly, objectively, ignoring the people around him. He did not seem particularly elated when he won or disturbed when he lost. All in a night's work, Beverly thought. The importing business indeed. She got up from her table to go and stand beside him.

He did not look up. After a moment, she said, "Mr. Kollias, I wonder if I might have another word with you." When he saw who it was, he inclined his dark, round head ironically.

They sat down at her table in the bar. "Perhaps my sister will come back to you," Beverly said pleasantly.

"Oh?" His dark eyes examined her curiously.

"I could not, of course, permit her to marry you right away. Long engagements are a tradition in our family, and a week's acquaintance is hardly a sufficient basis for matrimony even in Greece, is it?"

He was silent this time, clearly baffled as to what she was driving at.

"Of course, she's a well-brought-up girl. She couldn't come up here alone. It wouldn't look right. So, if she comes, I shall come with her." Beverly smiled and sipped her drink.

Kollias smiled faintly. "And how could you arrange that? I believe Sherry mentioned you are employed."

"I am, but I can always get time off," she lied. "Besides, I should occupy myself profitably while I was here studying your activities."

"What do you mean?"

"I believe the IRS people offer a nice reward to anyone turning in income-tax evaders."

Their glances met and held. After a moment, Kollias laughed shortly.

"Do not attempt to frighten me, madame. Do you think I have not been investigated by the IRS people before?"

"Probably not exhaustively," Beverly said calmly. "I doubt if they have the personnel to put a man full time on the trail of everyone like you. However, that is a service I should be happy to perform for them. Just so my chaperoning time won't be a total financial loss." She lit a cigarette, proud to see that her steady hands, in case he was watching, denoted that she felt herself in complete command of the situation.

"You are a very resourceful woman," he said at last.

He had made no move to light her cigarette for her. "Your sister will be fortunate if she finds a husband who looks after her interests so devoutedly. But perhaps, after all, she will not need such a husband if she has you."

"I'll consider that a compliment."

"Perhaps so. Perhaps not. No doubt an American woman would consider it a compliment." His eyes flickered briefly in anger and contempt.

"I've left a bracelet and three thousand dollars, which I believe belong to you, in the hotel safe in your name," Beverly said. "You can pick them up whenever you like."

He rose. "Convey my salutations to your sister. Since I shall not be seeing her again." Abruptly he turned and walked back toward the crap tables.

"So that takes care of him," Beverly concluded in triumph the following evening when she had finished telling the story of her trip to Sherry and Shirley.

"Beverly, you're wonderful," Sherry's blue eyes were limpid with admiration and gratitude. "I'm so relieved. What a ridiculous situation."

"Ridiculous? It could have been serious. Next time you just watch your step, young lady," Beverly said maternally.

"Why should she?" Shirley said acidly. "When she gets in trouble, she's always got you around to pull her out."

Beverly and Sherry turned to look at her. Shirley, in some subtle, undefinable way, was the not-so-pretty twin. She looked enough like Sherry so that their relationship was immediately apparent, yet somehow, mysteriously, she was not a beauty and Sherry was. Perhaps it was her features, which were a shade less harmoniously proportioned, or her hair, which she wore less becomingly, or her clothes, about which she was studiously careless. Most of all, she lacked the regal serenity, the absolute conviction of beauty which set Sherry apart.

"Don't be nasty," Beverly said calmly, still aglow with her triumph over evil. "What's a big sister for?"

"To keep people from growing up, apparently," Shirley said in the same tone. Her jeaned legs hung over the arm of her chair, and she was swinging one foot in a manner that was somehow insolent. "To keep them from ever having to face the consequences of their own foolishness."

"What do you mean?" Beverly asked indignantly. "You sound as though I was trying to run her life or something."

"Not run it," Shirley said. "Oh, no. If you were running it, there wouldn't be any mistakes in it for you to straighten out so you could feel important. No, you let her run it until it goes off the tracks. Then you come along, the great efficiency expert, and put everything right again."

"That's the most unfair thing I ever heard," Beverly cried. "What am I supposed to do? Sit by and let my family go to hell?"

"Why don't you, sometime? Why don't you let her stew in her own juices once in awhile? Then maybe she'd think before she started to do something stupid."

"I'm not going to listen to any more of this," Sherry said with dignity. She got up and crossed elegantly to the bedroom, shutting the door behind her.

"I don't know what's wrong with you, Shirley," Beverly said, trying to control her temper. "What makes you such a bitch about this? I've always been just as ready to help you as I have Sherry."

"But I never let you. Right? And you know why? Because I prefer to stand on my own two feet."

"You never liked me. You never let me help you because you didn't like me."

"Oh, no. That's not the way it was, sis. You never liked me because I wouldn't let you do things for me. You only wanted to be around people who lean on you and look up to you."

"You're jealous," Beverly said hotly. "Jealous of Sherry and me. More than ever since the folks died, you're jealous of our relationship."

"Good Lord! I wouldn't be either one of you. She's dependent on you, and what's worse, you're dependent on her and you don't even know it."

"Let's skip the amateur psychoanalysis, shall we? Just because you majored in psychology, you're not a Freud!"

"Maybe not, but at least it's helped me figure out my own family." Shirley looked at her contemptuously. "And I wish you'd let that girl grow up before it's too late. It's lucky for Belinda that you're so busy with your damn job, or she'd end up the same way."

"I'm packed," Sherry said, appearing at the bedroom door. "And I'm leaving. Are you coming, Beverly?"

"Right now," Beverly said. She stood up quickly.

"Thanks for the hospitality, Shirley," Sherry said without warmth.

"Any time," Shirley said. "Only next time, try not to be followed, huh? It makes me nervous to have men hanging around in the street staring up at my windows."

Nine

It was a cold, foggy Monday morning, but Vivian, driving downtown to work from Sid's house in Beverly Hills, felt no inclination to be depressed. She had on the red wool suit she had worn the day before, and the cheerful brightness of it reflected the warmth she felt within. It had been a wonderful night, full and satisfying. This morning she felt pleasantly conscious of her body, of its essential nakedness beneath the heavy winter clothing. In the few weeks they had been lovers, Sid had awakened in her a new awareness of the most intimate parts of herself, an awareness which stayed with her even when they were apart. It was that, she knew, which made the men at the office look at her with keener interest. Strange how men always seemed to sense when a woman was having a satisfying affair. It gave her a kind of aura. How many married woman of her acquaintance, she wondered a little smugly, were starting their morning with this warm, relaxed sense of completion? Dana, perhaps. Nobody else that she could think of. How beautiful it was to have a lover. She inhaled deliberately, dilating her nostrils slightly. Yes, she could still faintly catch the scent of Sid's body hovering on her skin. She had not showered purposedly this morning in order to have that scent and the memories it evoked accompany her through the day.

They saw each other nearly every night now. Sometimes they stayed in her apartment, sometimes in Sid's house in Beverly Hills, depending on which was more convenient. She liked his house except for the constant, vaguely disturbing realization that another woman had belonged in it. When she had first begun going there with him, she had insisted that he put away the pictures of his wife and children, but there were other, less tangible reminders, which remained. The crystal bottle of pink bubble bath on the tub ledge. The velvet-covered chaise in the bedroom with a lipstick smudge, not Vivian's shade, on one arm. The gold brush, comb, and mirror set on the dressing table.

"Why didn't she take these with her?" Vivian asked, fingering the hairbrush and feeling annoyed the first time she was in the master bedroom. A few black hairs still clung to the bristles.

"She left a lot. It's not like she really needs any of it. Her family has money."

"Is she living with them?"

Sid nodded. "She is now. They have a big house in New York. I guess it's good for the kids to get acquainted with their grandparents." He stood in the doorway, absentmindedly swinging a toy bear with long, white fur.

"What's that you've got?" Vivian asked sharply.

"Chris was crazy about this thing. I keep thinking I ought to send it to him."

"Well, do."

"All right, I will." He tossed the bear onto the chaise and, embracing her, walked her backward to the king-size bed and pushed her gently down on it.

"Here?" she asked in alarm. The quilted satin spread smelled of an unfamiliar perfume, and suddenly she felt like a trespasser.

"Here," Sid said firmly.

It had been only a few moments until his hands on her body had made her forget where she was.

Gradually, with repetition, the feeling of being an intruder in the house was fading. She knew the location of the pots in the kitchen, and where the liquor was kept under lock and key against the amoral maid who wandered in once a week to flick a feather duster over the furniture and listen to the record collection. She knew how to turn on the heat in the pool, and where Sid kept his underwear. She even had the key to the place. Occasionally, when she finished work before he did, she would get to the house in time to turn on the lights against the early twilight, build a fire in the mirrored fireplace, and get out the makings for martinis.

Once he had arrived to find her darning his socks.

"Christ," he said, surprised. "You're not going domestic on me!"

Vivian's head jerked up. "Certainly not. I simply noticed the ones you had on yesterday had a hole in them. I thought there might be more, and there are. As a matter of interest, your socks are a complete disaster. You know this town," she went on, sounding as practical as she could to neutralize the expression on his face. "If you go around looking down at the heels, you'll be out of a job in no time."

"Think big," Sid said.

"Exactly. Wealth is the best policy."

He came and sat beside her on the oversized sofa and watched. "Where'd you learn to do that?"

"At home when I was a little girl. We Midwestern types have all the homely virtues. I can also crochet, embroider, and tat. My grandmother taught me."

"Hell, Vivian, you don't have to go to all that trouble. I'll get Juanita to do it."

"Like hell you will. It's all Juanita can do to get the dust redistributed on her one day."

He spread his hands in resignation. "So I'll buy new ones already. Cut it out, baby, and mix me a drink. My ulcer's thirsty."

She regarded him solemnly for a moment, and he had the fleeting impression he had disappointed a child. "Okay," she said, getting up and going to the bar. "Booze coming up. Incidentally, we're all out of pickled onions."

On weekends when it was warm enough, they swam in the heated pool. The sun was too far south to produce a tan, but it was bright enough in the blue sky to give them a sense of tropical ease as they lay side by side on canvas pads on the warm concrete and looked at the glittering reflections the pool cast on the dark green leaves of the oleanders.

"Jesus, this is the life," Sid would say. "Sunshine, a pool, a beautiful girl. What bastard could ask for more?"

"Nebraska was never like this," Vivian would answer, smiling.

When they were thoroughly relaxed with the sun, the swimming, and the gin, they would go into the cool, dark house and lazily make love. These were the best times of all.

This last Sunday it had been too cold for swimming. The sky was gloomy, threatening rain but not producing it. After a late breakfast, they played gin rummy all afternoon in front of the fire. Around four, Vivian went to the kitchen to make fudge.

"Where's the chocolate? I know I saw some chocolate in here," she said, standing on a chair to peer into the cupboard. She had already tied on a blue apron she had brought from her apartment.

"It's so nice to have a broad around the house," Sid sang. He had a fairly passable baritone, with the same warm quality as his speaking voice.

"Please, your language," Vivian said. "I've led a sheltered life."

"I'll bet you have, working around newspapermen."

"No, but before that." She looked at him thoughtfully. "Do you know I never even said damn until after I was out of college? When I first went to work for the paper, I was appalled at the way everybody talked. I guess I looked shocked, because they kept apologizing to me all the time. Eventually I saw how nervous I was making them, so I just stopped paying any attention, and after a while things got back to normal. Now when the editor calls a reporter a stupid damn sonofabitch, I don't even think he's mad at him. Which of course, he isn't."

"You know something? You're a great girl."

The way he said it made her feel unexpectedly shy and self-conscious. "I am?"

"The greatest. You're gonna make some bastard a wonderful wife. Jesus, that was original."

"Well, don't count on it. I have no desire to spend the rest of my life waiting on some man."

"Don't you? You do it so well."

"I try to do everything well," she said a little edgily.

"And you do, baby, you do." He laughed meaningfully, putting his arms around her legs, then suddenly as he looked up at her, his eyes went dark with emotion. "Christ, Vivian. I don't know what would have happened to me if I hadn't met you. I was dying. I don't know what I would have done if you hadn't come along." His arms tightened, and he rested his head against her thighs in a gesture that seemed somehow defenseless.

As she looked down at him, a surge of deep feeling overwhelmed her. She did not give it a name, but it made her want to cradle his head in her arms and say a thousand tender things. She longed to kiss him, to comfort him, to protect him from everything cold and difficult and uncaring in the world, to give him everything he wanted and needed, everything, everything and more. "Sid," she whispered. She touched his face with her fingers and found him waiting, passive, receptive, hardly breathing. He was thirsting for tenderness. She caressed him gently. It was like pouring cool water onto dry, parched sand. "Oh, Sid."

Somewhere within her, an alarm sounded. Her heart began to beat irregularly, fluttering, then thudding like a frightened animal caged in her ribs. She caught herself up sharply. It was desire, of course. Only desire. Disengaging herself from his embrace, she got down off the chair and led him to the bedroom.

They had not had a night like that before. In the chilly, fog-darkened dawn, after they had gone together in silence one more time, Sid looked at her soberly. "You've got a lot of passion, Vivian. You can be a violent woman. But I never saw you tender before. Not like you've been tonight."

She laughed softly, rolling over to bite his shoulder. "It's you. It's because you're so beautiful."

"Beautiful? Me? Jesus, baby, you need glasses."

"No," she insisted, "you're beautiful. A beautiful, sexy man. Sensual. That's a better word. The sensuality of the European male. My beautiful, sensual European lover. Incidentally, have you been circumcised? I can never remember to check."

"What? Of course. Like I said, you need glasses." He continued to look at her soberly. "A great kidder, aren't you? A real crazy broad."

"Yes. A real crazy broad. Do you like me?"

"I like you," he said slowly. "But I'm not sure I understand you."

She had gotten out of bed then, and put on the red suit, and now she was driving down the freeway to work. She did not notice the gray day. She was too busy remembering how much he had pleased her and, even more important, how much she had pleased him. For this time, he had been deeply moved by her lovemaking, that she knew, and it gave her a sense of triumph. She prided herself on not being one of those women who passively allow themselves to be loved. On the contrary, she gave as much as she took, with the consequence that she possessed a man quite as thoroughly as he possessed her. It was, she felt, a credit to her strength of mind that she could be so uninhibited sexually after the strict way she had been brought up.

She walked into the office too absorbed in herself to notice any unusual bustle. Lou Adams got up from his desk and walked over to her immediately. "Have a nice weekend?" He looked her over insinuatingly.

"Lovely. Can't you tell?"

"Yeah," said Adams, who got around, himself. "You've got that look. I've been trying to get you on the phone for two hours, and you weren't home. Look, there's a plane down near the international airport. A 747. Crashed in the fog, knocked out a row of houses."

"My God. How many killed?"

"They're still counting. I want you to run on down there and get a human interest piece. On the double. Don't try to get back here with it. Phone it in. And make it good. It's the worst crash the L.A. airport's ever had." He looked at her carefully. "You'll be okay, won't you?"

"Of course."

"Good. Now beat it."

She was quite calm as she drove out the Harbor Freeway. In the southern section of the city, the fog was low and thick, smothering the dense morning flow of traffic. She proceeded carefully, watching out for rear-end collisions. In time she passed two, one involving three cars, the other five. The drivers stood helplessly arguing or jumping up and down on locked bumpers. A young man wearing a cowboy hat kept his hands in the pocket of his coat while he talked to a middle-aged man in an overcoat who was gesticulating angrily. The young one belongs to that truck, Vivian thought, seeing a red Ford pickup in the pile-up, and the older one belongs to the Cadillac sedan. Their breaths puffed out whitely in the cold morning air. She noted all these details clearly but from a distance, as though she saw them through the wrong end of opera glasses. Already she had assumed the attitude of mind which saw her through stories like the one ahead.

Traffic, as she approached the airport, came almost to a standstill. Motorcycle police threaded their way through it, trying hopelessly to unsnarl the traffic. On the sidewalk, people stood and stared into the blind sky. In the unmoving line of cars, Vivian waited and stared, too, but the fog obliterated any evidence of smoke.

A sign ahead on the right said Hamburger Heaven. Parking in Rear. There was a driveway just before the building which had the sign on it. She turned in and parked her car. She took her city street map from the glove compartment. The street where the plane crashed should not be far away. Yes, it was about five blocks.

She walked swiftly, wishing she did not have on high heels. Other people were hurrying in the same direction as she, but as she got closer, she began to meet people coming away. White-faced and silent, they were easy to recognize. One woman held her handkerchief to her mouth. Vivian increased her pace, cutting around slower walkers in front of her.

When she reached the street, a policeman barred her away. "No sightseers," he said angrily. "Haven't you people got anything else to do?"

Vivian showed him her credentials.

"Okay." He looked at her curiously. "But this is no place for a society reporter, lady."

"I'm not a society reporter."

The accident was one block up, and now the street was choked with police cars, fire trucks, and ambulances, leaving only a narrow passage through the center. The whine of a siren rose, and an ambulance came slowly down to the end of the street. As it passed, she could see a man sitting beside someone lying motionless inside.

The street was lined with small, similar houses. There were sparse, winter-brown lawns in front of them, but no trees and few bushes. Some of the lawns had low wire fences around them. The houses were white, mostly, and all of them were frame and looked as though they would burn easily.

When Vivian got to the end of the block, she paused for a moment and surveyed what lay before her. The houses on one side of the street had entirely disappeared. Where they had stood were blackened squares of ash which no longer even smoked. Gigantic gashes sliced across what had been the lawns, and bits of metal and unidentifiable debris lay scattered over the street. It's like a tornado, she thought. Like a tornado striking back home. Part of the tail section, the edges torn and ripped as though by a giant can opener, rose nearby from the midst of a small knot of people. Vivian went over to them. "Did anyone see the crash?"

Several people turned. "I didn't see it, but I came out of the house right afterward," one man said. He was middle-aged, with the tough, reddened skin of someone who had worked outdoors all his life, a carpenter perhaps.

"What happened? What was it like?" Vivian asked.

"Well ma'am, there was this terrible crash that shook the house. It went on a long time, the noise, seemed like, and then there was this big boom, like dynamite. I guess it was the plane blowin' up. I ran outside right away, and all the houses across there was smashed and on fire, and people were runnin' and screamin'. I never seen anything like it in my life." He paused, and Vivian waited silently for him to go on, giving him all her attention. He smelled, she noticed, rather strongly of whiskey.

"I looked up the street there, and the plane was burnin' away, and I ran up to see if I could do anything, but you couldn't help, you couldn't get anywhere near it. And then I see a cat runnin' and screamin' with its hair all on fire. A long-hair cat, it was. I tried to catch her, but she was goin' too fast, just screamin' and runnin'—I don't know where she got to." He paused again. "You a reporter?"

"Yes," Vivian said.

"You gonna write all this up for the paper?"

"Yes."

He jerked his head sideways. "Come on."

Vivian followed him up the driveway of one of the houses on the intact side of the street and in through the back door. On the sink in the kitchen stood a pint bottle of bourbon.

"Better have a swig of this. You'll need it."

"No. I have work to do. But thank you." She got his name and address as he accompanied her back down the driveway.

Farther up the street, the amount of debris seemed to increase. Brownish and blackened stains on the sidewalk showed where the clean-up crews had already been at work. Near the spot where the plane had exploded, a vast leveling process had taken place. The houses on both sides of the street had vanished here, leaving behind only an indistinguishable rubble of ashes, twisted metal, and broken mortar.

The front door of one of the last houses standing was open. Vivian went up to it and knocked. The woman who answered was in her forties, pale, plump, and red-eyed. She stared hostilely at Vivian, taking in the fashionable suit, the high heels.

"Excuse me," Vivian said. "I'm a reporter from the *Times*. I wonder if I could talk to you for a few minutes."

The woman unlatched the screen door and stood aside silently to let her into the living room. It was furnished in imitation maple, all of the same design.

"I'm sorry to trouble you," Vivian said. "Did you see the crash?"

"I heard it. I was in the kitchen getting breakfast. We thought the end of the world had come. There was this awful crash, and then the explosion." She shuddered.

"What did you do?"

"We didn't move at first. We were just frozen. 'It's the bomb,' my husband said. It's funny, living near the airport and all, we should have known it was a plane, but you always think first it's the bomb. Then my son, Wayne—he's fourteen—went tearing out the back door, and I yelled at him to come back. I didn't know what was out there, but I didn't want him to go. But he didn't come back, and then my husband and I went out and . . ." She put her hand to her mouth quickly, and her eyes filled with tears.

"Many of your neighbors have been killed," Vivian said. She simply stated it as a fact.

"If only it had happened a little later. At least the children would have been in school. If it had just happened at nine o'clock, they would all have been out of it, anyway. But six! At six o'clock in the morning, everybody's home." She took a Kleenex out of the pocket of her flowered housecoat and wept into it.

Several panes of glass were missing from the front windows. "Did the explosion break your windows?" Vivian asked, hoping to change the course of the woman's thoughts.

The woman glared at her. "What kind of a person are you, anyway?"

Startled, Vivian could not think of anything to say.

"Poking around a place like this. Snooping into people's grief. Aren't you human, or what?"

"Good-bye," Vivian said. She turned swiftly and walked out. She could not stop to ask the name, she had to get away immediately. The woman was trying to penetrate her, and she could afford to let nothing and no one penetrate, because then everything would.

She interviewed people for another hour, then she found a phone and dictated her story with mechanical precision. That was how she thought of herself on a story like this, as an infinitely complex machine which recorded every significant sight, sound, and smell and translated it into words. The most important part of the machine was the lens, the tiny, accurate lens which showed her everything clearly but at a great distance, where it could not really touch her.

The rewrite man who was taking the story down swore softly. "What a mess. You coming back here now?"

"Not yet. There may be more I can get for the late edition."

It was after three when she got back to the office. A copy of the first edition lay on her desk. Her story was at the bottom of the front page with "Good work" written across it in red grease pencil. She sat down and began reading it, lighting a cigarette and kicking off her shoes. Her feet, she realized, were so tired they throbbed.

"Hi," said Tim, the copy boy, stopping by her desk on his way home. "How was the plane crash? Pretty gory, huh? More fun, more people killed?"

There was no mistaking the look of rage on her tired, drawn face, as she stared up at him.

"Okay, I'm sorry." He left, swinging his coat by one finger over his shoulder.

"Why don't you go home, too? You've had a pretty rough day." With his sleeves rolled down and his tie pulled up, Adams looked like any respectable businessman leaving the office for the day.

"All right, I will," Vivian said. She wiggled with difficulty back into her shoes.

They walked out to the elevator together.

"You did a damn good job. Even if you did get out there two hours late." Adams never paid anybody a compliment without qualifying it in some way that made it seem less flattering.

"I wonder why something like that always happens just before the holidays," Vivian said in a faraway tone. "Did you ever notice?"

He glanced at her sharply. "You look tired. Get a good night's sleep?" He clapped her on the shoulder with his big paw as they left the elevator.

It was still too early for the freeway to be jammed, and the drive home to West Hollywood was easy. As soon as she had let herself in, she went to the bathroom and turned on the hot water in the tub. Then she poured in bath oil beads, staining the water turquoise, and went to the bedroom where she poured herself a large brandy from the decanter on the nightstand. She sipped it while she undressed. In the tub, she closed her eyes and let the heat combine with what she had drunk to make her absolutely numb. She was staggering a little, partly from fatigue, when she got out and began to dry herself. When she finished, she went dizzily back to the bedroom, pulled down the covers, and crept into bed. She was asleep almost instantly.

The insistent ringing of the phone awakened her. It was totally dark outside, and she could not imagine what time it might be.

"Hello?" she said fuzzily.

"Vivian? Jesus, what are you doing there?" It was Sid.

"Sleeping. Why?"

"It's seven-thirty. You were going to meet me at my place at six-thirty. What the hell happened?"

"Oh, Sid, I'm sorry." She paused to collect herself. Sid and the weekend seemed like things that had happened to her in another life. "I wasn't feeling well, and I came home from the office early and took a nap. I must have overslept."

"Oh?" He sounded immediately concerned. "You okay, baby?"

"As a matter of fact, I'm not. I think I'm getting the flu." She did not feel like describing her day. "Is it all right if we skip tonight?"

"Sure, baby. Take care. I'll call you tomorrow."

"Thank you." She was dimly grateful to him for not making more of a fuss. "Good-bye, dear."

After she hung up, she could not get back to sleep. Her head ached, and she lay staring at the barred pattern that the light coming through the window shades made on the ceiling. Finally she turned on the bedside lamp, took two aspirin, and poured herself another big brandy which she downed in three gulps. It hit her almost instantly, which surprised her until she remembered she had not had anything to eat all day. As the welcome numbness crept over her, she took the little piece of lead out of the nightstand drawer and looked at it. Lately, she had almost forgotten it.

"I did a good job today," she said, addressing it aloud. "Adams said I did a damn good job. So there."

She began to cry then, slowly and silently, as if from an infinite storehouse of woe. She cried for all of them on the plane, for the people on the smashed street, for everybody in the city, for the whole world; even, in a dim way she did not understand, for herself.

Ten

It was nearly Christmas. There was no snow, of course, but forests of fir and pine and spruce, their trunks firmly rooted to wooden cross-bars, had sprung up on vacant lots on all the main boulevards. Lampposts were wreathed in silver, encased in conical metal Christmas trees wired for lights, or faced with laughing Santa Clauses, depending on the whim and affluence of the merchants in each particular business district and suburban shopping center. All day long in the bright, unclouded sunlight, shoppers honked and crept and cursed their way in and out of parking lots. Once inside the stores, they elbowed through the jammed aisles between the laden counters while gilded angels and satin ribbons and plumed trees waved gently in the air-conditioned, carol-vibrant breeze overhead.

"It isn't worth it. It really isn't. Next year I'm going to have every single present bought and wrapped in September," Mrs. Fitzgerald said to her daughter, sounding grim. They had taken temporary refuge from the rigors of Christmas shopping in a Beverly Hills restaurant. It was nearly three. Most of the luncheon crowd had left, and they were enjoying their coffee in comparative peace.

"Oh, I don't know," Dana said. "I rather like all the bustle. It's part of the season somehow. How can you even be interested in September? It's still too hot to care about buying fall clothes, let alone Christmas presents."

"Believe me, I'll manage," Mrs. Fitzgerald said in the same tone. She glanced around imperiously. "Where's the waiter? I need just a drop more coffee. Wouldn't you think they could give better service when there's practically no one here? Waiter? Some coffee, please."

"He's not ours," Dana said.

"Well, he can just tell ours, then."

Dana sighed. She had listened to her mother being authoritative with waiters, busboys, elevator operators, porters, and salesgirls for as long as she could remember, and it still made her feel like hiding under the table.

"Well, now. Tell me about the acting class. Is it fun?"

"Not fun, exactly," Dana said. "Parker really makes us work, but—"

"If it isn't fun, I can't think why you bother doing it," her mother interrupted. "After all, it isn't as if you need a profession to support yourself. Although I suppose Don could be doing better."

"Don's doing very well." She said it quickly, feeling a fleeting twinge of pride that she could avoid adding, "And you know it." Today she was determined not to quarrel. "It has nothing to do with finances."

"Incidentally, did you check into that nursery school thoroughly? What do they feed Jeremy for lunch? Did you ever find out?"

"I've already told you, Mother, that it was highly recommended to me by two different people, and Jeremy is perfectly happy there. It's much better for him than being home alone with me all the time. He needs playmates his own age, and there aren't any small children in our neighborhood. As far as his lunches are concerned, they have a dietician planning the menus. Now what more could I ask?"

"I don't see why you need to take a class in acting anyway," Mrs. Fitzgerald said, switching topics again without warning, which was a habit of hers. "Why don't you just get a part? After all, we learn by doing."

"In the first place, I can't get a job. And in the second, there are techniques to acting, like any other art, that you can learn faster in a good class. Experience may be the best teacher, but it takes longer."

"And at your age, you have so little time." Mrs. Fitzgerald laughed gently.

"Don't laugh. I'm not that young."

Mrs. Fitzgerald laughed again. "You're a baby, darling. Just a baby." She took a sip of her coffee, added another lump of sugar, and shook her head in amusement.

Dana glanced at her resignedly. She wondered what it was about maternity. Was being the mother of an infant so traumatic an experience that most women never got over the emotional attitude it produced even when the child had long since disappeared into adulthood? Or was it simply that acknowledging a child was grown up involved some unpleasant acceptance of one's own increasing years? Neither theory seemed to fit her mother's case. Mrs. Fitzgerald was emphatically not a woman who lived in the past or clutched pathetically at bygone youth. On the contrary, you could tell just by looking at her that she lived most aggressively in the present. Her hair was gray rinsed delicately blue, her makeup was flawless, her clothes discreetly elegant and quite as much in keeping with her age as with her income and social position. No, it was some other emotional need, something she had yet to comprehend, that made her mother the way she was. God forbid I get that way with Jeremy, Dana thought to herself.

"Well, if it amuses you, why not?" Mrs. Fitzgerald said.

"What?"

"Acting. Why not, if it amuses you? But if you're just bored with being a housewife, I don't see why you don't take a trip. Go to Mexico. Come down to Palm Springs and visit your father and me. Run up to San Fran—"

Dana had stopped listening. A fat, dark-haired girl was coming toward them down the aisle between the booths, her arms stuffed with packages. It was several seconds before she could place who it was.

"Pam?" she said tentatively as the girl reached them.

"Dana Fitzgerald! Well, for heaven's sake, how are you?"

"Fine. My goodness! For a minute, I wasn't sure it was you. It's been so long," she added tactfully. "Besides, I thought you were living in Oakland."

"And I've put on some weight, haven't I?" Pam laughed self-consciously.

"Have you met my mother? No, I don't think you ever did. Mother, this is Pam—Oh, Pam, I should know your married name, but I've forgotten it."

Pam's name was King now. As they exchanged married names and vital statistics, Dana looked at Pam, who had been one of her close friends in college, with dismay. She had been so pretty, and now she was matronly and settled and dumpy. She certainly seemed to have gone domestic with a vengeance.

"Been down here five years now, and Jerry has a job in Van Nuys," Pam was saying. "If I'd known where to reach you, I would have."

"And do you have a big family like you planned?"

"Four. Home with a baby-sitter today, I'm happy to say, while I try to get my Christmas shopping done. Would you like to see their pictures?" She unloaded her packages on the table and got out her wallet.

The children were dark-haired and solemn and sturdy. The older girl, Dana thought, had a trace of Pam's former prettiness.

"We were living in San Gabriel," Pam said, "but now we've bought a place in Reseda—three bedrooms and a den. Right now the den's converted into a nursery, but soon as Gayle's older I can put her in with Suzy. Wasn't it clever of me to have two boys and two girls so we can get by on three bedrooms?"

"Good planning," Dana agreed.

"I wish you'd come out and see me sometimes," Pam said wistfully. "It's so nice running into you like this."

"Are you doing anything New Year's Eve?" Dana asked impulsively. "We're having a few people in, and I'd love to meet your husband—Jerry, is it?—and have you met Don."

Pam's face brightened. "That would be marvelous!"

"Then we'll expect you around nine," Dana said. She got a pen out of her purse and wrote down the address on the inside of a matchbook.

"You're not spending New Year's with us?" her mother asked after Pam King had gone on her way.

"No, just Christmas. I'm giving a party New Year's Eve."

"Well, that's disappointing." Her mother sounded vexed. "I've invited the Caines and the Terrals and the Nelsons, and I told them you and Don would be with us. It's been years since they've seen you."

"I really can't, Mother. I've already mentioned our party to several people."

"Well, I must say I don't think that's very nice of you. We were counting on your spending the holidays with us."

"We never talked about anything but Christmas. I don't know why you assumed we'd stay for New Year's too. Don has to work the week between, anyway."

"I would have asked the Caines to stay with us if I'd known you weren't staying over."

"Well, I'm sorry. Call them and ask them now."

"They've already made other plans." Mrs. Fitzgerald finished her coffee and stared moodily into the cool darkness on the other side of the deserted dining room.

"How's your league work coming?" Dana asked when the silence began to get on her nerves.

"Didn't I tell you? I'm going to be president again next year."

"Really? That's nice. I thought you said you absolutely wouldn't do it again. That it was too much work, and nobody appreciated it anyway."

"I know. That's what I told them. I told Rhonda Swift—she's chairperson of the nominating committee—when she called that I simply would not take on that headache again. But she talked me into it." Mrs. Fitzgerald permitted herself a small smile. "At the January meeting, they're giving me an award for my services in the past."

"Mother, that's wonderful!"

"Yes," Mrs. Fitzgerald said. "It is nice." Her expression altered perceptibly from smugness to something else. "It is heartwarming to be appreciated."

"Naturally they'd be grateful for all you've done for them," Dana said quickly.

"Not necessarily." Her mother stared off across the room again. "People don't always appreciate what's been done for them."

There was a slight pause.

"Don't you think I appreciate you, Mother?" Dana said wearily. She had long ago decided that the only way to deal with her mother's insinuations was head-on.

"I didn't say a word about you. Please don't feel guilty."

"I don't feel guilty."

"You must, or you wouldn't bring the subject up. But never mind. I know you have your own life to lead, just as your father and I have ours. It's just that we would have liked our only child to spend the holidays with us."

"I appreciate the invitation, Mother, and we are spending Christmas with you. I don't feel guilty about New Year's because there's no reason I should. Now let's drop the subject, shall we?"

"Certainly," Mrs. Fitzgerald said with dignity.

"You needn't sound so angry."

"I'm not angry," Dana said. Her head was beginning to ache with the effort to be calm.

"Waiter!" Mrs. Fitzgerald tapped her water goblet with a teaspoon. "Waiter? Give us our check immediately, please. We're in a hurry."

The sun was still shining when they got outside, but a cold wind made the outdoor yule decorations rattle and glitter.

"My, I'm chilly," Mrs. Fitzgerald said. "Fasten your coat. Incidentally, where did you get that coat?"

"Stokely's," Dana said. She felt her mother eyeing it. "What's wrong? Don't you like it?"

"It's a lovely coat, dear. But it's not you. No, I certainly don't feel it's you."

The old, familiar phrase. I will not say a word, Dana thought to herself. I will not ask. This time I will not ask. They walked west on Wilshire into the sun and the wind, their high heels clicking in unison on the sidewalk. Half a block in silence. The old feeling grew in her gradually, a hesitancy, a bewilderment. "What do you mean?" she asked at last, giving in. "What do you mean, it isn't me?"

"I don't know," her mother said. "It just isn't you."

I can cope with all the rest, Dana thought. I can overlook being treated like a child, I can handle insinuations that I don't know how to manage my life, I can resist being made to feel guilty when I don't do as she wishes. Why can't I cope with this? Another half block in silence. "What would be me, Mother?" She spoke abruptly, hating herself for asking, unable to resist. "What kind of coat would be me?"

"Well, I can't say offhand, but I'm sure I could find something if I looked. Why don't you take me with you the next time you shop?"

Dana did not answer her. "I'm getting tired," she said at last. "Why don't we call it a day."

"How did your shopping tour go?" Don asked. They

were having martinis in front of the fire.

"Oh, all right." As usual when she had been with her mother, she felt depressed and inordinately weary.

"Did you have a fight?"

"Sort of."

"What about?"

"She wanted us to stay over New Year's with them. She was very annoyed when I told her we couldn't."

"So now you feel guilty."

"Not really," Dana said defensively. "Why should I?"

"No reason. But you do, just the same. I don't see why you have all these problems with your mother."

"Why would you? You've lived halfway across the country from your family ever since you were eighteen, and before that you had a brother to help take up the pressure."

"What pressure?"

"The pressure of being the only one, the adored one. It's quite different when you have no one but you as the focus of all their dreams. When you're the only material they have to work on, to mold into whatever image it was they had in mind."

Don put his drink down on the hearth. "The trouble with you, honey, is you're too sensitive, too responsive to other people. It makes you vulnerable. Everybody has the power to make you react. That means that in a sense they can control you."

Dana frowned. "I never thought of it that way. I suppose it's true. But I like responding to people. I hate being isolated. I had that feeling enough as a child."

"You sacrifice something for it, though."

"Well, what's the alternative?"

Don paused to light his pipe, making little sucking noises as the flames licked into the tobacco. "I have twenty-four men under me at work. Some of them are nearly twice as old as I am. But I never have any trouble maintaining my superiority. They respect me. They're even a little in awe of me, and I think it's partially because I don't react to things the way they do. Take an example. You're always telling me I have no sense of humor. Do you know I think that's an asset of sorts? I walked in the other morning, and one of them was telling a story. When he got through, everybody laughed except me. When they saw I wasn't laughing, they all stopped gradually, and there was a kind of respect on their faces. Not responding had set me apart from them. And a little above them."

Dana stared at him. "Did you do it deliberately?"

"Not entirely. As a matter of fact, I didn't think the story was particularly funny. But then, I don't appreciate jokes as a general rule."

"Is that how you managed at school, too? Is that how you got to be such a big man on campus?"

"I suppose that had something to do with it. I never had any real inclination to horse around. I'd just watch while the rest of them did, and while it made them jittery, they ended up respecting me. When I saw what was happening, it was an easy step to take advantage of it. To take over."

Dana looked thoughtfully into the fire. "But you sacrifice something by your attitude, too, you know. You sacrifice just as much as I do."

"Maybe," Don acknowledged.

"Anyhow, there's no use debating about which is the better approach. I don't think I want to—or could —be like you, any more than you'd choose to be me. Take the fire," she went on, holding her hands close to the brass mesh curtain to warm them. "If you threw a piece of wood on it, it burns. That's me. But if you throw a stone into it, nothing much happens. The stone's impervious."

"That's me," Don said.

"Yes. We're made of two quite different materials."

"You don't have to look so serious about it."

"Am I looking serious?" She stood up suddenly, brushing the white lint from the carpet off her wool dress. "I have to go get dinner on. Tonight's my class."

Ryan Parker lived in Pueblo Canyon in a Spanish-style mansion of early 30s vintage with spaciously proportioned rooms, high, beamed ceilings, and floors of black tile which gleamed lustrously from many waxings. Against the white walls hung ponderous iron crucifixes, primitive paintings of blue-robed Madonnas, and other relics of the Spanish colonial period as well as Parker's famous collection of modern art.

After thirty years in Hollywood, he was a wealthy man. He had seldom received star billing, but that in itself was a secret of his success. When a picture in which he appeared was a hit, he enjoyed the general praise showered on everyone connected with it. If it was a flop, the stars were always blamed, not the supporting players. So he went on year after year, always just below the pinnacle, never in the abyss. He never appeared on Broadway, although he had frequent offers to do so. The risks were too great, the salaries too small to warrant leaving his pool and his paintings. Television attracted him only when the price was right, and it often was, for he was a performer of great skill and versatality.

Dana had been enchanted with him from their first meeting. He was a tall man with a thin, aristocratic face and somewhere in his early fifties. His closely cropped black hair was fading to grey at the temples, and his green eyes beginning to fan in lines at the corners. Behind those blade-bright eyes, she had quickly discovered, was a keen intelligence.

"Charming," he had said, bending over his hand, when Pete Hicks introduced them. "A modern Madonna." He had a rich, suave voice which poured over people like honey and warm oil.

"I do hope you'll let me work with you," Dana had replied warmly, liberated for once from her shyness by the courtliness of his manner.

"It will be a privilege," he had assured her. His style of speech, which would have sounded artificial in someone else, had the ring of sincerity, of authenticity coming from him.

Once the class began, however, his manner underwent a swift metamorphosis from courtier to drill master. He was scrupulously polite to his students as long as they worked earnestly, but he could be cruel and sarcastic when they did not. Too many transgressions, and they were thrown out of the class hastily with no appeal.

Dana welcomed the discipline. Rising to the challenges he presented made her feel that she was making some progress in her chosen field, although the possibilities of a job seemed as remote as ever. And on Tuesday nights, at least, she had work to do, an audience to play to, a chance to find out if the dimly remembered power she had once felt within herself was still there.

This particular night, much as she looked forward to the class, she could not quite calm the troubled emotions which the shopping tour with her mother had aroused. Talking it over with Don had done nothing to make her feel better. In fact, there was something about Don sometimes that upset her as much as her mother's attitude did. She could not place what it was, but the feeling nagged at her as she drove to class.

The class began promptly at eight o'clock. "Tonight we will exercise our memory of emotions," Ryan Parker said. He stood in front of the great fireplace, elegant in a navy-blue velvet smoking jacket, looking as though he were posing for a portrait. "Affective memory. The storehouse of the unconscious on which you will draw for every role you create. Essentially, it is this. When you are called upon to play a scene involving a given emotion, you will capture it by mentally reviving the circumstances which you obtained when you experienced a smiliar emotion."

"Like wow, man," muttered the boy sitting next to Dana. His name was Matt Stanley, and he was devastatingly sure of himself.

"What was that?" Parker asked sharply.

"Excuse me, sir."

"There will be no outside conversation. Perhaps, Mr. Stanley, you would like to be first since you are so communicative tonight. Enact for me a scene in which anger prompts you to beat someone you love. A friend. A lover. Anyone. Midway through the beating, you are overcome with remorse at what you are doing. You stop and beg forgiveness. All right. You have one minute to prepare yourself."

Stanley was a promising actor with considerable command of his body and voice, but the scene did not come off. Why is it, Dana thought, that some people move you, and some don't? I sit here and admire him with my mind, I think how well he's doing it, but he never touches me feelings.

There was a long pause when it was over. While Stanley fidgeted, Parker sat silently in a high-backed Spanish armchair, contemplating him. Dana smiled inwardly, admiring his timing. At last he spoke. "Mr. Stanley, you are lying."

The boy was startled. "Sir?"

"You are lying, Mr. Stanley. You did not do what I asked you to do. You did not summon a memory from your past to aid you in the scene. Instead, you used your superficial technique of which you are so proud to create a mechanical, external effect. Isn't that so?"

"Yes, sir." Stanley looked furious, partly, Dana guessed, because he was afraid to deny it.

"Do not think that I am so easily fooled. Nor is an audience. I shall call on you later, and I shall expect a more profound interpretation."

As the class went through its paces, Dana found herself becoming more and more nervous. The day had disturbed her, and tonight she felt she could not concentrate enough to do what he asked. What kind of memory would he demand of her? Wondering about it made her suddenly, inexplicably, want to run out of the room and go home.

"Mrs. Hurst. Mrs. Hurst? Ah, I thought you were not entirely with us. Here is your problem. You are searching for something you have lost, something very precious to you. Perhaps it is a letter from your lover, telling you the time and place to meet him for an elopement. You have forgotten the address he gave, the letter has disappeared, and you are searching frantically for it. If you do not find it, if you do not meet him, he will leave the country without you, and you will be separated forever. Your happiness, your future is at stake. Now, Mrs. Hurst, take a moment to prepare yourself, and then search for that letter."

Dana sat very still. Her mother's voice came back to her, saying, "It's a lovely coat, dear. But it's not you. No, I certainly don't feel it's you." A feeling of confusion began to grow in her. Mentally, she turned and felt her way back into the past.

She was in junior high school. She had saved her allowance and gone to the beauty shop in secret for her first professional hairdo. She had chosen it herself, and proudly she had returned home. "Oh, dear." Her mother's voice sounded amused and appalled at the same time. "Oh, Dana. Where did you get that awful set?" Hurt. Uncertainty. "Awful?" She remembered how timidly she had said it. "Why? Why is it awful?" "Darling, it's just not you. Next time, Mother will go with you and help."

Slowly, half hypnotized, she stood up and began to search Ryan Parker's drawing room for an imaginary letter. In the huge, ironbound chest, under the refectory tables, behind the linen draperies, searching, searching. Something very precious was lost to her. Her happiness, her very future was at stake.

Real panic began to possess her as she ransacked the room in utter silence. She was five, and she and her mother were shopping for her first party dress. Oh! There it was in the window, pale pink dotted Swiss with a ruffled skirt and a grosgrain ribbon sash and fabric roses all around the neckline. Oh, it was beautiful, beautiful. It was the most beautiful thing she had ever seen, it was the prettiest dress in the whole world, Mama, Mama, I want that one, that's the one I want! "Oh, darling, no. That's not for you." Her mother always sounded so positive when she was being negative. "That's too fussy and frilly. Let's try the blue. Or maybe the yellow. Such a nice, simple little frock. Now I wonder—Dana? Dana, why are you crying? Dana, stop that immediately! Stop it, or I'm going to have to take you home! I'm going to take you home immediately, do you hear? Dana!"

She could not find it. It was simply nowhere to be found. She was sobbing now in fright, in panic, in anguish. It was no use looking any longer. She would never find it. She stopped dead still in the center of the room and put her hands over her face, shaking violently.

Applause. They were applauding her. Someone even cried, "Bravo." She felt a hand on her shoulder and looked up. "That was very good," Ryan Parker said gently. "That was excellent. Now go and sit down. Do you want a handkerchief?"

She shook her head, unable to speak, and walked blindly out of the room, down the hall, into the powder room. Slowly, as she bathed her face in cold water, calm returned. She powdered her nose, combed her hair. She took several deep, steadying breaths. It was as though she had just returned from a painful, terrifying journey.

"Wait a moment," Parker said when the class was over, and she was leaving. "I want a word with you alone."

After the others had gone, he led her back into the

drawing room. She stood quietly and waited while he lit a cigarette.

"You will be a good actress," he said finally. "You can draw easily on your emotions. But you must learn to control them. When the scene is over, you must be able to replace them as easily as you put dishes in the cupboard when you have finished using them. Do you understand me?"

She nodded.

"You must not become this agitated. You still feel it now, don't you? You will burn yourself out if you continue to feel so intensely."

"I'm sorry. I couldn't help it."

"Don't be sorry," he said quickly. "It's a rare gift. But you must be its master, not the reverse."

They walked to the door without speaking. When they reached it, he looked at her curiously. "I should not ask you this. Ordinarily, I do not ask, but tonight I should like to know. You need not tell me if it is painful. But in your mind, what were you searching for?"

She was not sure she should tell him; it sounded so melodramatic. But she thought she knew. It had come to her afterward with a final, unmistakable aura of certainty. She looked at him intently, assessing him. Yes, if anyone were going to understand, he would.

"Myself, I guess," she said. She tried to smile, to pass it off, but against her will the maddening, uncontrollable tears stung her eyes once more, and she turned quickly and ran down the flagstone steps to her car.

Eleven

December thirty-first. Dana lit the last of the candles, using a long-stemmed match. Then she went to the fireplace and pushed the match into the wadded newspapers underneath the wood on the grate. The fire flared, augmenting the candles to fill the white-walled living room with golden light. She stood up and looked around, surveying the effect.

The Christmas decorations were still up, and now they reflected dozens of tiny pinpoints of fire, so that the whole room seemed alive with light, the gold globes on the white Christmas tree which still stood in the corner next to the fireplace, the golden stars which hung suspended over the mantel, the garlands that fell from the hands of gilded angels to outline the doorways. Glittering and festive, exactly the way a room should look for a New Year's Eve party.

Outside, the night was cold and clear. A white winter moon hung passively in the black sky over the sparkling lights of the city which somehow seemed festive, too, as though all the millions of colored bulbs with which people decorated their yards and the fronts of their houses could be seen and appreciated from this hilltop. After a moment's consideration, Dana pulled back the draperies, making the view part of the room.

As she looked down on it, she felt a little surge of anticipation. Perhaps before the new year was out, she would be part of the city again. Something had to happen this year; that much was certain. There was the bargain with Don. Nearly four months were gone already, and she was no closer to establishing herself as an actress than she had been in September. Somehow, something had to happen, and soon. She had to think of a way to make it happen. When life presented a blank wall to you, you had to keep pushing at it, testing the stones, chipping at the mortar, and eventually a spring was touched, a door sprang open, and you rushed through to the thing you desperately wanted and needed. Maybe. Anyway, there was nothing to do but keep trying.

Don came in, adjusting his tie, and she turned to him. "Doesn't it look beautiful?"

"It looks great." He came and put his arms around her, smelling pleasantly of the musk after-shave lotion she always bought for him.

She smiled, recognizing the look in his eyes. "And I look nice, too, don't I?" she prompted. Don rarely verbalized compliments unless encouraged to do so. He nodded, and satisfied, she hugged him in return, feeling, as always, slightly overwhelmed by his close physical presence. It was not only that he was so much taller than she was. His very body seemed denser, more solid, more palpable and robust. Being in his arms always made her feel fragile and weak and infinitely feminine, a maiden of the Middle Ages possessed by a sturdy and powerful knight. Silly idea, but nice somehow.

"Have we got enough ice?" Don asked.

"I think so. I've been making it all day and stashing it in the freezer. Would you fasten my sleeves?" The dress she wore was as red as lipstick and looked and felt like a silk nightgown. It was cut slashingly deep between her breasts, with a low back and long, pointed sleeves which buttoned at the wrist. She didn't need to wear dresses designed to hide a physical flaw; Dana had dressed instead to adorn the lines of her body.

"What time are they due?" Don asked.

"Any minute. If they're on time. But then, nobody ever is."

"Who are the ones I don't know, again?"

"The Kings."

"And you went to high school with her or something?"

"No, darling. College. I told you. Pam was a philosophy major, very intellectual, but fun, too. I always liked her, but she got married right after we graduated, and after that we lost track of each other."

"And what does her husband do?"

"He's some kind of engineer. Civil, I think. Don, don't you remember anything I tell you?"

"I do if it's important," Don said, sounding reasonable. "Last week, or whenever it was you told me you'd seen her, it wasn't important. Tonight, when they're coming here, it is."

She made a face at him. "The great man. So scientific. Can't clutter up his mind with the mundane details of existence."

"That's right," Don said. They smiled amiably at each other.

The bell rang, and Dana went to answer it. Prompt and beaming expectantly, the Kings stood at the front door.

"Come in!" Dana said. "Well, this is nice. Happy New Year, and meet my husband, Don. Don, Jerry and Pam King."

"Pleased to meet you," Jerry King said, holding out his hand to Don. He was a sandy-haired young man, pleasant-looking in an undistinguished way.

"My, what a beautiful place you have here," Pam said. "Jerry, look at the view. Do I get a guided tour, Dana?"

"Of course," Dana said. "Come and put your coat down."

In the bedroom, Pam King looked at herself in the full-length mirror and sighed. Then she glanced enviously at Dana. "You look marvelous. I don't see how you stay so thin."

"It's not any credit to me," Dana said tactfully. "I just have a tendency to be skinny."

"And then you've only had one child," Pam said. "Wait till you've had four. The doctor says it's upset my metabolism."

"I may never make it, but you have my wholehearted respect and admiration. How do you handle such a houseful?"

"Believe me, it's a full-time job. Incidentally, I'd love to see your Jeremy. Is he asleep?"

"We can go and look."

They tiptoed down the hall and into Jeremy's room. Flushed and limp, he lay sprawled like a starfish on his stomach, mouth slightly open.

"Isn't he darling?" Pam whispered.

"You don't have to be that quiet," Dana said in a low tone. "When he sleeps, he really puts his back into it."

"He looks like you."

"And like Don. But then people always think Don and I are brother and sister."

"He's very good-looking, Don. The glimpse I got of him as we came in. I gather you're happy."

"Very," Dana said. "Come sit down and let's have a talk before anybody else arrives."

"Pam, what can I get you to drink?" Don asked as they walked back into the living room.

"Scotch. On the rocks."

"Right."

"Need any help?" Jerry King asked, following Don into the kitchen.

Dana looked at Pam curiously. "My, your drinking habits have certainly changed. Correct me if I'm wrong, but weren't you a teetotaler in school?"

"Well, you know how it is when you get older." Pam laughed. "Boredom, I guess. After a day of changing diapers and aribitrating quarrels between four-year-olds and six-year-olds, I can hardly wait for that five-o'clock highball. Not that I don't adore the children, but let's face it, it's not like communicating with other adults."

"What about your neighbors? Don't you talk to them?"

"Oh, yes," Pam said brightly. "When we've got all the monsters down for naps, we gossip away. But let's not talk about me. I have nothing interesting to say. Tell me about you."

"I'm going to start acting again. That is, if I can ever find a job."

"You are?" A strange expression, the emotional origins of which Dana could identify, came over Pam's face. She opened her mouth to say something more, but before she could continue, the bell rang again.

"Excuse me," Dana said. She patted her friend's hand, feeling vaguely that Pam needed some sort of reassurance, and went to the door.

"Hi," Vivian said. "Is this the place?" She had on a tight black dress, immediately revealing to the experienced eye that it had been made especially to fit its owner. Her long lean left leg was almost entirely bare as the wrap-around dress stopped a bit higher than mid-thigh, but the other leg was nearly completely covered since the dress angled dramatically down to stop just above her right ankle. Every elegant, sensuous line of her body was either revealed by the clinging material so cleverly draped, or was completely bare. The overall effect of her appearance was of a fascinating, barbaric sexiness so potent that a satisfied smile lurked around the edges of her perfect lips.

"Don't you look wonderful," Dana said. "Hello, Sid. Come in, you two. We're just getting underway." As she started to shut the door behind them, two more figures appeared out of the darkness of the hill road.

"Hey, wait up," Beverly Connors called. "Don't

shut us out in the cold."

By eleven, the party was moving ahead under its own steam. The house was full of music and cigarette smoke and the spontaneous euphony of laughter and talk which occurs when the guests, full of alcohol and conviviality, are mixing well. Dana and Don gave remarkably successful parties considering the wide variety of their friends, Beverly Connors thought. Some of Don's colleagues from NASA and their wives; two couples that the Hursts had met skiing in Aspen; an actor that Dana had worked with on a TV show; a couple of people from her acting class and their dates; her friend, Pam What's-Her-Name from college; Vivian, Sid; an attorney from somewhere in Texas who had gone to high school with Don; and a rising young architect who had just remodeled the house where Dana's parents lived in Beverly Hills—it was a fairly all-embracing group, judging by those she'd been introduced to so far. You could just about tell by looking at them which were Don's friends and which were Dana's. The girls who were chic or striking or exciting in some way were Dana's friends, and the ordinary-looking ones were the wives of Don's friends. There were only two exceptions to this rule, Beverly thought. Pam What's-Her-Name and herself. She smoothed the full skirt of her black taffeta with the palm of her hand and told herself she really had to get back into it. With the party approaching its climax, she found herself sitting in Don's big easy chair in the corner without a soul to talk to. She couldn't just roost here forever. She had meant to have a good time, but it was proving to be one of those evenings when she somehow felt she had mysteriously become both invisible and inaudible. When people were introduced, they seemed to look right through her, and when she said something, nobody heard her.

Maybe I don't pay enough attention to my looks, she thought uneasily. She was not particularly self-conscious at work or among her neighbors in the valley, but Dana's friends always made her feel frumpy and unattractive. It didn't help, either, the way Bob took off with a gleam in his eye at parties like this which were full of pretty girls. He had left her the moment they arrived, and she had hardly seen him since. He must be in the dining room, dancing. As yet, nobody had asked Beverly to dance. This coming year I really have to lose weight, she told herself firmly. That'll be my New Year's resolution. Ten pounds. In the meantime, I have to get with this party. Parties were not her element, she acknowledged reluctantly to herself, and thought fleetingly and wistfully of Mayfield's.

Girding herself, she lifted her glass, which was beginning to make her fingers clammy, and took a sip. Nothing came except ice cubes, which banged against her lips unrewardingly. Good, she needed another drink. Going to the kitchen for it would give her something to do.

In the dining room, where the dancing was, the table was pushed against one wall, loaded with Dana's crystal and stainless steel in readiness for a midnight buffet. In front of it, Bob was dancing with Vivian.

"Hey, you dance pretty good for a hick," Beverly heard him say as she passed. Their eyes met, and Bob, looking defiant, pulled Vivian a little closer. He was holding his hand abnormally high on her back, so that it touched bare skin instead of her dress.

"So do you," Vivian said sweetly. "Only would you mind not dancing cheek-to-cheek? You're perspiring, and my hair's getting all wet."

So that's where he's been. Beverly passed them without speaking, and pushed open the swinging door to the kitchen.

"Hi," Dana said. "Have you met Vivian's friend, Sid Williamson? Beverly Connors, Sid."

"Are you an actress, too?" Sid asked.

"Thanks for the compliment. No, I'm in advertising. My sister's the pretty one in the family, but she's a model, not an actress."

"Hell, what do you mean, your sister's the pretty one?" Sid said gallantly.

"Nobody thinks I'm pretty, Mr. Williamson, except my husband. Anyway, he used to." Lordy, how sorry for herself she sounded. She smiled quickly to take the curse off.

"Do you need a drink, dear?" Dana said, taking her glass. "Yes, you do. Bourbon?"

"Don't put too much water in this one," Beverly said.

"Anyway," Dana said, pouring the whiskey, "as I was saying, Sid, I don't think Ryan's a phony. At least, not according to my definition."

Sid snorted. "Him and his Spanish mansion and his snobbish attitude."

"But that's the way he is. You want to know my idea of phoniness? These carefully unshaven kids that hang around Sunset Strip in their sandals and faded jeans. What are they trying to prove? That you have to be a slob to be real?"

"You got a point," Sid conceded. "But to a kid that grew up in the Bronx, the tough part of the Bronx, those fancy continental types always look artificial as hell. Christ, I guess I'm just jealous."

The door swung open again, and Pete Hicks appeared. "Now what are you two charming ladies doing in the kitchen?" he said amiably. "The dining room seemed chilly all of a sudden, and then I realized that two of the major sources of warmth had disappeared."

"Pete, you're a love," Dana said. "Tell me what shows you've done lately. I guess I told you I haven't worked since the one we did together."

"Patience, my dear, patience. It takes a long time to get one's foot in the door, but after that . . ."

As they went on talking, Beverly chewed her lip.

She wondered if she ought to go into the dining room. No, I won't give him the satisfaction, she decided. So tonight it was going to be Vivian that he had a Big Thing with. At parties like this, there was always some girl he spent the evening pursuing, groping, showering with attention, and none too subtly. He drank too much, and he laughed too loudly, and he had himself a ball while the other guests, never unperceptive of what was going on, stared curiously and sympathetically at Beverly. It was embarrassing even though she knew there was really nothing to it. She never took him to task for it, but she often wondered why he did it. It was almost as though he was deliberately punishing her for something. But what had she done? I'm being silly, she thought, dismissing the idea. Bob was attractive to women, and it was probably just that he wanted to use it, the way pretty girls did. He was still awfully cute, after all. She felt, through her annoyance, a touch of the old pride that Bob should ever have married an ordinary-looking girl like her.

"Would you like to dance?" Sid asked. "The people we came with seem to be living it up, so let's give them a little competition, what the hell."

"Thank you," Beverly said gratefully. She found it easy to return his smile. He had a nice, warm smile, as though he really saw you and liked what he saw.

As they went into the dining room, Vivian broke away from Bob and came past them toward the kitchen. She scarcely glanced at them, and she looked annoyed.

"Ah, another refugee from the merriment," Pete said as Vivian entered. "It's nearly midnight, is it not? The guests seem to be taking on the feverish gaiety of people who would rather not face the prospect of the coming year."

"What's happened to New Year's Eve, anyway?" Dana said. "When I was a little girl, I used to think it was when people had the most marvelous time of the whole year. Now we seem to be in a different era or something, and everybody just gets depressed. Do you get depressed, Pete?"

"Oh, sometimes, I suppose. It makes you conscious of the passage of time and how old one's getting. But you, you're young and beautiful, surely you're not depressed."

"No," Dana said. "Especially not this year. Just excited. I feel something's going to happen to me. I feel by next year, my life will be different."

"And better?"

"And better."

"What about you, Miss Hunt? You're being awfully quiet."

"I really don't feel much about it one way or other any more," Vivian said in a flat tone. "I used to, but then I reasoned that actually it's completely artificial. The days pass, and the years pass, and there's no more reason to consider the past and the future on December thirty-first than there is on, say, May third or August thirteenth."

"You used to get excited," Dana said teasingly. "Remember the New Year's Eve you and Joe Bales and that Dick Thornton and I went on a double date? And we ended up at midnight in the Sundance Club, and after everybody sang 'Auld Lang Syne' you sang "I Am Woman,' sitting on the bar, and everybody clapped?"

"I remember," Vivian said. "I learned it in high school, that song." She turned abruptly and walked out of the kitchen.

"Damn," Dana swore softly. "Why do I get so talkative when I drink? I should never have brought that up."

"Unpleasant memories?" Pete asked.

"Very."

"I'll just go and have a word with her," Pete said. "Perhaps I can take her mind off it."

As Dana was getting out more ice, Pam King walked somewhat unsteadily into the room. Her face was flush, and she put one hand on the stove to stabilize herself. "Dana. It's a lovely party. Just lovely. I'm so glad you asked us."

"Wasn't it lucky our running into each other like that," Dana said.

"I wish you'd come out and see me sometime. I really wish you would. I could use a little stimulating companionship. There's nobody out there to talk to. Absolutely nobody."

"I thought you had a big social thing with your neighbors."

Pam laughed bitterly. "That crowd? You should hear the conversations. Strictly PTA and toilet training. If you try to discuss ideas, they think you're a card-carrying feminist. Sometimes I think I'll go mad."

Dana looked at her carefully. "You used to read a lot."

"Read," Pam said. "Of course. Maybe I could flip through a good book with one hand while I change diapers with the other. Believe me, the minute the kids are all old enough to be in school, I'm going to get a job. Any kind of a job."

Dana leaned against the sink. "You surprise me, Pam. You never seemed very career-minded when you were in school. You always said philosophy was the most impractical major you could think of, vocationally speaking, but you didn't care because you were going to be a supermom and raise a flock of brilliant, intellectually unfettered children who would go out into the world and distinguish themselves."

"Oh, yes. I had a lot of theories, but they don't seem to be working out. They want Scooby Doo at bedtime, not Plato. And you know what I want? I want to use my mind again." She drained her glass.

"What about Jerry? Will he mind if you get a job?"

Pam laughed shortly. "He'd better not." She stopped and looked at Dana, focusing carefully. "Why? Does Don mind that you want to work?"

"Not really." Dana said quickly. She was thinking so

eagerly of her goal tonight that she did not want to consider any possible obstacle to it for even an instant.

Pam swirled the ice cubes in her empty glass. "You know what it is?" she said at last, a little thickly. "You spend four years developing your mind and getting an idea of the riches, intellectual and artistic, that the world has in store, and then you're supposed to forget the whole thing and submerge yourself in a way of life in which the major mental demand is fixing the baby's formula."

"It is frustrating, isn't it?" Dana said.

"Frustrating?" Pam stared at her. "Do you know what I do, Dana? Do you want to know what I do? I eat, that's what." Her voice shook a little.

"It's not your metabolism, then," Dana said gently.

Pam shook her head. "No. It's compensation. I can take just so much and then—I don't hit the bottle, you know, I don't let myself drink until just before dinner—but what I do, when it starts to get me down, I go out in the kitchen and eat a quart of chocolate ice cream." She burst into tears.

It was nearing midnight. In the dining room, Vivian was dancing what purported to be disco with a Mr. Sawey from Texas who had announced, cutting in on Pete, that he had gone to high school with Don. Vivian knew how to disco dance, but Mr. Sawey did not, as he had apologetically and unnecessarily explained, and so she was resolutely shutting out the music and concentrating instead on the steps Mr. Sawey was performing extemporaneously. Dancing that way, torn between the music and a bad partner, was a strain, but at least it took her mind off the occasion.

There was actually no reason at all for her to be depressed. She was having great success. She had danced with all of Don's business associates, somebody named Curtis who kept muttering about how he hadn't been able to get away skiing once during the holidays because the children had all had the flu, Pete Hicks,

Don Hurst, and of course, Bob Connors. She had been complimented on her dress, her figure, and her hair by various of the male and female guests present; and people she had not met before, on inquiring what she did, told her with enthusiasm and a little awe that she certainly had an interesting job. Sid, as usual, was attentive. He did not hover, but he came around from time to time and gave her an affectionate word or pat, and occasionally she caught him watching her with a warm look of approval in his dark eyes. It should have been enough to drown out the dismal feeling she had, but it wasn't.

The music stopped. "Shall we try another?" Mr. Sawey said, smiling uncertainly.

"I did promise the host a dance," Vivian said, "but let's dance again later, shall we?" She gave him a reassuring smile as she left.

Don was on the balcony outside with Bob Connors. "You should never let her go back to work," Bob was saying. "Believe me, it's a mistake. Especially if she ends up making more than you do."

Don looked at him coldly. "Oh?"

"The minute they have an income, they start wanting to wear the pants in the family. Not that I let Beverly get away with it, y'understand."

"I'm sure you don't," Don said. He sounded as if they were discussing garbage, or bedbugs.

"Not that I don't think career girls are wonderful," Bob said, putting his arms around Vivian as she came up. "Especially this one."

"Don, don't we have a dance coming?" Vivian said.

"I think I'd better check on the liquor first." Don's face had a set look, but beneath the slight plumpness of his jaw a muscle twitched. "Excuse me."

"Conceited bastard," Bob said after Don had left. "Come on. Let's have a little dance out here."

"We can't even hear the music, and besides, it's cold," Vivian said firmly. "Shall we try the dining room?"

He put his arm around her shoulders and left it there, heavily, as they went in. The music was slow now, a waltz with a languorous, insinuating beat. "You're the prettiest girl here, Vivian," he said as they started dancing. "You know that? You're the prettiest girl at this whole damn party."

"Thank you," Vivian chided through clenched teeth. "Would you mind not dancing that way? You're going to trip us both." As they moved he kept trying to pin her right leg between his thighs in a scissors grip.

"You don't have to prim with me, sweetheart." His voice was taunting. "I like you a lot. Can't you tell? Can't you feel it?"

"Only too well." Feeling slightly nauseated, she wrenched away from him and walked back into the living room. Something was all wrong. This was not the way things were supposed to be. She felt as though she might cry if she weren't careful.

"What's the matter, baby?" Sid said, coming up. "Is that perverted bastard bothering you? I'll knock him right on his ass."

"Please, no," Vivian said. "It's all right. He's the husband of one of my best friends. Don't make a scene."

"The son of a bitch. Not that I blame him. You are the sexiest-looking broad here."

Vivian looked at him strangely. "Thank you. You put it so well."

"It's midnight," somebody shouted. "Happy New Year!"

"Happy New Year, baby," Sid said. As he kissed her, someone switched the TV on loud, drowning out the record player. "Should auld acquaintance be forgot . . ."

Vivian turned and ran away from him, away from the party, down the hall and into the bedroom, slamming the door behind her.

"For Auld Lang Syne, my dear, for Auld Lang Syne . . ."

Another year. Panic gripped her. She was thirty years old, she had no home, no husband, no children, and life seemed to make less sense all the time. What's going to happen to me? she asked herself. How did I get here, and where am I going? I've got to take stock. Another part of her mind spoke sharply. It's an arbitrary date. Why New Year's Eve any more than May third or August thirteenth? Her heart began to beat irregularly, in the erratic way it had when she was frightened. Joe Bales. Whatever happened to me and Joe Bales? Would that have made all the difference? I wanted to take all life had to give . . . I did? Is that what I'm still doing? It's no different than any other night, her mind warned her. Pull yourself together. She shut her eyes and pressed her clenched fists against her forehead. The fear that hit her was intense and brief, like a knife stab in the stomach that was then miraculously healed. She went to the dressing table and powdered her nose, combed her hair, freshened her lipstick. After all, she had a reputation to live up to. Wasn't she the sexiest woman at the party?

When she went back to the living room, the kissing and the heartbreaking, nostalgic music had ended. Dana and Don still clung to each other, the happily married couple smiling benignly on their guests. Beverly Connors came toward her. Her face had a closed-in look, and her mouth was set.

"Excuse me, Vivian. I have to get my coat," she said as she walked past her into the hall. "We're leaving."

"I'm sorry," Vivian said.

"Oh, it's not your fault," Beverly said. "I know that. Husbands get that way at parties sometimes. I'll call you next week, and we'll have lunch, okay?"

"What happened to you, baby?" Sid stared at her, worried. "Jesus, you went tearing off. Did I say something?"

"No. It's all right. I just got to wondering where we'd all be a year from tonight. Where do you think we'll be, Sid?"

"Jesus, baby, how should I know? By that time maybe the bomb will have blown us all to hell and gone."

"The bomb," Vivian said. She laughed a little hysterically. "Yes, the bomb would solve everything, wouldn't it?"

Twelve

On New Year's Day, Vivian awoke around eleven with only a faint remnant of a hangover still with her. She had gotten up at five with a violent headache and the feeling that the liquor she had drunk at the Hursts's party had somehow burned all the moisture out of her body. After two glasses of water and two aspirin, she had gone back to bed and slept it all off.

She lay in bed, enjoying the unnatural quiet of the morning. She was in her own apartment, and she was alone. She had not wanted to spend the night with Sid, and he had taken her home and then left, somewhat annoyed, without making love to her. Later, perhaps, she would call him, but for the time being she wanted only her own company.

As soon as she had got used to the sensation of being awake, she got up, combed her hair, and wrapped herself in a pink silk dressing gown. It was a tailored robe, the sort of impersonal covering people buy to wear in hotels. Sid had never seen her in it, nor had any of her other lovers. It represented a different mood, neither sensual nor amorous, in which she wanted to belong solely to herself.

She went to the kitchen, put water in the teakettle for coffee, and poured herself a glass of orange juice which she sipped slowly, resting her elbows on the table. One more day to get through, and it would be all right again. The bad time would be over for another year. Tomorrow would mark the end of an emotional cycle which began every year with her birthday in December. At that time she went into a fit of depression which deepened throughout the holiday season, reaching its climax on New Year's Eve. This emotional cycle was not a childhood remnant; it was associated exclusively with her adult life, and it seemed to grow worse each year. To defend herself against it, she had taken the position that New Year's was an occasion with which it was ridiculous to have any emotional associations whatsoever. Today, with the worst over, she would abandon herself to memories and regrets, and tomorrow she would force herself to start living optimistically again.

The teakettle whistled, and she poured the boiling water over a double spoonful of instant coffee and put a slice of bread into the toaster. It was all very strange the way things worked out. Or didn't work out, whichever way you wanted to look at it. If she had married Joe, they might have been having breakfast together this morning, probably with two or three kids who would have to be told to drink their milk and not get crumbs in the butter. Pam King certainly looked placid and content. Vivian tried to imagine herself living in a tract in the Valley with Joe coming home at night from the TV station where he had his own local show, interviewing entertainment celebrities. No, that was not the kind of life they would have had. At first, they would have lived in a modern apartment, and later, after the children arrived, they would have bought a house in one of the canyons, an old house with lots of trees around it. It would have been rather run-down, and they would have fixed it up. I would have fixed it up, Vivian amended. Joe wouldn't know how to drive a nail in straight. That air of sophisticated assurance which was one of the things that made him so attractive disappeared entirely when he was confronted with a practical matter such as a leaky faucet, and he would grin with his boyish charm and spread out his thin hands and say, "Baby, that's not my line."

She heard him, she saw him make his gestures so vividly in her mind that she put down the coffee cup with a bang. It was frightening, being able to remember somebody that clearly after four years. Four years. That was as long as the whole time she had known him. Twenty-two to twenty-six. Those were the Joe Bales years. And twenty-six to thirty? There was nobody to name those years after, or rather, there were too many people and none of them, as she looked back, terribly important. She had run into John Majors the other day at a drugstore buying shampoo and looked at him with a degree of impersonality she would have thought impossible after only four months. He had gained weight since his marriage, and it was not becoming. She cared so little that she charitably forbore to tell him this as they chatted for a moment or two at the counter. Thinking of John, she found it hard to remember what it was like to sleep with him, but she could still recall the way Joe lit a cigarette, folding one match back, shutting the cover, and striking the match with his thumb while he kept the other arm around her.

The memories were tumbling back now. It was like opening the door to a closet you had stuffed with things you didn't want any more but couldn't bring yourself to throw away. Too full, too crowded, and the minute you gave them a chance they fell all over you, and you had to pick them up and put them back one by one. All right, she thought, taking a deep breath, if you're going to do it, be organized and start from the beginning.

Eight years ago. A tall, thin, unfashionable girl was being introduced around the city room of the *Times* by Arlene French, the society editor. "My new assistant," Arlene said, shoving her from desk to desk. Arlene was small and dark and energetic, and she made Vivian feel like a freighter of unwieldy size being shoved into an unfamiliar berth by an enthusastic tug. The other women in the society department greeted her with reserve and appraising stares. "You'll like it here," Arlene said briskly. "It's a good group."

"I'm sure I will," she said. Actually she was not sure at all, but she was determined to try. It had taken her four months to get a job in the editorial department, four months during which she had taken ads over the phone in classified and waited patiently for an opening upstairs. Getting a good job was important to her. It would make up for the fact that she didn't go out like other girls. If she had an exciting career now, it would serve the same purpose that being in the top ten of her graduating class at USC had done, making her feel that her life was significant and worthwhile, not wasted or deprived because there were no men in it.

During the time she had spent in classified, this big room had come to seem to her like Mecca. It was large and messy and noisy. The copy desk occupied vaguely the center of the room, and the reporters had desks along the wall. The various special departments, sports, drama, society, were tucked away in corners, partially screened off by glass-and-wood partitions. Important people like the managing editor had private offices that were completely screened off, but had lots of glass to allow them to watch over their preserve. She was surprised to learn that local columnists and feature writers with by-lines of their own sat at ordinary desks with the rest of the staff. In spite of the fact that the paper ran special ads exhorting people to read them and even put pictures of them on posters at the newsstands, in the office they were just like everybody else, prophets without honor in their own land.

"Don't tell me you're fascinated with your work," a male voice said, sounding amused. Startled, she looked up. He was sitting on a nearby desk where, she gathered, he had been talking to Liz Windom, who handled the club news. He filled up the room with his vitality and power of personality, the long-legged, masculine body dominating the space, commanding her attention. Vivian let her eyes roam over the smooth straight line of his jaw, the heavy, satirical brows, the sparkling blue eyes and the slightly arrogant hook to his strong nose. She did not remember having seen him that morning when she had been introduced around.

"Joe Bales. I'm on the drama desk," he said in a husky murmur, the low tones of his caressing voice sending a thrill down her spine. She shivered at the delicious sensation.

"How do you do. My name is Vivian Lee Hunt."

"Well, Vivian Lee Hunt. Can you tear yourself away long enough for a cup of coffee?"

In less than a week Vivian had heard all about him from other people: "He's twenty-four, he quit Harvard after two years to go into newspaper work, and he's been on the *Times* for three years now," she told Dana. "He missed out on Vietnam because of a lung lesion or something. He's from New York, and his father puts on Broadway shows. He has a sister who used to be on stage, but now she's married to a diplomat and lives in Paris. All the girls are trying to get him, but he's supposed to be very ambitious and not interested in marriage. Some people say he's spoiled rotten, but my goodness, it would be hard not to be with all he has to offer."

"I never heard you go on so about a man before," Dana said. "When do you think he'll ask you out?"

"Oh, he won't," Vivian said vehemently. "And even if he did, I wouldn't go."

"What do you mean, you wouldn't go? You like him, don't you?"

"That's just it," Vivian said, and fell silent. How could she explain, even to Dana, how she already felt about Joe Bales? When he talked to her, she was afraid she was going to faint. She thought of him night and day with an intensity that appalled her. She was even glad her work was not more demanding, because if it had been, she would not have been able to do it, she was so distracted.

It was nearly a year and a half before they had their first date, but from then on, they were together constantly. The ferocity of her carnal appetite staggered her. She felt she could never have enough of Joe, of his flesh, his warmth, his passionate invasions of her body. For the first time, she felt used for the purpose she had been born for, freed from invisible restrictions she had lived with almost without realizing them until she had met him. The bonds of some inner tension had been loosened, and she felt at peace with her own flesh in a way she had never been. She even seemed to move more easily than before.

Then the question of the job came up. It was, in a way, the most exciting one the paper would offer, a newly created post of roving reporter and special feature writer, with a by-line and an expense account. It meant a chance to cover the biggest local news stories, to interview all the visiting celebrities, to be, in a small, local way, a celebrity oneself. Joe was among those who wanted the job desperately and applied for it.

She would never know exactly what made her go to Hughes, the managing editor, and try to get it herself. The salestalk she gave him was brilliant, full of an unaccustomed boldness born of—was it frustration, or ambition? She explained why a woman, not a man, should have the job, and why she, Vivian Hunt, was the right woman. To prove she was capable of handling the roughest stories, she showed him a piece she had done on her own on child abuse. It was, she felt, the best feature she had ever written.

She got the job. The office buzzed with excitement and surprise when the news came out.

"Well, bravo!" said Arlene French, looking at her with new respect. "I'll be sorry to lose you, but I certainly can't begrudge you a wonderful deal like this. What did you do to old man Hughes, anyway?"

When she went to the composing room for proofs on a wedding story, even the printers crowded around to congratulate her. She was so excited she hardly had time to wonder what Joe's reaction would be.

Then suddenly he was beside her, pulling her around roughly by the arm, his blue eyes hard as marbles.

"You bitch!"

"What?" Surprise and the clatter of the machines made her unsure she had heard him correctly.

"I said you bitch!" He said it loud and clear this time. Startled, the printers stood silently watching them.

She felt as though he had kicked her in the stomach. "I'm sorry, Joe," she said weakly.

"Sorry? I'll bet you are. Well, you just fouled us up for good. If I'd gotten that job, I was going to marry you!" His eyes glittered, and he looked as though he wanted to hit her.

She looked at him for a long moment. A strange detachment came over her, as though she were suddenly very old and wise and completely removed from life.

"Well, you can have the job." His voice shook with rage. "In fact, you can have the whole damn paper. I'm quitting. I wouldn't work for this lousy sheet after what happened today."

"Good luck," she said. She felt very detached now, as if she were going to faint or die, as though she were bleeding to death right there on the lead-littered, concrete floor.

He turned and started to leave, and then he came back.

"You won't be able to handle it," he said. She would not have believed his handsome face could look so ugly. "You're a stupid little hick, and you're soft besides. You've got as much chance as a snowball in hell. You'll get fired, and you won't have me either. That's what's going to happen to you."

"Don't count on it," she said.

Those were the last words they had ever spoken to each other. He had cleaned out his desk and left the paper that morning, and she had never seen him again. The rest of that momentous day she had spent in such a state of shock that even now she could not remember what happened after the scene in the composing room.

Vivian took a deep swallow of hot coffee. It was strong and bitter and satisfying. She sat for a while, savoring it. In my whole life, nobody ever called me a bitch before, she thought. It was the funniest feeling. Like having filth thrown in your face.

The phone rang, unexpectedly loud in the quiet morning, calling her back to the present with a jolt. She ran to it eagerly.

"Hello?" she said breathlessly, expectantly.

"Hello, baby," Sid said. "Are you up?"

"Oh." She felt too deflated to say anything more.

"Why so disappointed?" He sounded annoyed. "You were expecting maybe President Reagan?"

"No, of course not. Are you coming here? Or shall I come over there?"

"Come here, baby. I'm still in bed, and you can make breakfast."

"All right," she murmured, a thread of laughter running through her pleasant voice. "I'll get dressed right away."

She hung up the phone and stared at is as though it were some kind of trap. Not again, after all this time. Not that wild, irrational hope that someday, somehow, it would be Joe calling. She had been all through that years ago. Well, it was her own fault for allowing herself to think about him all morning.

She went into the bathroom and took off her robe. After all, she thought wryly, she had a lot to thank Joe for. It was losing him that had turned the little hick from Nebraska into the sexiest broad at the party. It was ambition that had forced her to go after the wonderful job she had, but it was his parting taunt that had goaded her into making a success of it.

"You made me what I am today. I hope you're satisfied," she said in a conversational, almost thoughtful tone.

It was time to end her annual memorial service. Another year was beginning, and there would be interesting people to meet and places to go and things to do . . . After all, she had a full, busy, exciting life. She was really an extremely lucky person.

Mentally, she twisted the handle that turned off her feelings, all the sad, turbulent, soul-troubling emotions of love and regret and longing. At the same time, she reached out and twisted the shower faucets, turning the water on full force. When the temperature was right, she stepped, gasping, into the needlelike spray.

Thirteen

After the Christmas rush, January was a comparatively quiet month at Mayfield's. There were the January white sales, of course, but that involved only one department, not the whole store. The annual meeting of department store publicity and advertising directors from all over the country was held in New York, and Miss Bigelow was usually gone for a week or so attending that. While she was away, Beverly ran things and reveled in it. It was this particular Monday morning that Miss Bigelow was due to return.

"You know, it's a lot more peaceful around here with her away, but when she comes back, I'm always sort of glad to see her," Lynn remarked. She set Beverly's morning coffee down on a folded paper towel from the ladies' room so it wouldn't mar her desk. "Isn't that funny? How you can like having somebody around and at the same time they drive you crazy?"

"I know what you mean." Beverly smiled. She felt rather the same way about Miss Bigelow herself.

"She's so energetic. Being around somebody like that just tires me out, you know? But then, you're that way, too. Excuse me for saying so. Listen, tell me something. Were you always?"

"I guess so," Beverly said. She had never really thought about it.

"Well, some have it, and some don't," Lynn said comfortably. "Me, I could no more—"

"Well, kids." Miss Bigelow marched into the office on the stroke of nine. "How's it going?"

"Miss Bigelow!" said Lynn, her eyes brightening. "Welcome back."

"We missed you," Beverly said. "We were just saying so." As she got up and shook hands with the older woman, she realized with a shock that a subtle change had come over Miss Bigelow. It was not simply that she looked older, although strangely enough she did. There was also some indefinable loss of vitality, evident in her eyes and her handshake, which made her seem suddenly to be running out of whatever fuel had driven her all her life through the heavy seas of business competition.

"Come into my office and brief me on what's been happening," Miss Bigelow said brusquely.

Obediently, Beverly followed her through Lynn's cubicle into her own well-lighted office.

"Shut the door," ordered Miss Bigelow. She sat down at her huge, battle-scarred desk, unlocked it, and shoved her black calf handbag into a bottom drawer.

"Well," Beverly said. She got out her cigarettes and automatically offered the package to her boss.

"No thanks."

Beverly looked at her in surprise. Miss Bigelow had never been known to refuse a cigarette in her life. She put the package back without taking one herself. "Well," she said again, "it's been fairly quiet. The art department had a few problems. Both Horton and Marshall were out most of the week with the flu. I don't know if they're coming in today or not. The Bordeaux perfume ad got left out of the *Times* on Friday, but it was their fault, not ours, and not too serious anyway. They ran it Saturday instead."

"How's the new copywriter doing?"

"Chapman? Not bad. I've been going over his copy with him every day, explaining how we do things, and I think he's getting the idea."

"How are you coming with the schedule for the new store?"

"I haven't done much with you away. Filling your shoes is about all I can handle," Beverly said frankly.

"But you managed."

"Yes, I managed. Oh, one other thing. I only mention it because you may hear a different version from Sam. The Avanene ad, which was supposed to be ready Thursday, wasn't. I told Sam about it on Monday, and Lynn heard me. On Wednesday afternoon late when I went to him for it, he said I'd never mentioned it and got very indignant. We had a big fight about it. I know damn well he went and told Mr. Ladd that I was slipping up on the job and trying to blame other people for it. He even said he was going to."

"Sounds like it's the other way around."

"I don't think so. I think he did it deliberately to make me look bad while you were gone."

"He wants my job," Miss Bigelow said. She had folded her hands and was biting one knuckle thoughtfully.

Beverly was silent.

"Well, I have some news for you, too," Miss Bigelow said at last. "I'm going to have to take a leave of absence. I've been feeling rocky for some time, as you know. While I was in the East, it got bad enough so I decided to see a specialist. The news wasn't good. I'm going to need surgery right away."

"Oh, my," Beverly said. She looked at the older woman with concern, but she could not ask the question that came into her mind.

"Damn lungs," Miss Bigelow said briefly. "No more smoking. I left the last pack I'll ever buy in my New York hotel room."

"Is it hard to give up?" Beverly asked, thinking about her own health.

Miss Bigelow snorted. "Chewing gum isn't the same, I can tell you. Right after the morning meeting, I'm going in and talk to Ladd. I think you can handle this job while I'm away, and I'm going to bat for you. Sam'll get this office over my dead body."

"When are you leaving?"

"I'm going into the hospital as soon as I can make the arrangements. The doctor in New York gave me the name of a surgeon out here and I'm going to call right now. I'll be out two or three months at least."

"It's wonderful of you to trust me with the responsibility," Beverly said, frowning slightly. She had been half expecting something like this for months, but having it actually happen was still disturbing. She was genuinely fond of Miss Bigelow.

"Hell to that," Miss Bigelow said gruffly. "I think you can do it, or I wouldn't recommend you. Anyway, us old war-horses have to stick together. It's still a man's world, you know."

"Yes, it is." Her mind at last switched from Miss Bigelow's illness to what the implications might be for herself.

She sat through the morning meeting with her mind in a turmoil. She hardly dared hope that Ladd would approve of her taking over for Miss Bigelow, even temporarily. He was notoriously opposed to women in executive positions, and if Miss Bigelow herself had not preceded him at Mayfield's, it was extremely unlikely that she would ever have attained her present position. What was the matter with men? Beverly wondered. How many years was it going to be before they accepted the fact that women had as much right to run things in the world as men did? Well, times were changing, no matter how reluctant they were to admit it. Unfortunately, they hadn't changed quite enough yet, and the formula for feminine success in business was still a grim one. Act like a lady, think like a man, fight like a tiger, and work like a dog. And make less money than a man would if he had the same job.

When the meeting was over, she went up to the employees' cafeteria for coffee. Sam was sitting alone at a table, and he looked up as she came in. Ignoring him, she sat down at the opposite side of the room.

In a moment, he was at her side, smiling his yellow-toothed, chain-smoker's smile. "Good morning, Beverly. How's things? Okay if I join you?"

"Sure." She looked at him with loathing. His cheery, ingratiating phase was worse than his back-stabbing, which at least had the virgue of sincerity.

"So Biggie's back," he said chummily. "She looks bad these days, don't you think?"

"Does she? I hadn't noticed."

"She's getting old." He shook his head. "And that cough. When is she due to retire?"

"Oh, I think it's years yet. I don't really know, though."

"I should think you'd pay attention to things like that. After all, you might get her job when she leaves. If you last that long."

"Don't be ridiculous," Beverly said calmly. "They'd bring in somebody from the outside for a big job like hers. They always do. None of us locals have a chance."

"Oh, I wouldn't say that," he said, bristling. "I wouldn't say that." He leaned forward confidentially. "Anyway, I wouldn't be surprised if something was in the wind. She went into Ladd's office just now, looking grim. If you ask me, something's up." He threw her a sidelong, questioning glance.

"I imagine she's just giving him a report on her trip," Beverly said casually. "Incidentally, she said she had a wonderful time in New York."

"Well, great," Sam said. "Just great. I don't think the old girl gets much fun out of life."

"She manages. After all, she has lots of friends."

"Yes. Well, I'd better get back. See you around."

It was nearly eleven-thirty when Ladd sent word for Beverly to come to his office. As she walked through the advertising department with a pounding heart, she noticed that Sam was watching her sharply and that

WIVES AND LOVERS

several other people glanced around curiously. Apparently the word had spread that something was up.

Mr. Ladd stood up behind his desk to greet her as she came in. His glance was scrutinizing, and Beverly remembered with a qualm that in her preoccupation with what was going on, she had forgotten to check her makeup all morning. Undoubtedly she had nervously chewed all her lipstick off, and her nose was shiny.

"Sit down, Mrs. Connors." He indicated the armchair across from his desk next to the one where Miss Bigelow was sitting. "Miss Bigelow had just told me about her illness. I understand she has already informed you."

"Yes." She moistened her lips and looked attentive.

"In spite of the fact that her absence may be a prolonged one, I've decided, on the strength of her recommendation of your work, to let you take over while she is gone. You've been with us long enough to know the ropes, and if Miss Bigelow thinks you can handle them, I'm sure you can."

"Thank you, Mr. Ladd."

"We're going to give you an assistant, of course, to take over your usual duties. Rather than hire someone new, I'm going to give you Miss Eads of the art department. This has all come up quite suddenly, and she is, after all, at least familiar with the workings of the department."

"Oh," Beverly said, "Miss Eads."

"And now, Miss Bigelow, if you don't mind leaving Mrs. Connors and me alone for a few minutes?"

"Right," said Miss Bigelow. She strode to the door, giving Beverly a look of triumph.

"I'm sure you are aware of the serious nature of Miss Bigelow's illness," Mr. Ladd said when the door had closed. He paused and placed his well-manicured fingertips together. "I think we have to face facts, Mrs. Connors. Miss Bigelow may never rejoin the staff.

She's not a young woman, and it's obvious that she is quite ill. I would never consider replacing a woman like her with someone of your youth and inexperience, no matter how competent you may be. For the present, I have no choice. This whole matter has come up too suddenly. However, I want to make it clear to you that in the event Miss Bigelow does not recover sufficiently to rejoin us here, Mayfield's will have to search the country for a new director of advertising and publicity. In other words, your tenure is temporary, and it will end as soon as we learn—if we do learn—that Miss Bigelow is not coming back."

"Yes, Mr. Ladd," Beverly said. "I understand." With a little effort, she managed to give him a calm, direct, accepting look.

"Of course, if your work during Miss Bigelow's absence is satisfactory—as we have every reason to assume it will be—there is no need for you to worry about having to leave us if there is a new director. Such a person, conceivably, might want to choose a different assistant. That will be up to him. But if so, we'll find some other post for you. It may not be as elevated as you might hope, but it will be something. As you know, we like to stick by our employees here at Mayfield's. Give them the breaks when we possibly can. The team spirit."

"You're very kind," Beverly said. She hoped she didn't sound sarcastic.

"All this, of course, is confidential. There will be speculation among the other employees about what is going to happen, but I'd rather you didn't discuss the situation with them."

"No. Of course I won't."

"That will be all for now." Mr. Ladd stood up and held out his hand. "Good luck to you. Miss Eads will come to you tomorrow morning, and you can begin instructing her in her duties."

"Thank you for your trust," Beverly said. "I'll make every effort to live up to it for as long as you need me."

She went directly from Ladd's office to Miss Bigelow.

"Well, you look disgusted," Miss Bigelow said. "What happened after I left?"

"Nothing much," Beverly said. "Mostly I'm just stunned over falling heir to Cathy Eads."

Miss Bigelow gave a short bark of amusement. "She should be a lot of help. If you can get her nose out of her compact long enough."

"Not only that. She and Sam are big buddy pals. I can just imagine how busy they'll be planning ways to trip me up."

"Forewarned is forearmed," Miss Bigelow said. "You can handle the little bitch."

"I hope," Beverly said grimly. "I hope."

Cathy Eads reported the following day wearing her usual working uniform, a long-sleeved sheath that fit her well-developed body like water fits a glass. Her heels were so high and thin that she wobbled slightly as she walked, and the wobble did not detract from her general air of seductiveness. She was a dark girl with masses of curly hair and eyes that were either sullen or sultry, depending on whether she was looking at a man or a woman.

"Do I sit here?" she asked, tracing the back of Beverly's chair with a fingernail the color of dried blood.

"Not until next week," Bevery said, slamming the door of the filing cabinet for emphasis. "I won't be moving into Miss Bigelow's office until she leaves."

"You're glad she's leaving?"

"Certainly not," Beverly snapped. "I've very fond of her, and I'm extremely sorry she's ill."

Miss Eads smiled faintly in a way that expressed a subtle mixture of amusement, disbelief, and contempt, but she said nothing. Instead, she sat down in Beverly's chair and crossed her legs.

"Perhaps you'd better sit here." Beverly indicated the chair that stood against the wall near her desk.

Miss Eads shrugged, got up, and moved, swaying, to the new location.

"Now," Beverly said, sitting down at her desk, "here are the new ads and this is what you do with them."

"How did it go?" Miss Bigelow asked, as she and Beverly lunched together in a corner of the employee's cafeteria.

"She's not as dumb as she pretends," Beverly said. "She can learn fast enough when she wants to. As a matter of fact, she's rather shrewd. She puts on the act of not understanding often enough to annoy me, but not often enough so that I can run off to management screaming incompetence."

"If you did, she'd quick as a whip show them she knew exactly what was going on and make you look like a liar."

"Yes. And they'd believe her and not me, because she's pretty and I'm not. Men always think a plain woman is out to get a pretty one because she's jealous. It never occurs to them that possibly the pretty one could be the liar."

"There they are now," Miss Bigelow said. "The unholy twosome."

Beverly turned to see Cathy Eads and Sam walk into the cafeteria together. Cathy walked fluidly, her silver bangle bracelets jangling, and Sam followed her with the discreetly triumphant air of a man who has cornered the best deal in town.

"They're going to give me trouble," Beverly said slowly. "I just know it."

"What the hell," Miss Bigelow said. "You're smarter than both of them put together."

"I'd better be," Beverly said.

The week was a hectic one, and an hour after closing time Friday night, Beverly and Miss Bigelow were still finishing up the details of the work transfer. Miss Bigelow had explained everything to her in such elaborate detail that Beverly realized with a sinking heart that she knew she might not be coming back to work at all. It was with an unmistakable air of finality that she cleared her desk, locked it, and handed Beverly the key.

"Well, that's that. What time is it?"

"Nearly seven," Beverly said, looking at her watch.

"Let's get out of here before the janitor sweeps us up with the rest of the rubbish," Miss Bigelow said. She took her black topcoat down from the rack in the corner, slung it over the shoulders of her black-and-white tweed suit, and started for the door.

Beverly noticed that she did not look around her. But she would like to take a last look, she thought with sudden, painful insight. She's not doing it because I'm here. Oh, it's lucky I'm with her. They walked through the deserted advertising department, where the desks, chairs, and filing cabinets had the forlorn look of furnishings in an abandoned house. Nothing gives you such a desolate feeling as seeing empty a place that is usually full of people, Beverly reflected. Aloud she said cheerily to Miss Bigelow, "Looks like we're the last ones."

"Your family's probably champing at the bit. I'm sorry I kept you."

"Don't worry about that. This is more important than their dinner being a little late for once."

"Is it? Good."

After the long halls with their dark, deserted, silent offices, the creaking, lighted elevator seemed almost cozy.

"If there's anything I can do to help, call me," Miss Bigelow said. "I ought to have a little fight in me by Friday or so."

"The operation is Tuesday morning?"

"Right."

The elevator rumbled to a stop at the main floor and they pushed open the squeaky, grillwork door and stepped out.

Outside the streetlights were on and the night air

felt wintry and damp. Almost immediately Miss Bigelow began coughing with spasms that shook her short, sturdy body. "Damn smog," she grumbled.

"It is getting worse," Beverly said. She walked with Miss Bigelow as far as her car.

"Well, good luck." Miss Bigelow reached out and gripped her hand. "Don't let Eads get you down."

"Good luck to you." Beverly repressed an impulse to hug her. "I'll come and see you the second they let you have visitors."

It was past the evening rush hour, and the freeway was not crowded as Beverly drove home. She was glad because she felt inordinately tired, as though she were already facing all the responsibilities and pressures ahead of her in the weeks to come. She knew she would have to take work home at night quite often, at least for a while. That mean more trouble with Bob, but there was no way out. She was determined to show Ladd what a good job she could do.

Miss Bigelow's desk had caught her eye that night as the older woman was clearing out her belongings. It was a squat, tough-looking piece of furniture, scratched and scarred from years of hard use, unhandsome and sturdy. It looked as though it had been in the service of Mayfield's as long as Miss Bigelow had. In fact, it reminded her of Miss Bigelow. A strange feeling had come over Beverly as she looked at it. If Miss Bigelow was not coming back, she wanted that desk for herself. It looked as though it would take a lot of living up to, but she could do it. She knew she could. The trick would be to convince Mr. Ladd. Trick? It would take a miracle. Beverly's hands tightened on the steering wheel. All right. She'd give him a miracle. More than he asked for. More than he had any right to expect from a temporary executive. The challenge was tremendous, the odds against her overwhelming. All the same, she was going to try.

When she turned into the driveway, she saw a light in the kitchen. Bob must be getting dinner.

Belinda met her at the front door. "We've already eaten," she said importantly. "Daddy fixed scrambled eggs."

"Hello, stranger," Bob said as she walked into the kitchen. He was wearing an apron, and Beverly could tell immediately that he was angry but had decided to be jaunty about it.

"I tried to call and say I'd be late, but the line was busy for ages," she said.

"I was talking to Mary Beth," Belinda said. "Mary Beth's cat had kittens. She says I can have one."

"Isn't one cat enough?" Beverly said. "You wouldn't want Morris to be jealous, would you?"

"What new crisis today?" Bob asked. "What's the latest chapter in the life of Beverly Connors, girl executive?"

"It was Carol Bigelow's last day. We had some last-minute things to clear up. She goes into the hospital on Monday."

"And then you take over the whole shootin' match. I suppose after that we'll never see you again."

"Oh, I'll be home on time. But I may have to do some work in the evenings. At least for a while."

"Yeah. That's what you said before. Well, I may be doing some night work myself from now on."

"Oh?" She was surprised. "I thought you didn't believe in it."

"I don't, on principle. But sometimes it's more convenient to talk to people after business hours. You know. They're less distracted at home. No phone calls to interrupt, no secretaries with letters to sign."

"Well, that's wonderful. Yes. I'm sure you can get a lot more done that way."

"I don't know that I'll get a lot more done," Bob said casually. "I'll take some time off in the daytime to make up for it. Shoot a little golf or something. After all, I'm not crazy for work like you are. There's no need in both of us killing ourselves. And you like to."

"It's not that I like to," she said defensively. "Oh,

why do we have to go through all this again? I explained to you what the situation was. What Mr. Ladd said. All about Cathy Eads. I have to do a good job. If Carol Bigelow doesn't come back to work, and they bring in a new director, I may really be out in the cold."

"I understand, Beverly. I understand." He took the apron off and tossed it in her lap. "Now, why don't you fix yourself a bite? I'll see you later."

"Where are you going?"

"I have to see a man about a premium." He left, and five minutes later, Beverly heard him drive off. He had not come into the kitchen to kiss her goodbye.

She scrabbled two eggs and ate them with some cold string beans she was too tired to heat. After she had finished, she sat at the kitchen table, thinking, Maybe I should get some help with the house now. The idea made her feel guilty. If she couldn't manage a house and a job at the same time, then she shouldn't be working. And I *can* manage it, she told herself determinedly. I'll feel better in the morning. It's just that this has been a bad week.

"Mother?" Belinda stood in the doorway, twisting one leg up behind her like a crane and holding it with her hand. "Mother, are you sure I can't have one of Mary Beth's kittens?" She looked pleading. "It's a very small kitten."

In spite of her weariness, Beverly smiled. "All right," she said. "As long as it's a small one."

Fourteen

It was a rainy Tuesday night in February, and Dana drove slowly west on Mulholland Drive along the crest of the Hollywood hills toward Ryan Parker's house, watching for landslides. The hills had burned here less than six months ago and with the brush removed, they sometimes shed avalanches of mud during a heavy downpour. It would have been safer on a night like this to go out the Ventura Freeway, but she loved this road which so few cars used at night, solitary and deserted, winding among the hilltops high above the city.

It was fascinating how her senses seemed to have sharpened in the weeks she had been taking Parker's class. The drills he gave had unsheathed and honed a perception she never knew she had, so that everything she saw, heard, smelled, tasted, and touched registered with a new, fresh intensity. It was almost like being a child again, this ability to experience the world with the dullness of familiarity stripped away like the thick, flavorless skin of a fruit.

Dana had watched people with this intensity of observation for as long as she could remember. She had an endless curiosity about the way they looked and behaved, and a part of her brain seemed to record this information and file it away. She had never understood why she did this, but she did know it was an important part of her acting equipment. What Parker had done was to make her as aware of the rest of creation as she already was of human beings.

If her experience of everyday life had deepened and become richer because of Parker's class, this was minor compared to the excitement of attending the class itself. She went each week with an anticipation which could hardly have been headier if she were going to perform in a real theater. The other students were talented beyond the average, and under Parker's tutelage they were stimulated to give their best. Acting was rather like tennis, she thought. It was hard to play a superior game with a bad player, while a good one brought out skill you never knew you had. There were nights when a delicate rapport seemed to be achieved among those who were playing and those who watched. A current ran between them, binding them together, establishing invisible lines of communication along which they projected and received emotion with uncanny ease. It did not always happen, but when it did, the air in that odd, ornately furnished room was charged with the authentic excitement of the theater. Dana lived for those times. Afterward, she went home vitalized with a psychic energy, a sense of power so overwhelming that she could hardly sleep. Indeed, the feeling did not subside entirely for two or three days. The weekly practice, too, was restoring her confidence in herself.

She reached the top of Pueblo Canyon and turned downhill. Within a few minutes, she was at Parker's house. She had left home early because of the rain, but she had come across the hills more quickly than she had estimated, and none of the rest of the class had arrived. Parker was still at dinner, so at the maid's instruction, she went alone into the drawing room to wait.

Almost immediately, Parker came to join her. "Come in," he said, waving in the direction of the dining room. "I have a guest I'd like you to meet."

The man seated at the long refectory table was well-fed, ruddy-faced, and in his late forties.

"This is Dan Morgan," Parker said. "Dan, one of my students, Dana Hurst."

"How do you do?" Dana said. The name sounded familiar, but she was too busy wondering whether the man's exceptionally red face came from drinking or outdoor sports to place it.

"Mr. Morgan is an eminent dramatic writer," Parker explained, holding back a chair for her.

"Oh, yes," Dana said, remembering suddenly. "And an Academy Award winner, aren't you?"

"Not for some time," Dan Morgan said wryly. "I'm surprised you're old enough to remember."

"Oh, I'm old enough," Dana said. "The light in here is more flattering than you think."

Morgan burst out laughing. "Did you say this girl was an actress, Ryan? She's remarkably frank."

"Only one of her rare qualities," Parker said. "Dana, a little brandy? Wine?"

"Wine, please. Are you working on anything at present, Mr. Morgan?" Dana asked.

"I've just finished a play."

"A play? I didn't know you wrote for the theater."

"I haven't for twenty years. Not since my Broadway success brought me to Hollywood, where I've been ever since."

"May I ask what it's about?"

"Nuns." Everything he said had a slightly ironic tone. "Nuns in a hospital. A spiritually uplifting play which nobody will ever produce."

"Come, come, Dan. Don't be pessimistic," Parker said. "More coffee?"

"Thank you, no. I'm foundering on it now," Morgan said gloomily. "I'd better be running along."

"Why not stay and watch my class?"

"Wouldn't want to intrude. Frighten the poor little beasts."

"Not at all. It would put them on their mettle, having an outsider present. You wouldn't be frightened, would you, Dana?"

"Not in the least," Dana said. She smiled warmly at Morgan. "Please stay."

"All right. Since you put it so prettily." He returned her smile, his ruddy face wrinkling pleasantly.

A nice man, Dana decided, but a little strange. She would have thought he was drunk, but it seemed unlikely when he drank coffee while his host drank brandy.

"Tonight let us test your powers of observation," Parker said when the class had assembled. "I want each of you to re-create for me someone whom you have seen and talked with during the past two days. To make it more challenging, it must be someone of the opposite sex."

"How will you know how well we do when you don't know who we're imitating?" Jane Wilder asked. She was a blonde with a certain natural talent unfortified by much intelligence.

Parker looked at her with mild distaste. "An extraordinary question for anyone who has been in this class as long as you have, Miss Wilder. Mrs. Hurst, will you answer Miss Wilder, please?"

"If it's well done, it will have a ring of truth, of sincerity about it that's unmistakable," Dana said hesitantly.

"Precisely," Parker said.

Dana smiled and involuntarily, like a good pupil seeking approbation, looked at Dan Morgan, who nodded gravely at her. His face really was remarkably red. He looked, she thought, rather as though he'd been holding his breath.

It was one of the magical evenings. As each of them performed in turn, Dana felt the tide of excitement and enjoyment mounting within her and she searched her mind for a suitable characterization to present when her turn came. Perhaps because of the presence of a stranger, she felt impelled to some sort of tour de force. I want to be dazzling, she thought, moving restlessly in her chair. I want to outdo them all.

It was late, well after the intermission break, when Parker finally said, "Mrs. Hurst, do you have something for us?"

Silently she got to her feet. As she walked toward the great fireplace, she willed herself to seem taller, thinner. She turned, and her gaze swept the room with one quick, aristocratic movement of the head. "Perhaps, Mr. Stanley," she said in a voice unmistakably flavored with Parker's richness of tone, "you will be good enough to favor us with a visual reenactment of your breakfast?"

A murmur of amusement swept through the room, and she paused to let it die away. "No, no, Mr. Stanley," she went on, sounding annoyed. "We are not interested in seeing you eat your breakfast. We wish you to be your breakfast. What's that? You don't remember how you had the eggs? Then we'll let it be optional, Mr. Stanley. Whichever way you feel this evening. Fried or scrambled."

By the time she had finished, the room was in an uproar. Flushed and triumphant at the applause, Dana noted with satisfaction that Parker had so far lost his ordinary assurance that he was having to wipe tears from his eyes. Once again, she looked to Dan Morgan for approval. His face was redder than ever, and he was grinning like a pixie.

"I think we'll call it a night," Parker announced when order was restored. "I'm sure none of you want to follow that act. Good night." He walked over to Dana. "Will you stay behind for a moment?"

When everyone was gone except Dan Morgan, Parker said to Dana, "Well, my dear. You have an extraordinary talent for comedy that I never even suspected. Have you played much?"

"Only at home," Dana said, and then, when the two men looked puzzled, "For my little boy. He's a rather exacting audience."

Morgan and Parker exchanged glances.

"Would you be free to appear in a play?" Dan Morgan asked. "My play?"

Dana looked at him in bewilderment. "Why yes," she managed to say, "but I thought you said—"

"That nobody would ever produce it. That was something of a lie, Mrs. Hurst, which I told you in the hopes of preventing that appalling self-consciousness which seems to seize actresses in the presence of someone who might possibly have a part for them. The fact is, I came here tonight to see you at Ryan's suggestion. He's read the script, and he thought there might be something in it for you. I agree. It's not the lead, but it's a good part, a young nun whose warmth and spirit keep getting her into trouble with her superiors, although they endear her to the partients she nurses. Are you interested?" He had a certain quiet, intent eagerness.

"Yes, of course." She looked at him a little dazedly. "Of course I'm interested."

"Good. It's being produced locally in what we are hopefully calling a pre-Broadway run." There was the ironic tone again. "Actually, if it goes well here, I suppose there is a possibility that it might be done in New York later. They're holding readings all this week. Technically, I have no right to offer you a job, of course. But I'd certainly like to see you get it, and my word carries some weight. Could you read Thursday morning?"

"Yes. Oh, yes."

"Then come around eleven to the Pacific Playhouse on Wilshire. Incidentally, I'd like you to read the play first. Perhaps you could pick it up here at Ryan's tomorrow afternoon? I live in Malibu, but I'm coming to Beverly Hills in the morning for an appointment, and I'll drop it off." He looked at his watch. "I must go. May I see you to your car?"

The rain had stopped, and the air felt icy as they

went down the flagstone walk. It's snowed in the mountains, Dana thought, but there won't be any more skiing for me this year. I can't risk a twisted ankle. Aloud she said, "I'm very grateful to you."

"You needn't be," he said wryly. "Nobody does anybody any favors in this business. You must know that. I want you because I think you'll be good in the part, and I need a success rather badly."

When they reached her car, he stood without opening the door. "It's very difficult, casting nuns," he said thoughtfully. "People kept telling me I couldn't do it, have a block of black-and-white birds flapping around the stage. No variations in costume or makeup or hair to establish character. No close-ups like the movies or television. It takes a strong personality, a distinctive voice and manner. You've got those. Plus the eyes. Well. Good night." He opened the car door.

The next day she was too restless to stay home. After she had dropped Jeremy off at nursery school, she drove into Beverly Hills and wandered up and down the aisles of several department stores, hardly seeing the displays. This was a part she had to have. It sounded made to offer for her the way Dan Morgan had described it. Something about Dan Morgan fascinated her. She had the feeling that a lot had happened to him, some of it distinctly unpleasant. He sounded as though he had had career trouble, but he hardly looked down-at-the heels.

Eventually it was lunchtime. Most of the restaurants were crowded, and she didn't feel like driving home, so she ended by sliding onto a stool at a hamburger stand. She ordered a number ten rare and a Pepsi, and let her mind slide back to the reading. Waiting was maddening once you knew you were waiting for something specific. Today was longer than all of the last five months put together. I know I can do it, she thought, tapping her fingers nervously on the Formica counter. I know without reading it that I can do it. It is absolutely unbearable to contemplate that I might not get the chance. The hamburger came, and she bit into it absent-mindedly. How nice of Ryan Parker to tell Morgan about her. He wouldn't have, she realized with a sense of gratification, if he didn't think she was good. She wondered how long Parker and Morgan had known each other. If they were old friends, Parker would know all about him. Finishing her hamburger quickly and leaving the bag of potato chips behind, she got back into her car and drove up Pueblo Canyon.

Parker came into the drawing room to greet her wearing a tie and the smoking jacket that was his usual at-home attire.

"I was so excited last night that I'm afraid I forgot to thank you for telling Mr. Morgan about me," Dana said.

He laughed. "Quite understandable." He went to a table and picked up a brown manila envelope. "Here's the script Dan left this morning. He's very excited about you."

"Have you known each other a long time?"

"Oh, fifteen years or so, I suppose. I've appeared in a couple of pictures he's written. He has quite a list of credits, and two Academy Awards."

"I don't remember seeing his name lately."

"You wouldn't have. He hasn't done anything much for, oh, the past five years, I'd say."

"Has he been ill?"

Parker hesitated. "Yes, I believe alcoholism is considered an illness. He had rather a lengthy bout with it, which he eventually won. By then, of course, he couldn't get a job anywhere. So he sat down and wrote this play about the nuns who nursed him back to health. It's an interesting piece of work."

"Do you think it will be a success?"

He shrugged. "My dear, I've been in this business too long to make any predictions. I hope for his sake it will be. A success would bolster his ego and put him back into an active part in his profession. He needs to work, not for the money, but for his soul. He is not, fortunately, in financial need. He was extremely successful for a number of years.

"You know, last night at first I had the oddest feeling that he was drunk, and yet it seemed unlikely when he was sitting there with coffee while you drank brandy," Dana said.

"It's his manner. Perhaps it's due to having been an alcoholic for so many years."

"Is he married?"

"Not for some time. His wife left him years ago and took the children with her. They're both in college in the East now, and I believe she's living in the Bahamas."

"Then he has had a sad life. I sensed he had."

"Yes," Parker said soberly. "A man who has ruined his own life is always a more tragic figure than one who's been ruined by circumstances outside his control, don't you think? I'd like to see Dan make a come-back. He's a man of real talent, and I don't think he's reached the final expression of his potential by any means."

Thursday morning, at long last, arrived. Dressing early in order not to arrive in a frenzy of nervous haste, Dana put on her simplest black wool dress, the barest hint of makeup, and pulled her hair back into a bun. No jewels, she decided. Not even a string of pearls. She blotted her lipstick pale, and darkened her lashes and brows to bring out her eyes.

She drove to the theater feeling calm and desperate and excited and determined all at once. She felt as though she would like to command the part at gunpoint. That it was impossible to do this seemed one more unimportant custom of civilized life. Like red traffic lights. She missed four signals in a row and waited at each one in a mounting state of frustration. Obstacles. There were always obstacles. Well, they would simply have to be overcome, one by one, although patience was a virtue that seemed as impossible of attainment for her today as sainthood. Sainthood. That thought almost quieted her. It's a good thing it's a lively nun and not one of those resigned, spiritual ones, she thought grimly, or I'd never get the part.

The theater was a nice one, simple, uncluttered, not too large. She had entered it many times as a customer. The curtain was open now, revealing an empty stage in the isolated glare of a single naked bulb. A girl stood alone on it, reading from a script. Her voice sounded reedy and thin, swallowed up by the emptiness of the unpeopled auditorium. Dana started down the aisle toward the small group of heads she could see sticking up in the dimness of the front rows. When she got close enough, she could tell that one of them was Dan Morgan's. As she stood uncertainly wondering whether or not to join them, he turned and saw her. Immediately he came back, and after they had smiled a silent greeting, they sat down together in aisle seats and watched the reading in progress.

The girl was a king-sized, shiny-mouthed brunette. She, too, wore a black dress, the kind that involves truck drivers in rear-end collisions, and she stood with a boldness that belied the wavering uncertainty of her voice. What's the poor girl doing here? Dana thought, with a sensation almost of sympathy. She should be wearing feathers in Las Vegas. The lines she recognized; they were from the role that Dan Morgan wanted her to play. She turned to him with an inquiring look. He said nothing but gave her the pixie grin, and his face in the dim light seemed to get a little redder. He was obviously amused and Dana, as she watched, decided she could see his point.

When the girl had finished she stood still, waiting for further instructions.

"That was fine, Miss Purcell. Thank you," said a soft masculine voice in front of them.

WIVES AND LOVERS

Dan Morgan got up and held out his hand to Dana to help her from her seat, and together they walked down the aisle.

"Dana, this is Roger Deal, the director, and Mr. Boyd, the producer. Roger, this is Dana Hurst, whom I told you about."

"How do you do?" Dana said. Boyd was small and inconsequential-looking, but Deal really surprised her. He was young, certainly no more than twenty-five, tall, thin, spectacled, and shy.

"How are you?" he said in the soft voice she had heard a moment earlier. "Will you read for us now?"

On the stage alone under the work light, she stood quietly for a moment, mentally drawing her energies inward, assembling her powers of concentration. Nothing must distract her now; not the door at the back squeaking and opening a sudden rectangle of light in the blackness as someone came in, not Boyd in the front row coughing and feeling his pockets for cigarettes, not the sound of hammering which seemed to come from somewhere behind the stage. She must ignore all these things, she must neither see nor hear them, she must be utterly self-contained. When she had achieved this, she began. The words came easily, as though she had written them herself. The force she had gathered within her projected them as she willed, out of the tight circle of her being, sent them forth with power and authority until they filled the empty theater with invisible vibrations.

After she had finished, the odd clatter of handclaps, few but enthusiastic, reached her from below.

"Will you wait for us there a moment please, Mrs. Hurst?" Roger Deal called up to her.

She nodded. There was a chair at one side, but she did not sit down. She stood still, letting herself return to normal like an engine which has been turned off but continues to revolve awhile, more and more slowly, until it finally comes to a halt.

"All right, Mrs. Hurst. You can come down now."

She walked to them on legs that were just beginning to tremble a little.

"You have the part," Roger Deal said. "I've listened to fourteen people, and I don't want to hear any more."

"Congratulations," Boyd said, shaking her hand in a resigned way. "Very good."

Dan Morgan said nothing, but his blue eyes radiated approval. He took both her hands in his and nodded vigorously, seemingly unable to put his enthusiasm into words.

"If all goes well, we'll start rehearsing a week from Monday," Roger Deal said. "Will you give me your address and phone in case I have to contact you before then?"

She filled out the card he handed her with a pen borrowed from Mr. Boyd.

"We're going to celebrate," Dan Morgan said when she had finished. "I'm taking you out to lunch."

"Lovely. Let me powder my nose first." She walked up the aisle feeling as lightheaded as though she were high on a snowy mountain where the air was thin. A job. It seemed almost unbelievable, and she suddenly realized that unconsciously, during the months she had been waiting and hoping and preparing, she had somehow given up the idea of ever working and made a kind of career of the seeking itself. Now, this abrupt attainment of her goal required a wrenching mental readjustment.

She powdered her nose with a vague sense of misgiving. Broadway. Dan Morgan had mentioned that the show, if it were a success, might go East. What if she had the opportunity to go with it? What would Don say? And what about Jeremy?

I'm crossing all those bridges prematurely, she told herself. There was plenty of time to think about all that when the problem came up, if it ever did. Meanwhile, she was going to act. Act? Realization of what that meant burst on her, finally, like fireworks. She was going to appear in a professional show, in a real theater in front of people who had paid money to get in, she was going to wear a costume and makeup, she was going to rehearse, she was going to speak lines, she was going to play a role, my God, she was going to act! Act, at last! Feeling as though she had won the sweepstakes, feeling like Miss America, the First Lady, smiling bemusedly and a little foolishly to herself, she walked out into the lobby to meet Dan Morgan.

Fifteen

Beverly had never worked as hard as she did in the weeks after Miss Bigelow left for her operation. She found herself doing not only Miss Bigelow's work, but some of the duties connected with her old job as well. The schedule for the new store had to be completed, and Cathy Eads could not be trusted to do it. Because she did not like to stay late at the office and keep Bob and Belinda waiting for dinner, she often went in early in the morning instead. Generally, two or three nights a week, she took work home. Under the constant pressure, she ate more and began to gain, which disturbed her. Actually, though, she had so little time to think about herself that she was, for the most part, quite happy. There was a satisfaction like no other in meeting the demands of a difficult job, she thought. There was enormous pleasure in finding out how much you could handle, especially when it turned out to be considerably more than even you had suspected. She had power and, while it might be only temporary, it was real enough. It gave her a unique sense of exhilaration. She could understand why men with successful careers often became so absorbed that they neglected their families. Yet she could not, and would not, do this herself, although she had finally given in and hired a maid to clean the house once a week.

She was proud and happy to show off her domain the day that Sherry and Shirley came downtown to have lunch with her.

"How many people do you have working for you?" Sherry asked wonderingly, staring at the big room in which the artists and copywriters worked.

"Twenty-three," Beverly said.

"Do they have to ask your permission to go to the bathroom?" Shirley asked, a thread of laughter running through her voice.

Beverly ignored her. "And this is my office. Miss Bigelow's office, that is."

"How is she?" Sherry asked. "Will she be coming back soon?"

"I don't know," Beverly murmured throatily. "She's out of the hospital, but she's still awfully weak. She has a nurse taking care of her at home. I go over to see her once or twice a week on my lunch hour. Her apartment isn't far from here."

"This is a nice office," Sherry said. She sat down in the swivel chair behind the desk and crossed her elegant legs. "It must be fun being an executive."

"Fun isn't exactly the word," Beverly said, "but it does have its rewards." She laid her hand on the big, battle-scarred desk and gave it an affectionate pat, as though it were an ally.

A brown-haired man stuck his head in the door. "Mrs. Connors? Oh, excuse me. You're busy."

"That's all right, Mr. Chapman. These are my sisters. They're visiting me. Can I help you with something?"

"It wasn't important." He stood shyly in the doorway. "I just wanted to show you this. I think it's my best so far."

"Let's see it." Beverly held out her hand, and he gave her the copy he had brought with him. "Yes, that's good," she said. "That's very good. You've got the idea."

He looked pleased. "Thank you. I'm sorry I bothered you."

When he had gone, Shirley said, "Who was that?"

"Mr. Chapman. He's our newest copywriter. He

had a little trouble at first, but he's very anxious to do well, so I've sort of taken him under my wing," Beverly said. "He's coming alone nicely."

"With twenty-three people working for you, how do you have time for that kind of thing?"

"It's all in being organized," Beverly said crisply.

"He's sort of cute," Sherry said. "Not good-looking, exactly, but kind of appealing. You know?"

"I should have introduced you more thoroughly," Beverly said. "He might have asked you out."

Sherry shrugged, lifting her shoulders delicately. "Never mind. He undoubtedly hasn't got any money."

"Well, now," Beverly said reprovingly, "I hope that isn't your only criterion."

"No, just the first one." Sherry smiled at her older sister engagingly. "I'm spoiled. I admit it. But like Mother always used to say, it's just as easy to fall in love with a rich man as a poor one. And it's even easier if you have nothing but rich ones around."

"Only they aren't always too nice, are they?" Beverly said. "Remember your Las Vegas friend. No, the important thing is to marry a nice man. If you can find one."

"Incidentally, how's Bob these days?" Shirley asked suddenly with a look of amusement.

"Working hard."

"I forgot to tell you I saw him a couple of weeks ago. He was in a convertible, and some woman was driving."

Shock made her go prickly hot all over. "Oh?" she managed to say casually. "What did she look like?"

"I couldn't tell. She had on dark glasses and the top was up."

"I just thought maybe it was somebody we knew," Beverly lied. "But it was probably a client."

"Yes," Shirley said slowly, "probably it was a client."

Beverly looked at her narrowly. Shirley's expression was utterly devoid of malice, and it was frighteningly evident that she was telling the truth. "Well, let's take you two up and feed you," Beverly said abruptly. "I've got a lot to do this afternoon."

At lunch, she was careful to conceal how upset she was. She smiled brightly, chatted and laughed, discussed her new job in glowing terms. But for the first time that she could remember, she was not able to finish her dessert, no, not more than a bite of the delicious chocolate angel food, and the food she did eat seemed to turn sour as soon as she swallowed it.

When she was alone in her office after her sisters had left, she told Lynn she did not want to be disturbed and shut both doors. At first, a wave of such blistering anger swept over her that she broke out in perspiration. So Bob was playing around while she worked herself to death. How like him. How exactly like that miserable, spineless . . . . The furious adjectives formed a log jam in her brain and refused to come out in sequence. She lit a cigarette with shaking fingers. He had never been anything but weak. Why had she been such a fool as to fall in love with him when it was perfectly clear he had no character whatsoever? Just charm. Charm which he now, apparently, was using on somebody else. While I'm down here knocking myself out, she thought bitterly. I'm the man of the family. I've always had to be. Somebody has to be. I'm the man and the woman, the breadwinner and the housekeeper, while he skylarks around town with some bitch in a convertible. The bastard. "Damn him! Damn him! Damn him!" she burst out, crying, and as quickly as it had come out, it stopped.

The phone rang, but she did not answer it. Let Lynn take it. She was an executive now, with a right to a moment or two of solitude. She gave the store enough time they didn't have to pay for, taking work home night after night. Night after night, while her husband . . . . She realized, with a sinking sensation just how much Bob had been gone in the evenings lately. It had never occurred to her to be suspicious; she was merely relieved to have him out of the way so that she could work in peace. When he was home, and she had paper work, he was usually angry and irritated, and the edgy atmosphere kept her from concentrating. He had said that he was going to see clients, and she had never doubted him. She was not a mistrustful wife. Indeed, she never mistrusted anyone unless the person had done something to deserve it. A simple soul, that's what I am, she thought bitterly. Simpleminded, that is. I'm a damn fool, and it's high time I wised up.

An intense, frustrated fury welled up inside her and she immediately began to rebel against the self-characterization. It was true that if you were trusting, people sometimes took advantage of you, but what was the alternative? To become mean, small, suspicious? To go around forever expecting the worst of people? I suppose that's the only way to arm yourself, she thought, but I won't do it. I don't want to be that kind of person. I'd rather be hurt once in a while.

But when it was your own husband? He was a devil, she thought, agonizingly. He was an uncaring, insensitive devil. A surge of self-pity rose within her. What had she done to deserve this? She had loved Bob, she had helped him, she had always been a loyal wife. She had borne more than her share of the responsibilities of marriage from the start. And in spite of everything, he had turned away from her. The memory of the night they had quarreled after Belinda was born returned to her mind. "Damn the baby." What a dreadful thing to say. Then he had shaken her, and she had locked herself in the bedroom, and Belinda had heard and cried and cried. Suddenly she was crying herself, shaking silently, her hands over her face, and once again the telephone began to ring.

After a while, there was a knock on the door.

"Are you all right?" Lynn called.

"Fine," Beverly said, fighting to keep her voice normal. "Did you want something?"

"There's somebody here to see you. A Mr. Copeland."

"Just a minute." She had forgotten she had an appointment. She powdered her nose hastily and went to the door that led to Lynn's office. "Come in, Mr. Copeland," she said cordially. "I'm sorry to keep you waiting." As he followed her into the office, she seated herself quickly behind the big desk and gripped the edge of its solid, wooden bulk with her fingers.

By the time he left, she was much calmer. Perhaps, after all, the situation was not serious. Everybody knew that husbands, and even wives, had these little extramarital flings from time to time, and they didn't necessarily break up the marriage. Maybe Bob was just bored, and amusing himself. The idea was not palatable, but she forced herself to be realistic. Perhaps he had a right to feel neglected. Furthermore, she had been neglecting herself as well, she acknowledged uneasily. Involuntarily, she smoothed her hands over her hips, where the fabric of her suit skirt was stretched into tight horizontal folds. She really must go on a diet. Maybe find a new hair style, too. The women's magazines always advised you to pay extra attention to your looks if you thought your husband was straying. "Be the woman he married," was the way they put it. She sighed. After marriage, weren't adults supposed to forget about courtship and get on with the business of the world? Did you have to go on charming your husband forever? Well, maybe you did.

Sam stuck his head in the door. "Beverly, can you come out here for a minute?"

"Right with you," she said, getting up.

By quitting time she had herself completely under control. It had occurred to her, once the initial shock had worn off, that maybe it was nothing at all.

Perhaps the woman was a client. Or there could be other plausible explanations of why he was driving around in her car. She couldn't think of any offhand, but she knew this was just the kind of crazy thing that happened. A situation that looked sinister at first glance turned out to have a perfectly natural, simple explanation. Well, she would ask him who the woman was. She might even say kiddingly, "I hear you have a new girlfriend," and watch his puzzled reaction. Above all, she must not allow herself to sound snoopy or suspicious. That was so unattractive. If she did that, she would be terribly embarrassed when he explained that the woman was just a client, and it would put her at a disadvantage with him in the future. Whatever happened, she must keep her pride. Besides, there was going to be absolutely nothing to it! She had simply let her imagination run away with her.

When she got home, Bob had not yet arrived. Ordinarily, she would have thought nothing of it, although it did not happen often. Tonight it filled her with misgivings. Was he sitting in a bar somewhere, and if so, with whom? Perhaps he was only have a beer with the boys. She smiled ruefully at the old, familiar phrase. How grateful she would be if that were all he was doing.

While she was taking off her coat in the bedroom, she caught sight of herself in the big mirror over the chests of drawers. Her hair was stringy, her nose shiny, and she had eaten her lipstick off during the afternoon. She frowned. Why could she never remember to freshen her makeup more often at work? She always meant to, but then she became absorbed in what she was doing and forgot about how she looked. Even Miss Eads's glamorous presence failed to act as an incentive. Well, some women were good at that sort of thing, and some weren't. As a matter of fact, she doubted if Miss Eads's nose ever got shiny, even when she had a cold.

While she was repairing her makeup, Belinda came

and stood in the bedroom door. "What are you doing, Mother?" she asked curiously. "Are you going somewhere?"

"I'm just getting ready for dinner," Beverly replied, sounding more snappish than she meant to.

"What're we having tonight?"

"Liver and onions. And stop doing that." Her daughter was rubbing herself meditatively against the doorjamb.

"Ugh." Belinda made a face. "I hate liver. I just hate it."

"It's good for you," Beverly said automatically. She combed her hair, and as she did so, her eye fell on a small white card lying on Bob's chest of drawers. She picked it up. Phillip Barry, it read. Counsellor-at-Law. Just a man's business card. A telephone number was scribbled on it in pencil. Whose number was it? Phillip Barry's, of course. Who else?

"Why are you looking at that card?" Belinda asked.

Beverly put it down. "Belinda, I've told you to stop rubbing yourself against things all the time. You're a little girl, not a cat, and little girls don't do that."

Belinda giggled. "My arm itches."

"No doubt. Look. Go and watch television. Isn't Bugs Bunny on?"

"I guess so." She showed no inclination to move.

"Well, go and watch him. Please. I have things to do in here."

"What things?"

"Never mind. Go and watch Bugs Bunny."

"All right," Belinda sighed. She went lingeringly down the hall.

When she was out of sight, Beverly took a deep, courage-gathering breath. How do you search your husband's belongings for signs of philandering? What do you look for? A stray hair on a coat sleeve? Lipstick stains on a collar? A telephone number on a scrap of paper in an inside pocket? A letter? She had never done it before, and it made her feel sneaky and small. Nevertheless, she slid back the wardrobe door and began. She was still at it when she heard Bob at the front door. With guilty haste, she shut opened drawers and went to meet him. She had found nothing.

"Hi," Bob said, looking surprised at the big hug and kiss she gave him. "What's the idea?"

"Nothing." She laughed, and it came out sounding nervous although she had meant it to be light. "How are you?"

"Beat. What a day."

"Me, too," Beverly said, "I'll go fix us a drink."

She had planned not to bring the subject up until late in the evening after Belinda was in bed, just in case there was anything to it. By the time dinner was over, she had decided not to bring it up at all. Clearly, nothing was on Bob's mind. If anything, he seemed more affable than usual. Leave well enough alone, she told herself firmly. Don't be a fool.

They played gin rummy until bedtime, since she had brought no work home. Bob won, which made her obscurely glad and put him in an even more agreeable mood. They joked a little as they put away the cards and had a bedtime cup of cocoa. Oh, obviously there wasn't a thing wrong. Not a thing in the world.

Bob was sitting on the edge of the bed taking off his shoes when all of a sudden, she said, "The funniest thing happened. Shirley told me this morning that she saw you the other day in a convertible with a woman driving." Actually, she was astonished to hear herself say it.

Bob paused with a shoe in midair. Then he set it carefully on the floor and began taking off the other one. He said nothing. In time, the silence in the room became large and heavy.

"I told her it must have been a client," Beverly said. She was putting her hair in rollers. By shifting her eyes slightly, she could have looked at Bob behind her in the mirror, but she did not dare.

WIVES AND LOVERS

Still he said nothing.

Her fingers began to tremble so that she had difficulty winding the locks of hair. Bob got up from the bed, went to the wardrobe, and took out his terry cloth robe and slippers. After he had undressed and put them on, he came over to his chest of drawers, opened the top one, took out a package of cigarettes, and lit one. Although he was standing beside her now, he still did not meet her eyes.

"Well?" she said at last in desperation.

"Damn!" Bob exhaled violently, sticking his lower lip out so that the smoke blew upward. "A city this size, and you still don't have any privacy."

"Do you need it?" Beverly asked after a short pause.

"Yeah. I need it."

She was, it seemed, a manicurist, a divorcee, who liked to play golf on her day off. They had met two months before on only the second occasion that Bob had played that particular course. She was a good golfer, he had enjoyed playing with her, and eventually one thing had led to another.

"What's her name?" Beverly asked. She felt strangely calm and still.

"I'm not going to tell you," he said defensively. "She's a good person, and I'm not going to have you hunting her up and chewing her out."

"That's very sweet of you. Are you in love with her?"

"Hell, no." He paused. "She likes me quite a lot."

"Are you going to keep on seeing her?"

"Why shouldn't I?" His defiance reminded her, fleetingly, of a small boy brazening out an act of naughtiness. "What the hell is the harm in playing a little golf with somebody?"

"Is that all you're doing with her?"

He was silent, picking meaninglessly at a pulled thread in the sleeve of his robe.

"All right," Beverly said at last. "Would you like to leave now or in the morning? Personally, I vote for now."

His head jerked up. "You want me to leave?" he responded crisply, and his eyes darkened with quick anger.

"I don't want a husband who runs around. I might catch something."

He gave a mirthless sort of laughter. "Is that all that bothers you?"

"No, of course not," she said scathingly. "I've also come to the conclusion that I made a serious mistake when I married you."

He stared at her. "Maybe you did," he said sulkily. He pulled open his top drawer and began pulling underwear and socks out of it and throwing them on the bed.

"You're not a man," Beverly whispered through dry lips. "You never have been. You're just a little boy who wants all the fun and none of the responsibilities of being an adult."

He did not look at her, or answer. He took his clothes out of the wardrobe and began to dress.

"Your mother has a lot to answer for," she went on. She did not seem to be able to stop. "She spoiled you to death. I don't know why I couldn't have seen that from the first."

His mouth tightened ominously and his jaw flexed. When he spoke, it was with a threatening tone of voice that made her feel cold. "Leave my mother out of this. She was smart enough to see I shouldn't marry you! She told me it wouldn't work out."

"Oh, don't be ridiculous! She didn't want it to work out, you mean."

"She wanted me to be happy! That's all she ever said. She wanted me to be happy, and she knew I wouldn't be, married to a computer."

"Is that what she called me?" Beverly asked on a rising note. "A computer?"

"That's what I'm calling you! I know you better

than she does." Suddenly his voice was shaking with rage, and his face was flushed. "So I'm not a man, huh? Well, let me tell you something! You're not a woman! You haven't the faintest idea how to be a woman! You may be a red-hot executive, babycakes, but Betty could give you lessons in a lot of things!"

"Betty?" Beverly said shrilly. "Is that her name?"

"Betty! Betty Hale! On second thought, why don't you look her up sometime? You might learn something!"

"Anything I could learn from a woman like that," Beverly said, pulling the last shreds of her dignity around her, "I wouldn't be interested in."

He was very quick to move to her, jerking her arms down to her sides and shaking her roughly, hard, and she screamed at him furiously, "Get out!"

His hand cracked against her cheek domineeringly. "You bitch!" he said savagely.

Her hand flashed out, as swift as his had been, and smashed across his face with enough force to snap his head back. He stared down at her with eyes that seemed to be leaping right out at her with the force of his rage, his hands back to her shoulders, tightening until she felt sure that she would faint.

"Who," she spat at him, "gives you the right to strike me? Before God, you've gone too far! Now, I said get out, damn you! Get out!"

When he had gone, she sat down weakly on the edge of the bed. She sat there for quite a long time, not moving, not thinking. After a time, she became aware that Belinda was standing in the doorway in her pajamas.

"Mother?" Belinda said quaveringly. "What happened?"

Beverly took a deep breath. "Your father and I had a quarrel. He's—gone away for a while."

"Oh," Belinda said. She looked down attentively at her bare feet. Eventually, she lifted one and rubbed it over the top of the other. "He hasn't worked out very well, has he?"

Shocked, Beverly stared at her. What made the child say at thing like that? This was a crucial moment in her child's life. She must not give way to bitterness. She must not poison Belinda's mind against her father. She must say something cheerful, sensible, just, and reassuring. Something about Bob's being a fine man, but they just couldn't be happy together. Something about it being nobody's fault. She searched for the words, but they eluded her.

"No," she said finally. "He hasn't worked out very well."

Sixteen

"So it's over," Beverly said, "and that's that." Her voice sounded hard and businesslike.

"It's probably for the best," Vivian said carefully.

"Oh, sure. If he's going to start running around behind my back, I certainly don't want him. That's just too much." She mashed her cigarette into the ashtray with an air of finality.

"It would have been so easy to lie and say it was a client," Vivian said. "I wonder why he didn't."

"I thought of that, too, afterward." Beverly was silent for a few seconds, thinking. "It was almost like he was proud to have me know."

They were having lunch in Mayfield's Coffee Room. The decor was predominantly white and blue with a dark blue floor, table and chairs of chrome and light blue plastic. Along one wall ran a white-and-blue mural depicting the history of fashion, and on the opposite side of the big room, windows veiled in pale blue draperies looked out on the brown-hazed downtown skyline.

"How's Belinda taking it?" Vivian asked.

"I'm not sure. She seemed calm at first, but the last couple of days she's been a little strange. She keeps saying she doesn't feel well and doesn't want to go to school, but I don't think anything's really wrong with her. No temperatures, and she's very vague when I try to pin down symptoms."

"Have you heard anything from Bob?"

"No. And I don't want to." Beverly lit another cigarette. "I don't really need him, you know. I can run things by myself. Run them better, actually. Before, I was always depending on him to do things, and then he wouldn't, and it would create problems. Now that I know I have to do everything myself, I just go ahead and do it, and everything runs much more smoothly."

"Women like us shouldn't get married," Vivian drawled, sitting back and leisurely crossing one elegant leg over the other. "We can always take lovers."

"I can't quite imagine myself taking lovers." Beverly said calmly, sipping her coffee.

"If you don't want to, so much the better. That means even less emotional involvement to worry about. And freedom can be very exciting. Most women get married for financial security or they're sick of their boring job. But you like your work, and you can provide your own financial security, so why tie yourself down to a man? You're too intelligent, Beverly."

"I suppose," Beverly said vaguely. "I suppose." She put out her cigarette. "How's Sid these days?"

"Just wonderful. We're going away for the weekend."

"Where to?"

"I'm not sure. Probably Palm Springs. He mentioned Squaw Valley first, but I don't really care much for the mountains."

"Lots of snow right now. I talked to Dana the other day, and she and Don are going skiing this weekend. That is, Don's going to ski, and she's going to watch. She's afraid she might sprain something and lose the wonderful part she's got in this play."

"That's a good marriage," Vivian observed.

"I guess so," Beverly said, "although you never know. Marriages are like icebergs, seven-eighths underwater. It's only the tiniest fraction that outsiders ever see. Our next-door neighbor practically flipped when she heard Bob and I were separated. She thought we were an ideal couple." She laughed shortly.

"I know. I always think people are getting along if they're not actually breaking dishes over each other's heads in my presence."

"Even that doesn't necessarily mean anything," Beverly said soberly. "They could be doing that and still be crazy about each other. Hot anger's not so bad. It shows there's still some warmth left. Cold anger's the danger signal. That icy-polite business of slipping knives into each other over the bridge table or whereever. Or worse still, no communication at all."

The waitress appeared beside the table. "Dessert today?"

"I think I'll have cherry pie," Vivian said. "How about you?"

"I shouldn't," Beverly said doubtfully. "I'm gaining again."

"Oh, come on. Live a little."

"All right." She sighed. "I'll have the chocolate cake with mint ice cream and hot fudge sauce."

"Wow," Vivian said when the waitress had gone. "That's going the full route."

"Well, we all need some pleasures in life," Beverly said defensively. "Eating's mine. Anyway, lately I seem to have this empty feeling all the time."

"That's funny. When I'm unhappy, I practically stop eating altogether."

"I'm not unhappy," Beverly said quickly. "I'm just using up a lot of energy working so hard."

There was a pause in the conversation. Models, tall, sleek, meticulously curried, a class apart from the customers, circulated among the tables looking graceful and impersonal.

"That's not bad," Vivian said, to change the subject. "That black-and-white ensemble. I like that. And I could use something new for the weekend."

"Care to try it on? If you decide you want it," Beverly said automatically, "I can get you ten percent off."

Friday night Vivian and Sid drove down to Palm Springs in Sid's Cadillac. He drove fast and well with no unexpected stops, and Vivian, feeling pampered, relaxed and enjoyed the sensation of being in competent hands. They had the radio on, and she smoked a cigarette and listened to the music, staring out the window at the passing lights.

"You're quiet tonight, baby," Sid said. "You okay?"

"Yes. Happy quiet. Not sad quiet."

"Come here and sit by me." He took his right hand off the steering wheel and held it out to her.

She moved close to him, resting her hand on his thigh with a feeling of possessiveness. They had not been away together before, she reflected. It made her feel closer to him to be going out of the city like this. In town, they were still separate entities, both with their homes, jobs, friends, business associates. Now it was as if they were really alone together for the first time.

"Where are we staying?" she asked.

"A little place called the Beach Inn."

"Have you been there before?"

"No. Somebody at the studio told me about it." He hesitated. "When I used to come down here with Joan and the kids, we always stayed at the Oasis. They like kids there, got a special pool and playground for them, all that stuff. It's a different kind of a place entirely."

"You know, I've never been to Palm Springs before, all the years I've lived in Los Angeles."

"No kidding. You mean I'm the first guy's brought you here?"

She turned quickly and looked at him. "I don't like the way you said that. I could have come with a girlfriend, too."

"Hell, baby, a good-looking woman like you, spending your own money for an out-of-town weekend?"

"I've gone out of town for a weekend lots of times on my own," she said stiffly. "Or with another girl. Dana, for instance. We used to go away together before she got married."

He chuckled. "Okay. Don't get on your high horse. I was only kidding."

She took her hand off his leg and moved away a little. The occasion seemed, suddenly, less agreeable than before. "Sid," she said after a moment, "tell me something."

"What?"

"Do you think I'm a whore?"

"Do I think you're a whore? Christ, Vivian, what kind of a question is that? Of course I don't think you're a whore."

"Oh. But you do think I let men take me away on weekends all the time."

"Why the hell shouldn't you? You're young and single."

She was silent. "You don't think I'm promiscuous, do you?"

"Promiscuous? What the hell is that?"

"You know. Sleeping around. More than one man at a time."

"Hell, baby, why should I think that? I don't think you're two-timing me. What is this all of a sudden, anyway?"

"Nothing. Never mind. Skip it."

The silence between them now was not as comfortable as it had been before. Vivian leaned her head against the back of the seat, feeling inexplicably tired. It was not, as a matter of fact, a unique experience for her to be going away with a man. There had been many weekends since the ones with Joe Bales. Recalling them, she realized that the sensations she was experiencing were familiar. It always seemed exciting and romantic beforehand, a weekend away with one's lover. Then when it was actually happening, there was always a vague sensation of unease, a feeling that what she was doing was slightly sordid. It exasperated her, this feeling, yet she could never quite drive it away. It remained in the back of her consciousness the whole time, blighting the carefree gaiety she had anticipated, casting a shadow over the cocktails and dining and dancing, even over the lovemaking. Especially over the lovemaking.

Sid looked over at her uneasily. "Want to stop for a drink?"

"No, let's just get there."

It was nearly eleven when they arrived. Sid went in and signed the register while Vivian waited in the car. The Beach Inn was U-shaped, low and modern with full-length windows that looked out over the pool area in the center. The pool, lighted a brilliant turquoise, looked uninviting in the cold desert night. Mr. and Mrs. Sid Williamson is what he's signing, Vivian thought. Only I'm not Mrs. Sid Williamson. I wonder if he feels funny about it. I wonder if things like this bother men at all.

The room was cold, but it was not unattractive. The walls were white and happily pictureless, and there was a brown carpet on the floor. Twin beds with brown covers extended at right angles from a large corner table with a lamp.

"Christ," Sid said in exasperation. "I told them a double bed." He started for the door.

"Never mind," Vivian said sharply. "Let's not make a fuss."

"Why the hell not? There are married couples, too, that like to sleep together."

"I know, Sid. I just wish you wouldn't."

He shrugged. "Okay."

They unpacked their bags and hung their clothes in the closet. Sid looked at his watch. "It's only eleven-thirty. Want to go out for a nightcap?"

"That's a good idea."

They got the car out and drove to the main street of town. It was brightly lighted, and there was a lot of traffic, and people were walking up and down looking into the shopwindows.

"In the summer it's a little town. In the winter it's a madhouse."

They went into a bar called the Starbuck and had a brandy, sitting on stools around a grand piano where a young man with a voluptuous mouth was singing Barry Manilow songs. In time, Vivian began to feel better. It was the kind of bar she liked best, warm and cozy with mellow wood paneling and candles on the tables and customers that seemed relaxed and friendly. "I write the songs that make the whole world sing," sang the pianist, flirting with her in a way that made her feel more masculine than feminine. She smiled back at him provocatively, and winked at Sid.

"So," he said. "You don't hate me any more." In the warm, dim light, his eyes were dark and appealing.

"I didn't hate you."

"Yes, you did. You hated me for seducing you and dragging you down here for a little sin. A nice girl like you."

"I did not."

They smiled at each other.

"You want another brandy, or you want to go?" Sid asked.

"I want another brandy, and then I want to go."

They had two more brandies apiece, and then they drove back to the Beach Inn.

"Let's push them together," Vivian said when they were in their room.

"What?"

"The beds. Let's push them together and make one kingsize. It'll be much cozier."

"Yeah. And about the bedding?" Sid said. Nevertheless, he pushed one bed over beside the other and, laughing, they took off the brown slipcovers and arranged the bedding.

"I hope nobody falls down through the crack in the middle. It'd be a helluvan embarrasing way to get a broken back."

When the light was out, she slid quickly across the

crack to his side and hugged him with all her strength.

"Jesus, what was that for?" he asked in the growly way he had when he was pleased.

"I don't know," Vivian said, smiling in the dark. "I guess I just like you."

The next day was warm and sunny. They had a big, late breakfast, and then they sat beside the pool and soaked up sunshine. The air was clear and fresh, and beyond the immediate noises of the swimmers and poolside loungers, Vivian was aware of the immense, serene silence of the desert. After awhile, they got up and walked down to the end of the road where it began, half a block or so beyond the motel. The colors were delicate, as though they had been faded by the constant sun. Pale beige sand, pale blue sky. At the edge of the desert was a pasture tinged with the faint green of spring, and in it a couple of horses stood lazily flicking their tails.

"Here boy," Vivian called, and one of the horses ambled over and nuzzled her outstretched hand. Finding nothing to eat in it, he nevertheless allowed her to stroke his velvety nose and the sleek hair of his long cheeks. "I miss animals, living in the city," she said.

"Hell, baby, I'll buy you a kitten."

"No. They don't allow pets where I live or I'd have one now."

"Listen, baby. When we drove down here last night, I didn't like the way the engine sounded. I'm gonna take the car over to the garage. You want to come?"

"I guess not. I think I'll have a swim, and then get dressed for lunch. Are you taking me someplace wonderful for lunch?"

"You know it. When you've got a good-looking woman, you want to show her off."

When they got back to the Beach Inn, Vivian put on her cap and dived into the pool. It felt cold for only a minute or two, then it seemed as warm as bath water. She swam lazily for quite a long time, turning over occasionally to float on her back and look up at the sky. Her body, free of weight and tension, seemed hardly to exist at all. When she got out and began to dry herself, she was pleasantly aware that several of the male guests were eyeing her admiringly.

"Mrs. Williamson. Mrs. Williamson."

It was not until a hand touched her arm that she realized someone was addressing her. The woman was short and middle-aged with dyed red hair. "Didn't you hear me calling you?"

"No, I—I didn't," Vivian said. To her annoyance, she felt herself blushing.

The woman looked at her penetratingly, but her face remained blank. "There's a telephone call for your husband. Mr. Williamson, that is. From Los Angeles."

"He isn't here," Vivian said. "He went to have something done to the car. Tell them to call back in an hour."

"Don't you want to talk to them?"

"No."

The woman shrugged and went back to the office.

Without looking around, Vivian picked up her towel and walked swiftly to their room. She was sure everyone was watching her and laughing, having guessed the meaning of the incident. Inside, she locked the door and leaned against it, putting her hands, still cool and damp from the pool, against her burning cheeks.

Mrs. Williamson? No, I'm not Mrs. Williamson. I'm Vivian Hunt, and I'm just having an illicit weekend with Mr. Williamson. What would the woman have done if she had said that? All the unpleasantness she had felt the night before on the drive down came flooding back.

"What's with you?" Sid asked when he came back.

She smiled faintly. "How can you tell so fast that something's wrong?"

"I ought to know you pretty well by this time, shouldn't I? What's up?"

"Oh, nothing. The clerk just called me Mrs. Williamson, and it threw me, that's all. It was quite some time before it dawned on me I was the one she was talking to. Now I'm sure she thinks things. Not that they're not true." Vivian felt suddenly as if she was suffocating and she flushed brightly.

"Oh, hell, baby, don't worry about that."

"I can't help it. It's embarrassing."

"Well, you don't have to worry in this place."

"What do you mean?"

"It's their specialty."

Vivian licked her lips and stared at him. "You mean they cater to unmarried couples?"

"Sure. You've got nothing to worry about. She wasn't shocked, believe me."

"I see," she said slowly.

There was a long silence.

"Vivian, what the hell is wrong with you?" Sid said at last. "You're thirty years old, and you're acting like a kid that's never been around."

"I know. I'm annoyed with myself. I don't know what's wrong with me. I don't know why I can't throw off the stupid, tiresome, middle-class, midwestern morals I was brought up with. God knows I've been trying to long enough."

"Still a nice girl at heart, huh? You think nice girls don't do this? This is the 1980s, baby."

"Where I come from, they don't," Vivian said bitterly. "Nice girls get married and lead respectable lives."

"Well, for Christ's sake, if you didn't want to come, why didn't you say so?" He ran a hand over his hair in exasperation.

"I did want to come." Suddenly she was contrite. "I'm sorry, darling. It's ridiculous for me to behave like this. I know it is."

"Well, you're making me feel like a bum," he said shortly.

She looked up at him, her eyes clearly expressing some of the turmoil she felt. "I said I was sorry." She kissed him. "Listen. Somebody called you from L.A. They should be calling back about now. Then let's have lunch."

They each had two gin-and-tonics before lunch, and a bottle of wine with it. Afterward, they spent the rest of the afternoon wandering up and down looking in the shopwindows in a euphoric haze of sunshine and alcohol.

By the time they got back to the Beach Inn, a cool breeze had sprung up, and most of the sunbathers had gone inside. Only a middle-aged man with a well-tanned paunch and a young redhead still sat in the deck chairs.

"They're not married," Vivian said clearly.

"Sssssh," Sid murmured. "For Christ's sake." The couple had turned and were looking at them.

Vivian giggled. "It's all right. We're all in the same boat," she said in a lower tone. "Aren't we?"

When they were in the room, she took her clothes off deliberately and stood before him naked. "Make love to me, Sid." It was whispered, but it was a command. She was feeling the way she liked to feel, regal, authoritative, wielding the controls. He stared at her, and she could not tell what he was thinking.

"Sid," she said again, insistently. "I want you now." She put her arms around his neck lightly to pull him to the couch.

Resisting, he ran his hands down her sides from the armpits to the hips, touching her in the sensuous way he had, so that she knew his fingertips were aware of every aspect of her flesh. She took a tortured breath and could not stop herself from looking down. And it seemed as if her passion was doubled, to see and to feel his lean, strong fingers touching her nipples delicately, then moving away to cup each breast with a caressing gentleness, and to see each rosy bud harden in a response that she felt with a trembling down the whole length of her body. He touched her the way a miser touches money, the way an art collector touches a fragile, priceless bit of sculpture. She shivered under his touch, and her belly muscles convulsed in a delicious spasm of hot desire.

"Sid," she murmured, touching his ear with her tongue. "Come on."

He did not move. Standing there, he continued to caress her until, nearly fainting with pleasure, she had to be half led, half carried to the bed. His weight on top of her was so delicious and erotic, and her need so intense, that there was no time for gentleness or the luxury of leisurely lovemaking.

After they had made love, and slept, and made love again, it was time for dinner.

"God! I'm sober," Vivian said gaily. "Didn't we bring anything to drink?"

"There's a flask in my suitcase," Sid called from the bathroom.

The drink warmed her and numbed the slight headache she had felt on awakening. She took a couple of aspirin with it just to make sure.

They went to one of the posh places for dinner.

"Mr. Williamson. Haven't seen you in a long time," the maitre d' said, taking down the velvet rope. He gave Vivian the briefest, most discreet glance, which she saw but ignored, staring haughtily over his head.

"What do you want to drink?" Sid asked when they were seated at a table.

"A Black Russian. No, wait. That was bourbon in your flask. I'd better have a Manhattan."

"It doesn't make any difference, baby," Sid said. "It's all booze."

"You should never mix your drinks," Vivian said. "That's an old wives' tale, and I have the greatest respect for old wives."

"Okay. A Manhattan. With two cherries," he told the waiter.

"Well, lover boy," she said, smiling at him. "You know the way to a girl's heart, don't you?"

The salad was crisp, the lobster beautifully delicious. For dessert, they had cherries jubilee prepared in a chafing dish at the table.

"I adore having my food fixed right before my eyes," Vivian murmured, watching the blue flames. "It makes me feel like royalty. You know. If you're watching, they can't slip any poison in."

"Don't kid yourself," Sid said. "Doesn't prove a thing. Maybe they slipped it in the brandy beforehand, who knows?"

There was a good band, and they danced while the fringe on Vivian's black dress swayed and shook. Sid was a good dancer, and several couples stopped to watch them. When they finished, there was a splattering of applause.

Laughing, they were making their way back to the table when an improbably tall, broad-shouldered, lean-jawed young man barred their way.

"Sid," he said. A little unsteadily, he clapped Sid on the back, holding a drink in his other hand.

"Tom, boy, how are you?" Sid said. "Nice to see you." He tried to pass.

"What're you doing down here? Business or pleasure? Pleasure, I guess," he said, looking at Vivian. "Who's this?"

"Vivian, this is Tom Gardner, our new 'Private Detective' series star. Vivian Hunt."

"How do you do?" Vivian said.

Tom Gardner stared down at her, trying to focus. "Mighty nice," he said, drawling. "Where you from, honey?"

"Nebraska," Vivian said.

"I'd like to lay you," he said without further ado and with a wicked glint in his green-flecked eyes.

"All right, Tom, forget it," Sid said.

"I'd like to lay you," he repeated loudly, holding his long arms out so they could not pass. "Why are you running around with this middle-aged creep? You can do better than that, sweetheart."

"I'm not interested," Vivian snapped furiously. The people at nearby tables, she was aware, were beginning to listen.

"Not interested?" he queried derisively. "What do you mean, you're not interested?"

"Just what she said, boy, now forget it," Sid said.

"Crap," Tom said. "You can be bought, can't you, honey? Isn't that how he got you? Well, I'm making more money than he is any day of the week."

The band had finished, and half the room heard. Abruptly, Vivian turned and fled, pushing blindly among the tables to the front door.

"Now what's wrong with her?" she could hear Tom saying in loud, plaintive tones. "I finally meet a girl who comes up past my navel, and then she doesn't like me." There was a general ripple of laughter.

When she had burst through the front door onto the sidewalk, she stopped short. Heart thumping irregularly, she realized for the first time that she was crying and brushed the tears away impatiently. How long would it take Sid to pay the check?

In a few minutes, he joined her, looking angry and concerned and generally upset. "That lousy bastard. His series is shooting near here, and I heard at the studio he was boozing it up and chasing broads till they can hardly get him sobered up when it's time to work. You all right?"

"I'm fine. Could we go?"

When they got back to the Beach Inn, she went to the closet and began taking out her clothes. "I want to go home, Sid," she said without looking at him. "I want to go back right now."

"Okay." He sounded neither surprised nor angry.

Neither of them talked much on the long drive home. What's going to happen to me? Vivian thought. Am I going to go on living like this all my life? I never meant to wind up being insulted in public by men who think I'm a whore. The whole thing was extraordinary, and sad. She remembered the child she had been in Nebraska, cuddling a baby chick, the girl she had been at college, shy, idealistic, fiercely innocent. Could this Vivian be the same person? Yes, that was the trouble, she saw with a sudden flash of comprehension. They were all the same person. People were like trees, they grew new outer layers every year, but nearer the core, buried and hidden, were all the other selves they had been when they were younger. That was why, she realized, remembering her complaint to Sid about her middle-class, Midwestern morals, it was impossible to escape your past. You were always carrying it around in the deepest part of you.

The car stopped in front of her apartment. She turned and looked at Sid. "Thank you. I'm sorry about everything."

There was a pause. "Do you want to get married?" Sid said slowly.

"Are you asking me to?"

"I'm asking you to."

"But what about Jo—what about your wife?"

"I'll write and tell her to get on with the divorce."

"Oh, Sid," she whispered. "Do you want to?"

He nodded. "This is a lousy situation for somebody like you. I'm finally getting that through my thick head."

The idea took getting used to. Proposals were new to her. "Maybe we could be happy," she said slowly. "All right. Do it."

The kiss they exchanged was curiously gentle.

"You're something very special," he murmured. The street lamp shone on his hands holding the steering wheel, but she could not see his face.

They got out of the car, and he carried her suitcase up to her apartment. It was nearly four.

"Come in?" Vivian asked. The early morning stillness made her feel a little lonely.

He hesitated. "No. Sleep alone tonight, baby. It will do you good."

Seventeen

The weeks that *The Sisters* was in rehearsal were the happiest Dana could remember. With deep excitement, she felt the role of Sister Martinette becoming more and more hers. What in the beginning had been only words printed in a script became in time a living person, and that person an extension of herself. She felt an explicable sympathy for this nun whose nature battled an authoritarian environment to find expression. As she worked and studied, she felt an increasing admiration for Dan Morgan, and gratitude toward him as well. He had given her a lot to work with. For him as well as for herself, she devoted all the intensity of her growing ambition toward bringing Sister Martinette to life.

At last the night of the premiere arrived. She had slept until one that day after a late dress rehearsal the night before. The rest of the afternoon, to keep herself calm, she had worked at minor tasks around the house, dusting books, rearranging drawers, vacuuming, making a tuna casserole. When Don got home at five-thirty, she had dinner ready for the table.

"What's this?" he said, raising his eyebrows at the sight of food. "No time for a drink?"

"Mama's gonna act," Jeremy said importantly, clutching his father's trousered leg at knee level.

"I want to be at the theater by six-thirty," Dana said apologetically.

Don ruffled his son's hair absently and gave her a

sharp look. "Don't tell me it takes you two hours to put on your makeup."

"No. I just want some time to compose myself before I go on." She started for the kitchen.

"Look, Dana." His tone indicated he was about to bring up something he had thought about for a long time. "Aren't you taking yourself a little seriously?"

She turned quickly. "Don't you take your work seriously?"

"Naturally. But that's different."

"No, it isn't. Acting is just as important to me as space shuttles are to you."

"Maybe so. But how important is acting compared to what I'm doing? Keep your perspective."

Dana gave him a long look. "Don't be patronizing, darling," she said slowly. "Molding people's minds, arousing their emotions, giving them new ideas, helping them to understand each other better—what makes you think that's less significant than a space program? And those are the things a great play does."

"And this is a great play you're in?"

"It could be. I think it is. And I want to do it justice."

"All right, touché." He started back toward the bedroom. "What time am I supposed to show up? Eight-thirty?"

She was still a little disturbed when she arrived at the theater. Don's condescension was irritating, but the feelings it aroused in her went deeper than that. If he loved her, how could he shrug off something that was obviously so important to her? Then the thought occurred, He hasn't seen me act. When he does, if I'm good, he will underststand.

Neither of the two girls with whom she shared a dressing room had arrived. Slowly and in the quiet, she pinned her hair back and put on her makeup. The concentration this required helped to still her troubled mind. Then her nun's habit. The heavy folds of fabric felt unfamiliar and strange; she had only worn the costume once, at the dress rehearsal the night before. She walked back and forth across the dressing room to accustom herself to moving in it. Then she opened the door and listened. It was still so early that there was no sound of activity. She walked slowly down the hall to the wings.

The curtain was open, the work light burning above the stage. It all looked much as it had the night before when they had finished. Four o'clock this morning, Dana thought. It seemed years ago. Calculating how little sleep she had managed to get the past few nights, she realized that by rights she should be worn out. Excitement, however, made her feverishly wide-awake, and she suddenly remembered from her earlier acting days that the exhaustion underneath had its usefulness. It seemed to break down the barriers between the conscious and unconscious, so that the acting flowed more easily. You become less inhibited the more tired you were, at least up to a point.

Silently she stood stage center and drew herself inward into a compact entity, focused, energized, concentrated. Sister Martinette, come. You must be me, and I you. It was like bringing two nearly identical images into focus as one, which would have more depth and dimension than either had alone. That image, larger than life, was a mysterious creation which possessed the power to move the mind and emotions of a roomful of strangers for a brief hour or two. When she had completed this process, which was like self-hypnosis, she went back to her dressing room.

Soon the rest of the cast began to arrive. Almost like a visitor from another world, she watched the other girls dress, heard the bustling confusion in the hall outside, smelled makeup and freshly ironed linen and human perspiration and electric bulbs burning. As she had brought Sister Martinette's world to a high pitch of reality, the actual world had correspondingly faded to mere illusion.

"Wake up, honey." One of the girls was talking to

her, standing, incongruously, in panties and bra and a nun's white coif. "If you don't snap out of it, you'll miss your cue."

"I'm all right," Dana said. When she spoke, the two images separated slightly, but even so, Sister Martinette remained as real and alive as she herself was.

"Curtain!"

She heard the call from a great distance. In fifteen minutes, she would be on. She waited, noting impersonally that her hands were trembling and she felt cold all over. Stage fright. That was to be expected. It was nothing to be alarmed about if you did not let it get out of control. Like exhaustion, it could be an ally.

"Mrs. Hurst. Five minutes."

Will I be good? I must not think about that. I must not try too hard, or I'll spoil it. I must relax just a little, or it will not happen. But I must be good because this is my chance. Nonsense, there will be other chances. No, there is just this one. Just tonight. Tonight.

"You're on, Mrs. Hurst."

Abruptly, she turned the interior dialogue off. Smoothing the perspiration from her palms against the rough folds of her skirt, she walked swiftly onstage.

It was odd how quickly the first act passed, a timeless blur during which she was aware of dazzling lights, of the murmurous, unseen crowd in the black auditorium, of her own voice sounding strangely unfamiliar. Then the curtains were closing, and she was back in the feverish, babbling excitement of backstage, so different from the measured calm of the performance. Have I done it? she wondered confusedly. Had it gone well? All she knew for sure was that she had not forgotten her lines or missed any cues.

The second act began almost before she had time to think. This time when she went on, it was easier to keep her mind on what was happening on the stage and forget the black void out front. This time, so deeply was she absorbed that the applause at the end startled her. As she hurried back to her dressing room, a hand on her arm stopped her. "Good, dear. Very good." The soft voice, barely audible in the confusion, belonged to Roger Deal. He gave her a vague smile and moved on quickly, preoccupied.

It was in the third act that the miracle happened. She had a scene, a long one, her best in the play. She had barely begun it when she realized that the subtle communication which had been achieved between her and the other students on good nights in Ryan Parker's drawing room had somehow been established between herself, her fellow players, and this crowd of paying strangers. It was almost as if the audience were part of the play itself. She felt their interest, their absorption, intensify her own experience of what she was doing. She spoke with more authority, more conviction. Again they responded. Yes, yes, they were really on the same wavelength.

An overwhelming sense of power sprang into being within her, of power over herself, power over others. It was tremendous. She felt like a hurricane, calm at the center, radiating force and energy to a distant, dazzling place. Sister Martinette was like that, too, the way she herself felt now, vibrant with life, bursting with power, longing to assert her individual being with all the strength within her.

When she exited, there was a burst of applause. The sound of it followed her all the way to her dressing room.

"Dana. You were great." One of the girls had followed her from the wings, and Dana saw awe and respect in her face.

"Yes. I mean, thank you." She bit her lip. She knew beyond any doubt that she had been good, so that the compliment, in a sense, seemed superfluous.

"I didn't know you had it in you."

Dana smiled and did not answer. I did, she thought.

Oh, I knew. I just wasn't sure I could command it. She sat down at her dressing table and looked in the mirror. For a moment, she hardly recognized herself. Her face was incredibly beautiful, as though the energy burning within her had illuminated it. She had never seen herself look that way before, not even on her wedding day. But of course, she thought, with a little chill of recognition, I am not looking just at myself. I am looking at Sister Martinette.

The noise outside intensified. The play was over. Quickly she went back down the hall to the stage for the curtain calls. The applause rose and fell and rose again. Above the thunder of clapping hands, there were even a few bravos.

When she got back to her dressing room, the deluge began.

Her mother in mink, pearls, and pale gray brocade, opulent as a duchess and just as condescending. "You were very nice, dear." Then looking around, "Is this where you have to dress? Heavens, how messy! Couldn't they arrange something a little nicer? After all, you do have rather a large part."

Ryan Parker, elegant, tall, aware of being recognized. "You had them there in the third act." A measured nod. She could tell he was proud of her. "My dear, you really had them."

Then Don, looking formal and subdued, even more stolid than usual. "You did very well." He sounded as though he were addressing an utter stranger.

"Thank you." Without meaning to, she sounded equally impersonal.

"Will you be ready to go soon? I have a big day tomorrow. I want to get to bed."

"But there's a party!" she exclaimed. "Mr. Boyd, the producer, is giving a party for the cast at his house."

"Dana, Dana, what can I say?" Dan Morgan, lobster-colored, perspiring, took her hands, and for a second, they smiled at each other like conspirators.

"You haven't met my husband, Don," Dana said. "Don, this is Dan Morgan, the man who wrote the play."

"You must be very proud of your wife," Dan said before Don had a chance to speak. "She's a fine actress with a wonderful future ahead of her. She proved that tonight."

"Yes," Don said stiffly. "Of course, acting is only a hobby with her." He adjusted the knot of his tie, and his face, as he looked at Dan, was absolutely expressionless.

"Oh?" Dan glanced at Dana. "Well, it should be more than that. She has genuine talent."

"Dana, how long will it take you to get dressed?" Don said with a sudden, daggerlike glance at her.

She changed quickly without stopping to remove her stage makeup. Strange how quickly the evening's luster had dimmed. She felt really exhausted now, at last, and more disappointed than she could have put into words.

"All right. I'm ready," she said with an effort.

Don cleared his throat. "You can go to the party by yourself, I suppose, if you want to. You have your car."

"No," she said briefly. "I don't want to go alone."

"All right. Where are you parked? I'll walk you there."

They went out the stage door and up the dark side street beside the theater without speaking. The night was cold and damp, and moisture glistened on the hoods and tops and windshields of the parked cars. When they reached Dana's car, they stopped and looked at each other.

"Look," Don muttered. "If it's going to break your heart not to, I wish you would go to the party."

"Oh, the party's not a vital issue," she forced herself to say unemotionally.

"You're acting as though it is."

"No. I'm just wondering what's wrong with you."

"Nothing's wrong. I told you. I have an important meeting tomorrow at nine, and I don't want to go to it half asleep. You can understand that, can't you?"

"Of course. That isn't what I meant. Only you seem —you are glad I did well, aren't you?"

"Naturally. Just so long as it doesn't give you any crazy ideas about having a career."

She was startled. "But you said if I proved my ability within a year, I could go on acting! And I think now maybe I'm going to be able to do that."

"I said you could go on playing around with it if you wanted to. That's all. I expect a woman who is married to me to concentrate—"

"What do you mean, 'a woman'?" she interrupted angrily, unable to keep the annoyance out of her voice. "We're talking about me."

"All right. We're talking about you." His voice was curt. "I expect you to put me and my son first in your life at all times."

"Haven't I always? Have I ever neglected my home?"

"I'm not saying it's happened," Don surveyed her unsmilingly. "I'm just saying it's not going to happen."

She stared at him as he studied her sardonically, but she did not answer. The flat, peremptory way he spoke reminded her unpleasantly of the way her mother addressed her, commanding, imperious, as though she were not an individual with rights of her own to be considered. Whether he was right or wrong, he didn't have to put it the way he did. "I'll see you at home," she said shortly, and bent over to unlock the car.

By the time he returned from taking the baby-sitter home, she was wiping the last of the stage makeup from her face. Brown stains on a heap of cleansing tissues were all that remained, at the moment, of Sister Martinette. Her long, blond hair was brushed neatly back and held with a ribbon. It hung straight down her back like a child's hair, lower than the back of her pale blue nightgown. She looked up, aware Don was watching her.

"That's more like it," he said. "Now you look like my wife again."

She put down the tissue. "Don, I'm your wife all the time. The acting has nothing to do with—"

His eyebrows had shot up at her words, and he interrupted gently, "Doesn't it? Tonight when I was watching you up there, I got the feeling you were somebody else entirely. Somebody I didn't even know. It scared me."

Hearing the anxiety in his voice, she frowned a little. "I suppose that's true, in a way. That's a side of me you don't know very well. But I want you to. I want you to know all of me."

"One side is enough. I know the side I want to know." He kissed her and began to undress, as though the subject was closed.

"Don," she said helplessly, and then stopped. She wanted to warn him that what he had just said was a dangerous thing, that if he refused to know her as a whole person their happiness was threatened.

"What?"

She hesitated. "Nothing." Perhaps tonight was not the time to discuss it. Later, when he got used to the idea of her performing regularly, when he saw how happy it made her, it would be easier to make him understand.

As she got into bed, a gratifying thought occurred. He is possessive because he loves me, and he is jealous of my work because he's afraid it might take me away from him. The idea softened the anger she had felt toward him. After all, if he loved her, in time everything would work itself out. A marriage had to be flexible. Little by little she would help him to change, to adapt himself to this new situation in their lives. Down the hall in the bathroom, he was brushing his teeth.

Inexplicably, the homely, familiar sound pleased and comforted her. She was smiling to herself when he came back into the room naked and turned off the light.

But as the weeks passed and the play continued to run, it was she, not Don, who began to change, imperceptibly at first, then with a metamorphosis as emphatic as the blossoming of a bare tree. Her notices had been good. She had an agent now, and she had done two more television shows. Her self-confidence was growing, and she no longer felt weak with fright when she walked into a producer's office to ask for a job. Don, on the other hand, showed no signs of increasing tolerance toward her professional aspirations. Seeing her happy seemed to anger rather than soften him, and he was often cold and abrupt with her for no apparent reason. Puzzled and hurt, she worked harder than ever, and because she could not discuss her ambitions with Don, she discussed them with Dan Morgan.

"I'm beginning to have mixed feelings about our long run," she told him one night. They were sitting in a small bar across from the theater after the evening performance. Dan had come in to see how the show was going, as he liked to do occasionally, and he had asked her to join him for a drink. It was a Tuesday night, and the place was nearly deserted. They sat at the bar alone, glancing from time to time at the TV screen above their heads where anonymous people sang and danced and grimaced in silence. At their request, the bartender had turned the sound down until it was inaudible.

"How do you mean?" Dan asked.

"It's wonderful to be working regularly after being idle and frustrated all that time, but—don't strike me, Dan—I'm getting impatient to go on to something else." She shrugged and laughed. "I suppose it's like playing the violin. As you improve, you want to learn new numbers, not just play the same old one over and over."

He smiled. "You don't shock me. You're an ambitious woman, all the more so because your desires along those lines are slightly belated. Ambition's like certain diseases, you know. More virulent if you contract it as an adult than when it strikes early."

That made her serious. "It is a disease. A fever, really. There's nothing you can do about it, even if you wanted to. Once I'd discovered acting, I don't know how I ever left it for those five years. It's inconceivable to me now that I could have."

"You have a real sense of vocation in the theater. I've known that ever since opening night when you came early and stood by yourself on the stage."

She was surprised. "Were you there? Where?"

"Sitting out in the house in the dark."

"Why didn't you say something?"

"I didn't want to disturb you. You were hypnotizing yourself, weren't you?"

"Yes. I was putting myself in character."

"I thought so. I do the same thing before I begin writing."

"Really?"

"Of course. Acting and writing are very much alike, you know. It's the same business of transporting oneself into an imaginary world, inhabiting the minds and bodies of other persons, so you can think and feel as they do and bring them to life."

"I see. Yes, of course. I never thought of that before." She smiled at him. "It's hard, isn't it?"

"Yes. Very hard." Dan revolved his glass of ginger ale slowly between his palms. "How does your husband feel by now about your career?" he asked unexpectedly. He had not mentioned Don since meeting him backstage on opening night.

"I don't really know," Dana said cautiously. "He hasn't said much about it lately."

"What would he think of your going to New York with the show?"

"What?"

"I have a producer who is very interested. He saw the show Saturday night and liked it. Naturally, he wants to recast the leads with bigger names, but he's thinking of taking two of the local cast along. You and Jackie Wyatt."

"Oh, my." Here it was, at last.

"It would be an excellent chance for you. Unless you would be content to stay here indefinitely doing an occasional TV show and hoping for a chance at the movies."

"I don't know what to say," Dana murmured. "I'm quite sure Don wouldn't like it at all."

"That was my feeling, meeting him the night of our premiere," Dan said wryly. "Probably he wants to keep you all to himself, and I don't blame him. But how do you feel about it?"

"I'd love it. Oh, you know I'd love it. I can't tell you what being in the play has meant to me."

"I have an idea, watching you change these past few weeks."

She looked at him, startled. "Have I changed?"

"Rather radically, I'd say. It's as though you're coming into focus as an individual."

"It's interesting that you should say that. I know I feel much surer of myself than I ever have. Much more content within myself."

"Success can do that. If it's the right kind of success."

"It's wonderful for you, having the play produced in New York, isn't it?"

"Yes. If it's successful there, it will mean a lot to me."

"Don't you have children in school in the East?" Dana asked hesitantly. He had never mentioned his family to her.

He nodded. "A son in Harvard, a daughter in Vassar."

"Do you see them often?"

"I haven't seen them in years. Their mother felt it was better that way. Quite some time ago she managed to have the court revoke any visiting privileges for me."

"How dreadful. You must miss them a great deal."

"I do. However, I bear her no ill will. She was quite justified in feeling I was an unfit parent at the time." He paused. "I was an alcoholic."

"It must have been a horrible thing to go through."

"A nightmare. But I'm making no excuses for myself. As a matter of fact, when I stopped making excuses, I stopped drinking. The nuns taught me that."

"I've always wanted to ask you. Are you a Catholic?"

"No. Actually, I'm nothing. When I finally realized I had a problem, I started seeing a psychiatrist five times a week. He helped, but not enough. In the end it was the nuns that pulled me through."

"Yes," said Dana. "As the play says."

"As the play says." He emptied his glass and set it down thoughtfully. "Do you love your husband?" he asked after a moment.

"Very much."

"I thought so. And if it came to a choice, you would sacrifice your career for your marriage?"

She stirred uneasily on the stool. "I hope I never have to make that decision. It's impossible to contemplate. Besides, I hate wasting my energies on hypothetical questions."

"It may not be hypothetical much longer."

"I guess not." She frowned a little, twisting the tiny glass in her fingers so that the heavy liqueur hung like a transparent curtain against the sides.

"I suppose," Dan said, "that with a woman, a

perfect marriage would always take precedence over a career."

"Yes," Dana said slowly. "I suppose a perfect marriage would."

Eighteen

It was March, it was Sunday, and it was raining. Breakfast was over, and Beverly was doing the dishes while Belinda read the funny papers on the living room floor. A long, purplish scar, freshly unscabbed, ran along the inside of her left arm from the wrist halfway to the elbow. Two weeks ago she had fallen in the playground at school and cut herself on a piece of broken glass. They had called Beverly at work, and she had rushed over to find Belinda sitting, pale but self-possessed with blood all over her skirt, in the nurse's office. The injury, the doctor declared, was not serious, although it had required eight stitches.

"Thank goodness," Beverly said, shaking with relief. "I've been afraid for years she might really hurt herself someday. She's always been such a tomboy."

"It could have happened to anybody," the doctor said reassuringly. He patted Belinda on the shoulder. "Well, young lady. Now you can play hooky the rest of the day."

Belinda looked at him with unsmiling eyes and said nothing.

"Does it hurt much?" Beverly asked anxiously when they were in the car going home.

"No. They gave me a pill."

"Would—would you like to stop for a sundae before we go home?" She felt, irrationally, that Belinda had suffered an injustice which should be made up to her somehow.

"Yes," Belinda said after a moment's consideration. "That would be nice."

The counterman constructed a special confection in honor of Belinda's misfortune. Architecturally impressive, it consisted of three kinds of ice cream, a banana, chocolate sauce, and chopped nuts, surmounted by a dome of whipped cream with a cupola of maraschino cherries.

"Wow!" Beverly said brightly. "Doesn't that look good!"

Belinda regarded it soberly. "I didn't cry," she said.

"I know. They told me. That was very brave of you."

"It bled a lot, too." She peered down into her lap. "Look at my skirt."

"Eat your ice cream, dear," Beverly said hastily. "Before it melts." Belinda's solemn face made her feel like crying herself.

She had tried to call Bob immediately when they got home. The office said he was out of town attending a convention. She decided not to mention him at all, but later that night Belinda said unexpectedly, "Isn't Daddy coming to see my arm?"

"He can't dear," Beverly told her. "I called him this afternoon when we got home, but he's out of town."

"Oh." Belinda's eyes got very shiny.

"Now, honey. He'd come if he knew. He'll be back Saturday, and I'll call him to come right over then."

"I want him now," Belinda said, starting to cry. "I want him now!"

"Goodness, what's happened to my brave girl?" Beverly said, chiding gently. "Come on, now. You're not dying or anything. He'll come and see you just as soon as he can."

Bob had not entered the house since the night he had packed and departed a month before. They had decided, by phone, that a clean break would be better all around, at least until the divorce suit was filed. When he arrived, Beverly was as nervous as though she were going on her first date with a strange man. They inquired stiffly after each other's health and careers in Belinda's presence, which precluded any overt unpleasantness. After these amenities had been taken care of, Bob played cards with Belinda and read to her most of the afternoon. Busying herself about the house in order to leave them alone, Beverly debated whether she would ask him to stay for dinner. In the end, she had decided against it. Having him around made her too uncomfortable.

After he had gone, Belinda said in a small voice, "He didn't stay very long, did he?"

"Oh, quite awhile," Beverly said. "Over two hours."

Belinda fingered her bandage. "I thought—I thought he might spend the night."

"Oh, he couldn't do that," Beverly exclaimed, sounding more emphatic than she meant to. "He doesn't live here any more."

"I know," Belinda said.

They had an early dinner and watched television. Then as Beverly was helping her get ready for bed, Belinda turned suddenly. "I—sort of miss him." It was the first time she had acknowledged it. She looked at Beverly curiously. "Don't you?"

Seeing Bob that afternoon had weakened Beverly's defenses. Now the question caught her completely off guard. "Yes," she said, and to her horror, her voice broke.

"Then couldn't we invite him back?" Belinda asked eagerly. "I mean if we both miss him?"

"Belinda, I've told you it didn't work out," Beverly said, fighting for control. "Your father and I simply can't live together any more."

"But—"

"Belinda! I don't want to discuss it!"

Since that night two weeks ago, the initial bravado with which she had faced Bob's departure had never returned. Although she catalogued his faults in her mind as regularly and meticulously as ever, the list seemed to have less meaning every day. Furthermore, although she retained the conviction that she was not exaggerating his shortcomings, she could not escape the suspicion that there had been some failure on her own part, too. She found this failure harder to pin down than Bob's. She had done her duty as a wife and mother. She had worked hard. In the beginning, she had loved Bob very much, and if she had stopped, it was his fault, not hers.

Along with the vague sense of failure, there was a peculiar emptiness and flatness about her life. It was not that she had too little to do. She was as busy as ever at work and at home. But this morning, for instance, as she washed the Sunday breakfast dishes, how long and gray the day stretched ahead of her. She felt tired just thinking about it, although she had gone to bed early the night before. Life seemed somehow to have lost its point.

As usual, she caught herself thinking in this fashion before it had gone on too long, and firmly switched channels. At least it was restful not to have the customary Sunday quarrel going on. She and Belinda always got along well together. Fleetingly, it occurred to her that perhaps it was the absence of that tension which had existed so long between her and Bob that made life seem so slack, so lacking in vibrancy. Their quarreling had become so much a habit that she might well miss it, disagreeable though it was. However, if that were the case, she told herself firmly, it was extremely unhealthy. She would have to learn to appreciate peace and quiet again.

"Mother." Belinda was standing in the doorway to the kitchen. "What are we going to do today?"

"I don't know," Beverly said. "What would you like to do?"

Belinda considered. "Go to the zoo?"

"Not in the rain."

"Why?"

"It wouldn't be very pleasant. It would be wet, and anyway, you couldn't see the animals. They'd all be back in their caves keeping dry."

"Well, let's go to a movie, then."

Beverly sighed. "It's so far, honey. I don't feel like driving all that way in the rain. Tell you what. Think of something we can do right here. There aren't many days we can stay home together."

"I don't want to stay home." Lately Belinda had taken to whining when she didn't get her way. She did it deliberately, affectedly, putting pathos into her voice like some child actress.

"Stop that," Beverly said sharply.

Belinda looked at her with an unfathomable expression. Then she began rubbing herself against the door like a cat.

"And stop that, too," Beverly said in exasperation. "Look. Here's what we'll do. We'll build a fire in the fireplace, and we'll play some gin rummy, and then we'll have cocoa later on."

The fire, when she had it going, made the room seem cozier, and Beverly thought, It's not going to be such a bad day, after all. They sat crosslegged on the hearthrug with the footstool between them for a card table. Belinda won quite regularly, which made her a little less solemn than usual. Letting her do it, Beverly thought uneasily, I'm violating a principle, but after all . . . She did not finish the thought, but once again she had the feeling that Belinda had suffered an injustice which should somehow be made up to her.

"A six, Mother?" Belinda exclaimed, pouncing triumphantly on her last discard. "Goodness, didn't you know I was saving sixes?"

"No," Beverly said. For once it was the truth. "I guess I haven't been paying attention."

"Well, do," Belinda said severely. "It's no fun

beating you if you're not trying."

I wonder if I didn't try with Bob, Beverly thought. The most innocent remark sent her mind back to the painful topic of her broken marriage, the way one's tongue goes incessantly to the sore spot in the mouth, worrying it, prodding it, investigating it until the pain starts again. Nonsense, of course I tried. I've always tried, all my life, to make a success of everything. Stingingly, she felt now that it was she as well as Belinda who had suffered an injustice.

"Gin," Belinda said. Smugly she spread her cards out on the footstool.

"You are getting good," Beverly said. "Your deal again, huh?"

"Yes," Belinda said with satisfaction. "Winner always deals, loser draws first."

As the afternoon wore on, the rain continued to come down steadily. "This should be good for the lawn," Beverly said, "if it doesn't drown it out entirely." She stretched painfully. Her back and legs ached from sitting on the floor for so long.

"Could it? Would the little grasses drown?" Belinda got to her feet and went to the sliding glass door that looked out over the backyard.

Beverly lay on the floor, sighing with relief. It was still early afternoon, but the greyish darkness outside made it seem like twilight. The fire had died down, and the room seemed gloomy again. Winner always deals, loser draws first. Games were fairer than life, weren't they? She wondered who the loser was, she or Bob. Apparently he felt like playing another hand with a new partner. She wondered if she ever would. She was getting quite depressed again. Quickly she sat up. "Belinda, turn the light on, will you? It's like night in here."

Listlessly Belinda left the window, wandered over to the table by the sofa, and turned on the lamp. She seemed to have grown pensive, too. "I'm tired of cards," she said flatly.

"So am I," Beverly replied.

"Then let's stop." Belinda sighed noisily and flung herself on the sofa. Picking up the end of one of her pigtails, she began rubbing it absentmindedly against her chin like a little brush.

It grew darker still, and a wind sprang up, rattling the glass, sending a chilling draft into the room. Abruptly the sound of the rain grew louder, sharper, turned into a staccato clatter.

"Look," Beverly said. "It's hailing."

Belinda's little face beamed. "Can I go out?" she asked eagerly.

"Better not," Beverly said. "That stuff can sting."

"Little teeny ice cubes. Is that what snow is like, Mother?"

"No," Beverly said. "Snowflakes are soft. Remember last winter when we went up to the mountains to see the snow?"

"We didn't see any coming down. I thought maybe it was like this."

Gradually the storm passed, the hail subsided, and even the rain diminished to a fine drizzle. Reluctantly, they turned back to the room.

Belinda sighed. "Mother, what did you do on rainy days when you were a little girl?"

Beverly tried to remember. "Well, there were three of us, of course. We played cards. Watched TV. And we cut out paper dolls. And oh, yes, sometimes my mother would get out her photograph album and show us."

Belinda looked up with interest. "Do we have a photograph album?"

"Of course we do. Don't you remember? I've showed it to you."

"Show me again. Come on, please show me again."

After a search, Beverly located it on the bottom shelf of the bookcase next to the fireplace. They sat down on the sofa and opened it. "See," she said. "It's the very same one my mother had."

"Show me everything," Belinda said, wiggling in anticipation. "Start from the beginning."

The first page showed a group of young ladies and young men standing around a large white tablecloth laid on the ground. There were trees in the background, and the remains of a picnic lunch on the cloth. In the foreground, one of the young men lay gracefully on his side, supporting his head with one arm, while one of the young ladies tickled his ear with a flower.

"This is your great-grandmother and grandfather and some of their friends on a picnic," Beverly said. "Do you remember which ones they are?"

Belinda pointed.

"That's right. And here's another." The next picture showed the same group arranged around a car.

"Why is that man lying on top of the car?" Belinda asked curiously.

"Just clowning," Beverly said. The whole crowd looked singularly happy and carefree. She wondered why people never took pictures like that any more.

On the next page was a bridal party. The darkhaired bride wore a short, loose-fitting gown, a skirt ending in scallops like the petals of a flower. The groom, serious and unsmiling, had his arm around her, and behind them beamed a joyful assortment of relatives and friends.

"That's your grandma and grandpa on their wedding day," Beverly said. It seemed strange to be referring to that couple, so radiantly young, as grandparents.

"I thought wedding dresses were long," Belinda said.

"Not always. Especially in those days."

"Is that you?" Belinda said, pointing to the little flower girl who stood in front of the bride.

"No," Beverly said smiling. "I didn't come along for several years." She turned the page. "See? Here I am now, in my bassinet."

Belinda giggled. "You were a funny-looking baby."

"I looked happy, though, didn't I?" Beverly said thoughtfully.

After that, there were pictures of the baby gradually growing into a little girl. Beverly in a new dress and bonnet being admired by doting parents; Beverly sitting on the front steps holding a Barbie doll in her fat little arms; Beverly riding a tricycle down the sidewalk and squinting into the sun.

Then there were two new babies, in their baby carriages, with Beverly, a scrawny seven-year-old with teeth missing, standing beside them with a proprietary air. "That's Aunt Sherry and Aunt Shirley when they were babies," Beverly said. "Weren't they darling? And look at me. I was so ugly." She turned the page slowly.

"What was it like, having baby sisters?"

Beverly was silent a moment, thinking back. "Mother was terribly busy after they came. She hardly had a second."

"Didn't she like you any more?"

"Of course she did," Beverly said quickly. "Only, new babies need a lot of attention, so she didn't spend as much time with me as she did before."

Belinda turned from the pictures to look up into her face. "Were you lonely?"

"Yes." She said it reluctantly, knowing the admission would bring back emotions she did not want to remember. Loneliness, yes, more than loneliness, a panicky feeling of being thrust out to the perimeter of the tight circle of love and warmth of which she had so long been the center. Lost. Left out. Unwanted. She blinked. But she had managed to find her way back. "So do you know what I did then?"

"What?"

"I learned how to help my mother take care of

them. I was a regular little nursemaid. I used to give them their bottles, and take them for rides in their carriages, and even change their diapers." Her voice had a brittle, falsely cheery sound. "Everybody thought I was wonderful, such an efficient little girl. And later on, when Grandpa died and Grandma had to go to work, I used to get dinner for all of us, and I helped them with their homework, and I braided their hair, which was so long and pretty, I did everything for them, really. And Mother was so proud of me. She said I was absolutely indispensable. And everybody thought I was wonderful. I was so efficient and well organized and—and efficient . . ."

"Mother," Belinda said in alarm, "why are you crying? Mother? Mother! Please don't cry!"

She wanted to stop, she truly wanted to, but she could not. The loneliness, the panic of more than twenty years ago returned, as strong as ever, to reinforce the loneliness and bitterness of the present. The rejected child, the rejected wife, merged and mingled until she could not separate them or control the intensity of their combined grief. She covered her face with her hands. Outside, the drumming rain seemed an extension of her own tears.

"Mother," Belinda sobbed. "Oh, Mother, please don't feel so bad."

She had tried. She really had tried, hadn't she? Being efficient had won her love and acceptance as a child, why did the same methods seem to work against her now? A computer, not a woman, Bob had called her. That was how he felt about her, when all she wanted was to be loved and needed. It wasn't fair. Or had she, somehow, done it all wrong this time?

When the spell was over, she sat numbly on the sofa, staring at nothing. She had cried like that only a few times in her life. The violence of the emotion had exhausted her, but at the same time, she felt dimly relieved. The house seemed empty, and sad. Belinda had gone out somewhere. In the midst of her tears, she had heard the front door slam. She hoped she had put on her raincoat and galoshes. It was dreadful of her to break down like that before Belinda, but the outburst had come upon her so unexpectedly. You can never trust you feelings, she thought. You can suppress them for months, years even, until you think they aren't there at all any more, and then one day they come bursting out to overwhelm you all over again.

Four o'clock. The day, finally, was nearly over. It had been a bad one after all, but then, Sundays usually were. Tomorrow she would have the office problems to face again, but they would help to take her mind off her personal difficulties. She felt grateful, all at once, for her job. The warmth of a big office, even with Sam and Miss Eads, was preferable to the coldness of this nearly deserted house.

She put the photograph album back and threw some wood on the fire. It was time she and Belinda had something to eat. She would fix some cocoa and cheese sandwiches, she decided, and then maybe they would go out to an early movie. Something of Disney's was playing at the theater nearby. It would be good for Belinda and for her, too. Disney movies were always cheerful and optimistic, and even though things might look bad for a while, they always came out right in the end. I wonder if he'd like to take over my life? she thought wryly.

She put the cocoa to heating while she looked for the marshmallows. Belinda always liked them put on the fire along with the cocoa, so they were already melted by the time they were poured into the cups. As she dropped them in, she was reminded of childhood parties. It would be nice to have a party right now, in the rain, she thought wistfully. Maybe she should call Sherry and see if she wanted to come over.

The doorbell rang, startling her. Who could it be? Bob, she thought eagerly. Maybe it was Bob. No, that was ridiculous. It might be Sherry, though. Anyway, it was somebody dropping in. How wonderful. She stopped to powder her tear-shiny face before opening the door.

"Beverly?" It was Barbara Stevens from next door, her face oddly tense.

Beverly looked at her blankly. "What is it?"

Barbara twisted her hands together nervously. "I think you'd better come."

A chill of premonition seemed to halt all her vital processes. "What's happened?"

"Now, Beverly, don't get excited," Barbara said rapidly. "It's going to be all right, she's not dead, she's just—"

Before she had finished, Beverly was pushing past her and running down the wet walk.

"Beverly, take it easy!" Pat Stevens, who was just coming up, intercepted her and grabbed her firmly by the arms.

"What is it?" Beverly cried wildly. "For God's sake, tell me!"

"She jumped in the river." His face was taut with sympathy.

Beverly gasped. Then she saw the little knot of people at the end of the street where the high wire fence marked the flood control causeway. There was a twenty-foot drop from the top of that fence to the concrete below. Concrete. She broke into a run. The people parted to let her through, through to the center, the focus of their attention where Belinda lay unnaturally quiet and still, wet, muddy, with one leg twisted at a strange angle. Her glasses were gone, and her white face looked younger than usual. Beverly knelt beside her and grasped her wrist. She seemed to feel a faint pulse, but she was not sure. Oh, God, she said silently to herself. She took a corner of the apron she still wore and wiped the water from her daughter's face.

"Somebody's called an ambulance," a voice said.

"Here's her glasses. She must have taken them off first."

"It's lucky Walter saw her when she jumped. She would have drowned for sure."

Beverly looked up. "Jumped?" she repeated stupidly.

"She climbed the fence and jumped. Walter Kahn saw her and went right in after her. All he stopped for was a ladder."

"Lucky they both didn't drown, all the rainwater that's going down there today."

"Lucky it was raining, or she would have been killed for sure, hitting that concrete."

Beverly looked at her daughter. Belinda's nostrils were pinched and blue, and her skin felt clammy. She has drowned, Beverly thought. Still, there might be a chance. Gently, handling the strangely bent leg with care, she turned her over on her stomach and began rhythmically pressing her hands down against Belinda's back and releasing them. Press and release. Press and release.

"You shouldn't do that!" a woman's voice gasped. "You shouldn't touch her until the ambulance comes!"

"If there's water in her lungs," Beverly said, "that can't wait."

"But suppose she has broken ribs!"

"I'll take the responsibility. I'm her mother."

Press and release. Press and release. There's a newer method, Beverly thought. Mouth-to-mouth resuscitation. I'm a fool not to know it. Press and release. Where's Bob? Somebody should call him. Did we do this to her? Is it our fault this happened? Press and release. Her arms ached, and the rain ran down them. She was chilled through, but she did not notice it. All of her being was absorbed in trying to detect some sign of life in the prostrate body beneath her. She mustn't die. Oh, God, don't let her die. Press and release. Somebody threw a coat over her shoulders. An umbrella was held over her head.

"Let me do that for a while," somebody offered after what seemed hours, but she shook her head. She had to do it herself. This much, at least, she had to do. Press and release. Press and release. Where was that ambulance? Her vision began to fade, and she wondered giddily if it were getting dark already.

At last she dimly heard the wail of a siren which drew closer, growing louder in volume, lower in tone as it slowed to a stop. Press and release. Press and release.

Someone touched her shoulder. "All right, lady. We'll take over now."

Many hands helped her to her feet.

"Beverly, are you okay?"

"I'm fine," she said clearly. She lifted her head, bent for so long over Belinda, and as she did, blood throbbed violently in her temples. How strange. It seemed to be quite dark all of a sudden. Yes, it was dark at last.

She was not aware of the hands that caught her as she fell.

Nineteen

"I've got a nice one for you today, Vivian," Lou Adams said. "You get to go out to Disneyland and enjoy the sunshine."

"Oh, wonderful," Vivian said cheerfully. "Who with?"

"Madame Ahmed Ben Bella and her kids. She's the wife of some Algerian government official. He's going to be tied up with Mayor Bradley this afternoon, and she wants to take in the sights. You go along and do an interview. It shouldn't be hard. They say she speaks good English."

"Lovely. I've never met an Algerian before, and it's been months since you sent me to Disneyland with somebody. It'll be almost like having the day off."

Adams grinned at her. "Don't let the old man hear you say that, you'll get docked a day's worth. They're at the Hilton on Wilshire. Be there by eleven."

It was a bright spring day, windy and clear. Freed from filthy air, the city had a clean look, as though all the buildings had just been thoroughly hosed down, and the snow-covered mountains visible from the *Times*'s windows seemed close enough for lunch-hour skiing. In view of how nice it was, Vivian decided to walk to the hotel. The sun was warm between the sheltering tall buildings, and she unbuttoned the jacket of her suit as she walked along, experiencing that sense of harmony that she was always aware of when the weather matched her mood. It was a marvelous feeling being engaged at last, or almost so. Sid had called his wife in New York, and she had agreed to file for divorce.

"She's coming out here to do it," Sid had said. "I don't know whether she'll file in California or go to Vegas. That's one thing we're going to have to talk about. If she files here, it will take a year, baby."

"I know," Vivian said, kissing him on the nose. "It's all right. Just so it's good and legal."

"Good and legal is how it's gonna be. We'll make an honest dame of you yet."

She did not laugh, she was thinking of something else. "How do you feel about her now? I mean—do you think about her at all?"

"I've hardly thought about her for months, thank God," Sid smiled slightly, a smile that was more an expression of pain. "After all the hell we went through. You don't know what it's like when a marriage breaks up."

"I hope I never do."

They looked at each other soberly.

"We'll be nice to each other, won't we?" Vivian asked wistfully.

"I'll be nice to you. And if you aren't nice to me, I'll beat the hell out of you. How's that?" He seized her in a hug so tight she could not breathe.

The high-ceilinged, ornate lobby of the Hilton was busy with the usual bustle of people going up and down the double staircase to the upstairs lobby.

"Madame Ahmed Ben Bella," Vivian said to the desk clerk.

"Over there." He nodded toward where a woman stood with two little boys, and Vivian experienced a faint surprise.

What had she been expecting, harem pants? she wondered as they introduced themselves. Somehow she had not been prepared to find Madame Ben Bella slender and fair, with a hat and suit she recognized as being from the spring Paris collections. Nothing about her, not even the pearls at her throat and ears, had an Arabian look. The boys, who apparently resembled their father, were dark with large, languourous brown eyes.

"Ferhat and Hebib," Madame Ben Bella said, presenting them. "Shall we go? The limousine is waiting."

"I'd like you to tell me how it is with women in your country," Vivian said as the big Cadillac pushed through the downtown traffic and onto the Santa Ana Freeway. In front of them on the jump seats, the two boys were already conversing quietly in their own language. "Do many of them have jobs? Do they want careers?"

"They work, yes. Since the election of Chadli Benjedid, Algeria is a very modern country. You know of Chadli Benjedid?"

"President Berjedid? He took the fezzes off the men and the veils off the women and did away with arranged marriages."

Madame Ben Bella laughed. "Yes, but he did much more than that. Before Chadli Benjedid, Algeria was a socialist state." She paused. "Of course, though laws change, customs remain. And attitudes."

"What do you mean?"

Madame Ben Bella took a silver case from her handbag and offered her a cigarette. As she did, Vivian noticed for the first time that her eyes were penetrating and intelligent. "I have not met an American career woman to converse with privately before. Only the wives of various dignitaries." She spoke slowly and precisely. "I have just arrived in your country, and this is the first time I have been here. I have been most eager to meet someone like you and to ask questions, so if you would not object . . ."

"Fine," Vivian said. "You interview me, and then I'll interview you."

Madame Ben Bella inclined her head in a gracious little nod of satisfaction, and Vivian thought, She's charming. As long as they had all afternoon, it would pay her to answer the woman's questions first. By that time they would be acquainted, and her own interview would go better. Aloud she said, "What would you like to know?"

"Tell me first what it is you do?"

Vivian told her.

"And you like this work?"

"Yes. It's exciting."

"Ah. Now. I apologize if I am too personal, but are you married?"

"No," Vivian said. She was happy to be able to add, "But I'm going to be."

"And will you continue with this work after your marriage?"

"I don't know." She was a little surprised to realize she had not given the matter any thought. "I suppose so. That is, at least until—if I have any children. Then I guess I'd have to stop. Anyway for a while."

"I see. You have a great passion to do the work of the world?"

"I don't know that I'd describe it that way. I think it's more a matter of having intelligence and wanting to use it."

Madame Ben Bella nodded. "I see. It is not enough simply to maintain a household for one's husband and children."

"I'm sure that's very rewarding," Vivian said quickly. "Particularly if you love the man. It must have been dreadful in the days of arranged marriages."

"Perhaps." Madame Ben Bella shrugged. "And yet can one assume, with your American divorce rate of 50 percent, that marriage based on romantic love leads to happier results?"

"It doesn't look that way, does it?" Vivian was quiet for a moment, thinking. "There's another reason for working. It's a matter or pride, I suppose. Of not wanting to live only through a man."

"Not even if you love the man?"

"Not—I don't know," Vivian said, breaking off suddenly. Something about the conversation was beginning to disturb her. "Maybe now you will answer a question for me. You are obviously an intellgent woman. Is it enough for you to live through your husband only?"

Madame Ben Bella looked out the window, smiling a little. "It is. But I shall have to think awhile how to explain it to someone like you."

Leaving the topic, Vivian asked her other questions, and then finally, "Look," she said. "Over there on the right. That's the Matterhorn. In a minute or two, we'll be in Disneyland."

They took the Jungle Ride and rode up the river on the Showboat, and then it was time for lunch. The little boys were fascinated. They said little, even to each other, but they looked at everything with a dark-eyed intensity that delighted Vivian, and the smiles they gave her were more eloquent than chatter. "How well behaved they are," she remarked. "Better than most American children."

"It takes patience," Madame Ben Bella observed. "And a strong will."

The last comment surprised Vivian a little, but her companion did not elaborate.

After lunch, they went on the Submarine Ride. "It's a question of power, isn't it?" Madame Ben Bella said unexpectedly as they peered out the little windows into the green bottom of an artificial ocean where sunken treasure gleamed and the hair of mermaids floated languidly on the current.

"How do you mean?"

"It is a question of how best to obtain power. You choose to do it, like so many American women, though your own achievement."

"Yes. I think it's better that way. It would offend my dignity to hold power only through a man. Would you have liked living in a harem?"

"I should have managed. I should have managed quite nicely."

"Well, I would have hated it," Vivian said vehemently. "I'd probably have gotten my head chopped off the first week."

"No, you would have found it an excellent testing ground for the intelligence of which you speak. You could, perhaps, have used it to rule the land and raise a leader."

"But I'd still be a slave with no freedom."

"Freedom." Madame Ben Bella shrugged gently. "What is freedom? It is an illusion. Your job, your career, holds you in bondage as much as a marriage would."

"But not the same kind."

"No. Not the same kind."

As the afternoon wore on, Vivian found herself watching her companion with uneasy admiration. She's so much more relaxed than we are, she thought, considering herself and her friends in comparison. Madame Ben Bella moved with such ease and elegance, she managed to control her children without once raising her voice. She was gentle, feminine, and serene, and yet the quickness of her mind prevented any impression of bovine placidity. They discussed politics, world affairs, art, fashion, and as they did, small, disconcerting fragments of self-criticism flashed intermittently through Vivian's mind. I smoke too much. My voice is too loud. I sound too adamant about things. Next to this woman, she felt less and less like a woman herself, and the sensation was deeply disturbing.

"We must go," Madame Ben Bella said suddenly, when the sun was halfway down the afternoon sky. "I told my husband we would return by five."

They were both tired, and the ride began in silence. As the car purred along, Vivian's mind went back once more to the major topic of the day.

"Perhaps it is partially a question of power. But it's

also a question of identity," she said.

Madame Ben Bella looked at her quickly. "Identity?"

"Yes. To lose one's identity and become simply somebody or other's wife—I find that idea degrading. There is a psychological game people have been playing lately in this country at parties. The person is asked to describe himself, to tell the most significant, revealing things, in three words or phrases. I asked this of a married friend of mine, and do you know what she said? She said, 'I am Leslie. I am Mark's wife. I am Debbie and Gary's mother.' She thought of herself only in relation to her husband and children. I was appalled."

"Was she happy?"

"Yes. But I couldn't be. Not that way."

"Not even if you loved the man?"

"No," Vivian said violently.

"Why not?" Madame Ben Bella's eyes were deeply questioning.

Vivian looked at her in consternation. "I don't know," she said. It frightened her a little not to know the answer. Perhaps she would be even more frightened if she knew it. "I don't know," she said again, helplessly.

Madame Ben Bella reached out quickly and patted her arm. "Come. We talk no more about it." The curiosity in her eyes had turned to sympathy.

By the time they reached the hotel, the lights along the street were beginning to come on.

"It's been an interesting day," Vivian said.

Madame Ben Bella looked at her thoughtfully. "Yes. But I think we have not convinced each other."

"You don't envy me my freedom."

"No. Because I do not think it makes you happy."

"All the same," Vivian said, "I couldn't do without it."

"How fortunate that we do not have to lead each other's lives. But there is one thing I think you do not understand. Within our sphere, we have great power, and the men let us have it because we do not challenge them in theirs. They do not have to fear us as possible usurpers."

"Do you think we frighten our men?"

She hesitated. "I sense in this country a great antagonism between men and women, especially on the part of the men. And hatred is born of fear, is it not?"

"I haven't been hated," Vivian said, but even as she spoke, Joe Bales came into her mind. How strangely he had behaved when she had begun to get recognition in the office, even though she had done it just to impress him. And when she had been given the job he wanted . . . You bitch. She closed her eyes.

"I wish you joy in your marriage." Madame Ben Bella said, moving to get out of the car.

Vivian got out too, and they stood for a moment on the crowded sidewalk. "I wonder what you would have been like if you had grown up in this country instead of Algeria," Vivian said unexpectedly.

The question took Madame Ben Bella by surprise. She stood there, slender and chic, oblivious of the passing traffic, considering it, and looking at her Vivian thought, It's only the eyes that give her away, those penetrating eyes and the mind behind them. "I don't know," Madame Ben Bella said at last. She gave Vivian a strange little smile. "Perhaps—like you?"

The wind had blown up clouds, and it was cold now. Vivian shivered as she walked back to the office and hugged herself to keep warm. It had been a disturbing day. She liked Madame Ben Bella, she felt a kinship with her in spite of their opposing views, and yet the woman had somehow made her feel angular, brittle, aggressive, the typical American career woman. But after all, Vivian acknowledged reluctantly, I suppose that's what I am. On the outside, at least. But on the inside? Suddenly she had an overpowering desire to see Sid, to make love to him, to be reassured of her womanhood. If only I could lose myself in a man, she thought. The idea surprised her so that she stopped dead in the middle of the hurrying sidewalk, while pedestrians brushed by her on both sides. Yes. All at once she felt that was what she wanted more than anything else in the world.

As soon as she got to her desk, she telephoned Sid at the studio.

"I've been calling you all day," he said. "Where you been?"

"On an assignment. Sid, I want to see you tonight."

"I want to see you too." His voice was guardedly low. "Look, I'm in a conference, and it's going to break up late. Suppose I come by your place around seven, seven-thirty."

"All right," she said. "Hurry."

When she got home, she undressed immediately, feeling a distinct dissatisfaction with her practical black suit. Newspaper work was dirty, and she wore dark colors a lot at the office. She washed the soft carbon of copy pencils off her hands a dozen times a day, and still it was hard not to smudge her clothes accidentally. In the bathroom, she turned on the water in the tub. Showers were for working girls. She poured a capful of bubble bath under the brisk stream from the faucets, and the bubbles rose, hissing gently, while the water turned milky.

When she got into the tub, she soaped idly, letting the hot water draw the tiredness of a day's walking from her body. What would it be like to be simply and beautifully a woman, the way Madame Ben Bella was? She thought about Sid. It would change every aspect of her relationship with him. How would he react if she were tender rather than violent, submissive rather than demanding in love? It will make him happy, she thought with quick, instinctive conviction. As she dressed, putting on a pale pink negligee and a lot of Sophia, an unaccustomed gentle mood took possession of her.

When the door bell sounded, she went to the door

feeling almost shy. She had decided not to tell Sid about the day's conversation and how it had changed her. She would simply let him discover for himself how different she was. But when she saw him standing there, something made her throw her arms around him and hug him fiercely. All the love she had withheld so long, protecting herself, seemed to want to come out at once.

He was startled. "What's all this?"

"Nothing. I just missed you terribly today, that's all. I've been wanting like crazy to talk to you."

Gently he took her arms down. "Yeah. I want to talk to you, too." He walked into the room and turned around, and for the first time she saw how serious his face was, and how tired.

A shudder of premonition ran through her. "What about?"

"About Joan. About my marriage." He ran a stubby hand over his dark hair and looked away from her. "Vivian, baby, I don't know how to tell you this. We're going back together."

The shock took immediate effect. Like someone smashed in an accident, she was so dazed that she did not realize at first how seriously she was injured. Automatically her mind threw its usual safety switch, and she saw him as if from a great distance, through the wrong end of opera glasses. "Oh? How did that happen? Maybe you'd better sit down." Her voice was calm, even flat, and certainly not indicative of the kind of tension that was gripping her stomach.

He sat heavily on the sofa. "She got here last night. With the kids. I went to meet them at the airport." He said hesitantly, the words having a tendency to stick in his throat. This was going to be harder than he had first supposed.

"How are they?"

"Oh, fine. I—Vivian, I didn't know what it was going to be like to see them again. It's been so damn long. Over six months." He fumbled in his pocket for a cigarette.

She opened the box on the coffee table and handed it to him. As he took a cigarette and lit it, she noted from the deep recess of her detachment that his hand was shaking. "So you still love her."

"I don't know. I'm not even sure it's love any more. Maybe it's just habit. When you live with somebody for fifteen years . . . Oh, hell, who knows after all that time what to call it? Maybe you just have too big an equity in each other's lives. And then there's the kids. Jesus, you don't know how I've missed them. I don't know if it's so much her as it's them. I want them back, Vivian. They're my family."

"Of course," she said quietly. "That's understandable."

He stared down at his hands. "I want you to know the reconciliation wasn't my idea. It's hers. She says she still loves me. She didn't realize it until I told her I wanted the divorce. She says she needs me."

"Does she know you've been—seeing somebody else?"

"Yeah. I told her when I talked to her on the phone the other night."

"Did you tell her we loved each other? Never mind," she added quickly. "I suppose that's none of my business."

"I told her last night when she got here. We sat up half the night talking. Then she went to bed, and I sat up the rest of the night thinking about you."

He was silent. After a moment, Vivian said, "Yes? And what did you think?"

"I thought maybe it wouldn't work anyway," he finally said. "I don't know what it is, Vivian, but something about you scares the hell out of me. You give your body so freely and so well, but there's some other part of you that I never got to at all. There's some kind of closeness people have that we never managed. Christ, I don't know why. Maybe it was my fault. But there were times when I wanted it like hell."

"Yes. I suppose you're right." She smiled, but her heart wasn't in it.

"You're a hell of a woman, Vivian. I've never known anybody so passionate. Jesus, I just don't know anymore. Maybe it was my fault."

"No. It's mine." She might as well be generous. It was too late to be anything else. Besides, it was true. Her eyes went unfocused and she stared off into nothing for a moment as she realized how barren her life would be without Sid.

He turned and looked at her at last, and his dark eyes had the warm, appealing look that had always drawn her. She had a sudden, insane desire to kiss him.

"I better go." He got up. "What's the use of dragging this out?"

"Must you?" Her tone was conversationally polite. "Wouldn't you like a drink?" She did not want him to go, she could not let him walk out the door even though it was all over and done with.

"Yeah, I'd love a drink." He started for the door. "But I better not have it here. I'm not so damn calm as you are."

"I'm not calm," she said slowly.

"Aren't you?" He stared into her eyes and looked quickly away. "Oh, Christ, Vivian. I'm sorry. I don't know what else to say."

"Is anything of yours here?" Her mind was racing now, searching for excuses to keep him from opening the door. "Haven't I got some of your pajamas? Wait, I'll get them for you."

"No. Never mind. Send them to me at the studio."

"I think there are some things of mine at your house," she went on deliberately.

"Yeah, I know. I should have gotten them out before. Of course, I thought she'd stay at a hotel. But she's at the house."

"I hope it didn't cause you any embarrassment."

"Look," he said abruptly. "I'll mail them to you, okay?" His hand was on the knob.

"All right." She took a quick deep breath. "I think there's a blue silk nightgown, and a pair of slippers, and a toothbrush. Oh yes, and my zebra-striped bathing suit."

"Vivian." The tone of his voice silenced her. "For Christ's sake, cut it out."

"All right." She was beginning to be aware, dimly, of internal injuries.

They looked at each other.

"Take it easy," he said.

Then he opened the door and closed it behind him.

She stood perfectly still. It's a bad one, something informed her. Oh, it's a bad one. When the shock wore off, the pain would be unbearable. "Well, don't let it wear off," she said aloud to herself in a practical tone. Briskly she went to the kitchen and opened a bottle of Scotch. The time to start administering the anesthetic was before the pain started. She poured herself half a glass, put one ice cube in it, then drank most of it down without waiting for it to chill. There. Now, what else in the way of first aid? Carrying her glass, she went to the bedroom and took off the pink negligee, exchanging it for the tailored dressing gown she wore when she belonged exclusively to herself. As she tied the sash, the thought came that she should dress and go somewhere, anywhere at all. No. That was out of the question when she was so badly injured. She took another gulp of Scotch. How much would it take to put her out completely? The first gulp, on an empty stomach, was already making her dizzy. She must hurry and get settled. From the nightstand drawer she took the piece of lead. Holding it tightly, she went to the kitchen for the Scotch bottle, which she took into the living room and set carefully on the coffee table. Sitting on the sofa, she finished the first glass. Yes, that was better. A kind of numbness was coming over her. She reached up and touched her forehead experimentally. Already it felt like somebody else's skin. She looked down at her hand, which clutched the piece of lead. Opening it, she found that the lead had dug into it, leaving two long red marks.

"I don't do very well," she said to it. Her voice sounded terribly loud in the silence of the empty apartment. "I don't do well at all."

She examined her inner self anxiously for signs of the beginning of pain. Still none. So far, so good. Perhaps, if she were clever, she would be able to escape it for some time, but she would have to be awfully clever. Awfully clever. Because this was a bad one.

She would be lucky to climb out of the wreckage alive.

Twenty

The telephone woke Dana, and she fumbled a hand loose from her bedclothes, pulled the receiver down to her ear, and fuzzily murmured, "Hello," with the vague feeling that it had been ringing a long time.

"Hi. Did I wake you? I'm sorry." It was Vivian's voice.

"It's all right," Dana said, twisting sleepily to look at the clock on the nightstand. "It's eleven. I should have been up long before this."

"I waited as long as I could. The thing is, I'm coming out your way this afternoon for an interview, and I thought maybe we could have lunch first."

"Wonderful. Where and when?"

"How about Jeno's at twelve?"

"Okay. I'll meet you there."

Jeno's was crowded, but Vivian already had a table when Dana arrived. The day was cold and windy, and she was happy to see a fire burning in the hearth. Vivian was smoking, and there was already a snuffed-out stub in the ashtray.

"Hi," Dana said, sliding into the booth. "What's new? How's Sid?"

"Sid's gone back to his wife."

She said it so matter-of-factly that Dana could not believe what she heard. "You're kidding. I thought he asked her for a divorce."

"He did. That's when she came back from New York, and they got together again."

"My God," Dana said. She looked at Vivian closely, but her friend's face showed no sign of emotion. "Well, I must say you're taking it very well."

Vivian shrugged. "What else can I do? Wives have a priority, don't they?" Her tone indicated she was not particularly anxious to go on discussing it. "Let's have a drink."

When they had ordered, Vivian asked brightly, "What's with you? How's the play going?"

"Fine. Just fantastically good."

"That's wonderful. You must be pleased after the way you've worked."

"Oh, I'm pleased, all right." She said it without enthusiasm.

"You don't sound like it," Vivian said, giving her a sharp look. "What's the problem—Don?"

"How did you guess?"

Vivian laughed shortly. "He wouldn't be the first husband to be jealous of his wife's career."

"Jealous? You think that's it? But why? It isn't as if he weren't successful himself, so that he'd feel I was outstripping him in some way."

"You're thinking of Beverly's problem with Bob? That's not the only one. Some men—most men, probably—have to be the center of the universe where their wives are concerned."

"But lots of wives work," Dana said bewilderedly. "Good Lord, look at the statistics."

"Work, yes. To augment the family income. Or get away from the kids. But having a job isn't the same thing as having a career. You're working because you love what you're doing, and that's far more dangerous from Don's standpoint than if you were just selling dresses at Saks for an excuse to get out of the house every day."

"He keeps telling me I've changed since I've been in the play. That I'm different. But you know what I think? I haven't changed so much as I've developed. I'm more the person I was meant to be now than I was before."

"Well, that's a good thing, isn't it?"

"I don't know," Dana said frowning. "It would seem to me that it is, but I hate what it's doing to Don and me." At the moment, she did not want Vivian to know how upset she was. Looking around, she concentrated on the other diners to calm herself. They were career people, slick and well-dressed, and they were arranging deals over their daiquiris, and the atmosphere was full of laughter and talk and the urgency of many ambitions. "How's Beverly these days?" she said at last, to change the subject.

"I don't know. I haven't talked to her for a week or so."

"I just wondered how she was taking the separation."

"All right, probably. You know Beverly. She always has everything under control."

Their drinks came, and they sipped them absentmindedly without proposing a toast to anything or anybody as they often did in fun. "They want me to go to New York with the play," Dana said at last.

"Really? But that's wonderful! When did you find out?"

"Three days ago. I haven't had the nerve to tell Don about it yet. I'm so worried I haven't been sleeping. I took a sedative last night. That's why I was still asleep this morning when you called."

"You're going to do it, aren't you?"

"I want to, of course. I want terribly to do it. If only I could make him understand how important it is to me."

Vivian lit another cigarette and looked at her. "Just how important is it? Worth sacrificing your marriage for?"

"Vivian, I couldn't bear to have it come to that. Don and Jeremy. . . . Up until a few months ago I wouldn't have dreamed anything in life could mean as much to me as they do, and now . . ."

"It's not fair, is it? Men never have to choose between their jobs and their families. With them, everybody's willing to admit the job comes first. But if a woman puts her job first, she's a wicked person."

"What about this interview you're doing this afternoon?" Dana asked abruptly.

"The *Times* Woman of the Year. Mrs. Elias Howe. Head of one of Los Angeles' largest advertising agencies, outstanding hostess, devoted wife, mother of four. The whole bit."

"Do me a favor," Dana asked. "Ask her how she does it."

"I know," Vivian said. "I've met Mr. Elias Howe."

Dana looked at her.

"Behind every successful married carrier woman, there's the right kind of man," Vivian said lightly. "Didn't you know that?" She took the mint cherry out of her gimlet, ate it, and finished the drink in a gulp. "Come on, we'd better order. I have to be in Beverly Hills at two."

After lunch, Dana drove to the nursery school and picked up Jeremy. Don took him in the mornings now on his way to work, and she brought him home early in the afternoon in order to have more time with him. He clambered into the car waving a large sheet of paper. On it was scribbled in brown crayon, with a red crayon border, an unidentifiable animal.

"It's lovely," Dana said, curiously looking at it. "What is it?"

"A groundhog," Jeremy said triumphantly. "This is Groundhog Day, Mama. Didn't you know?"

"No, is it? I didn't read the paper this morning. That's very interesting. Do you know about groundhogs, Jeremy? They say that on Groundhog Day they come out of their burrows to look around. If they can see their shadows, there'll be six weeks more of winter before spring really arrives. If they can't see their shadows because it's cloudy, it's spring already."

Jeremy thought it over. "Is that a true story?"

"I don't know, dear. But it's a story people always tell."

"Could we look for a groundhog this afternoon?"

"All right. But first you have to take your nap."

While he slept, Dana wandered restlessly around the house. If she went to New York, she would take Jeremy with her. She could not bear to be separated from him for longer than a week. It was a strange thing about children. When they were tiny and demanding, there were times when you felt you had to get away from them or go mad. Then when you did, left them with somebody and went off for a weekend, you spent the whole time thinking about them and missing them and wondering if they were all right and longing to get back to them. She and Jeremy had never been separated for longer than a week, and that only once. Don would miss him, of course, she thought guiltily. But when a child was as young as Jeremy, it was more important for him to be with his mother. Surely Don would see that.

Tonight they would have to discuss the whole thing. It was cowardly and pointless to postpone it any longer. Somehow she must find a way to make him understand. It would not be easy for, she was dimly aware, she did not fully understand it herself. She twisted her hands together nervously and wished that she had a cigarette. Ordinarily she did not smoke, but this afternoon she could have lit one from the other in her anxiety. The full ashtray at Jeno's when they left came into her mind. Vivian was certainly smoking a lot these days. How badly had she been hurt by Sid? She had been so preoccupied with herself that she had not been sensitive as usual to her friend's state of mind.

"Mama?" Jeremy stood in the doorway. "Can we go look for groundhogs now?"

Dana looked at her watch. "Oh, Jeremy. You've only been down half an hour."

He gave her a steady stare exactly like Don's. "I want to look for groundhogs," he said stubbornly.

WIVES AND LOVERS

"All right," Dana said with a sigh. She was eager for a walk herself. "Put your shoes on." She went to the closet and got out a ski sweater, dark blue with red and white stripes, for herself and a heavy coat for Jeremy.

They walked up an unpaved fire road that climbed the brush-covered hillside, briefly green with the rains of springs, above their house. Dana was surprised at how many wildflowers there were, tiny ones dotted almost invisibly in the gray-green shrubs.

"Here, groundhog! Here, groundhog!" Jeremy shouted, running ahead of her.

"Sssssh, you'll scare them, if there are any," Dana told him. "You must look quietly along the edge of the road for their burrows."

"What's a burrow?"

"A hole in the ground. It's where little animals like rabbits and groundhogs live."

"Don't they have any windows?" he said, wrinkling his nose. "It must be dark down there."

"No windows," Dana said. She thought of New York. "I know a city where the people have burrows."

Jeremy stopped dead and looked back at her. "People? People live in burrows?"

"They don't live in them, but they travel back and forth in them. There are trains running through to take people where they want to go."

"Oh." He looked dubious.

"Would you like to see that?" Dana asked. The false brightness of her tone disgusted her faintly. "Would you like me to take you there?"

"I guess so," he said without enthusiasm. He ran ahead, stopping on his fat legs every few yards to peer at the raw yellow rock where the road had been cut through the decomposed granite of the hillside.

At last they reached the end of the road. It disappeared into a weed-grown, leveled-off hilltop lot where no house had yet been built. The view over the city at this level, so much higher than their own house, was staggering and made even more dramatic on this afternoon by the weather. Clouds, the big, well-defined ones which follow the breakup of a storm, crowded the sky, casting enormous shadows on the city below, and between the shadows, tiny, select areas gleamed in golden sunlight like the Promised Land. Looking out over it from this vantage point, which was windy and cold, Dana felt a deep satisfaction. The sense of isolation that being above the city had once given her had disappeared. Even up here, she could still hear the faint, vast rumble of traffic and see cars moving steadily along the palm-lined boulevards.

The wind blew fitfully, penetrating the thick sweater she wore, and higher still, it shifted the ponderous clouds until the sun shone brilliantly on the place where she stood. She laughed. It was like a spotlight on her, and the city in cloudy darkness below like an audience before a stage. The familiar scene of power rose within her. Look at me, she commanded the city silently. Look up at me, and I will play to you. How wonderful it would be to play to them all, to communicate with them all in this one way she knew how, she who had always been so shy. She would be a hundred different people for them, she would help them to understand themselves and each other better than before, they would feel joy and compassion because of what she had made them see. Oh, it was a magnificent profession, acting. It was a way of giving, of reaching out, of contributing. Impulsively, she stretched out her arms.

"What are you doing, Mama?" Jeremy said, coming up to her.

"Playing games," she said lightly. " Being silly."

"Can I play, too?"

"We have to go back down now. It's getting colder." She turned her back on the city and started down the road.

When Jeremy had been put to bed that night, she brought it up at last.

"Something wonderful has happened." After three days of consideration, she had decided to begin without any preamble. "The play is going to be produced in New York."

"Oh?" He put down the *Wall Street Journal* and looked at her so intently that she knew he suspected what was coming next.

"Only two people from the local cast have been asked to go back with it, and I'm one of them."

"That's very flattering, isn't it?" he said evenly. "Naturally you told them it was impossible."

"Impossible?" The word sent a chill through her. "Why impossible?"

"Because you have a husband and child."

"It would only be for about three months, less if it flopped," she said quietly. "Dan Morgan is so eager to have me do the part in New York that he'd arrange for me to have a twelve-week contract instead of the usual run-of-the-play."

"That's very thoughtful of Mr. Morgan, but I cannot spare my wife for three months under any circumstances," Don said doggedly. His face had already settled into the closed-in, stubborn expression she knew so well.

"Don. This is a wonderful opportunity for me, but beyond that, I feel I owe a debt to Dan Morgan. If it weren't for him, I wouldn't have had the part in the first place. He understands how much my home means to me, and he's gone to a great deal of trouble to make this arrangement. It's practically unheard-of, and the producer, needless to say, was reluctant. I explained to Dan that I couldn't consider being gone an indefinite length of time when your work keeps you here, and you see that I didn't even mention the subject to you until what I thought was a feasible arrangement was all worked out."

Don picked up his pipe. "It's a pity you didn't check with me first. Then you would have known it wasn't a feasible arrangement at all." He began tamping tobacco into the pipe bowl with great deliberateness.

Desperation began to take hold of her. "I wish I could make you understand how much this means to me," she said in a low voice. "The chance to prove myself where a success really counts. More than that. The part itself. I may never get another like it. I really understand this nun, Sister Martinette. Interpreting her does something for me I can't explain, but I need it. Just this one time, and I'll never go away again. Oh, Don—" She stopped. He was not even looking at her.

"No." The word dropped with a thud.

Dana looked at him for a long time without speaking. How strange it was, she thought, that the very qualities which attracted you to a person in the beginning sometimes became the ones you disliked the most as time went on. When she had first known Don, how she had adored his masterful ways, his authoritative air. Now she found him dogmatic instead of masterful, tyrannical instead of authoritative. He was, she realized, as domineering as her mother, only in a different way. When she detested it in her mother, how could she have found it so attractive in Don? She studied his face as though she had never really seen it before. Was it strong, or had she merely mistaken inflexibility for strength?

"What are you looking at?" he asked at last.

"You."

"I can see that. Well, I'm sorry if you think I'm a monster. I probably made a mistake in the beginning, being so lenient with you when you decided to go back on the stage." He put the pipe in his mouth and picked up his paper with a gesture which closed the conversation.

"Lenient?" Rage boiled up in her. "What do you mean, lenient? You sound like a strict father with a delinquent child, or a warden with a misbehaving prisoner. We're husband and wife, you know. It's not quite the same sort of relationship." She paused, but he kept on reading without so much as a glance at her.

"Will you put that paper down, please?" she asked on a rising note. "We're discussing something of considerable importance to me, and we're not through."

He looked up. "I'm through. As far as I'm concerned, the subject is closed." As he spoke, his face seemed to become quite unfamiliar. It was as though someone who merely resembled him had somehow taken his place in the big chair.

"Well, I have one more thing to say," she said, trying to control her voice which was beginning to tremble. "I will not be given orders in this Victorian way. I'm going to New York with the play whether you like it or not."

Now, at last, he put down the paper. "If you do," he said softly, eyes glittering, "you don't need to bother coming back."

She could not believe her ears. She stared at him, seeking some sign that he himself was as astonished by those words as she was, but his face was closed-in, expressionless. He waited a moment or two as though expecting a word from her. When none came, he picked up the paper and once more began to read.

Pride drew her to her feet. She would not let him close her out so icily. Quite as deliberately as he had picked up his paper, she got up and walked out of the room, put on her coat, and left the house.

Twenty-one

They met awkwardly, as people do who have been divided by more than time and space. It was evening, and in the subdued light of the hospital corridor nurses rustled past efficiently on their rounds, looking calm and organized in contrast to the visitors who shuffled along, patently ill-at-ease, peering half fearfully into the open doors beyond which their friends and relatives, alienated by illness, lay propped on high, white beds.

"She's sleeping," Beverly said, indicating with a nod the door she had just shut behind her. Bob had come up just as she was leaving Belinda's room, and although she had known he was coming to the hospital tonight, the sight of him still startled her so that she felt herself begin to perspire a little.

"How is she?" Bob asked. In the uncertain light, his face looked sallow and thinner than it used to be.

"All right. She ate a good dinner. The leg hurts her, though."

"She cried when I came in this morning after I got your call," Bob said. He bit nervously at his lip.

"She was very glad to see you. She told me so tonight."

A nurse came up to them. "If you'd like to talk, there's a waiting room just down the hall."

The waiting room was depressingly cheerful with worn fabric covers on the furniture and artificial plants in tarnished brass planters. They sat down at opposite ends of the sofa and looked carefully away from each other.

"I can't get over it," Bob said. "Ever since you called this morning, I've been trying to get it through my head, and I just can't believe it."

"You should have been through yesterday." The image of her daughter, lying wet and still with her leg twisted under her, rose up in Beverly's mind for the hundredth time in twenty-four hours. "I couldn't believe it while it was happening. I'll never get over it as long as I live."

"The nurse said you saved her life."

"I know. You always wonder how you're going to react in an emergency. Well, now I know. You don't think. You just act. It was Walter Kahn who really saved her, though, by pulling her out of the river."

"River. My God. When you stop to think that three hundred and sixty days out of the year there's nothing down there except concrete—" His voice broke, and he reached into his pocket for cigarettes. "I can't get over it. A little kid like that. Trying to commit suicide because we—"

"Is that what she told you?" Beverly said curiously. He nodded.

"It's not exactly the truth."

Bob looked at her uncomprehendingly. "What do you mean? It sure as hell wasn't just an accident."

"No, it wasn't an accident. She—staged it. Only, it didn't work out the way she planned."

"Go on." A match had burned down close to his fingers, and he lit his cigarette and blew it out without taking his eyes off her.

"She—thought I was very unhappy without you," Beverly said hesitantly. "So she tried to think of some way of bringing us back together. She decided that if she jumped in the river and pretended she was committing suicide because we were separated, that would do the trick. She wouldn't have jumped if there hadn't been all that water and silt to break her fall, and after all, she does know how to swim."

"Where did she think she was going to swim to? Those concrete walls go on for miles."

"Oh, she was only planning on keeping afloat until Walter Kahn or somebody rescued her."

"Walter Kahn?"

"She climbed the fence and sat on top of it until he happened to come out for the car. She waited until he saw her and yelled at her, and then she went off. With a good, loud scream, just in case."

"Good Lord," Bob said, looking stunned. "The self-possessed little devil."

"Brave, too. Only, she miscalculated a little. She was very annoyed about that when she told me the whole thing this afternoon."

"How did she happen to tell you?"

"Well, I pried a little. After the first shock wore off, when I thought it over I realized she wasn't the suicidal type. She's too much like me. So I asked a few questions, and pretty soon it all came out."

"What did you do—laugh or cry?"

"Both. I also told her that the only thing that was saving her from a good spanking was that broken leg."

Bob sighed shakily. "Well. What do we do now?"

"I don't know." Beverly ran her fingers along the top of her black handbag and watched what she was doing with great interest. "I suppose we shouldn't let her make the sacrifice in vain."

"Does that mean you want me to come back?"

"What about your friend?"

"Friend?"

"The manicurist. Or whatever she was."

"Oh." He looked embarrassed. "I haven't been seeing too much of her lately."

"Well," Beverly said at last, "if you want to come back, it's all right with me."

He stood up quickly. "Let's wake up Belinda and tell her." He started for the door.

"No, I don't want her disturbed tonight," Beverly

said firmly. "She's had a lot of pain today and she needs her rest. I'll tell her tomorrow."

Bob looked disappointed. "I thought we should tell her together."

"If we wake her now and get her all excited, it may be hours before she gets back to sleep. Please, Bob, we mustn't be selfish about this."

"Okay. Where's your car? I'll take you to it."

On the way to the parking lot, he said, "How's the job going?"

"Still fighting for my life. It looks as though Miss Bigelow's not coming back, but I don't think I have a chance in a hundred of getting her job."

"What'll we do when Belinda gets out of the hospital? Can you take time off to look after her? She sure won't be able to get around by herself for awhile."

"I don't dare leave work the way things are," Beverly said, frowning, "but I'll manage. I'll just have to get someone to come in during the day."

So they went back to living together, gingerly at first, and then with a gradual diminution of unnaturalness and strain. Beverly was relieved that the crisis was past. With her personal life on an even keel, she had more time and energy to give to the battle going on at Mayfields, a battle which gave her more cause for alarm with every passing week. What was happening, she saw, was that a subtle form of psychological warfare was being employed against her. There was, and would be, no major plot. Instead, she was continually harassed by a series of small incidents as monotonously repetitious and maddening as Chinese water torture. Orders she gave were misinterpreted or not carried out at all. Memos she issued vanished before reaching their destination. Phone messages left on her desk by Lynn disappeared before she saw them, and when the parties eventually called back, irate and complaining, she could only stammer an apology. It was not Sam, although he disrupted the smooth operation of the department as often as he dared, but Miss Eads, his lieutenant, who was the major troublemaker from her vantage point as Beverly's assistant.

"I know she takes things off my desk," Beverly told Lynn when the sixth phone message had been mislaid. "Watch her."

"I'll try, but I don't know what I can do," Lynn said, her round eyes troubled. "She has to go into your office a lot, and I can't just follow her around like a bloodhound."

"I suppose not," Beverly said ruefully. She thought she knew what they had in mind. If they could get her so upset that she began making real mistakes, or if she lost her head and complained to Mr. Ladd that there was a plot against her, her own behavior would seem so erratic that he would never dream of considering her for an executive position. If, on the other hand, she could beat them at their own game and catch them in one of their tricks, Mr. Ladd might be willing to consider the possibility that she could handle the job after all.

It would not be easy, Beverly realized. Cathy Eads was no fool. She sat in Beverly's old office, legs seductively crossed, knit blouse stretched tight across her high breasts, and languidly fluffed her curly black hair with her red-tipped fingers, looking Beverly up and down with a faint smile of scorn and amusement. And Beverly, in the midst of issuing instructions, would suddenly become aware that her nervousness these days was making her overeat, that she was gaining weight, and that in Miss Eads's sharp eyes she was a dumpy, bossy, self-important little woman who had almost lost her husband and was about to lose her job.

She kept her head, but as the weeks passed, anxiety made her emphasize more and more the aggressive, authoritative side of her character. To keep the situation under control and to bolster her own self-confidence, she became increasingly a female martinet like Miss Bigelow, barking orders, ferociously dressing down any unfortunates who did not carry out her instructions exactly, insisting mercilessly on perfection at all times from every member of her staff.

It was not easy to turn it off once she got home. "I thought I asked you to put out the trash," she snapped at Bob in exasperation one night.

Her tone brought him about sharply. "Okay. So I forgot it. But don't talk to me like a drill sergeant."

She scarcely heard him. "With all the things I have to do to keep this household going, I should think you could manage your one or two without constantly being reminded."

"Dammit!" he swore softly. "Don't nag, Beverly. Don't nag."

"I don't want to nag. But if I don't keep after you until you've actually done something, you don't do it at all. I reminded you just once last night, and look what happened. Now it'll be three weeks before they come around for the trash again, and by that time we'll be buried in garbage."

"So fire me," Bob said, his face flushing. "I'm obviously not worthy to be on your staff."

March was becoming April, and "Easter at Mayfield's" was moving into high gear. Lilacs were its theme, and under Beverly's supervision, a tremendous, coordinated advertising and publicity campaign was in progress. Fresh lilacs bloomed in the store's aisles, and the scent of lilac perfume was wafted through the air conditioning to the noses of springtime shoppers. At least one of the store's daily ads was printed in lilac ink in all the major metropolitcan newspapers, and on Sundays, the ink itself was scented with lilacs. Salesgirls wore sprigs of imitation lilac on their dresses or in their hair, and Easter gifts purchased at Mayfield's came wrapped in the theme color, even down to being packed in lilac tissue paper.

The details of planning and running this campaign occupied Beverly's mind to the fullest. If it was a success and pre-Easter sales increased noticeably, it would be a mark in her favor with management. She worked doggedly, staying late in the evenings, coming in early in the mornings. Much that she should have been able to delegate to Cathy Eads she did herself because she could not trust her assistant.

Healthy though she was, the strain began to tell. When she came home at night, there were dark circles under her eyes, and her face began to look haggard in spite of its plumpness. Even Bob turned sympathetic. "Take it easier, sweetheart. It's not worth killing yourself over," he said one night when Beverly, too tired for once even to eat, had pushed her plate aside and laid her head on the table.

"It won't go on like this forever," she said, sitting up with a sigh. She put a hand absently to her hair. It needed a set, but she had not found time to get to the beauty salon that week. "Only a couple of weeks more."

"Just about when Belinda will be up and walking again. Listen, Beverly, I have an idea. I'm going to make her some crutches. They're always so damn heavy, you know? I think I can make her some light ones that will be easier to use."

"Why bother? They have metal ones now—aluminum, I think they are—that are much lighter than the old wooden ones. We can get her some of those."

"Well, I'd like to." Since his return, Bob had taken to working a little in his shop again. "That's all. I'd just like to."

"All right," Beverly said, swallowing a yawn. "I think I'll go to bed. I'm bushed."

The last two weeks before Easter, her work increased in volume. Lately it seemed to be getting more complicated in a dozen little ways. Her memos, for example. In order to protect herself, she had taken to making them out in duplicate and keeping the carbon copy in her desk in case any question arose later. Also, she relied more and more on memos instead of verbal orders which her two enemies could misinterpret. Lynn, worried, harassed, but utterly loyal, was her only ally. She still refused to go to Mr. Ladd with the story of her woes. She was determined to handle them herself with no help from above.

It was not until just before Easter that she finally, under the pressure of overwork and exhaustion, tripped and fell. Good Friday's color ad was to show a gigantic lilac bunny, nearly two feet tall in actual size, which was a material copy of the rabbit which had been used as a trademark in the corner of all the "Easter at Mayfield's" ads. The bunny, with wistful pink eyes and an orange carrot clutched in one paw, had been proclaimed absolutely adorable by every female employee of the store who had seen the sample, inflatable soft plastic made in Japan especially for Mayfield's. The bunny in the ads had been commented upon enthusiastically by numerous Mayfield's customers, most of whom would presumably be eager to buy the original. So at only $5.99, a ridiculously low price, Mayfield's expected it to be a big seller. Beverly hoped it would be. It was her idea.

Misfortune, however, had haunted Mayfield's Easter Bunny almost from the time the order had arrived at the manufacturer's in Japan. First a fire at the factory had delayed production; then a dock workers' strike in Yokohama had prevented shipment. The final result was that the bunnies, which were to have arrived a month before Easter and a good three weeks before the start of the Easter advertising campaign, were still somewhere on the Pacific at the very start of Holy Week. Word had come on Tuesday that the ship on which they were arriving would dock in San Pedro late Wednesday night. The bunnies would be unloaded and brought to the store on Thursday, and on Friday the ad would run, soliciting phone orders and promising delivery on Saturday just before Easter. It was a tight schedule, but it couldn't be helped. At least they're getting here before Easter,

Beverly thought.

Thursday morning was hectic. Her phone rang incessantly, keeping her from doing needed paper work. She would have skipped lunch or had it sent in, but the advertising manager of a big Boston department store was in town, and she was taking him to lunch. When he arrived at noon, Beverly was just finishing her check of the ad schedule for the remainder of the week. She picked up her gloves and bag and was about to leave when the phone rang one more time.

"Lynn, will you take this? Tell them I've gone to lunch." As she stuck her head through the door into Lynn's office, she saw Lynn was not there. She must have gone on an errand; she was not scheduled to leave for lunch until one. The phone rang again, and with a glance of apology at her guest, she answered it.

"What?" As she listened, horror seized her. "Oh, no." In another moment, she hung up, stunned.

"Bad news?" Mr. Leach, the visiting manager, looked sympathetic.

"Horrible," Beverly said. The rabbits had not arrived. They were not on board the ship, which had arrived the night before as scheduled, and the Captain had no knowledge of them. It was clear that, in order to put a stop to the frantic cables from Mayfield's, the manufacturer must have simply said they were arriving when they were not. "Lynn," Beverly said distractedly again, going to the door. Then she remembered that Lynn was not there. She went on through Lynn's office to where Cathy Eads sat languidly twisting her necklace and examining the Mayfield's ads in the morning papers.

"Cathy, the rabbits aren't coming in time for Easter. That ad for tomorrow has to be canceled immediately. You'll have to do it, I'm just leaving for lunch. Tell the papers to run the Saturday color ads instead. They have them."

"All right," Miss Eads said. Something in her tone made Beverly pause.

"Just a minute. I'll give you a memo on it."

"That won't be necessary," Miss Eads said.

Without answering her, Beverly went back to her own office, scribbled the memo, and slapped the carbon in her desk drawer. "Here," she said to Miss Eads, who had followed her.

There was a knock at the door. "Mrs. Connors, could I see you for a minute?" Mr. Chapman, the copywriter, asked, sticking his head in.

"Can it possibly wait until I get back from lunch? I have a guest."

"Oh, sure. Sorry."

"Mr. Leach, shall we go before anything else happens?" Beverly said.

"What time will you be back?" Miss Eads asked. Her black eyes sized up Mr. Leach as she spoke in a manner that made him adjust his glasses self-consciously.

"One-fifteen or one-thirty," Beverly called, going out the door. "And be sure you kill those rabbit ads right away."

Friday morning, the blow fell. She was in the usual morning conference with the copy chiefs, the art and advertising managers, and the production managers when the phone rang. It was the buyer for the toy department.

"What's going on? We're getting calls for those rabbits that didn't come in."

Beverly's heart stopped. She had not yet had time to scan the morning papers. "Just a minute." She whipped them open now. Yes. The ad was there, of course, in both papers. The bunny gazed out at her wistfully, appealingly. Damn that Cathy Eads. "There's been a mistake," she said into the phone. "I'll have to call you back," and she hung up on the angry protests of the toy buyer.

Cathy Eads smiled faintly as Beverly strode into her office. She must have been expecting me all morning, Beverly thought. "Well?" she demanded.

Miss Eads's eyes opened wide. "Well what?"

"I told you to kill those ads yesterday."

Miss Eads's eyes opened even wider, registering surprise. "No you didn't, Mrs. Connors."

Beverly gasped. Somehow she had not expected such a bald-faced lie. "Yes, I did," she said slowly, shaking her head, "and furthermore, I gave you a memo on it."

"No, you didn't, Mrs. Connors." The eyes were now registering injury as well as astonishment.

Before Beverly could reply, the phone rang in her own office. "Mrs. Connors, what's going on?" Mr. Ladd's voice said. "That rabbit ad's in the papers today even though you learned yesterday morning that they weren't coming in. The toy department's going crazy. The manager just called me."

Beverly took a deep breath. "Mr. Ladd, maybe I'd better come and see you."

As soon as she walked into Mr. Ladd's office, she began her story. In spite of her anger, she did not accuse Cathy Eads of any but this one misdemeanor. Mr. Ladd listened silently, tapping a pencil on his blotter and chewing the corner of his lip.

When she had finished, he picked up the phone. "Ask Cathy Eads to come to my office immediately."

Miss Eads arrived still projecting hurt and astonishment. Beverly noted that Mr. Ladd stood up when Cathy came in, as he had not for her.

"Would you repeat to Miss Eads what you have just told me?" he asked Beverly.

When Beverly had finished, Miss Eads looked at her sadly. "I knew you were jealous of me, Mrs. Connors, but I did not think you would do a thing like this. I thought you were a nice person."

"I am a nice person," Beverly snapped, "or I would

have complained to Mr. Ladd about you long before this. The fact is, I've been far too generous."

Miss Eads turned to Mr. Ladd with the countenance of a sorrowing Madonna. "It is always like this with me. Always. The women, they try to hurt me—"

"Oh, nonsense," Beverly interrupted, her voice rising.

"Ladies, please," said Mr. Ladd.

Beverly rose. "If you'll excuse me a minute, Mr. Ladd, I'll get the carbon I kept of the memo in question. That's the quickest way to prove who's telling the truth."

She was halfway back to her office before the sickening thought struck her. Then she trotted, almost ran, to her desk and jerked open the top drawer. It was gone, of course. She stared at the little pile of carbons in the paper clip and remembered putting that particular one on top yesterday. She had been in a hurry, so she had not slid it under the clip but had placed it on top. Now it had disappeared.

She remembered Cathy Eads standing in the doorway, watching her. Had she known before that, or hadn't she, that Beverly kept carbons on the memos? She remembered, too, going to lunch without locking her desk because she did not want to keep Mr. Leach waiting.

Slowly she went back to Mr. Ladd's office.

"Well?" Mr. Ladd asked impatiently.

"It isn't there. Someone's taken it."

Cathy Eads gave him a quick look of triumph.

"Women in business," Mr. Ladd said, frowning. "This is the sort of thing that happens. You may go, Miss Eads."

When he and Beverly were alone, there was a short silence. "You realize, of course, Mrs. Connors, how much embarrassment this mistake is going to cause Mayfield's. Every customer who wants one of those rabbits and doesn't get it is going to feel ill toward the whole store." He looked annoyed. "For that matter, the rabbits have been a headache from the start."

"Yes, Mr. Ladd," Beverly said quietly. She realized that, irrational as it was to blame her for the rabbit's delayed arrival, that was exactly what Mr. Ladd and everybody else would do. Especially now. Human nature was like that, and it was futile to expect it to be otherwise. She bit her lip and waited.

"Up until now, I've been quite pleased with the way the Easter campaign was going. However, this makes it clear that you've bitten off a little more than you can chew." He paused. "That, however, does not disgust me as much as your attempt to put the blame for your negligence on Miss Eads. A good executive, Mrs. Connors, knows how to accept the consequencs of his mistakes as well as the rewards of his successes."

Beverly's eyes flashed. "I'm only sorry that you see fit to take Miss Eads's words instead of mine," she spoke through her teeth, not caring if he saw through her facade to the anger pulsing underneath.

"What else can I do? You claimed to have a copy of the memo in question, you failed to produce it."

"My only mistake is my honesty."

Mr. Ladd looked at her questioningly.

"If I were a little more devious, I might have taken time in my office just now to produce a carbon copy of a memo like the one I discovered missing, mightn't I?"

Mr. Ladd stared hard at her. "Yes, you might have. Unless the idea didn't occur to you until just now?"

Beverly got to her feet. Her knees were shaking with anger, but they held her up. "Will that be all?"

"That will be all," Mr. Ladd responded crisply. "For now."

She walked blindly back to her office, ignoring the stares and whispers that followed her through the department. She got her coat and picked up a pile of ads. "I'm going to take these to the printer myself," she told Lynn. "Then I'm going on some other errands. I won't be back today."

WIVES AND LOVERS

"Is there anything I can do?" Lynn asked anxiously. Her round face was full of affectionate concern.

"No," Beverly said briefly. "I'll see you Monday." She wondered how much Lynn knew of what had happened, but she did not feel like staying to discuss it. All she wanted to do was get out of the building.

In the car, she forced herself to control her rage. She did not want to have an accident. If she put her mind firmly on other things for a while, in time she would be calm enough to figure out what to do next. The injustice of it was so staggering she could not cope with it for the moment. All those weeks of hard work canceled out by this one incident. Then the thought struck her, If I leave Mayfield's under a cloud, they won't be likely to give me a good reference for a job elsewhere either. Her face flushed, and she set her jaw.

"Well, hello," Shorty said in delighted surprise when she arrived at the printer's. "How's my girlfriend? Haven't seen you in weeks."

Beverly smiled, grateful for a friendly face. "I know. I've been too busy. Besides, I—don't have the same job I used to."

"No kidding? Got a promotion, I bet."

"Sort of," Beverly said. Hanging onto the smile suddenly became an effort. "It's nice to see you again." She laid the ads on the counter.

"Nice to see you." He eyed her in a way that was fatherly and appraising at the same time. "Putting on a little weight, I see."

"Yes," Beverly replied.

Shorty chuckled. "That's my girl. Not like those skinny models." As she started for the door, he called after her. "Come back soon. Don't be such a stranger."

"Okay." She had a sudden memory of herself coming here as Miss Bigelow's assistant. Those carefree days seemed like part of another life. If she ever had occasion to come here again now, it would be a wonder.

She did the other errands she had downtown, and then she drove home to pick up Belinda and take her to the doctor.

"Do you think he'll let me walk now, Mother? Do you?" Belinda asked, bouncing up and down on the car seat, cast and all.

"If everything's all right, yes. Today's the day."

"Oh, boy." Belinda rolled her upper lip up to her nose as she always did when she pleased. "And Daddy has the crutches done."

"And Monday you can start back to school," Beverly said.

"It's about time. I'm sure getting lonesome."

The doctor had good news for them. "The leg seems to be knitting properly. I think we can let you have some crutches now."

"Daddy's made me some," Belinda said importantly.

"Oh? Well, that's fine." To Beverly he added, "Have her take it easy at first. Getting used to crutches is a strain on the arm muscles. Don't let her overdo it."

"I won't," Beverly replied.

As they drove home, the tension that had been building in Beverly all day seemed to increase still more. What was she going to tell Bob? That the budding executive had goofed and was about to lose her job entirely? She remembered the taunts of the past and pressed her lips together. He would almost certainly be, secretly, a little pleased. He would be glad she'd stubbed her toe. People who weren't making it themselves were always glad when somebody else tried and failed. Well, she couldn't take that just now. She would postpone telling him until the blow actually fell, which would probably be Monday. All weekend she would be an actress and pretend nothing was wrong. Tonight, tired and depressed as she was, that would not be easy. Perhaps if they went out to cocktails and dinner.

Bob was already there when they arrived, lying on

the sofa with his shoes off. "Hi. How's the girl executive?"

She looked at him sharply, but he was grinning good-naturedly and there was no sarcasm in his expression. "Fine," she said warily.

"What's wrong?"

"Nothing." She tried for a bright smile. "Why?"

"I don't know. You seem a little tense."

"Just tired." As she went to the bedroom to take off her coat, she was annoyed with herself. A fine actress she was. She'd better call Dana for some instructions.

"Daddy! The doctor says I can go on crutches now," Belinda was saying in the living room.

"Great," Bob said. "They're all done. We'll try them right after dinner, okay?"

"Now! Now! Oh please, Daddy, now!"

"Okay, okay. I'll go get them."

Beverly went back into the living room. "Bob, could we go out to dinner tonight? I'm too tired to cook."

"Sure. We'll celebrate Belinda's promotion. You got any money?"

"I thought you were going to the bank today."

"I didn't get around to it."

Beverly opened her purse. "I only have five or six dollars. That's not enough to eat any place decent."

"We'll get a hamburger somewhere."

"All right," Beverly said, sighing. "Let's have a drink here first."

As she went to the kitchen to make them, she felt unreasonably disappointed. It was the end of the day now, and weariness, depression, anger, and a bitter sense of injustice had tightened into a hard knot inside of her. It would have been nice to go somewhere restful for cocktails and a leisurely dinner, somewhere dark and soothing. It would have made it easier to play her role. Tomorrow, after a good night's rest, it would not be so hard, but tonight . . . She sighed again, getting out the ice cubes. He didn't get to the bank. Well, all right, he didn't get there. That was nothing to be resentful about. Even as she struggled with the resentment, however, she realized that it came from something deeper. What she really resented was having to play a role for Bob, having to pretend there was nothing wrong when everything was. If only she could trust him to be sympathetic and understanding about what had happened. She made the drinks strong.

"Here they are," Bob said, back in the living room with the crutches.

"Oh, boy," Belinda said.

"Take it easy. Don't slip. Beverly? Come here for the debut."

"Coming," Beverly said. She put the glasses on a tray and walked into the living room just as Belinda started hesitantly off on the crutches.

"Oh, boy!" Belinda shouted, her voice shrill with joy. "They work!"

Suddenly there was a sharp crack of splitting wood, and the next second Belinda was on the floor, screaming.

Beverly slammed the tray onto a table and ran to her. "Belinda! Are you all right?"

"They broke," Belinda sobbed, her face twisted.

"My God." Bob was standing absolutely still, paralyzed with shock.

Kneeling beside Belinda, Beverly turned on him, the rage she had kept under control all day bursting out violently. "You idiot! You stupid idiot! Can't you ever do anything right?"

"I . . . I made them out of light wood so they wouldn't be too heavy for her to manage—"

"Fine! Balsa wood, I suppose! Something sturdy like that!"

"My God." He looked bewildered, and horrified. "My God, I never thought—"

"That's just it!" Beverly was so furious she shook. "You never do think! Why don't you just give up?"

"Mother, I'm all right," Belinda said in a trembling

voice. "I don't think I broke anything."

Beverly turned back to her. "Are you sure?"

"I was just scared," Belinda said.

"Come on, put your arm around my neck," Beverly said gently. "I'll help you to the sofa."

As she settled Belinda against the cushions and wiped the tears from her face, Beverly's rage subsided a little. "My goodness, you really gave us a scare."

"They broke," Belinda said. Her eyes filled with tears again.

"That's all right. We'll go out tomorrow and get you some regular ones. That's what we should have done in the first place."

"I wanted to use Daddy's," Belinda said. It was odd how heartbroken a child could sound over a trifle.

The front door slammed, and a moment later, Beverly heard Bob's car start. The noise gave her a curious feeling of apprehension. "Daddy's upset," she said slowly. "I think we're going to have to go out to dinner by ourselves."

They had a drive-in dinner and went to a drive-in movie afterward. By the time it was over, Beverly was feeling thoroughly contrite. She shouldn't have spoken to Bob so sharply. He had been so proud of making the crutches. If only she hadn't been so upset by what had happened at the office. She would have to tell him about it now, she realized. Maybe it was the best thing to do, anyway. She hoped he would still be awake by the time they got home.

His car was not in the garage, she was disappointed to see as they drove up. She unlocked the front door wearily, thinking how empty the house always seemed when she came home and he was out. Tired as she was, she would wait up for him, she decided. Take a nice hot bath, and then read in bed until . . . As she walked into the bedroom, she was seized with the conviction that something was wrong even before her eyes told her what it was. The drawers of Bob's chest were open and emptied, a vacant hole gaped in the wardrobe where his clothes usually hung.

She looked around stupidly. A sheet of lined notebook paper leaned limply against the lamp on her chest of drawers. Of course. People always left notes under these circumstances, didn't they? She picked it up. The message was short and to the point.

"I'm taking your advice and giving up," it said. "Lots of luck. You're a better man than I am, Gunga Din."

Twenty-two

There are no clearly defined seasons in California; spring drifts into summer, and summer is sometimes never followed by winter, but turns to a days-old spring that melts into summer again. In April there is always a brief spell of premature summer in Los Angeles, and for a week or so heaters are turned on in swimming pools, tans are begun which will fade to nothing in the endless fogs of May and June, and even on weekdays the beaches fill with sun lovers at liberty —mothers with preschool children, the old pensioners who live in the shore towns of Venice and Ocean Park, and those young men, blank of face and splendid of physique, who mysteriously never seem to have anything to do in the daytime.

On a hot Saturday morning in the midst of one of these spells, Vivian and Dana lay on their backs in the sand, skin ritually bared and oiled. It was only eleven o'clock, and the beach was not yet crowded. At their feet small, dirty waves broke steeply with an abrupt slap on the hard, damp sand, and beyond the waves the green Pacific sparkled silently in the sunshine. In the direction in which their heads pointed, buff-colored cliffs rose against the morning sky, and below them trucks rumbled along the Coast Highway, their air brakes hissing as they stopped for the signal at Sunset. Vivian lay flat, her eyes covered by little plastic cups attached to each other by a nosepiece. Dana, propped up on her elbow, gazed somberly down the length of her own body to where Jeremy was dragging a necklace of yellow-brown seaweed along the edge of the water.

"I don't know what's going to happen," Dana was saying, keeping her voice low. "It's dreadful. We hardly speak to each other. I can't believe he's going to stick by what he said."

"When do you leave?" Vivian asked.

"Next weekend. If I'm going. Oh, I don't know why I say that. I have to go now. I can't let him adopt this chauvinist attitude with me. It's too—barbaric."

"Will you take Jeremy?"

"Of course. I wouldn't dream of being separated from him for three months. I'll have lots of time in New York when we can be together, and when I'm working I'll get somebody to come in and look after him."

"What does Don say about that?"

"We haven't discussed it. We've hardly talked at all since the night he issued his ultimatum." She picked up a handful of sand and threw it down on the smooth, glistening surface a wave had just washed. In an instant, another wave came and melted it away. "The dreadful thing is, I can see his point. Of course he doesn't want me gone all that time. But I have to do it. I can't help myself, I just have to."

"You're going to divorce Don," Vivian said.

"Oh, no."

"Of course you are. You've outgrown him. There's nothing else for you to do."

"Oh, God," Dana murmured.

"And when you do, do you know what I think? You should learn to live without men. Or at least, in the same degree that they can live nicely without us. When's the only time they really need us? In bed. All right. You play it that way, too. It will save you a lot of time, trouble, and litigation in the future, and you can concentrate better on your career."

Dana said nothing. The twin furrows of a frown

appeared above the nosepiece of her dark glasses, and she rubbed the bottom of one foot absently across the instep of the other, getting sand on it.

Vivian stretched lazily. The air was still, and the sun beat down insistently, penetrating her cotton bathing suit, warming her very organs. I want someone, she thought. Right now. If Dana weren't here, I'd look for one of those muscular, willing beach bums. The imperious quality of her desire pleased her obscurely. It reminded her of the priestesses of the fertility goddess in the days before Rome who threw men down in the furrows of the spring fields and rode them astride like stallions. If she had a man right now she would take him in just that way, fiercely, ruthlessly. The masculine way.

After Sid left her, she had made a resolution. There was going to be no more weak, feminine involvements. Give the body, but keep the heart free had been her motto ever since Joe. Unfortunately, it had not been easy to achieve. Love and tenderness kept welling up and getting in the way in spite of her efforts to sublimate them—no, it was the reverse of sublimation—into pure lust. She had been upset about Sid, so much that it frightened her. For three days she had stayed home from work, drinking brandy in her apartment, not eating, not sleeping, not answering the phone. At the end of the third day, she caught a glimpse of herself in the mirror. Haggard, disheveled, red-eyed from liquor and lack of sleep, she looked ten years older, and the sight sobered her like a slap. Feminine pride came to her rescue, and she took a long, hot shower followed by a cold one, combed her hair, powdered her nose, and went out for a hamburger and black coffee, since there was nothing in the refrigerator. Sitting in the restaurant, she began to take an objective view of things. Clearly a change in her design for living was indicated. If she couldn't have a steady boyfriend without getting emotionally involved, she would just have to play the field for now on.

Safety in numbers. It was stupid not to have thought of it before. After all that was the way men did it. Some of them even made it a rule never to take a girl out more than three times. That was how they stayed clear of entanglements, and she saw no reason why it wouldn't work for her as well. For the first time, she felt she understood the psychology of the femme fatale. She was simply a woman who took the masculine approach to sex. Conquests. Love 'em and leave 'em. As long as you kept the upper hand, you couldn't get hurt. As she sat thinking about it, she began to smile. It could be rather like a game. Yes, it might be fun to see how destructive one could be. How pleasant to think of some man crying into his little pillow over you instead of the other way around. How satisfying to leave a trail of bleeding hearts and battered egos after having been the victim yourself so damn many times. She had gone back to work the following day, and had begun her little project at once.

"What time did you say you had to leave?" Dana asked.

"About three. I have a dinner date at six, and I have to wash the sand out of my hair and all that jazz first."

Dana sighed. "I was hoping you could come back and have dinner with us. It might relieve the strain a little. Who's your date with?"

"Adams. My city editor."

"Isn't he married?"

"Yes. His wife's out of state looking after her sick father."

"Is that a good idea? Dating a married man again?"

"Now don't be stuffy. It's nothing serious. He's been giving me the eye for a long time, so I just thought I'd give him a break. He's been married for centuries and has four kids."

"Is he unhappy with his wife?"

"Oh, I don't think so," Vivian said, yawning. "Just bored. He thinks I'm terribly young and vital and all that crap."

"Who else are you seeing these days?"

"Just little Tim Dodd."

"Who's he?"

"The copy boy."

Dana stared. "You're joking. You mean that kid with the pimples?"

"He's charming," Vivian said, unperturbed.

"But how old is he?"

"Nineteen."

"Good Lord! Eleven years younger than we are?"

"For heaven's sake, Dana, I'm not going to marry him. I'm just—introducing him to life. Haven't you ever seen any French movies?"

"And how does he like being introduced to life?"

"He thinks I'm the most beautiful woman who ever lived, and he'll never meet anybody like me again."

"Suppose he and Adams find out about each other?"

Vivian laughed, letting it sound nasty, and rubbed her back on the warm sand like a cat. "Maybe they'll fight a duel. Typewriters at ten paces."

As she dressed for dinner with Adams that night, she was in an agreeable frame of mind. He was turning out to be one of her more interesting lovers. Tough, intelligent, fifteen years older than she, he was completely baffled by her, a state of affairs which she found infinitely amusing, particularly in view of the fact that he was an experienced woman-chaser.

Getting on intimate terms with him had been simple. She had said nothing. She merely let her eyes rest on his face an instant too long once or twice when he was giving her assignments. Then one day when they had passed each other in one of the narrow aisles in the composing room, she had come unnecessarily close, brushing him with her body. That same afternoon he asked her out for a drink after work. Twisting the short glass of Scotch and ice in his big hands, playing it safe, he asked warily, "What are you doing for laughs these days?"

"Nothing," she said, deliberately looking him in the eye, waiting.

"Nothing? A good-looking woman like you?"

She shrugged negligently. "I'd rather watch TV than go out with someone who bores me."

He took two cigarettes out, lit them, handed her one. "Do I bore you?" he asked matter-of-factly, knowing the answer.

She shook her head, her eyes on him, smiling a little.

He stood up abruptly, pushing the table back.

"Where are you going?" she asked.

"To call home. I'm taking you to dinner."

It was, of course, convenient that his wife happened to be out of town just now, Vivian reflected. However, when she got back they would still find ways to see each other. Adams was not a man who spent a lot of time at home in any case. If he wasn't with a woman, he was boozing it up at the Press Club or playing late, late poker with a select group of disreputable professional cronies.

The doorbell rang, and she strolled out to answer it.

"Hi." Adams handed her a brown paper bag. "Brought you a present."

She opened the bag and took out a bottle of Scotch. "Lovely. I have trouble keeping enough in stock with you around."

He laughed, a room-warming baritone rumble that Vivian found enormously attractive because it suited him so well. He was a big man, awkward and slow as a bear, with shaggy brown hair and a pair of arresting blue eyes. Their depths held a warm gleam that had a dancing charm all its own. Awareness of his sexual magnetism quivered pleasantly along her nerve ends. He put his hands on her shoulders, and they were like paws even when he was trying to be gentle. It took a tremendous force of will to pull her gaze from his roughly hewn features, but Vivian succeeded in doing so.

"Want a drink now?" she asked.

"Yeah, but let's go to a bar. I feel like going to a bar."

"Oh?" Vivian said. Still holding the bottle, she put her arms around his neck and fitted herself wickedly against him, breasts, belly, thighs.

When he pulled back to look at her, to make sure, she kissed him, a provocative, invitational kiss that promised more than it gave. Still he hesitated, so she kissed him again, stepping up the voltage. This time she felt him quiver all over, like a machine that has just been turned on.

"Come on," he said gruffly, and pulled her toward the bedroom.

Following him, she smiled in inward satisfaction. How beautifully he responded. She had made it a rule that if he wanted to make love immediately when he arrived, she would not, but if he didn't seem to be thinking of it, she seduced him. So far she had not failed in exercising her power.

Afterward, as they lay side by side having a cigarette, she found him looking at her speculatively.

"What's wrong?" she asked.

"Nothing. I just can't figure you out."

"You never dreamed I was so sexy," she said, teasing.

"I never dreamed you were so—available."

"Disappointed?"

"Hell, no. Surprised, that's all. I thought you were —oh, like a volcano in a cold country. Plenty of fire down below, but first you have to climb six glaciers to get there."

"And you didn't think it was worth the trouble."

"I would now. Believe me." He turned on his side to reach for her, but she rolled quickly off the bed and stood looking down at him.

"Let's go have dinner, Adams. I'm starved."

With Tim, the copy boy, she wielded her power in a different way by never letting him know until the last minute whether she was going to see him or not. Her behavior was partially dictated by necessity. She was more interested in seeing Adams, and he could not always get away. She kept her evening more or less open for him, and if he was unavailable, and she still felt like seeing someone, she gave Tim the sign. Usually she did not know until around five, and Tim, who was technically off at three-thirty since he came in at six-thirty in the morning, took to hanging around the extra hour and a half in hopes of getting a date with her.

Nobody in the office knew Adams was interested in her, but everybody knew Tim was. He hovered gawkily like a hungry crane waiting for crumbs. He emptied her ashtray three times an hour, made special trips to the composing room to bring her proofs, and blushed every time she spoke to him. He even took to wearing a tie and a clean white shirt every day, which got him kidded unmercifully by every reporter and rewrite man in the place. Shy as he was, he took in manfully and never bragged to anyone that he was actually dating Vivian, since she had asked him not to on the grounds that everyone would disapprove of the difference in their ages.

He had been virgin when they began seeing each other. Vivian had suspected it, but she had not known for sure until the first time he made love to her. Afterward, he had lain with his head turned away from her for such a long time that she finally reached out and touched his face. It was wet with tears.

"Whatever is the matter?" she asked in astonishment.

He was embarrassed. "I'm sorry. I guess it's just relief. I was so afraid I—wouldn't be able to or something. That happens sometimes. I've heard about it. I would've killed myself if I'd—failed you."

"Oh, come on," Vivian said gently, wiping his cheeks with her fingertips. "It's not that important. If you've heard about it happening a lot, you must know that."

"It would've been important to me." He turned his face away again. "You see, I've never done this before."

"Done what? Made love, you mean?"

He nodded. "I guess I'm backward or something. Not that I'm afraid of girls. It's not that. But I was afraid of . . ." He stopped.

"Of what?"

"Of getting involved, I guess. Of caring too much. I—well, you see, I'm pretty intense."

"I see."

"I knew that—well, not only that I couldn't sleep with a girl I didn't love, but that if I did sleep with her, I'd love her more than ever. I'd be gone, that's all. I'd just be gone." He took Vivian's hand. "And I am," he said in a low voice.

She was disturbed. This was only their third date. She had not expected so much emotion so fast, and the revelation found her strangely vulnerable. It was difficult not to respond to love, she would have to act quickly.

She reached out and turned on the light. "Now you listen to me. I'm not in love with you, and I'm not going to be. I like you, and I think you're a nice boy, and that's about it. Furthermore, I don't want you to love me. I doubt if you really do, but I don't want you thinking you do just because I'm the first girl you've been to bed with. Pull yourself together, Tim, and do it right now. We can have a lot of fun together if nobody gets serious. But only if nobody does. Understand?"

"No." The look he gave her was straight and a little angry. "What do you want to sleep with me for if you only just like me?"

"I don't know. Well, maybe I do, but it's too complicated to explain. You'll just have to take my word for it."

"I see. And supposing I don't want to play it that way?"

"Then there's no game at all," Vivian said firmly. "I'm sorry to sound so brutal, but I think we'd better get everything straight right from the start."

For a long time, he said nothing. His body, young and thin and beach-tanned, white where his trunks had been, looked exposed, unprotected. Not used to a woman's eyes, Vivian thought, and felt a strange little twinge of compassion. He rested his head on one arm, eyes downcast, and she could tell nothing from his expression.

"Okay," he said finally. "If that's the way you want it."

"Good," Vivian said briskly.

He looked up at her. "Only, would you please stop sounding like a schoolteacher or something?"

"All right." She smiled and held her arms out to him.

"I think I better go home now." Not looking at her, he got up and began putting on his clothes.

After he left, Vivian lay awake thinking about him for a long time. The episode had nearly moved her, but she had handled it well and forcefully, she thought. Maybe too forcefully. When he'd had a chance to think it over, he might not come back. That would be too bad because he was very sweet, and furthermore, he made a nice contrast to Adams.

The next morning, she wore one of her most becoming outfits to work, a blue linen suit, and a black silk blouse. He took one quick look at her as she walked in, and then kept his eyes resolutely away the rest of the day, although he emptied her ashtray and brought her proofs as usual. Neither of them spoke. When three-thirty came, he left the city room abruptly, still without glancing at her, and she felt a slight sag of disappointment. Bending her head, she concentrated fiercely on her work. In a few minutes, she saw out of the tip of her eye that someone was standing beside her desk. She looked up.

"Are you doing anything tonight?" Tim asked. His

face looked fresh, as though recently in contact with water, and his hair was wetly combed. Clearly he had been no farther than the men's room.

Vivian sat back in her chair. She was not busy that evening, but she had no intention of seeing him. He must be punished for not speaking to her all day. "I'm not sure," she said. "Could you wait around until five, and I'll let you know then?"

And so, by keeping herself free, she made both of them prisoners in a manner of speaking. Adams was not in love with her, she knew, but he spent a remarkable amount of time with her considering that he had a wife, and Tim was openly devoted. Still, there was something missing from her life. She debated it, drinking brandy and watching an old Taylor movie on television one of the rare nights she stayed home alone. She was not as happy as she had expected to be when she started playing the field. Sometimes, in spite of her two admirers, she felt strangely depressed, almost despairing. Well, there was only one cure for that. Live it up a little more.

Twenty-three

It was a long drive to the airport, but neither of them spoke. Dana sat tight against the car door, holding Jeremy against her and as far from his father as possible. Her stomach was knotted so tightly that it was difficult even to breathe, but she felt if she tried to relax it she would become physically ill. Besides, that rigid mass of muscle was the center, the focal point, of a fight for self-control so desperate that it occupied her entire being.

"Mama," Jeremy said, breaking abruptly into the taut silence. "Are you going on a jet?"

"Yes. A jet. All the way to New York."

"Why can't I come?"

"I've already told you, dear. Because Daddy would be lonesome. He wants you to stay here and keep him company." She did not look at Don. *Yes. Daddy wants you here so much that he got a court order to keep you. An order restraining me from taking you out of the state.*

"Who will keep you company?"

"Your mother has work to do. She doesn't need anybody." Don's voice, as he spoke, sounded utterly emotionless and impersonal.

"Maybe later on, Daddy will bring you to New York for a visit," Dana said. Out of the corner of her eye, she saw Don glance quickly, angrily in her direction. They had agreed not to bring this subject up. Don had already refused to come East, but she felt compelled to reassure her son as well as herself. She could not bear to think they were going to be separated for three months.

Silently Jeremy pressed himself closer to her, and she gave him a little squeeze and looked resolutely out the window, fighting back tears.

It had degenerated finally, shockingly, into a power struggle between her and Don. She had not recognized it until the night, a week before she left, when she had told Don that she planned to take Jeremy with her.

"No, you're not," he had said matter-of-factly, maddeningly calm.

The flat tone of finality which he had used more and more often in the past few months made her want to hit him, but she mastered herself and said reasonably, "Don, a child his age needs to be with his mother."

"You should have thought of that before you took the job. You are not taking my son away from me." As he spoke, he worked industriously at lighting his pipe, seeming to devote only second place in his attention to their discussion. It was, Dana suddenly began to see, a favorite ploy of his, another of the devices he used to maintain psychological control over those around him.

Instantaneously, fury seized her, "Yes, I am taking him—" she began hotly, but he cut her off.

"I thought you might insist." He did not smile, but triumph seemed almost to emanate from him. Then he told her about the court order.

At first, she was too stunned to speak. She could not have been more astonished if he had suddenly unmasked himself as a homosexual or a Soviet spy. "You're a bastard," she burst out, anxious to try and send him as far away as possible from her, so that she could go and lick her wounds in private.

"Don't be dramatic," Don said drily.

"You are." Then another thought came. "Do you love us, Jeremy and me, only because you can control us? And when you can control us?"

He had not answered.

From that time on, she had seen him in a new depth and dimension, seen him as he really was for the first time since their marriage. This new image shocked and fascinated her. It was as though all these years she had been mistaking a lighted scrim for the actual set, and then suddenly the lighting had been changed so that she saw through the scrim into the reality behind it. Don was, she now felt, one of those people whose real pleasure in life is the manipulation of other human beings, not solely for personal advantage to gain but for the rich sense of power to be derived from it. He did it at work, intimidating the men under him in a dozen subtle ways. He had done it at school, too, undoubtedly. The big man on campus. She had not known him then, but she had heard all about his successes in college politics, and she could imagine him managing the callow adolescents around him like a young aristocrat, suave but authoritative, using the good looks, the friendly hand on the back, the impressive reserve of manner to control first his fraternity, then his class, then the whole campus. Probably he had done it as a child. It must have been easy, Dana thought, remembering his sweet, rather vague-headed mother, his genial, preoccupied doctor father. She wondered about his brother, whom she had never met and whom Don rarely mentioned. What had happened between them that they never even wrote? She felt a small chill. What had Don seen in her, she wondered in the light of this new insight into his character, and what had he offered her so dazzling that it had blinded her and obscured her vision of him until now?

He played life like a chess game, constantly seeking new opponents. Unwittingly, by opposing her will to his, she had become one of them, and cunningly he was using Jeremy as a pawn against her. Now it was her move. Pride would have kept her from retreating even if the needs of her own nature had not been so deeply involved. She went ahead with her plans to leave.

They were nearly at the airport. "See the airplanes, Jeremy?" she said with false brightness. Jeremy looked, but he did not react, and she felt a spasm of anguish. They had been careful, they had not quarreled in front of him, but a child's emotions are sensitive. Surely he had sensed the strained atmosphere of the past few weeks.

"I put Dr. Long's number on a card and pasted it on the wall by the phone where it's easy to see," she said to Don. Dr. Long was the pediatrician. "Also the phone and address of the closest emergency hospital to where we— to the house."

"You've told me that three times already," Don said.

"I've told Mrs. Gill, too," Dana said with a slight tremor in her voice, "but she seems absent-minded, so if you'd just remind her occasionally when you think of it?"

Mrs. Gill was the housekeeper that Don had engaged, with Dana's dubious approval. Six other women had applied before her, and none of them had seemed right. Not bright enough, not motherly enough, not conscientious—Dana had finally realized that no one was ever going to seem capable of looking after her son, no one. Time was growing short, and finally they had engaged Mrs. Gill, who was no better or worse than the others and who seemed, vaguely, not to live up to the glowing letters of recommendation she had brought with her. She had steel-rimmed glasses and a habit of sniffing every few minutes as though she were coming down with a cold. If only she's careful with him, Dana thought bleakly. A black panic gripped her whenever she pictured something happening to Jeremy during her absence. What if he fell down the hill, what if he caught something at nursery school, what if . . . The possibilities which her anxious imagination conceived were endless. And if something happened, would it be her fault, or Don's for not letting her take Jeremy with her?

She glanced at Don's immobile profile. She could not imagine how all this was making him feel. This was another source of his power, this ability to repress and conceal emotion, to maintain a maddening calm in the deepest crisis. His granitic stubbornness sent a shudder of frustration through her. There were times, now, when she almost hated him, and this was the worst of all, this terrible sense of benign love turning malignant, curdling into bitterness and a wish to hurt. Her own tendency was to express her emotions freely and fully, but she was beginning to sense dimly that the only way to fight Don was with his own weapons. So she had held herself in, and the turmoil inside her became in time a tangible, physical pain. It's a good thing I'm leaving, she thought. This is the way people get ulcers.

International Airport, the sign said, and Don turned. "Why don't you go and check in?" he said briefly. "I'll park the car."

The night are was damp and smelled of the nearby ocean. She walked into the lighted, crowded, bustling terminal with a growing, bewildered wonder that this could actually be happening. To combat the peculiar sense of unreality which seemed to be overtaking her, she concentrated studiously on what she had to do. First, check in at the airline counter; then the insurance. She took out twenty-five thousand dollars' worth in Jeremy's name with the distinct awareness that nothing was going to happen to the plane. She had a destiny, but that was not it. Something else was in store for her.

They had left the house at the latest possible moment; she had seen to that. She wanted no extra time at the airport. The flight was called just as Don and Jeremy came in from the parking lot.

"Will you write and tell me how you're all getting along?" she asked.

Don gazed slightly over her head, his expression impenetrable.

"All right," she said tightly, past the ache in her throat. "I'll phone occasionally."

The flight call came again, the voice loud, distorted, impersonal over the public-address system, the subdued turmoil of the big room, electric with the urgency of many departures.

"Well, goodbye," Don said, and held out his hand. He looked directly at her for what seemed the first time in weeks, but his eyes were expressionless.

"Don." Suddenly, helplessly, she was crying, the tears overflowing and running down her cheeks, mascara stinging her eyes. "Why don't you—" She stopped. *Why don't you ask me to stay? Oh, God, and even if you did, how could I?*

"You'd better go if you want a window seat," Don said.

Unseeing, she knelt and hugged Jeremy. "Goodbye baby," she whispered. "Do what Mrs. Gills says. I'll see you soon." She stood up swiftly and looked once more at Don. *If he would soften just a little,* she thought wildly, *if he would just unbend that terrible iron will . . . but he won't. And neither will I.* "Don't come with me to the plane," she said, and turning, ran, fled from them both blindly.

So it was done. After the takeoff, separated, isolated from the earth and the realities thereof by the blessed emptiness of space, she began, minutely, to relax. As she did so, the conviction grew in her that, difficult and painful though it was, she had done the right thing. "This above all, to thine own self be true," she had written in her college notebook as a motto, and now it came back to her. She had not realized then how much being true to oneself entailed. At the time, it had seemed that anything that sounded so right must be easy to achieve.

When did maturity begin and what did it consist of?

There had been a time when she had naively assumed that it was automatically conferred on anyone old enough to have a home, a family, a job. She had felt herself an adult when she had married Don and borne Jeremy, but those events, significant as they were, were only way stations, she realized now. The goal was still somewhere ahead of her; perhaps it was merely an abstract ideal like perfection, never to be fully achieved. She was thirty years old, yet only in the past few months had she begun to grasp who she was and what she was meant to be.

The stewardess came down the aisle swaying, sure-footed, moving with the unconscious emphasis on equilibrium which people develop who walk in moving vehicles. "Would you like some coffee?"

"No, thank you," Dana said. Automatically, she turned and studied that walk, fascinated, as the stewardess went on toward the back of the plane. She walks, Dana thought, as though she is completely unaware that only a thin metal skin and thirty thousand feet of air separate her feet from solid ground, but just the same, there's a tiny segment of her mind that always remembers.

Sitting back, the walk and the attitude behind it memorized, filed away in her mental storehouse for future use, she noted, I'm doing it again. How often she had exercised this special perception of hers the past few weeks in regard to her own life and emotions. All through the agonies of decision and conflict and separation, a part of her consciousness had stood aside impersonally and observed. At first, she had found this disconcerting. It seemed somehow to cheapen and invalidate what she felt, to make of her own life merely another part she was playing. Do I never stop acting? she asked herself, appalled at what appeared to be a kind of insincerity. Behind the deeply emotional scenes through which she had just lived, the thought had constantly run, This is how it feels when you begin to hate a man you once loved, this is how it feels to have to go away and leave your child, this is how it feels to be so dedicated to what you are doing that no human being, no matter how dear, can stand in your way. Always there was the realization that someday she would play these roles in the theater, or similar ones, and when she did, the emotional fuel would be stored and ready for her.

This is how I am, she thought now, accepting it. It was how she had always been. Was it, then, a question of identity? Was that what was driving her away from the persons she loved most into the difficult pursuit of an uncertain and demanding career? She considered it for a long time and then, exhausted, with the continent passing swiftly and silently beneath her, she fell asleep.

Dan Morgan met her at the airport in New York. He kissed her on the forehead, hugged her, and then stood back and looked at her, his face reddish and affectionate as ever. "Where's Jeremy?"

"Don wouldn't let me bring him. He got a court order."

"No!" He gave her a glance of such quick compassion that Dana was reminded he was not inexperienced in just that kind of bitter domestic litigation. He took her arm. "Come on. You look exhausted. I've found a nice little apartment for you."

As they drove in, Dana looked silently at the overwhelming, legendary skyline. New York. This was the city to beat.

Dan glanced at her. "Have you ever been here before?"

"Yes. Once with my parents when I was a child, and once on a business trip with Don. Never alone before."

"It's a great town."

"Yes." She gave a strange little laugh. "The proving ground for all the nuts, isn't it? I suppose I was destined to end up here."

"What are you talking about?"

"You know, Dan. The more you have to prove, the bigger the city you look for to do it in. If you're just a little bit neurotic, Chicago will do, or San Francisco, or Los Angeles. But if you really have a point to make, then there's no place like New York, is there?"

"Do you have a point to make, Dana?"

"Yes. Yes, I'm really beginning to think I do. I'm not sure what it is yet, but I'll find out."

The apartment was just three blocks from Central Park.

"I thought it would be a good location for Jeremy," Dan said, unlocking the door. "There are two bedrooms. I didn't know whether you'd have a nurse live in."

There were two big vases of red roses in the living room.

"Oh, Dan." Dana put her hands to her face and swallowed. "This is a bad time for kindness. I'm feeling terribly—vulnerable. I may just dissolve all over you."

"I wouldn't object." He looked at her hard for a moment, but when she did not move, he went quietly about the room turning on lights. "I think it's rather pleasant here. And quiet. You'll need your sleep."

"Yes. Yes." His thoughtfulness touched her beyond words.

He finished with the lights and came back to her. "There's serious trouble between you and Don?"

"He told me if I came here, I needn't bother to come back."

Dan gave a soundless little exhalation of amazement. "But you came anyway."

"I had to." She did not feel like going into details just then. "The things that have happened—the incredible gulf that's opened between us the past two weeks. Honestly, Dan, I can hardly believe it."

"Then you're finished with each other."

"I can't bring myself to accept that just yet," Dana said slowly, "in spite of everything. Faith in love dies hard, doesn't it? I see Don in a way I never saw him before, but I think I could accept him the way he is, if he'd just accept me the way I really am. That's the way it should be, isn't it? After five years of marriage? Good Lord, how can it have taken us so long to get acquainted with each other?"

Dan smiled wryly. "It's not unusual."

"Do you know how I think marriage ought to be?" she went on, frowning. "There must be enough trust, or faith, in the relationship so that each can give the other the freedom to realize himself."

"I quite agree with you. But the people who can live together that way, without adorning each other in lovingly handwrought chains, are rare."

"And a chain's a chain, no matter how tenderly they fasten it on to you."

"Yes. And even when they assure you it's for your own good. It's a strange thing," Dan said, walking about. "But I think, in marriage, you've even got to give your partner the freedom to go the devil, if that's what he wants. When I started drinking heavily, if my wife had just left me alone, I might have stopped by myself. Yes, I'm sure I would have in time. But she couldn't do that. She pleaded, she preached, she threatened, wept, persuaded, argued, pounded me into the wall until I drank as much to escape her accusations as anything else. God knows I was conscious enough of my own inadequacies at the time. The last thing I needed was to be reminded of them in ringing tones a dozen times a day. In the end, I was so pulverized it took a whole corps of kind and loving people to assemble the bleeding fragments into a man again."

"Yet always done from the right motives. Always done out of love. These terrible, crippling things."

They were silent a moment. Outside the window, Dana could hear a taxi honk above the faint, vast rumble of the city, closer, ominously closer, than the sound of Los Angeles which reached her hilltop living room at home.

"Fortunately, you have a great deal of work to do," Dan said finally. "Better still, it's work that you love. I think you'll find the new cast exciting to work with. They're enormously capable performers who'll bring out the best that's in you." He went toward the door. "I'm going to go now and let you get some sleep. I'll call you around noon tomorrow and see if you'd like to go out and take a look around."

She followed him to the door and squeezed his hand in gratitude. "You're a good friend, Dan. I don't deserve you."

"Of course you do." He kissed her forehead again. "Sleep well. What is it, Dana? Why do you look that way?"

"Maybe he won't disappoint me," she said in a low voice. "Maybe when he realizes he can't intimidate me, he'll have more respect for me and for my work. He's an intelligent man, Dan. Maybe it will come to him, the kind of insight we've been talking about?" She looked up at him pleadingly.

Dan Morgan caught his breath. She was one of those rare women whose beauty deepens through sorrow, not happiness. He had never seen her eyes like that before, shadowed with longing, troubled by a new and painful understanding. "Maybe," he said. To himself, he thought that only the most obstinate and unperceptive of men would give up a woman like Dana so easily.

"Good night, Dan. Thank you for everything."

"Good night." He turned from her with an abruptness she did not notice and walked quickly to the elevator.

When she had closed the door behind her, she began to feel a kind of terror. For the first time in her life she was alone, without the great, overshadowing fortress of another, dominating personality at hand to shelter and protect her. She would have to prove herself as an actress now; it was all she had left. She had sacrificed everything for it. The situation had radically altered. Before, serious as she had been, she was still Mrs. Don Hurst with the financial and emotional security of a solid marriage to fall back on if her career did not work out. Now there was nothing behind her for support, and before her was this staggering, ruthless metropolis to find her place in, to win over, to impress.

Outside the open window, late as it was, the city still hummed, a voracious sound. I'm going to be fed into it, she thought faintly, reminded of the rubbish trucks at home which took the city's leavings and pulverized them with a grinding roar in the quiet of early morning. New York, from the sound and size of it, could take people and reduce them to a mass of unidentifiable debris in just the same way.

Shuddering, she closed all the windows and pulled the draperies across them. Then she undressed quickly and got into bed where she lay, heart beating frantically, curled in a tight fetal bundle with the covers pulled over her head.

Twenty-four

Monday morning, Beverly walked into the office determined that no matter what happened, she would take it like a man. She would not cry, she would not utter recriminations, she would not give Mr. Ladd the slightest opportunity to indulge in any more slurs about women executives. That much, at least, she owed herself.

Easter Sunday she had spent struggling violently with her feelings. She had cried, then, until the floor beside her bed blossomed with damp tissue papers like a scattering of white roses. She had lost her husband, and she was about to lose her job. Perhaps because of the job, she had lost Bob, and now the job was going too, and she had not even had time to tell him. She was tough, though, and by the time she had cried herself out and had a nap, her natural determination reasserted itself. Whatever happened, she would see it through, and afterward she would pick herself up quickly and go on.

So now, on Monday morning, she walked into the office with her usual efficient stride, ignoring the heads that snapped up and the eyes that stared as she made her way through the advertising department to her office.

She had hardly seated herself at her desk when Lynn came in. "Mr. Ladd wants to see you right away."

"All right." In a way, she was glad. Better to get it over with quickly, while her courage was still high.

"Good morning, Mrs. Connors. Sit down." He did not smile, and Beverly thought, He looks even less friendly than he did on Friday, if that's possible. She said good morning and waited, while he sat for a moment not looking at her, tapping his manicured fingertips together. He seemed to be having trouble finding the right phrases for what he had to say. Good, she thought grimly. At least he's uncomfortable.

"You have some good friends in this office," he said at last.

That surprised her, but she restrained herself from asking what he meant. Again she merely waited.

Mr. Ladd cleared his throat. Obviously he had expected her to open the way for him with a question. "Both Mr. Chapman and your secretary paid me visits Friday afternoon," he said. "What they told me throws an entirely different light on this entire—ah—situation." He glanced at Beverly, but realizing quickly this time that he was going to get no help from her, he continued almost at once. "News of your little difficulty with Miss Eads over the memo apparently reached Mr. Chapman, and he came to me of his own accord and told me he had heard you ask Miss Eads to cancel the ad."

"Mr. Chapman?" Beverly exclaimed, startled. Then she remembered. He had come to the office just as she was leaving for lunch with Mr. Leach from Boston.

"Shortly after his visit, your secretary came and told me the whole story of your difficulties with Miss Eads." He paused. "Tell me. What prevented you from discussing this matter with me?"

"I felt I could handle it myself," Beverly said. "I didn't think a man in your position should be bothered about a personality conflict between employees."

"Personality conflict? I think that's understating it a little, don't you?" Mr. Ladd said drily. "In any case, Miss Eads has been relieved of her duties with this organization, and you will have a new assistant as soon as we can find one. I have several possibilities in mind, but I want you to make the final choice since this time it will be more or less permanent."

"Yes, Mr. Ladd. Thank you," Beverly said, and then stared at him in astonishment as the full significance of what he had said began to dawn on her.

"It has been decided that you will be Mayfield's new publicity and advertising director," Mr. Ladd said sonorously. "As, I gather from your expression, you have just guessed. The matter has been under consideration for some time, and I was, I confess, the one most strongly opposed to it. However, you conduct in this affair with Miss Eads gives me confidence that you have the emotional stability to handle the job. Your efficiency and enterprise are, of course, already established beyond any doubt."

"There will naturally be a considerable increase in your salary," he went on. "I daresay you won't find that amiss even though, being married, you don't have to support yourself."

"No." This was not the time to reveal her marital problems to Mr. Ladd.

"Well, I guess that covers it." He stood up and held out his hand, and for the first time, he permitted himself a small smile. "Welcome to Mayfield's executive circle."

Beverly pressed his hand firmly. "Thank you. I hope I can continue to justify your confidence in me." The formal, conventional words sounded to her as though she were reciting them in a play. Surely this couldn't actually be happening?

She walked back to her office in a daze. Miss Bigelow's big desk, hers now, stood waiting for her, loaded with papers, layouts, proofs, the glass full of sharpened pencils, the telephone with its shoulder-rest attachment, all the equipment of authority. She sat down and ran her fingers along the front edge, where the nicked wood showed through white here and there under the dark mahogany stain. Hers at last. All hers. She waited for a sense of triumph, but emotion of any sort seemed oddly nonexistent within her. Thoughtfully, almost gently, she fingered the scars on the big desk, as one fingers human bruises to see how sore and tender they are.

Lynn burst in. "Excuse me, Beverly, but I just couldn't stand it a minute longer. Is everything all right?"

"I got the job," Beverly said. "I'm staying here. This is really my office now." She had hoped that saying the words would intensify her grasp of this new reality, but nothing happened.

"Oh, Beverly, I'm so glad!" Lynn pressed her hands to her cheeks and beamed between them like a child. "I went to him—did he tell you?—and told him all about that bitchy Eads. I tried to get you all Friday afternoon on the phone, but you weren't home."

"You're a great friend, going to bat for me like that," Beverly said gratefully. "You could have made yourself a lot of trouble getting into this mess."

"I don't care," Lynn said, still beaming. "I mean, I would have done it anyway to help you, but it really wouldn't have mattered whether I got into hot water or not." She paused with an anticipatory, news-imparting look. "You see, I'm quitting anyway. I'm getting married."

"Lynn!" Beverly got up, went around the desk, and hugged her. "That's wonderful! Did it just happen over the weekend?"

Lynn nodded and held out her hand, where a sparkling, tiny chip of diamond twinkled in a silver setting. "We've been talking about it a long time, but he just gave me the ring yesterday. See?"

"It's beautiful," Beverly said, examining it. "Oh, dear. You're not quitting right away, are you?"

"Not until just before the wedding. In June. Some of my friends think I should keep on till I get pregnant, for the extra income, but Jonathan doesn't want me to. He doesn't believe in wives working." There was a kind of pride in the way she said it.

"And what about you? Don't you think you'll miss Mayfield's? After all, you've been here almost as long as I have."

"Oh, I'll miss you. But after all, I can drop in here and see you sometimes and bring my kids around to show you. And as far as the rest of it's concerned," Lynn went on happily, "I've had the white-collar-girl bit. All I want from now on is to be a plain old housewife. It may not be glamorous, but it sounds great to me."

"You're lucky," Beverly said. The wistfulness in her tone made Lynn glance at her quickly.

"Beverly, you don't have to work if you don't want to, do you?"

"I didn't mean that. I mean you're lucky to feel the way you do. That it's enough just to be a wife."

"You don't feel that way, do you? No, I guess you don't. That's why you got where you are." Lynn looked thoughtful. "You know something, Beverly? I think it's wonderful you have Bigelow's job, I really do, but I don't envy you. I mean, I wouldn't want it. I wouldn't know what to do with it. I'm happier with what I'm going to have. I really am."

"Well, good," Beverly said, forcing a smile. "Then everything's worked out nicely for everybody, hasn't it?"

When she went to thank Mr. Chapman for his part in saving her job, he waved her gratitude aside vehemently. "Nice of me? Why was it nice of me? I was only doing the just thing. And I owe you a lot, Mrs. Connors. You were so helpful to me when I first came to work here that I'll never be able to repay you. You went out of your way to be kind."

"Not really," Beverly said. "It was just part of my job."

"You didn't have to take that much of your time," he said firmly. "You're a very rare person, and if you don't make you permanent head of this whole damn thing, they're crazy."

"They just did."

"They did? Well, that's just great!" Smiling, he pumped her hand with genuine enthusiasm. "I hope I'm the first to congratulate you."

"My secretary beat you to it," Beverly said, smiling back at him. "But I'm glad the two of you are first, because if it weren't for you, I'd probably be clearing my desk out this morning instead of settling at it permanently. Thank you."

"You're welcome, Mrs. Connors." He surveyed her as though she were his own personal discovery. "Now it'll really be a pleasure to work here. I hope you won't think I'm just flattering you when I say that."

"Of course not," Beverly said warmly. His sincerity was obvious, and the pleasure he was taking in her triumph kindled, at last, the expected enthusiasm in her own heart. She was glad that he worked for Mayfield's. His brown eyes behind the glasses had a sweet expression, and the way his hair fell over his forehead was really quite appealing. It's too bad he's so young, went through her mind. He was only twenty-four or twenty-five, five or six years younger than she. She did not complete the thought with any specific reason why it was too bad.

Within three weeks she was dating him. His first name was Steve, and he lived alone in an apartment in the Culver City area. His only close living relative was a married sister ten years older than he who lived in Palo Alto. He had a dog, an elderly terrier that he was very fond of, and he liked Italian restaurants and stamp collecting and taking long walks in Griffith Park. Best of all, Beverly learned to her delighted surprise, he liked Beverly Connors.

"Right from the beginning," he told her seriously after their first embrace. "Right from when I first started working at Mayfield's, I thought you were wonderful."

They were sitting in a parked car on Mullholland

Drive, and it was quarter to twelve on a Saturday night. Steve had stopped the car at the farthest edge of the road, facing the east. Turning the ignition off, he combed his fingers through his wind-rumpled hair to restore it to some semblance of order. The hush of the night seemed to spill over Beverly, the coolness of a breeze softly stirring the air. She stared at the brightness of the Los Angeles skyline.

"It seems too beautiful to be real, doesn't it?" She half glanced at Steve.

"It can be like that," he agreed, and stretched his arm along the seat top. "If an artist tried to put it on canvas, it would look artificial."

"That's true." Beverly realized that her voice was barely above a murmur and laughed softly. "Why are we talking so quietly?"

"Probably because we're the only ones here." Steve smiled. His glance swept the road ahead and behind.

His head bent toward her and she knew instinctively that he was going to kiss her. The tips of his fingers rested lightly along her jaw and the curve of her throat, holding her motionless with no pressure. Excitement danced through her senses, but Beverly willed them to stay under control.

The first brush of his lips was soft and teasing, but they came back to claim her mouth with warm ease. Beverly was hesitant to respond, unwilling to have him discover how much she wanted this, but he coaxed a response from her.

Her lips were clinging to his by the time he finally drew back a few inches to study the result. She was motionless, but inside she was straining to be closer to him. Beverly was too unsure of herself—and him—to take the initiative.

"Steve?" The rising inflection of her voice put a question mark at the end of his name. She was feeling fluttery and confused and a little guilty. After all, she was technically still married. She should never have let him bring her up here.

His mouth curved in a compelling smile that seemed to take her breath away. "Beverly, don't be cold. You're businesslike and efficient at the office, but you're not cold, are you?" Steve murmured, and started to close the distance between them again.

"No." Beverly admitted, turning her head to end the tantalizing nearness of his mouth.

It moved onto her lips with a sureness of purpose, claiming them as if it had long been his right to do so. There was no resistance to its commanding pressure. Her lips parted willingly to deepen the kiss as his hand curved itself to her spine. A heady tide of feeling seemed to swamp her, and she reeled at the whirling mist of glorious sensation. She felt drunk with his kiss.

Then there was no room for thinking, only feeling. Beverly was weightless, floating in a mindless bliss. She wasn't conscious of sinking backward onto the seat, only that her hands were now free to glide around his shoulders and curl into the thickness of his hair.

Tiny little moans of pleasure came from her throat when he nibbled sensually at her earlobe and made an intimate study of her neck and throat. The contours of his body pressed their male shape onto her flesh while the stroking caress of his hands wandered over her.

Desire seemed a natural extension of all the raw emotion his embrace was disclosing to her. It was the purest form of passion she'd ever know, and the beauty of it swelled her heart until she ached for him. The need inside her strained to be released.

His hand glided smoothly across her ribs, nearing the heated fullness of her breasts. The sensation of his hand against her breasts suddenly shocked her into an awareness of how far out of control she'd gone.

"You're wonderful," he murmured and rubbed his cheek against the lapel of her dress, pushing it back so that he could kiss the place where her breasts were pushed together by her brassiere. Burrowing his nose into the crease, he groaned.

"Steve, this is crazy," she said breathlessly. "I'm too old for you." She felt secure enough to mention it now.

He raised his head indignantly. "Age doesn't matter. It's how people feel about each other that counts." He put his head back in its former location and nuzzled some more. Beverly stiffened in a delayed attack of modesty.

"I have to go," she said at last. "I promised the baby-sitter I'd be home by one. Take me home, Steve."

"Not till you tell me when I can see you again." His boyish determination made her smile. He was really more like eighteen than twenty-five. "Tomorrow?"

"Tomorrow I'm going to spend with my little girl."

"Well, what about Monday night?"

"I can't go out during the week," she told him. "I have to be fresh for work."

"Friday then."

"All right. Friday."

He sat up and began to comb his hair, looking in the rearview mirror. "I get to see you Monday anyway at the office," he said seriously.

Eventually, she talked briefly to Bob. He wanted her to file for divorce right away, and she promised, but she did not do so. She told herself that it was because she was so busy, but the real reason was quite different. Filing would bring home to her inescapably the painful conviction that she had failed as a wife. It was all very well to count the beads of Bob's weaknesses over in her mind. He was lazy, he was careless, he was resentful and abusive to her, true, but somewhere in their marriage was a secret area in which she had been proven unfit, too, although she defiantly refused to talk about it. In this connection, Steve's attentions were a godsend. He admired her achievements in the business world, and he was attracted to her as a woman. It was the perfect balm to soothe the wound in her ego which Bob's departure had caused, and it gratified her needs. She did not stop to think what deeper motives might be involved.

His youth, which had disturbed her a little at first, came in a short time to seem a significant part of his charm. She liked his undergraduate fervor about things which interested him, his earnestness, even a certain naivete which gave him the air of an unsophisticated teen-ager. At the same time, he seemed exceptionally mature in other ways. He had no passion for cars, showing off his capacity for alcohol, or any of the other conventional status symbols of the young American male. Girls his own age bored him, he claimed. They had nothing to offer. He and Beverly sat up far into the night discussing such topics as the flaws of the American educational system, the future of labor unions, and whether or not Madonna's sex appeal was a synthetic product or the real thing. Steve maintained it was an example of inspired press agentry. "You know what? I doubt if she even likes men very much, really," he said, shaking his head wisely.

"She certainly projects sensuality," Beverly said magnanimously.

"Anybody with a shred of singing talent could learn to do that," Steve said, slipping his arm under her head.

In time, they began dating on week nights, too. Steve would come home from work with her, and while she got dinner, he would read to Belinda. When he was in the house, Belinda was not allowed to watch television. Youngsters got too much TV these days, he said. It was one of his theories. After Belinda had gone to bed, he and Beverly would sit up until ten-thirty or so, engaged in serious conversation and petting, in that order, and then he would go home. It was all rather refreshing. It had been years, Beverly realized, since she and Bob had spent any time discussing anything.

On Saturday nights they went to the movies, and on Sundays, they took a picnic to Griffith Park and lay peacefully on the grass brushing the ants off each other while Belinda happily skinned her knees while playing.

In a remarkably short time, he asked her to marry him. "I need you, Beverly," he said soberly. "I could look around forever and not find another woman like you."

She was as dazzled as she had been when Bob proposed. It always seemed miraculous to her that a man could be seriously interested in anybody as utterly lacking in glamour as she. The years of comparing her own uninspired, if pleasant, features with Sherry's exquisite beauty had left an indelible impression.

Miracles were not to be sneezed at. Weeks of flattering attention and increasing intimacy had brainwashed her of any doubts she might have entertained about his suitability as a husband, and she considered the proposal seriously. After all, she liked him a lot. She wasn't at all sure she didn't love him a little already, and she was positive she would in time. He and Belinda got along well together, and Belinda needed a man around the house. Best of all, he had convinced her that she was indispensable to him. Almost hidden behind all these encouraging reflections lay a final, half-formed inducement: Won't everybody be surprised if I marry again right away!

She accepted after thinking it over for only a week, and her suitor was overjoyed.

"We'll have to wait a year," she pointed out. "I can't take the time to go to Nevada."

"That's okay," he said, hugging her exuberantly. "I can wait."

Anchored, fortified with a new love, at last she went to court for her divorce.

The day was unusually hot for May, and smoggy. As

she waited outside the courtroom for Vivian, who was to be her witness, she noted apprehensively that she was far more nervous than she had expected to be. All through the talks with the attorney, the disagreeable meetings with Bob over the propertly settlement, she had maintained her self-possesion to what she felt was a commendable degree. Now it was really all over but the formalities. The details were decided upon, she had won custody of Belinda without difficulty, Bob would not even be present today. Taking out a handkerchief, she blotted the beads of perspiration from her upper lip and tried to calm herself by watching the throngs of people who passed to and fro in front of her in the wide corridor. Their very numbers were depressing. Are all of them here for a divorce? she wondered. Are that many marriages going down the drain on just this one morning?

"Hi," Vivian said, coming up breathlessly. She looked cool and fashionable in a slim, black cotton dress. "I thought I'd never make it."

"It's just ten," Beverly said. "Let's go in."

"Are you nervous?"

"No, of course not. What is there to be nervous about?" She was asking the question to herself, really.

"Mrs. Connors." She was startled to hear her name called promptly just as they entered the courtroom. Heart pounding, she walked up to the stand and sat down. Her attorney, Mr. Carr, who was short and bald and had a gray, bushy mustache, smiled at her encouragingly. "Now, Mrs. Connors, in your own words tell the court . . ."

Her own words, as she described the incidents which had brought her to this room, had a familiar ring. "Embarrassed me in front of my friends . . ." How many women before her had uttered that timehonored accusation? She described how Bob had behaved with Vivian at the Hurst's New Year's Eve party. How trivial "incidents" were compared to the real causes of a broken marriage. At best they were only symptoms, feeble and makeshift illustrations of the subtle disintegration of a relationship. "Resented my work . . . didn't come home nights . . . verbally and physically abused me," she heard herself saying. How many people told what actually happened? How many of them even knew? Maybe the stock phrases covered a tragic, unfathomable ignorance. When Vivian took the stand and corroborated her testimony, she went red with the indignity of it all.

At last it was over, and they were back in the corridor with all the other people who were legally putting asunder whom God had joined together. Beverly looked at her watch and was astonished to see that it was only ten after ten. "It didn't take long, did it?" she said.

"No," said Vivian, watching her. "Are you all right, Beverly?"

"I'm fine." She was deeply grateful that she had to go directly back to the office to work, issue instructions, make decisions.

Once she had the divorce decree, she told Sherry and Shirley about her engagement to Steve Chapman.

"Oh, Beverly, that's lovely," Sherry said at once, enveloping her in a hug. "I think he's just darling."

"My God," Shirley said. "Not really. You never learn, do you?"

A little of the happy excitement drained out of Beverly, as though Shirley had stuck a pin in her and made her spring a leak. "All right. What do you mean by that?"

"Wasn't one mama's boy enough?"

"Mama's boy!" Beverly exploded indignantly. "Well, I never heard anything so ridiculous in all my life! Bob loathes his mother, and I don't get the impression Steve was very crazy about his, either!"

Shirley blew the cigarette smoke from her mouth in a short, contemptuous puff. "Naturally. Of course, they loathe their mothers. They loathe them for spoiling them, and waiting on them, and dominating them until they didn't have any guts left. They loathe them for turning them into spineless little—not homosexuals, but ineffectuals."

"That's completely unfair," Beverly said. "Steve's mother died years ago and—"

"And he's probably been looking for another one ever since," Shirley said. "It was plain the day he walked into your office when we were there that he felt like your little boy. Look at my work, Mrs. Connors. Did I do a good thing? Huh? Did I? Wanting to be patted on the head. I could see you loved it, but I didn't think you'd take it on as a full-time job. I would've thought you'd had enough of that."

"Look"—Beverly was so angry it was hard to talk coherently—"they are nothing alike, Bob and Steve. Bob resented my work, Steve admires me for it."

"Uh-huh," Shirley said maddeningly. "Bob did too, at first, didn't he? And he loved having you take care of him. Isn't that how you ended up doing everything around here yourself? And didn't he start resenting it even while he let you do it?"

"Well, Steve does not resent my taking care of him!"

"He will." Shirley snuffed out her cigarette disgustedly. "And when he starts, man, he'll really resent you. After all, you're his boss lady at the office too, which means he'll be under your supervision twenty-four hours a day."

"You're a witch, Shirley," Sherry murmured. "Why are you so mean?"

"Yes, why are you?" Beverly said.

"I'm just trying to get you to see what you're doing before you make another mistake," Shirley said impatiently. "If you're going to marry this kid, you might as well have stuck it out with Bob."

"I'll be the judge of that," Beverly said hotly.

Shirley shook her head. "These guys are the worst booby traps of all. They aren't gay, and they have managed to untie the old apron string, but they never feel right about it. They keep looking around for more apron strings."

"In other words, I'm just a mother substitute," Beverly snapped.

"Exactly. And remembering how they feel about Mama should scare the hell out of you."

"I don't care to discuss it any more," Beverly said. Under her arms, the sleeves of her dress were damp with angry perspiration. "It's none of your business, and anyway, you're completely wrong. Completely."

"Okay," Shirley said. She gave her sister a look of mixed pity, contempt, and resignation. "Only one of these days, why don't you stop and have a good long think about what you're getting out of these strange relationships?"

Twenty-five

Fun? It was a ball. Vivian did not know when she had enjoyed herself as much as she did that spring. She drank, she danced, she played in the surf at Malibu and rode horseback in the cool, pine-strong air at Lake Arrowhead, she went out nearly every night. Somewhere along the line she had picked up two more men friends, a psychiatrist and a rising young attorney.

The psychiatrist, William McDermott, had the place at Malibu, a comfortable place with the slightly mildewed air of old beach houses. He was divorced, and he lived alone with two dogs and a vast collection of records and books. Vivian liked to go to Will's place. Unlike most bachelors, he kept things fairly neat, possibly as a result of previous marital training, and he was a good cook with an impressive array of herbs, spices, and offbeat liquors, all of which he used expertly. His personality was as soothing as his surroundings. He showed no interest whatsoever in clinically observing and cataloguing her reactions. On the contrary, Vivian realized after their fourth or fifth date that he had erected an impenetrable but deftly camouflaged barrier between himself and other people, including her. He was affability itself, friendly, amusing, and polite, but his deeper feelings were never anywhere in evidence. There was a wall around the estate, she thought to herself, not out in front of the property line where it could be seen immediately, but set back and concealed by delightful landscaping. In the beginning, she felt that nothing could suit her better than this man who was obviously every bit as eager as she was to avoid emotional involvements.

The attorney, Scott Palmer, was an incredible synthesis of all those qualities which mothers interested in locating a good catch for their daughters find irresistible. He was young, brilliant, good-looking and ambitious, and he did, and apparently always had done, all the right things. Graduated from Harvard Law School at twenty-five, he had almost immediately on his return to Beverly Hills been taken in by a local law firm which specialized in the incessant litigation of film stars: divorces, tax suits, the setting-up of corporations. Scott was excellent for the film stars, particularly the female ones. He was blond, blue-eyed, and impressively built, and the movie people, instinctively from their own experience equating good looks and success, liked and trusted him. If he had been a little taller, he might have been one of them himself. As it was, he lived almost the way they did, playing tennis at the Racquet Club in Palm Springs, driving a Mercedes, lunching at the best restaurants at least twice a week. Most of the girls he dated were starlets or models, carefully selected for their decorative qualities. While Vivian was attractive, she was not in that class, and it took her a little while to figure out just what Scott saw in her. Eventually, the dates he took her on gave it away. Young Republican dinners, museum openings, Junior Chamber of Commerce balls—Scott had political ambitions, and when he was enlarging his sphere of social activities with this goal in mind, she was the girl he chose to escort.

"Not that I'm an intellectual," Vivian told Beverly over lunch, "but I fit the category better than the usual type he dates. I do have a by-line, and he always introduces me as the *Times*'s brilliant young feature writer. Then I smile, and try delicately to convey the impression that while I am indeed a superior intellect, I am overshadowed completely by his genius. That's just what he wants."

In spite of the constant dating, her work had never been better. She wrote a series on big-city prostitution which was picked up for distribution around the country by one of the major wire services. When Adams had given her the assignment, she had been secretly amused. She felt defiantly rather like a whore herself these days. My sisters under the skin, she thought ironically, but when she had interviewed a few of them, her attitude changed. Pity and revulsion invaded and shook her until she was compelled to withdraw as usual into the state of self-hypnotic detachment which she used to protect herself on painful assignments. She went on, then, into one obscene bedroom after another from Figueroa to the Sunset Strip with the calm, thorough eye of the professional observer, and the story that emerged was at once so objective and so vibrant underneath with compassion that several of her associates made flattering remarks about the Pulitzer Prize.

She looked marvelous. Lack of sleep gave her a feverish, restless quality that enhanced her seductiveness. She lost weight, she became thin as a mannequin, but men still crossed the room to find out who she was at cocktail parties. They scent me, she thought, like a bitch in heat, and she laughed to herself and gazed at them provocatively out of eyes alluringly dilated by the drugs she took to keep alert in the daytime.

Adams and Tim were still her steadiest admirers. Neither knew about the other, although they were both aware that they were not alone in her life. She had told Will about dating the city editor and the copy boy simultaneously, and he thought it as funny as she did. To arouse them both, he ordered a rose sent to her desk at the paper every afternoon for a week. Adams said nothing. He flexed his jaw muscles and became terse and abrupt, but Tim was completely undone. His face flushed, and tears came into his eyes when he saw the rose on her desk. Usually he had to deliver it to her.

"I'm being a witch and a bitch," she said, lounging in front of a driftwood fire after a foggy Sunday afternoon on the beach. "But the little bastard might as well find out early in life how fickle we all are. Don't you think it's bad for the young to be overprotected?"

"Right." Will grinned around his pipestem. He was young for a psychiatrist, only thirty, and he had taken up pipe-smoking as one of several devices to give his patients the proper impression of maturity and wisdom. He wore glasses, too, although he didn't much need them.

Vivian lay on the bear rug and looked at him. He was so admirable in every way that she didn't quite know why it was that from time to time a wave of annoyance with him rose in her. She felt it now.

"What was your wife like?" she asked abruptly. Any sort of personal question would, she knew, be a curse, and she felt like vexing him.

"She was a wonderful girl," he said promptly. At the same time, his eyes seemed to become dark.

"Then why couldn't you work things out?" She made her expression puzzled and innocent.

"Well, Vivian, it was just one of those things." His tone made it sound as though he were imparting a great confidence. "You know? Just one of those things. How about some coffee?"

Unreachable though he was emotionally, Will was at least accessible on the physical and intellectual planes. They had stimulating conversations and a certain rapport in bed. Boudoir pals was the term Vivian used in her own mind. She preferred either Adam or Tim, but for that very reason, she kept on with Will. She was determined to play the field.

Scott, in his own way, was quite as baffling. He talked endlessly about his cases, never asked her opinion on anything, never made a pass. It was exactly as stimulating as going out with a computer, which also provides intelligent answers if you ask it the right questions. In time she came to feel that his emotions had withered from lack of exercise, while he had been cultivating his mind and body so assiduously. He did not seem to be homosexual. He did not seem to be anything in particular, just a long list of admirable attributes typed out on a sheet of paper.

After a time he, too, began to annoy her. She decided to try breaking through to him with the elemental approach, although flirting with Scott had always seemed as unpromising as playing tennis alone. They were sitting in a lush Polynesian restaurant where the Hollywood crowd went a lot. The atmosphere was romantic in a synthetic sort of way, and Vivian decided it was as good a setting as any. She began mildly, using her eyes, but Scott was deep in an explanation of the Reagan budget setup and seemed not to notice. After a while she leaned forward in a manner which she knew displayed tastefully a certain amount of cleavage, and asked him for a cigarette. As he lit it for her, she steadied his hand with hers and gazed into his eyes.

"Lot of people are interested in the new tax reforms," he was saying. A startled look came into his eyes. "Why are you staring at me like that?"

"I'm sorry," she said demurely. "Go on."

He drank more than usual that night. When he took her home he stopped the car with a jerk and quickly turned and took her in his arms. He was as rigid as a robot, and his heart pounded with what Vivian sensed was more fear than desire. He kissed her moistly and inexpertly, and then sat back panting. "Well. Good night." He got out and went around the car to let her out.

As they climbed the stairs, she stifled a hysterical desire to laugh. The young man-about-town. It was absolutely ridiculous. She ought to really scare him to death by inviting him in. He'd probably faint.

At the door, he took the key from her and did the

unlocking. "Well, good night," he said again, stiffly. Fear and anxiety struggled to express themselves in a face he was trying hard to keep expressionless. He looked at her as a stranger might, as though they had never talked, never had dinner, never sat together in a car.

"Good night," Vivian said.

As she closed the door, the laughter went out of her, and she felt deeply depressed. How many of the dates that kept the nighttime city humming ended this same way, with a silent room and an empty feeling? When there was no communication of any kind, just two people all dressed up and driving around in search of amusement, there was nothing. It was deadly and defeating. Anything is better than this, she thought, leaning wearily against the doorjamb, but at once she caught herself. "Dammit!" she swore softly, anything was not better than this. Better numbness than pain.

He did not call her again, of course, and Will was the next to go. She drove him away herself, fully conscious of what she was doing, unable to stop. Quite simply, she asked too many questions. It was partly habit. After all, it was her job to interview people, bring them out, make them reveal themselves. But it was also increasing frustration at being shut out. She had grown up in a town where everybody knew everybody else, where people talked freely, and secrets were few. Will was the opposite extreme. In fact, he was simply not normal. He never discussed his boyhood, the schools he had attended, or his parents. From his conversations, one would not have guessed that he had a personal life. The more she saw of him, the more it upset Vivian. It became a compulsion with her, an obsession, to get him to tell her one little thing that would shed some light on what he was really like.

Finally she gave up. "Tell me," she said one night, "is it an outgrowth of your profession, do you think— this impersonal way you have?"

His mouth tightened ominously and his jaw flexed.

When he spoke, it was with a silky, threatening tone of voice that made her feel cold. "I wasn't aware I was impersonal."

"Well, that's how you strike me." Her eyes began to fill up. "I never met anybody before who gave me the feeling they were reluctant to tell me the name of the dog they had when they were a little boy."

He changed the subject. "Have you been taking a lot of drugs, Vivian?" he said, sounding professional. "I've noticed lately that your pupils are unnaturally dilated."

"Yes, I have. Sleeping pills." Crying openly now, she got up and started for the door. "And if you don't mind, I think I'll go home and take one now."

For some time, it had been increasingly difficult for her to sleep. On the rare nights when she got to bed early, she lay staring at the ceiling and feeling an inexplicable tension build inside her. It seemed to be caused by fear, panic even, but she did not know its cause; indeed, it seemed to be related to the future, not the past. Something dreadful is going to happen, she thought to herself, and her heart fluttered irregularly. It was a premonition. Perhaps she was going to die.

At first the feeling came only at night, when she had insomnia, but gradually it crept into the daytime hours as well, a shadow over the busy reality of life. It insinuated itself into her consciousness when she was sitting at her desk in the office or having an early cocktail with Adams. It came even after she had made love, and that particularly frightened her because ordinarily it was the time when she felt most relaxed and happy.

She took drugs around the clock now: uppers in the morning, downers at night. Her life became less busy without either Will or Scott. On the evenings when she was free, she could not stay in the apartment; she walked or went to a bar alone. Anxiety and restlessness drove her. It was as though a motor ran in her that could not be turned off, she felt that at any time she might lose the ability to sleep altogether.

"God, you're getting thin," Tim said. "I never used to be able to feel your hipbone like that." He sounded concerned, but there was accusation in his eyes. "Do you have to run around so much?"

"I'm not running around so much. I don't run around at all any more, except with you." She lied, she was still seeing Adams, but she was tired and wanted to preserve peace.

"And you don't sleep with anybody else? You don't ever do that, do you? I couldn't stand it."

"Sleep with anybody?" She laughed on the fine edge of tears. "I hardly sleep at all."

Adams, too, began to sense that there was something seriously wrong with her.

"Vivian, why in hell don't you go back home and get married?" he asked her suddenly late one Friday night when they were having a nightcap in her apartment.

Her head jerked around. "Why?" she snapped. "Do you want to get rid of me?" It was not like her to speak that way. She did not know why she did it.

"Of course not. You just don't seem happy."

"And I suppose you think darning some man's socks while I rode herd on a flock of nasty little brats would represent heaven. You men. That's what you all smugly suppose. Well, I'm damned fed up with it. Have you ever talked to any of the more intelligent women who are stuck with that life? Hell no. If you had, you'd know they're climbing the walls with frustration while their minds rot and their figures go to pot."

"Okay, okay. Don't bite my head off."

"I have a brain, and I want to use it for something besides figuring out grocery lists. Incidentally, how happy is your wife—really?"

"Okay, Vivian. Christ. Let's drop the whole thing."

She was shaking with unreasonable anger. She did not know herself why his words made her so furious.

She could have struck him. She hated him, hated all men for their arrogance, their condescension, their maddening smugness in assuming that no woman could be happy without one of their sex under her roof to wait on and look after. Well, she had better things to do with her life. Viciously, she stabbed out her cigarette and lit another.

There was a knock at the door. Startled, they looked at each other. "You expecting anybody?" Adams asked in a low tone, eyeing her negligee.

"No. Just be quiet, and maybe they'll go away."

The knocking persisted. "Vivian?" It was Tim's voice. Adams threw her a look of surprise. Vivian shrugged. She was still vibrating with hostility toward men, and it extended itself to Adams and Tim with all the rest.

"Vivian!" He called more peremptorily this time. "Let me in. I know you're there."

VIvian bit her lip. She motioned silently toward the bedroom, and Adams got up, putting down his cigarette, and tiptoed into it, shutting the door behind him.

She went to the front door and opened it a little. "Now what do you want?" she said crossly. "We didn't have a date tonight."

"I know." He looked hurt at her unfriendliness. "I just got lonesome and thought I'd drop by." He swallowed nervously, and his Adam's apple moved up and down in his thin throat.

"Well, you'll just have to drop on out. I have a headache, and I don't feel like seeing anybody."

"Vivian, what's wrong? I only wanted—" His eyes went past her into the room, fell on something, stopped. Vivian turned quickly and looked. Two cigarettes smoked in the ashtray on the sofa, and two highball glasses stood on the coffee table. "You've got somebody here." He said it slowly and unbelievingly, then accusingly, "You've got somebody here!"

"All right. So I've got somebody here. I have a right

to, after all."

"It's a man. You've got a man here. And you told me you weren't seeing anybody but me!"

"Please! Go away, Tim. It's none of your business!"

"What do you mean, it's none of my business? We're going steady!"

"Not any more, we're not," she snapped. "I just changed my mind."

Bewilderment, anger, and hurt struggled in his face. Suddenly he pushed past her into the room.

"Tim!" Her voice was shrill. "How dare you?"

Ignoring her, he ran to the bedroom and yanked the door open. Adams was sitting on the bed. For a shocked second, the two men stared at each other. "Mr. Adams!" Tim gasped. He let go of the doorknob as though it had burned him. "Mr. Adams, I . . ."

"Hello, kid." Adams's tone was gruff, and he looked angry and embarrassed.

Without another word, Tim turned and ran out as violently as he had burst in, slamming the door behind him. In the humming silence, Vivian and Adams looked at each other in consternation.

"What a fool I was," he hissed through his teeth. "Are you playing around with kids, too?"

She did not know what to say.

He got up from the bed. He seemed more bemused than angry. "Who else, Vivian? Am I by any chance sharing you with my whole goddamn staff?"

"No," she said evenly. "Only with Tim." Her anger had gone, and in its place was a grim satisfaction that at last they had found out about each other.

"I'll be damned," Adams said. "The poor kid. I take it back, Vivian. I guess you don't belong down on the farm. Any woman that operates like you do needs a big city."

Neither of them called over the weekend. Adams was busy with his family, and Tim did not appear for their Saturday night date. All right, let him be angry, she thought defiantly. It serves him right for dropping in unannounced. As far as finding her with Adams was concerned, that was the way life was, and he might as well learn it while he was young. After all, she had. She went out alone, took a furious walk on Wilshire, and ended up at a bar. Anger and irritation were all she felt; she was not aware of the pity and guilt below the surface.

By the time she arrived at the office on Monday morning, she had formed a plan. She would take the offensive with Tim, be angrier than he at his intrusion. He was young and easily swayed; in a few days, he would be eating out of her hand again. Adams apparently was not so much angry as surprised at her. Fine, let him be. If she played it right, he would wind up more intrigued with her than ever. Then she could continue with them both, and any strain in the situation would be felt by them, not her.

She had just sat down at her desk when Adams walked over to her. She gave him a radiant smile with just a hint of knowing amusement over the secret they shared.

He did not smile back. "Vivian, I think I better tell you this before somebody else does. Tim's dead. He smashed up his car Friday night, apparently after he left us. You didn't see a paper over the weekend?"

Dumbly she shook her head.

"He went over a cliff up on Mulholland. The car landed in somebody's swimming pool, and he drowned before they could get him out. His parents are on the warpath. They seem to think it had something to do with you because they've called up here already this morning, wanting me to fire you. I told them—Are you all right?"

She nodded. She did not seem to be able to speak.

"I tried to calm them down, but you may hear from them anyway. They were calling you some pretty uncomplimentary names. I thought I'd better warn you. Have the switchboard filter your calls, and maybe—" Even as he spoke, Vivian's phone rang. She picked it up.

"Miss Hunt? This is Tim's mother." The woman's voice was shaky but determined. "I suppose you know by now our son was killed Friday night."

"Yes," Vivian said. Her own voice sounded far off and strange to her. "I'm terribly sorry."

"He was killed Friday night, and we are wondering if you know why. He went to see you, but you weren't with him when it happened."

"I wasn't home Friday night," she managed to say.

"Weren't you? I wonder where you were. Tim was always afraid you were not being faithful to him. He told me once he'd—kill himself if he ever found out you weren't." The voice on the phone broke. "Why were you going around with my son, anyway, Miss Hunt? An older woman like you, so much more experienced—"

"He had an accident," Vivian said. Her own voice was shaking now. "It's ridiculous to blame me for it. I wasn't even with him at the time—"

"He was a careful driver, Miss Hunt, not reckless like so many boys. He was a good boy, and he was very much in love with you. Were you in love with him? Were you, Miss Hunt? Were you? Or are you just a whore who likes to amuse herself playing around with young boys who—"

Vivian slammed the receiver down. Her face was colorless, and her mouth trembled.

"Come on," Adams said roughly. He pulled her from her chair and out of the city room into the corridor. When they were alone, he shook her. "Pull yourself together."

She leaned against the wall. Her knees were weak, and she felt sick to her stomach.

"Listen to me, Vivian. I think you better get out of here for a while. Take a little vacation. Go out of town, and try to get yourself under control. I've been worried about you a long time. It doesn't make any sense, a woman like you running around the way you do. You're not the type, no matter what you think."

"Where do you want me to go?" she asked faintly.

"Hell, I don't care. Just get away. Go back to your hometown for a visit. Go to San Francisco. Get out of here for a while and give things a chance to cool down. Yourself and everybody else."

"I don't know where to go."

"It doesn't matter, Vivian. Just get the hell out. And do it right now. Today. I give you the day off. Go to a travel agency, buy yourself a ticket, and be on a plane tonight." He shook her again. Through the shock, the faintness and nausea, she was dimly grateful for his masculine authoritativeness.

"All right." She put her hand to her mouth. "Do you hate me?" she whispered.

He stared at her. She spoke like a frightened child to a stern father, pleadingly, and her eyes were wild with fear of not being loved.

"Hell no," he said gruffly. "Now get out of here before somebody sees you like this."

She walked unsteadily back to her desk and picked up her handbag. As she went toward the door of the city room, she met him coming in from the corridor. They did not look at each other as they passed.

Twenty-six

"It's almost like a new play," Dana said. "I don't just mean all the script changes. I mean the new cast. She's wonderful, Sylvia. Emily Eastwick was a good mother superior, but Sylvia's superb."

"You're good," Dan observed. "I think I might even say you're better than you were in Los Angeles."

"Thank you." She gave him a small smile without really looking at him. His eyes lately, his very manner, were telling her something she did not yet wish to know.

They were sitting at the bar of a small Italian restaurant on 43rd Street near the theater where *The Sisters* was in rehearsal. The late afternoon sunshine that fell along the sidewalk outside was reflected through the white curtained windows set just about street level.

"New York is good for you." He was still looking at her in the same intent way. "You have great serenity, so it doesn't rev you to fever pitch the way it does some people, but you have a vitality here you didn't have in California."

Interested, she looked him full in the face for the first time. "Do you know how I feel here? As though I'm living inside an enormous dynamo. I can feel energy being generated around me, the energy of all these millions crammed into so little space. It's wonderful when I'm working, but at night—you know, at night I can still feel it? Even in my remarkably quiet apartment? Sometimes it's so strong I can't sleep, I feel as though I must get up and prowl the streets to keep my batteries from overcharging."

"I can't sleep either, but I doubt if it's the restless millions." He turned his glass of ginger ale slowly, leaving a pattern of wet rings on the polished wood of the bar.

"Are you worried about the play? That's a stupid question, of course you are. Do you think Lederers is weakening it?"

"I honestly don't know any more. Cliff is a great director, I respect his work as I've seen it in the past, and let's be honest, he's had considerably more experience in the theater the past few years than I have. I don't even question his right to make a few changes. But it played well in California. I felt I had molded it into its final form, and now something's happening to it that seems alive. Perhaps it's still a good play, but it's not the same play."

"Have you told Cliff how you feel?"

"No."

"Why not?"

He was a long time answering. "I suppose I lack the sense of authority about my work I used to have. There was a time when I put up a good fight. But Dana, remember, before this play I hadn't written anything in five years. That's an appalling vacuum in a writer's life. And it's been fifteen years—my God, fifteen!—since I last wrote for the theater."

"So you're not sure any more just how good you are."

"No. I'm not sure any more."

"Remember the reviews in California?"

"My dear, this is New York."

Both of them were silent. Through the closed door, the sound of traffic was insistent, chaotic. Dana looked out. Beyond the curtains on their whiny brass rods, she could see the hurrying legs of the city's homebound workers. The door opened, and two men in business suits came down the short flight of steps and sat at the opposite end of the bar from where they were. It was nearly five; the place would begin to fill up now.

"I wish I knew what to say to you," she said finally. "There's no point in my telling you that I liked the play better the way it was, because my opinion is of no important, anyway."

"Don't say that, Dana. You're an intelligent woman with training in the theater. Of course your opinion matters, particularly to me."

"Well then, that's what I think. I don't think Cliff's changes are necessarily improvements. If he wants to write a play, why doesn't he write one of his own?"

Dan burst out laughing. "Dana, I love you for that. Every playwright who ever lived loves you for that."

"Well, it's true." She smiled fondly at the way he looked when he laughed. His blue eyes twinkled, and his face got redder in the most engaging way. "It's true, and I think you should tell him so yourself. And now, listen. I have something to tell you. I've decided on my stage name."

"Still Dana, I hope." He looked apprehensive. "I'm fond of that name. It suits you."

"Yes, still Dana, but a new last name. Landon. Dana Landon. Do you like it?"

"Dana Landon. Yes, it's very nice. When did you decide to do this?"

"I've been thinking about it ever since I left Los Angeles. My old names, my maiden name and my married name, didn't seem to fit me any more."

"I see." He hesitated. "Have you talked to your husband lately?"

"I call him every few nights to see how Jeremy is. Last night I invited him to come for our opening."

"Did he accept?"

"No." She forced herself to look calmly at him, concealing what she felt. "He said he wasn't interested."

"Maybe he'll change his mind. After all, it's still

three weeks off."

"Yes, maybe he will." She gave a short laugh which sounded more bitter than she meant it to. "Of course, he's never yet been known to change his mind about anything, once it's made up, but miracles do still happen occasionally, don't they?"

Cliff Lederers was young and thin with a delicate, supple neck and eyes as soft and black as charcoal, with the same capacity for combustion. He had grown up in New York, and his gift for the theater, according to the critics, was extraordinary and rare. He did not lash performances out of his players; he coaxed them out, flattered them out, fairly worshiped them out.

"Miss Landon, you have a voice men will remember in their old age," he told Dana. His voice was low, but the intensity of his eyes as he spoke burned the words in. "What a voice, my God, a heart and soul made audible. Let it go, let it soar, let them hear it and carry it in their hearts forever."

Spellbound, Dana worked harder, played better than she ever had. She did not have the ego for criticism, but faith—faith made her give the best of herself. It was as though he saw and shared the image she held of what she wished to be, an instrument with power and range and exquisite subtlety. He had the same effect on the rest of the cast. He found the inner vision they had of themselves, called it forth, made it a reality. He burned with an evangelistic fire that ignited them, gave them a towering confidence, and Dana, more and more excited, saw, felt, knew that she, that all of them, were probably going to give the performance of their lives.

The play was another matter entirely. What was happening to the play troubled her. Speeches were out, rearranged, shifted. Whole scenes changed their point and meaning. Lines were altered from day to day, and the cast murmured, but Lederer's incandescent belief in himself and in them burned away their doubts, and they went on. Only Dan grew more and more agitated, pacing in the aisle, smoking one cigarette after aother.

"Please, Mr. Morgan," Lederers said one afternoon slightly more than a week before they were due to open. "Your agitation distresses me very much. I'm afraid I must ask you to leave." His voice was as soft as ever, but his black eyes snapped.

Dana caught her breath. In the shocked quiet, someone giggled, and she saw Dan's head snap up. He did not move from where he was standing: he simply stood and stared.

"Mr. Morgan." This time Lederer's voice was a shade louder and infinitely more commanding. "If you do not go, this rehearsal cannot continue."

Dana shut her eyes. Say something back, Dan, she pleaded silently. Oh, please say something.

"Very well. Now we can continue." Lederer's voice was soft again, and triumphant.

She opened her eyes in time to see Dan walking swiftly back up the aisle and out the door.

They had a dinner date that night at seven. When Dan did not appear, she phoned his hotel. The room did not answer. She went to bed early and then, troubled, could not get to sleep until well after midnight.

The next day he did not appear at the theater.

"Have you seen Mr. Morgan?" she asked Art Novik, the stage manager, who lived in the same hotel as Dan.

"Not since he left yesterday. Why?"

"I have a message for him from somebody just in from the coast," she said, and did not pursue the subject. She was aware that there was considerable speculation around the theater about her and Dan. They all knew he had been responsible for bringing her to New York. Although the obvious motive they assigned to this annoyed her, she had avoided explanations, realizing how futile they would be.

He did not come to the theater that day either, and she spent the evening phoning his hotel without results. On the third day when he did not appear, she became thoroughly alarmed. When rehearsal was over, she went directly to his hotel.

It was a long time before he answered her frantic knocking. When at last he opened the door, a shock ran through her even though she had been prepared for what she might find. Red-eyed, unshaven, in a stained shirt and rumpled trousers, he stared at her with a hopelessness that twisted her heart.

"Dana," he murmured. "My God." His face, already slack with fatigue and alcohol, crumpled completely and tears came into his eyes.

"Dan, I've been so worried about you." She said it gently, without reproach. Then she walked past him into the apartment.

The room was a shambles. Bottles and glasses, half-filled, empty, spilled, stood on the tables, the chair arms, the floor. Dark, sour stains disfigured the carpet, the back of a chair, one of the gold cushions of the sofa. Cigarette butts floated in half-emptied glasses and littered the coffee table around an overflowing ashtray. The air reeked of whiskey, stale cigarette smoke, and vomit. Sickened, she walked to the windows and started to pull back the closed draperies, but his hand grasped her roughly by the elbow and stopped her.

"Go away." His red face was sticky-wet with tears, liquor, and the residue of nausea. "Get out of here, and leave me alone."

Briefly her mind flicked to Don, who was always neat, always in control, who had never had too much to drink in his life. Don, who had never needed her, nor ever would need her, as this man did now. "No," she said. "I'm going to stay with you."

The next three days, whenever she thought of them

afterward, had in spite of their nightmare quality a dreadful, heartbreaking intimacy deeper than anything she head ever shared with another person. The Dan she had known, so kind, so civilized, so perceptive, had vanished; it was as though the alcohol had eaten away the surface veneer like an acid, and all that was left was a human core so pitted and scarred, so stained and corroded by a lifetime of despair, frustration, and self-doubt that the sight of him left her faint with pity. He was no longer a man. He clung to her like a child, terrified, bewildered, shrinking from life as a fetus might shrink from premature exposure to the bitter glare of existence, weeping, whimpering. At times he was less than human, an animal raging incoherently at memories he could not articulate, falling, groveling, pulling himself from the floor to lie with his head in the seat of a chair while his fists beat fitfully, impotently against the cushion.

He told her everything, sometimes in a voice so broken she could not comprehend his meaning, all the shameful defeats, mistakes, dishonors, that darken confessionals and the walls of analysts' offices with an invisible brown stain of anguish; everything, from the beginning. Still drinking, he talked. He vomited a lifetime of bitter experience, and she let him go on, knowing it was the only thing to do, watching him, listening, weeping herself sometimes with horrified compassion. She did not sleep, she left him only long enough to go to rehearsals, she told no one what was happening. At times she was so frightened that she longed to call a doctor, but she remembered what he had told her about the drinking, and so she allowed him to battle his demon to the finish, waiting patiently, near exhaustion, until the time should come when she would be able to reach him. If he did not die first.

On the third day, she came back from rehearsals to find him collapsed on the bed with one hand in a dark, drying spread of blood. "Dan!" She heard the hysteria in her own voice as she ran to him. He lay heavily on his face, his neck twisted at an unnatural angle, breathing laboriously. The hand had been sliced sharply across three fingers, and a broken tumbler lay on the floor beside the bed in a stinking puddle of Scotch. She turned him over, but he did not stir or awaken. His pulse felt weak and uncertain, and his forehead was clammy with an unnatural sweat.

She found his overcoat in the closet and spread it over him. Then she washed the hand and bandaged it with a clean handkerchief from his drawer. Opening all the windows wide, she cleaned the apartment, hearing the noise of the busy, dinnertime streets as it came faintly up from below. When she had finished, she went and sat beside him. His breathing seemed easier now, and a trace of normal color had returned to his face.

Suddenly she was so dizzy with weariness and relief that she felt she was going to faint. Making her way to the windows, she leaned her head against the jamb. The sky was darkening, and lights were beginning to come on in the tall, peopled buildings across the way. It was over now. She could go out to dinner and get a good night's sleep. The plan was infinitely appealing, but somehow she did not seem to have the strength to put it into effect. Perhaps if I lie down and rest for just a minute, she thought. She walked unsteadily into the living room and stretched out on the sofa.

The smell of coffee awoke her, and she stared, bewildered and disoriented, at daylight filtering weakly into the room, slitted by the venetian blinds. There were sounds of activity in the kitchen, and she went out to find Dan, shaven, washed, in clean clothes, standing by the stove.

"Good morning," he said gravely.

"Good morning." Her shoulders and neck ached, her body felt as leaden as though she had not slept at all, but a kind of joy stirred in her at the sight of him restored to normal. While she watched, he poured coffee into two cups, opened the blinds slightly to let more of the morning in, and put the cups on the chrome-legged table by the window.

"You shouldn't bother with me, Dana," he said as they sat down together. "It should be clear to you by now that I'm not worth it." There was no self-pity in his tone, only regret.

"I think you are," she said matter-of-factly. Something warned her not to be too emotional.

"Once a drunk, always a drunk." He took a sip of coffee and put the cup down.

"That's silly, Dan. You haven't had a drink in months."

"No, but the moment there's any pressure—I can't seem to stand pressure."

"Lots of people can't."

"What can I do then? Go into some line of work where there isn't any? Perhaps I should be a plumber."

"That would be the worst pressure of all. That would kill you."

"Oh?"

She took a sip of coffee. "Don't you know what the pressure is that you can't stand? It isn't having a play produced on Broadway. You could handle that. The pressure you can't stand is not doing what you were meant to do, what you were born to do."

He looked at her curiously. "What do you mean?"

"Why did you start drinking in the first place? Wasn't it because you had lost all respect for what you were doing? And why are you drinking now? Not because you can't stand the suspense of not knowing whether the play will be successful, but because you're standing by and letting somebody else make a mess of it without saying a word."

"And why am I doing this? Go on."

She put her cup down. "I suppose because your confidence in yourself has been badly shaken by all the years you drank and did work you didn't believe in.

That's bad for anybody, Dan, but for somebody with your talent, it's destructive. The odd thing is, beneath all that, you still do have an essential faith in yourself. I'm sure that's why you went on this binge. You think you're right about the play, and Cliff is wrong, and you hate yourself for not telling him. If you really had no belief in your own abilities, wouldn't you be delighted to have this bright young man fixing things so you'll be a huge success?"

They looked at each other for a long time without saying anything.

"How do you know these things, Dana?" Dan asked finally.

"Because I'm like you, I suppose. I know how it feels to have something to give and not be giving it. People compromise, they compromise all the time because they think it's going to be easier. But in the end, it's not easier at all. If you don't commit yourself to the best that's in you, you head straight for a very personal kind of disaster."

"You think I should talk to Cliff?" Dan said after another short silence.

"What have you got to lose? If the play goes on as he's rewritten it and fails, you'll have no one but yourself to blame. And everyone else will blame you, too. If it's a success, you won't have any real feeling of triumph because it's not your play any more. Commit yourself, Dan. Fight for your work. There's no other way."

"And if I get my way, and it fails anyway?"

"My dear, that's a hazard of your profession that you've always had to deal with. If it fails, you'll write another. Because that's what you do in this life. You write plays." She waited a moment, then she finished her coffee and stood. "I'm starved. Do you suppose I could persuade you to take me out to a really tremendous breakfast?"

"I'd be delighted," he said slowly. "But would you be kind enough to wait ten minutes while I telephone our esteemed producer and director and ask them to meet me at the theater in an hour?"

The conference took all morning. It was still going on when Dana, who had gone back to her apartment to change after breakfast, arrived at the theater for rehearsal.

"There's some kind of trouble," Art Novik told her. "Morgan blew in there with blood in his eyes. Or maybe it was just bloodshot eyes. Where's he been the last three days? On a binge?"

Dana shrugged and did not reply, and Art, after looking at her for a second, grinned significantly and turned away. He thinks I've been sleeping with Dan, she thought wearily. But it's much more than that. She was closer now to Dan, she realized, than she had ever been to Don, closer than most people ever got to another human being. It made her strangely happy, this deep intimacy. It was almost worth coming to New York for, whatever else happened. She was a little surprised at herself for thinking that.

When the three of them came onstage at last, the cast stopped chattering immediately, and a curious, expectant silence fell. They all looked grim; it was impossible to tell who had won. Lederer's black eyes smoldered in his pale face, and Dan was red and shiny with perspiration.

"Ladies and gentlemen." It was the producer who spoke. "It has been decided to do the play as originally rehearsed. This will mean a lot of work for all of you the next three days before we open. I'm sorry, but I know I can count on your cooperation . . ."

Looking at Dan, Dana stopped listening. She felt like crying with relief. Hardly knowing what she was doing, she walked toward him, and he pulled her quickly into the wings.

"We won," he whispered, gripping her shoulders. "We won."

"Dan, I'm so proud of you." The "we" warmed her heart, although she did not say so.

"It will mean hard work for you. Damnably hard work. I'm sorry."

"It'll be a pleasure." She stood on tiptoe, not caring if anyone saw, and kissed him on the cheek. "Don't worry about it."

Twenty-seven

VISIT MEXICO, the travel poster said in red letters splashed against a blue sky, beneath which sparkled a bay rimmed by trees and mountains and the glittering cubes of luxury hotels.

Vivian leaned against the counter and looked at it blankly.

"May I help you?" The travel agent was an efficient-looking older woman with silver-rinsed gray hair and glasses with frames that matched it.

"I want to fly to Mexico," Vivian said.

"When?"

"Today."

The woman's eyebrows lifted. "I'm not sure we can get you on a flight that fast. However, I'll try." She retreated from the counter to a desk and picked up a phone.

Mexico. Yes, that was a good idea. Get out of the city, get out of the whole country, have a complete change. Adams was right. She needed to get herself under control. If she could just rest, if she could just have a nice, quiet relationship with a man and no emotional involvement, just have fun and not think about anything . . . No, that was wrong. No more men for a while. Just rest and quiet. Maybe she could find some little village with a small hotel where she would wake up in the morning to the sound of birds, no traffic.

"Well, I can get you a flight to Mexico City this

afternoon, but it's not the direct flight." The clerk's voice across the counter startled her. "It makes two stops, Tijuana and Guadalajara. You leave here at three-ten and get to Mexico City around one-thirty tomorrow morning. Is that all right?"

She nodded and got out her checkbook.

By the time she walked out of the travel agency into the gray spring morning, she had stopped trembling, but another, more frightening reaction had begun. She felt quite literally as though all the nerve endings of her body were exposed, raw and quivering, to the assault of every passing stimulus. The bright, whitish light of the sky, where the sun was flimsily veiled by high fog, hurt her eyes. The rumble and screech of the passing traffic struck her with almost physical force, and when a bus horn blasted behind her, she jumped as though a gun had been fired. She put on her dark glasses and hurried back to the parking lot, walking as close as possible to the buildings.

Luggage. Vaccination. Fortunately, she had the vaccination already. She had intended to go to Mexico last summer on her vacation, but John had talked her into going with him to San Francisco while he did a bit in a movie. John. What a long time ago that seemed. John was married now. Sid was married. Adams was married. And the others were—What was wrong with all the others? What was wrong with her?

She quickly drove home and packed. What kind of clothes did you take to Mexico in May? It was the rainy season, wasn't it? Did that mean it was cold? She pulled dresses and suits off their hangers automatically, hardly noticing what she chose, and when the suitcase was full, she snapped it shut and locked it. Looking at her watch, she was appalled to discover that it was only noon. Still three hours until flight time. The idea of waiting in her apartment alone terrified her. Taking her bags down to the car, she headed for the airport.

When she had checked in at the flight counter, she

went to the bar. Actually, she was hungry, but the thought of food nauseated her. A brandy would be more comforting; it would numb her, sheathe the exposed nerves so that she would stop seeing, feeling, hearing everything with such dreadful intensity.

"That'll be two seventy-five," the bartender said, and she jumped as though he had pinched her. "What're you so nervous about, miss? First flight?"

She managed a smile and nod. It was as good a reason as any.

"It won't be that bad."

"Won't it?"

He paused, leaning his hand on the damp, folded towel he had been using to wipe the bar, and looked at her. He was tall and freckled and reminded her of a football player she had had a crush on her first year in high school. "If I could, I'd come along and hold your hand," he said sympathetically.

"Thank you." She tried another smile, but her mouth was trembling at the unexpected kindness, and it didn't come off, so she raised the little glass and emptied it.

She had four more brandies before the flight was called, and when she got down off the stool, she found she had to concentrate on walking steadily. Somewhere she remembered having heard that if they thought you were drunk, they wouldn't let you on the plane. Outside, the sun was fully out now, shining blindingly in a sky still pale with remnants of fog. When the plane was airborne, the hum of the engines vibrating in her head numbed her brain, completing the anesthesia begun by the brandy. Finally, blessedly, it was impossible to think. Closing her eyes, she turned her head toward the window and slept.

It seemed only a short time until they were landing in Tijuana. She awoke, feeling sick at her stomach, and stared down at the bare brown hills tilting up toward them from below. As they got off the plane for customs inspection, she noticed for the first time that a young couple who had been in the travel agency that morning were traveling with her.

Nausea rose inexorably in her as they stood waiting for the bags to be searched. Shock, lack of food, too much brandy, the plane's motion—as she catalogued its causes, it became clear to her that she was not going to be able to fight it off. She looked around desperately. Across the way was a door marked DAMAS. She began walking toward it, it seemed an infinite distance, finally she was running, her hand to her mouth. Pushing the door open, she flung herself into one of the metal stalls and dropped to her knees.

The vomiting lasted a long time, or so it seemed. When it was over, she rested her cheek on the toilet seat, bathed in sweat, feeling a faint sense of peace. The physical crisis had momentarily blotted out the emotional one. Limp, exhausted, she felt in her handbag for a tissue and whiped her mouth off.

"Miss? Miss, are you all right?"

In time she became aware that the question was addressed to her. She got up wearily and straightened her skirt. A piece of damp toilet paper clung to it, and she brushed it loose with a shudder of distaste.

The girl who had been in the travel agency was waiting anxiously for her beside the lavatory. "Are you all right? I saw you run in here, and you looked so sick."

"I'm all right now," Vivian said. She caught sight of herself in the lavatory mirror, face greenish-white, hair clinging damply to her cheeks, lipstick smeared. She opened her handbag.

"You better not stop for that now," the girl said. "The plane's leaving any minute."

They walked out of the rest room together and found a young man waiting.

"This is my—my husband," the girl said, stumbling over the new phrase. "Brad Kingsbury. I'm Diana Kingsbury. We're on our honeymoon."

"We better go," Brad Kingsbury said, nodding at

Vivian. "Come on. I think they're holding it for us."

They walked her to the plane, one on each side. She felt their concern as clearly as she felt the solidarity of their love. It made her feel infinitely old and lonely. Could she really be only thirty? She felt as though she had lived a long, long time.

They put her in a seat, an aisle seat this time, and looked at her worriedly.

"We'll be right here if you need anything." Diana Kingsbury said. She looked calm and responsible and organized, in spite of her youth, with the dignity of matrimony newly upon her. "Just don't hesitate to ask." As she spoke, her husband put his arm around her.

"Thank you," Vivian said. She watched as they took seats across the aisle and in front of her. She could not take her eyes off them. They were on their honeymoon, but already they were acting as a couple, a unity of two, a team with doubled resources to meet the challenges of the world. They were so secure in their love that they could afford to be kind. What makes people think that unhappiness builds character? Vivian thought. Happy people are always nicer. Unhappiness, if you aren't careful, turns you into a monster. The thought of Tim, which she had carefully avoided until now, came into her mind without warning, and shame and anguish made her catch her breath.

"So. You are traveling alone?" The man who sat beside her in the window seat was examining her with interest.

"Yes, I am." She was grateful to have her thoughts interrupted before they became unbearable.

He offered her a cigarette, and she thought, in spite of her distress, that she had never seen a more arresting face. He was brown and thin with thick, gray hair that fairly jutted back from his low forehead. The hollowed-out cheeks, the sharp-ridged nose, the deep creases like parentheses between his nose and mouth, gave him the world-weary look of an Egyptian pharaoh.

"Permit me to introduce myself." The German accent was unmistakable and somehow sinister. "Kurt Schmidt."

"Vivian Hunt."

"Delighted to know you. You are going to Mexico for pleasure?"

"I guess so," she said. "And you?"

"I go on business. I am an archeologist."

"Really? Then you should be in Egypt. You remind me of a pharaoh's head I once saw, carved in stone. Khufu, I think it was."

He laughed. "By this time I should have begun to resemble the ancient Maya."

He began to talk about his work. Isolated by the turmoil within her, Vivian only half heard what he said, but the place names came through to her with eerie clarity. Tikal, Bonampak, Palenque, Uxmal—they conjured up images of steep-walled temples strangled by the jungle growth of centuries. Places to lose oneself. Or maybe that was not what she needed. Maybe she had been lost for some time already. I'm not making sense, she thought confusedly, I must pull myself together. Adams said so.

"But I am boring you." He had stopped talking.

"Oh, no," she said quickly. "No, not at all."

Aware, appraising, he looked at her. It was a gaze she was infinitely familiar with by now, the look of the interested, about-to-go-on-the-make male. In a second, he would ask the name of her hotel.

"Excuse me." She got up and walked toward the rest rooms at the front of the plane. The door marked WOMEN was locked. Bracing herself against the partition, she waited.

"How are you feeling now?" Diana Kingsbury was right behind her.

"Just fine."

"You're going to Mexico all by yourself?"

Vivian nodded.

"Aren't you afraid?"

"What is there to be afraid of?"

"I don't know." Diana laughed and shrugged. "I'd just be scared to, that's all. But I suppose if you're not married, you get used to doing things all alone. Traveling and all, I mean."

"Yes," Vivian said. "You get used to it."

When she had locked herself in the tiny lavatory, she began to feel panicky. She was alone, it was true, and she did not want to be alone, she did not dare to. Not now. What would happen to her? How would she be able to avoid thinking? No, the situation was intolerable. Anything would be better, even getting involved with Kurt Schmidt. After all, he was an attractive, interesting man. She did not know why she had already begun to dislike him. Never mind, he was a man, someone to talk to. She got her compact and lipstick.

"Ah. I see you have refreshed yourself," he said when she returned to her seat. "I was about to ask where you are staying in Mexico City."

"To tell the truth, I don't know. I don't have a reservation."

"That is very foolish when the city is full of tourists. I myself am at the Rivera. Perhaps, if you like me to, I could get you a room there."

"That would be very kind," Vivian said.

The Rivera proved to be old and comfortable and right in the midst of things. She took two sleeping pills when she went to bed, and it was noon the next day before she awoke. The room was incredibly noisy. Outside the three floors below, the traffic roared and rumbled. Half-groggy still, she went to the window and looked out. Sunshine struck her; she could not bear the sight of the cars, the trees, the buildings. She began to tremble and feel her nerve endings exposed all over again. It was too much. She could not stand all these new, unfamiliar, bruising sights and sounds. She shut the window, pulled the blinds, and fled back to bed, smothering her head with the pillow. The darkness, the muffled silence, soothed and comforted her. She would stay here all day. She would hibernate like a bear until her nerves were calmer. After a while, when she stopped trembling, she went back to sleep.

Abruptly the telephone rang, and she jumped as though someone had screamed in her ear. She looked at her watch, squinting to see its hands in the room's semidarkness. Four o'clock. The phone screamed again, and she snatched at it wildly. "What is it?"

"It's Kurt. Are you all right?"

"Yes. Why?" She could not keep the strain out of her voice.

"You sounded so desperate when you answered. I called to see if you will have dinner with me."

"No, I'm afraid I can't. I'm not feeling very well."

"That's is a pity." He sounded politely concerned. "Have you called a doctor?"

"No. It's nothing serious. I'm just a little—tired. Thank you for calling, though."

"I'll try again tomorrow. Perhaps you will be better by then."

"Yes. Yes, I'm sure I will."

When she had hung up, she stuffed her head under the pillow again and lay, breathing fast, listening to the sound of her own pulse in her ears. This was intolerable. Why had she come down here, anyway? What she needed was not a trip, but a hospital. Something was dreadfully wrong with her, some kind of nervous disease must be making her feel so painfully exposed, so agonizingly invaded by the external world. She hated even to feel the dry, cottony texture of the pillowcase against her cheek. What she wanted, what she needed and longed for, was oblivion, complete and impenetrable. She shook a red capsule out of the sleeping pill bottle and swallowed it without water. Then she shut her eyes and waited.

Half an hour later, she was still awake, but the drowsy numbness had sheathed her raw senses a little. She took the pillow off her head and lay staring at the unfamiliar ceiling. Mexico. She had come all the way to Mexico. It was silly to stay in bed the whole time, even though that was what she longed to do. If she weren't going to sleep, she'd better be up and doing. But not alone. Not alone.

She reached for the phone and asked for Kurt Schmidt's room. "Is the dinner invitation still open? I'm feeling better."

Dazedly, she lay in bed an other hour, and then it was time to dress. He was taking her to the Hilton for cocktails, and then some place called Miguel's for dinner. She painted her face on with the studied, meticulous care of a drunk. Her eyes didn't focus properly, and she had to brace her unsteady hand against her chin to wield the lipstick brush. Her heart was behaving strangely, pounding in intricate, unsettling rhythms that visibly shook her breast. Was it the sleeping pills, she wondered, or the altitude? Mexico City was supposed to be very high. Also very cosmopolitan, she thought disconnectedly, shaking out the fringed black dress.

They met in the lobby. In her spike-heeled evening pumps, she towered over him, but he didn't seem to mind. "Charming," he murmured, assessing her half-bared bosom which was at his eye level.

The lounge at the Hilton was warm and luxurious and full of worldly-looking people, and oddly, through the numbness of sedation, she began to enjoy herself. She could not keep her mind on what he was saying, although she was convinced it was fascinating, but the sound of his voice, masculine and European and surprisingly resonant for such a little man, pleased her. Gratefully she sat back and listened to it as to music, admiring his predatory face.

"You are quite beautiful," he said finally, as flatly as though he were settling an argument.

"You're pretty glamorous yourself," she said boldly. The remark seemed to surprise him, but he didn't look displeased. No, not at all.

Going into Miguel's, she stumbled and he caught her arm. "I'm a little dizzy," she said. Everything seemed dim and lovely and unreal. "It must be the altitude."

"It does sometimes intensify the effect of liquor. I'll see to it you do not have any more."

He did not allow her to have any wine with her dinner, although he ordered a bottle for himself.

Watching him drink it, she smiled vaguely and said, "You remind me of my father."

"Oh?"

"You're so authoritative," she explained, seeing she had offended him. "You make me feel I—better be good."

"And were you good?"

"I always got very good grades," she said, feeling a distant pride. "An odd thing to expect of a little girl."

She frowned slightly, and an indefinable uneasiness worked its way through the paralysis that had seized her brain. "Yes. It was odd, wasn't it?"

The lights dimmed, and the violinists came and played, standing all around the elegant room between the tables. It was beautiful; it was the way she had always imagined restaurants in Paris to be. She applauded, she smiled appreciatively at Kurt, she adjusted the spaghetti-thin straps of her gown. She ate her dinner without knowing what was on the plate.

Then they were in a taxi again, and Kurt's arm was around her. In the moving car, he seemed solid and stable, and she slid down in the seat so that she could put her head on his shoulder.

"Do you want to go back to the hotel?" he asked.

"Yes."

He went up in the elevator with her, and unlocked the door for her, and when the door was closed, she was mildly surprised to find he was still in the room.

"Do you want me to go?" he asked, seeing her puzzled look.

"Oh, no." Definitely, she did not want that. When he went, she would be alone. Her legs were still unsteady, and she sat down on the bed.

It was only a moment—or was it longer?—before he was behind her, quietly, expertly unzipping her dress, slipping the straps from her shoulders, unfastening her bra.

"You mustn't," she said faintly. It seemed indecent. Something about him reminded her of her father. She looked down to see his hands slide under her breasts and cup them as if weighing them.

"As firm as a young girl," he said softly, almost hissing it.

"Kurt." Helplessly, she watched him undress and throw his clothes over a chair. She could not think of what she wanted to say. Then he strode over to her, already excited, his penis rigid, ready.

"Come. Your clothes."

Her brain was numb, paralyzed. She felt incapable of making a decision, of resisting, of arguing.

"Come." Did he really snap his fingers, or did she only imagine it? Dazed, she stood up and let her dress fall to the floor.

Standing before her, he seized her hands and began forcing her fingers backward.

Incredulous, she stared at him. Pain and shock cut through her numbness. "No!" Suddenly she was furious. "Let go of me!"

"Kneel!"

He was stronger than he looked. Her wrists were beginning to ache unbearably. "Stop it!" she gasped. Then, unable to stand the pain any longer, she sank to her knees.

"Now." He sounded pleased. "Now we—"

She bit his wrist as hard as she could. "Get out," she said. "Get out of here, and don't come back!"

For a moment, he stared at her as though he could

not believe what had happened, rubbing his wrist. Then, without a word, he began putting his clothes on. He fastened his tie, looking in the mirror of the bureau, and combed his gray hair meticulously. When he finally turned to her, his eyes were icy with rage and contempt.

"You are not a woman," he said. "You are . . ." He searched for the word. Finding it, he snatched up her lipstick and wrote it in German on the mirror in slashing, angular script.

"Get out!" she screamed. "Get out of here!"

He left.

Trembling, she looked at what he had written. She did not know what it meant, but the very handwriting sickened and terrified her. The numbness had vanished, the protective, narcotic sheath had been ripped away, she was naked now, and more than naked, flayed alive, her flesh stripped off to expose the raw, quivering nerves underneath. "You are not a woman. You are . . ." Sobbing, she snatched up a handful of cleansing tissues and rubbed the word out, rubbed until the red grease disappeared, leaving only a faint smear on the glass. "It isn't true, it isn't true, it isn't true," she chanted softly over and over to herself as she rubbed. When she finished, she put her hands to her temples as if to ward off an unbearable pain.

This was the last straw. She could not bear any more. It was too painful to be awake, to be alive. She wanted to sleep, to forget, to escape forever. She simply could not take any more.

There were still quite a few sleeping pills in the bottle, she noted as she emptied them into her hand and swallowed them, one by one, with a glass of water from the bathroom.

Joe. Where was Joe? Going to her jewel case, she got out the little slab of lead. Bales . . . Film, it said in miniscule letters along one edge, a type slug that had once identified a proof of one of Joe's stories. A ridiculous souvenir. A mundane, slightly greasy item that happened to be the only tangible memento of Joe that she had left. She wondered if the letters would print themselves on her hand if she held it tightly enough. Getting into bed, she pulled the covers up to her chin. Now the waiting began.

I wonder if it's safe to drink the water? She thought dimly, irrelevantly, remembering just before she lost consciousness that she had filled the glass from the tap for the sleeping pills. But then, it really didn't matter much, did it? "Joe . . .?" Her lips moved, but no sound came.

Twenty-eight

The doorbell rang, and when Beverly answered it, she found Steve standing on the porch with a lumpy, full blue laundry bag under one arm.

"Well, hi!" She sounded more surprised than she meant to. There was a slight, awkward pause. "I didn't know whether you were coming or not after last night," she added finally.

"Oh. Well, I'm sorry about that." He looked uncomfortable. "I was going to call you, but then I thought I'd just come over instead."

"Well, fine. Come in." She detached the laundry bag from him as he walked past her into the living room. "I see you brought your clothes. I'll just put them in to soak right away."

He followed her to the laundry room and watched while she opened the bag, sorted his dirty clothes, put a selection into the washer, and added washing powder.

"I don't know what comes over me." He still sounded embarrassed. "When you're so good to me and all, its—"

"Just forget it," Beverly interrupted lightly. "We all have our moods." She did not want to discuss it; she did not want even to think about how often lately Steve had been sullen and discontented. Their quarrel the night before had been trifling, which in a way made it all the more disconcerting. When she had first known him, he had seemed so endlessly good-natured.

"Kiss and make up?" Sometimes he sounded like a wistful child.

"Sure," Beverly said. Still preserving the offhand touch, she gave him a quick hug and a matching peck, but he seized her and held her tightly, prolonging the embrace.

Arms around each other, they walked back into the living room.

"This afternoon would you come with me while I look for a car?" Steve asked. "The Dodge's about had it, and I've been meaning to check the lots out here."

"All right. Let me get a sweater and make sure Belinda's still next door."

The sky was pale with high, thin fog, and a cool breeze whipped the strings of red, blue, green, and yellow pennants over the used-car lots into a frenzied fluttering. Through the congested, crawling Sunday traffic they cruised Ventura, Van Nuys, and Brand Boulevard in Glendale, stopping from time to time to compare prices, kick tires, and fight through the honeyed gabble of the salesmen to an approximation of facts. Steve was a little vague about what he wanted, and after two hours of tentative searching, they stopped, tired, for a snack at a pizza parlor which bore a sign saying, HAD A PIECE LATELY? on its roof.

"I don't know," Steve said, slumping in the cracked red leatherette booth and frowning at the menu. "It's between the mushrooms and the pepperoni. What're you having on yours?"

"Pepperoni," Beverly said. She took out her compact and surreptitiously checked her makeup while he was occupied. Lately she was paying more attention to how she looked.

"Hmmm. If I had that too, we could just get one big one instead of two small—Oh, I don't know."

The waitress, dark-haired and with an ill-tempered face, came up, pad and pencil at the ready.

"I'll have a small pizza with pepperoni," Beverly said promptly.

Steve hesitated, and the waitress, tapping pencil on pad, looked at him impatiently. "Well, I think I'll have the mushr—" he began hastily, catching her glance, and then stopped. Unexpectedly, he blushed. "No, I guess I'll have the pepperoni, too."

"A small one, sir?"

"Yes. No! Make it one big one as long as we're having the same thing. And coffee. You want coffee, Beverly?"

"Coffee."

When the waitress had sullenly departed, he stared out the window, twitching his mouth a little and frowning.

"What's the matter?"

"Oh, nothing." He did not look at her, he began drumming his fingers fretfully on the red Formica top.

Beverly smiled tenderly at him. He looked particularly boyish when he was annoyed. "Oh, come on. Tell me."

"It's nothing. It just always makes me so mad when I can't make up my mind like that."

"Well, it's probably just a habit you could get over if you tried," Beverly said reasonably. "Just make a decision—snap! like that—and stick to it. Don't allow yourself to hesitate."

"But that's just what I can't do," he said in exasperation. "I always hesitate, and the more I hesitate, the harder it gets until finally—well, I just don't think I'm going to be able to make my mind up at all. Ever. And it seems like the littler the decisions are, the harder it is to make them. Like what kind of pizza I want. That's what really gripes me."

"Illogical," Beverly agreed. "But I'm sure you could get over it if you put your mind to it."

"You just say that because it's easy for you," he said gloomily. He took his glasses off and wiped them, a gesture he habitually made when he was feeling uncertain.

The pizza came, and Beverly bit into hers, feeling

the crust scratch the bony ridge behind her upper front teeth. Eating pizza always gave her a sore mouth. "What did you think about the cars?" she said, to change the subject.

"Well, I guess it's between the Volkswagen convertible—remember that one with the white top?—and the Toyota station wagon we saw at the last place." He tore off a chunk of pizza, using his forefinger to disconnect the gluey, semiliquid cheese, and stuck it gloomily in his mouth. "I suppose I'll never be able to make up my mind about that either."

"Do you want to know what I think?"

He nodded, chewing.

"Get the station wagon. After all, I already have a convertible, and we are going to be married, and a station wagon would be a handy second car for camping and trips to the beach and things like that."

He thought it over. "When we get through here, let's go back and look at both of them again."

The salesman at the lot where the station wagon waited for adoption hailed them enthusiastically. "I was afraid you folks wouldn't make it. Right after you left, another party came in and almost bought it outright, but then he decided to have his wife take a look at it. He's gone home to get her now. I was hoping you folks would make it back. After all, you did see it first, and I'd hate to have you disappointed."

Beverly and Steve looked at each other. "I wish he had bought it outright," Steve said. "It would have solved my problem."

They stood there while the salesman did a reprise of his initial eulogy of the car. Beverly tapped her foot impatiently. It was getting cold, it was getting late, she was anxious to get home and put her roast in the oven. It was pork, and would take a long time.

"There's this other car," Steve was saying. "I want to take one more look at it before I made a decision."

"Okay," the saleman said reluctantly, shaking his

head, which was getting bald on top. "But hurry. The other party will be back any minute now. With his wife."

For the dozenth time that afternoon, they walked back to Steve's beatup Dodge and got in.

"Honestly," Beverly said. "The line those people give you. Does he really think we're going to believe somebody else is right on the point of buying it? What a tired old pitch."

"Maybe they are," Steve said. "The thing is, you can't be sure, so it makes you nervous anyway." Glumly he pulled out into the traffic.

After they had looked at the convertible one more time, he was still undecided.

"Look, you don't have to make up your mind today," Beverly said, hugging her arms and shivering.

"Yes, I do," he said stubbornly. "I'm sick of being indecisive. Damn, if I just knew . . . !" He walked around and around the car, staring at it as though it were Pandora's box.

"Steve," Beverly said at last. "Look at it this way. Isn't it much more sensible to get the station wagon? After all, the station wagon—"

"Sensible!" The word seemed unexpectedly to tap some hidden spring of resentment in him, and he turned on her. She was astonished to see real anger in his face. "I hate that word!"

At first she was too baffled to answer. "Well, there's nothing wrong with being sensible," she said finally. "It's just—"

"Yes, there is," he interrupted again, glaring at her. "For one thing, it's boring. It's just the most boring thing in the whole world."

"Well, it's a good thing everybody doesn't feel that way," she said chidingly. "If nobody was sensible, the world would be a pretty—"

"Beverly, for Pete's sake!" He fairly snapped the words. "Cut it out. You sound just like my mother."

Aghast, she stared at him. He had never spoken to

her so sharply before. He had never looked at her with such defiant resentment, almost hatred. "All right," she said quietly.

Nobody said a word on the way home. Beverly felt as though he had slapped her. What was wrong with him, anyway? Hadn't he asked her to come along and help him decide? She couldn't understand it. His anger seemed from some long-buried, unwholesome reservoir that had never been properly drained.

When they got to the house, she turned to him. "Steve, I'd rather you didn't stay for dinner. You seem to be in a bad mood, so why don't you just go home, and I'll see you at the office."

Sullenly, he scratched at a chipped spot on the steering wheel. "Okay," he said at last. He drove off without looking back.

Monday was dreary from start to finish. Steve avoided her, and she made no move for a reconciliation either, although it was hard for her to keep her mind on her work. Hurt as she was, she found herself becoming just a little annoyed with him, too. After all, was it her fault he had trouble making decisions? He didn't need to take it out on her just because not being able to make up his mind put him in a nasty mood.

That evening she made one of her biweekly visits to the hospital to see Miss Bigelow. As always when she walked into the bare, quiet, sterile-looking room, she felt a shock of horrified pity. Carol Bigelow was dying. She was drawn, she was wasted, she was as a winter apple, dryed-out as a tree from which the sap had gradually withdrawn. In six months, she had aged ten years.

Beverly took her hand, which lay motionless on the sheet. It was hot and dry, as though it had lain buried in desert sand.

Miss Bigelow opened her eyes. "Beverly?"

"How are you feeling tonight?"

"I feel like the devil." She smiled faintly.

WIVES AND LOVERS

"We certainly miss you at the office." Always, at some point in the conversation, Beverly said that.

Miss Bigelow's eyes brightened momentarily. "I got the card. The one everybody sighed." She motioned vaguely, without turning her head, in the direction of the bedside stand. The office card stood upright, half-opened, next to the plastic water carafe. Another card lay beside it. There were no flowers on the stand, or anywhere in the room.

Beverly brought a chair over to the bed, placing it so that Miss Bigelow could see her easily, and sat down.

"How's your fiance?" Miss Bigelow asked.

"Oh, just fine," Beverly said. She tried a smile, felt it hopelessly artificial, let it die, then looked at the floor.

"Come on, Beverly. Is something wrong?"

Beverly hesitated. She had not discussed her personal problems of the past few months with Miss Bigelow, feeling that the older woman already had an overwhelming burden to bear with her own illness. Now, as she found her former boss looking at her expectantly, almost eagerly, out of her weary, old bulldog face, she changed her mind. Perhaps it would be good for her, after all, cut off as she had been so long by the deadly, antiseptic monotony of hospital routine.

And so Beverly told her, not only about Steve, but about Bob. There seemed to be no connection, no resemblance even now between the two of them in her own mind, and yet, and yet . . . She remembered what Shirley had said, and was frightened.

"So I'm thinking maybe I should break our engagement," she concluded tentatively. "Only, then I'll be all alone."

"Well, Beverly, you're a strong woman. You can manage."

"I suppose I can," Beverly said, disconcerted. Somehow she had hoped Miss Bigelow would argue with her. "I guess I'll have to, if the only kind of man who's attracted to me is a weakling who'll end up resenting me. I don't want another marriage like that."

"You can manage." Miss Bigelow said again. "Learn to get along without needing anybody. Everybody's alone, sooner or later." Her eyes wandered over the bare, impersonal room. "You might as well face that right now, while you're young, and learn to live with it."

"How?" Beverly asked. The idea depressed her immeasurably.

"Think about your work. You're one of the lucky ones, having work to do. Love that, live for that. It's the only thing that never deserts you."

"Has it been enough for you?" Beverly asked hesitantly. "Have you been happy?"

"Happy as most people, I suppose."

"But doesn't everybody need people to love, too?"

"If you need love, there's always someone." Miss Bigelow paused. "I had you," she said gruffly. "And you have your daughter. Love never has to go to waste."

Beverly did not answer. Without a man, the future seemed bleak beyond words. Maybe when you got as old as Miss Bigelow, it didn't matter, but now . . .

"I suppose you think I don't know anything about all this," Miss Bigelow said.

Beverly looked at her.

"I suppose you think I'm just a tough old maid who never had a man. Well, I did, but not for very long." Miss Bigelow smoothed the sheet with her dry hand, making a faint, rasping sound. "Our marriage lasted just three years, but in that time I managed to turn my husband into a drunkard. I was too strong for him, too. I made him feel like a fool and a weakling, and when he started drinking, I even called him those things."

"And eventually you left him?"

Miss Bigelow nodded. "The situation got past tolerating, and I decided I could go it better alone.

Well, I did. I've done pretty well. I've had a full life, and I haven't missed being married very much. Maybe I'm one of those women who never should have married in the first place." She paused, struggling with memories, or perhaps she was only trying to get her breath. "I do regret one thing. I might have helped him if I'd shown a little more understanding, but I didn't. He died years ago in a sanitarium."

"You couldn't help it," Beverly said impulsively. "We can't be blamed for things we don't see, can we?"

"I don't know," Miss Bigelow said soberly. "I've thought about him a lot since I've been in here. More than I have in years."

"Maybe I'm one of those women who shouldn't be married either," Beverly said. Everything in her rebelled against the idea.

"Only you know the answer to that. Personally, I've always thought we were a lot alike. I suppose that's why I've been so fond of you."

Although she spoke bravely, Miss Bigelow's voice had weakened noticeably, and Beverly realized guiltily that they had probably been talking far too long for the older woman's waning strength.

She reached over and patted Miss Bigelow's hand. "I'd better go. You must be sick of listening to my troubles."

"You know better than that," Miss Bigelow whispered gruffly.

The two women smiled at each other affectionately.

"It's sure taken us a long time to get acquainted, hasn't it?" Miss Bigelow said unexpectedly.

"I was just thinking the same thing. All those years in the office, we just knew one side of each other, the professional side," Beverly said. "Now I feel like I know you as a whole person. And I guess you know me that way, too."

"Well, better late than never," Miss Bigelow said.

"Yes." Suddenly she felt that she was not going to be able to keep from crying. She patted Miss Bigelow's hand one more time. "Goodnight, Miss Bigelow."

"Carol."

"Goodnight, Carol. I'll come again soon." She turned and walked swiftly out of the room.

Outside, the May night was damp and foggy. As she swung onto the freeway for the long trip home, an unbearable loneliness weighed her down. What if Miss Bigelow was right, and she wasn't the type who should marry? It seemed so unreasonable. She wanted to love. She wanted to be loved. Why couldn't she find the right kind of man to live with? There must be a solution. She could not stand the prospect of being alone all her life. She wanted—yes, now that her career was established, she even wanted to have more children. It was wonderful to be loved and needed and looked up to.

All at once she wanted terribly to talk to Steve, who loved her, she knew, in spite of his moods and tantrums. The quarrel had been too silly. What difference did it make what car he got as long as he was happy?

She would call him the minute she got home, and make up. Maybe he would even come over. Checking the traffic flow in the side-view mirror, she pulled over into the left-land, fast lane and stepped a little harder, a little desperately, on the gas.

Twenty-nine

Leaving Tickets In Your Name At Box Office, she had wired Don. Please Come. Through the last three soul-wearing days of rehearsals, the conviction that he would not fail to appear buoyed Dana up, kept her going. Now it was opening night, and she had heard nothing from him. She was so tired, she felt drugged. Her head buzzed; her face in the ruthless, naked light of the dressing table mirror with its caged bulbs looked dispirited and ill. God willing, makeup would cover the bluish shadows, like fading bruises, under her eyes, the haggardness that made the normal, delicate hollows of her cheeks look cavernous and desperate. She uncapped the greasepaint, dotted it over her forehead, cheeks, and chin, and began to smooth it in.

He absolutely had to come. It would be the happy ending that would make the pain of their separation seem unimportant, worthwhile even, if it led to a better understanding in the future. They had met in a theater; wouldn't he remember that? He had come to Drama Arts with a friend who had a girl in the cast, and after the performance they had come back to the dressing rooms. He had stood there, blond and stolid and handsome, and looked at her and said nothing until finally she had asked, "Did you enjoy the show?" "I thought you were beautiful," he had said seriously. Involuntarily she had turned toward the long, narrow, green-framed mirror that ran horizontally along the wall, and they were reflected, looking like brother and sister, like a prince and princess of Arthur's Camelot which had been the source of all the romantic fantasies of her girlhood. Children began dreaming of love at a far earlier age than most adults suspected. She had started in the third grade, or was it the fourth, and now here she stood in medieval costume with a tall, pointed hat that had a veil floating from the peak. She looked at him and thought, A white, gentle knight. She had not known then, and she still did not understand, the mystic effect—could it perhaps have been born of narcissism?—that the circumstance of their looking alike had on her. She had only felt, looking at his fairness, at his classically Anglo-Saxon features, that here was her masculine counterpart. Did he feel the same thing toward her. Why had they fallen in love so suddenly?

"Five minutes, Miss Landon." No telegram had arrived from him, although she had one from her parents. That proved he was definitely coming. She rose from the dressing table and walked a few steps in the measured gait with just a hint of restrained lightness that was Sister Martinette's walk. Did he really love her? Oh, she was certain he did, and wasn't accepting people the way they were a part of loving them? That was how Dan felt about it. And they had created a child together. Didn't that bind them mystically, irrevocably together in his mind as it did in hers? If we do not spend our lives together, I still cannot have another child with someone else, she thought, and wondered at herself for feeling that way. Perhaps, again, it had something to do with the conviction that he was her male counterpart.

She frowned, hearing the restrained, urgent activity outside in the corridor that meant the show had started. She was not concentrated at all the way she should be. She should be Sister Martinette completely now, and Dana, all the Danas past and present, should be forgotten. Maybe if she sent word to the box office to see if the tickets had been picked up . . . She was, she realized, afraid to know. How could she perform, after the ordeal she had been through the past few days, if he were not there to see her? Panic rose in her. She was simply too exhausted to be single-minded and ready for work. Don, Jeremy, Dan wandered in and out of her consciousness like spirits to whom it was impossible to refuse entrance. How was she going to perform when she could not focus her mind any better than this?

Maybe a little more coffee. It was lukewarm, but she cupped her chilly hands around the damp mug and finished it anyway thinking, I wonder if I'll ever drink coffee again that doesn't taste like mud? How many gallons had she swallowed these last three days? They didn't seem like days at all, or nights, but only a long twilight blur during which she had forgotten she was in New York, forgotten who she was, forgotten everything but the penciled, crossed out script, the work light blaring feebly over the stage, the endless, echoing reiterations of lines that had so little meaning for her any more that they hardly seemed to be written in English. It was devastating. She felt as though in trespassing the boundaries of her own strength she had entered a nightmare realm over which she had no control. No, she had to will control over it. He was coming, wasn't he?

"Miss Landon, you're on."

When she was back in her dressing room after the first act, she had the disquieting sensation that the play had not yet begun. She looked for the yellow rectangle of a telegram on her dressing table. Surely if he weren't coming, he would have wired . . . ?

"Dana." Dan knocked, said her name, and came through the door almost simultaneously, and she heard the concern in his voice even before she saw his face.

"I'm not being very good, am I?" she said quietly.

"What's wrong?"

"I'm tired, and I'm worried about Don. I keep wondering if he's here, but I—"

"Hasn't he contacted you?"

She shook her head.

Dan hesitated. He looked very nice in evening clothes, she thought irrelevantly, a very distinguished lobster. "Then he wants to surprise you," he said. "Of course he's here. I checked myself just before curtain time, and the tickets have been picked up. I shouldn't tell you, but if it's upsetting you not knowing—"

"Thank God." Surprise, joy, and relief jolted through her like electricity. "Oh, and I was so bad just now!"

"Never mind. You have two more acts to redeem yourself."

She rubbed her forehead distractedly, forgetting the makeup. "Do you think I can? Dan, I don't know. I'm so exhausted I can't focus, I feel all diluted and dispersed—"

"Dana, my dear." He came over to her and gripped her shoulders strongly, and she was surprised, having seen him in complete defeat such a short time before, to feel the authority, the security he could project. "You can do it. You have the talent and the will. They won't desert you now."

"I'm so frightened—"

"For yourself?"

She nodded.

"Think about your audience," he said quietly. "You told me once—do you remember?—that acting was something you wanted to do not only for yourself, but for others. Think about what you want to communicate to them. It will help."

"Yes." Even as he spoke, a little of the fright seemed to leave her. Odd how one felt stronger doing for others; there was less ego involved, and more heart. How wise he was to remind her of that at this moment. Still, she was so desperately weary . . . In her need, she looked at him searchingly. It was vital to know if he were merely saying he believed in her. No, there was unmistakable conviction in his eyes. If he thinks I can do it, I can, she thought, and the warm, firm clasp of his hands on her shoulders seemed to be communicating the strength she lacked.

"All right," she said. "I'm ready."

How strange that he should pull her through a major emotional crisis when only a few days before, she had done the same thing for him. The thought of it warmed her so that as she turned back to the mirror, she felt restored, recharged. Now, for the benefit of all of them—Don, Dan, the audience—she could give the play what she wanted to give. She felt grateful, humble, filled with joy that she had a contribution to make, a gift, however modest, to give the world. Tears of thankfulness came into her eyes, and she had to blot them quickly with a cleansing tissue to keep them from streaking her makeup.

"My dear, you were wonderful. . . ." "Absolutely brilliant. . . ." How they talked, how they exclaimed. Smiling, she accepted the cheers, the compliments, the applause, still half dazed by the towering realization of what she could do. From time to time, while her hand was being shaken and her cheeks kissed, her eyes sought the door. How very like him to delay until everyone else had gone. He would be too proud to arrive with these enthusiastic strangers simply as one of a crowd. Dizzily, she allowed the long-sought, glittering waves of triumph to swirl around her and bear her up, and it was not until Dan came in, with something in his face which warned her, that she began to face things as they were.

"I'm sorry," he said when they were finally alone. "I didn't know what else to do but lie to you. I couldn't let you spoil your debut when you've sacrificed so much for it."

"It's all right," she said slowly. "Actually, I suppose I'm grateful. I should be, shouldn't I?"

"Of course, there's always a chance something happened at the last minute to prevent him," he said, watching her face. "He might even have missed the plane."

"No, Don doesn't miss planes. He never intended to come, and he didn't. And that's that." Without meeting her own eyes in the mirror, she dipped her fingers into the thick, transparent cleansing cream and began removing her makeup.

"What are you going to do now?"

"I don't know." She paused. "Yes, I do. I'm going to fulfill my contract here, and then I'm going back to California and ask him for a divorce."

Behind her, she heard him sigh. "I wish there was something I could do, or say, or . . ."

"I know, Dan, and it's dear of you, but there isn't. All these months while I've been hoping things would work out, I suppose I've known in the back of my mind that they wouldn't. And then I'd have to do this. Understand that, I mean *have* to, not *want* to. It's a strange thing," she went on, "and maybe it's going to sound monumentally selfish, but from now on nobody on earth—nobody—is going to keep me from acting. From doing what I do, and feeling what I felt on that stage tonight." Her mouth was trembling. To conceal it from him, she reached for a tissue and began wiping off the cream. When the stage makeup was off, she began applying her regular makeup. Behind her, Dan walked up and down, radiating sympathy and affection until it almost warmed her.

"As soon as you're ready, I'll take you home. I don't imagine you feel much like a party."

"I don't want to go home," she said quickly.

"Dana, my darling, a couple of hours ago you weren't even sure you had the strength to get through the performance."

"I don't care. I want to go to the party, and I want to go with you."

"Dana—"

"Don't you think we should share this evening?"

For a moment, he stared at her. "I'd like nothing better," he said then, softly.

When they were in the cab, she threw her head back unexpectedly and laughed, loudly, in a way she never did. It sounded hysterical, but even hysterical laughter was better than tears.

"Do you know how I feel, Dan?" she said. "As though we'd been through some terrible catastrophe together—a war or an earthquake—and survived!"

It was July, and so hot and humid the air seemed to have no oxygen in it, merely moisture. All the time she had lived in New York now had not prepared her for this, and Dana, on her way to the airport to take a plane to California, leaned forward and rolled down the cab window, feeling half-stifled.

"I'll be glad to get out of here for a few days. New York summers are even worse than everybody's always said they were."

Dan looked at her apprehensively. "You are coming back?"

She patted his hand reassuringly. "Of course. I have to, don't I? Didn't I sign a run-of-the-play contract in return for getting a week off?"

"Yes, but I mean permanently."

"I don't know, Dan," she said restlessly. It always hurt her not to be able to give him the answer he wanted.

"You know how much I love you, don't you?"

"I know," she said, frowning, "but you realize, don't you, that what makes it so hard for me to give you an answer is that I've changed so much and so quickly this past year? Not so much changed, I guess, as developed. I know myself better now than I did, but the discoveries I've made—I'm not used to them yet."

"You've never really told me what these discoveries are."

"I guess that's because they're difficult to describe."

She paused. Perhaps, since she was leaving, it would be easier to tell him now. "I think I know finally, why I have to act. Why it's more important to me than staying married to a man I once loved so much. It goes back to the time when I was the typical confused teen-ager—no, worse than typical. That's the time, tradi-tionally, when you struggle to find out who you are, but in my case the problem was complicated by my mother."

She smiled a little. "You'll have to meet her some-time, Dan. She still does what she did to me then. That dress isn't you, Dana, dear. No, that hair style isn't you. She was always positive of what I wasn't, but she never seemed to know what I was. And heaven knows, I didn't. I spent my adolescence trying on different personalities like clothes to see if I could find one that fit. I looked at people, and studied them, and thought, Is that what I'm like? Am I you? I copied one model after another with a kind of desperation that frightens me even now when I think about it. I suppose that's why I decided to major in drama in college. In every role I played, I was looking for myself, too."

"Was all this still going on when you met Don?"

"Yes. And looking back, I think what really attracted me to him, beneath the obvious things, was the fact that he had a definite image of what I was like. And I liked that image."

"Those are always the people we love, aren't they?" Dan murmured. "The ones who see us in a way that appeals to us."

"Well, there it was." She stared out at the jungle of buildings, bridges, skyscrapers, the river, pricked by lights out of the stifling darkness. "Don saw me as his lovely, adoring wife, as the devoted mother of his children. And I saw myself that way too, yes, I could see myself clearly in that role. In a way, I suppose I was grateful that someone saw me in any well-defined role. I thought I had found myself at last."

"But you hadn't."

"No. It wasn't until we'd been married several years and Jeremy had come along that I began to sense that Don's image of me was limited. There was a whole lot more of me, and it wasn't being used. Do you know what I now think had happened? All those years that I was studying other people, other roles, looking for myself, I was learning something. Acting."

They were nearing the airport.

"Wish me luck," she said suddenly. "Wish that I may have my child with me when I come back."

He kissed her on the forehead. "Wish me luck, too. Wish that I may have a wife someday when you come back."

All the way back to California, she brooded over what they had said to each other. Dan had made sense, but she was afraid to take the chance, afraid to love him for fear the same thing would happen, that someday she would have to sacrifice him as she had sacrificed Don to the career which she was certain was the most vital thing in the world to her. I shall always be alone, she told herself. It was the price a woman paid for inordinate ambition. She resented it, it made her feel sad and bitter, but she was going to have to accept it.

Thirty

It seemed strange to be back in her quiet, white living room again with the city stretched out, sparkling and murmuring in the summer night, beyond the big windows. She had chosen the slender teak furniture in this room, hung the pictures, vacuumed the carpet a hundred times and more, but in just a few months the city, the outside world, had drawn her so completely away that it seemed to her now almost as impersonal as a hotel room. It was hard to remember the kind of life she had here, hard to recall the existence bounded by Don and Jeremy, by cleaning the house, phoning a friend, giving a party. Or perhaps, she thought almost guiltily, some inner defense was keeping her from remembering. Superficially, she felt quite calm, but there was a knot in her stomach which ached with tension, and she could not seem to relax it.

Don cleared his throat, and she looked at him warily. If she could just keep her guard up for a little while longer, the worst would be over. Tonight she was determined to control herself as rigidly as he did, particularly when they reached the dangerous part of this discussion.

"What about Jeremy?" he said.

There it was. She drew her breath carefully. "I want him, Don. Even if I can't be the kind of wife you need, I can be the kind of mother he needs. You know that, don't you?"

He began to fill his pipe, calmly, deliberately. You

can't rattle me with that ploy any longer, she thought, watching him, but as the silence lengthened, she felt her heart begin to pound.

"I think you could be a good mother if that's what you were concentrating on," he said at last. "But you're not, are you? You're thinking about your career."

"Not to the point where I'd neglect my child. Surely you know I'd never do that."

"Do I? You've just left him without a mother for several months."

"But Don? That was your fault! I wanted—I planned—to take him to New York, and you stopped me!"

"Yes. And it seems to me that you really put motherhood first, as you say, that would have prevented you from leaving, too."

"But it was too late! I'd signed a contract! I was committed by then, I—" She could not finish.

"You had a choice to make, and you made it." He looked at her levelly. "If you want to leave me, I can't stop you. But I'm going to do everything in my power to prevent you from taking my son away, too. You might as well face that."

"You mean we're going to have one of those messy custody battles? Fighting over our child like two dogs over a bone? Is that what you want?"

"No, that isn't what I want. But I'll do it if I have to. As a matter of fact, I think I'd stand a pretty good chance in court if I told them you deserted him for four months. Even in California, the mother doesn't get the child if she's proven unfit."

For a moment, she almost hated him. Such anger engulfed her that she could have shouted like a fishwife, thrown a vase, done anything to shatter that stubborn imperturbability. He's made of stone, she thought, gripping the arms of her chair to control herself. Then, as she stared at him, all at once she understood, and pity dissolved anger.

"It won't work," she said quietly. "It didn't keep me home from New York, and it won't keep me home now. Don't use Jeremy as a weapon against me, Don, because you know how much I love him."

"Dana!" Astonished, she saw the pipe go down with a clatter and heard his voice break as he spoke her name. "I don't want to use any weapons against you! I love you!" He leaned forward in the chair, driving one fist into the palm of the other hand so violently that the cords in his neck stood out.

A wild, unlooked-for hope rose in her, and she caught her breath. "Do you?"

"Do I have to say it? Don't you know?"

"You were so cold, so abrupt the last few weeks before I left that I—"

"My God, Dana, I was afraid of losing you! Can't you understand that?" There was despair in his face, unmasked at last. "You're my wife! I need you to be my wife!"

"Oh, Don, I want to be! Truly I do, but—"

"Then forget it! Forget the career! You've proved yourself now, haven't you? Haven't you?"

She shut her eyes. "Do you love me?"

"Yes! I said that! Of course I do!"

"Then why can't you let me be myself?"

There was a long silence. Eventually, she opened her eyes. He was by the window overlooking the city, his back toward her, and although he stood quite still, she had the impression that he was crying. "Because I can't," he said.

"Why not?"

"I don't know." He turned, and his eyes were unnaturally bright. "I just can't."

"I wish I could change. But I know myself and my needs too well now to think it would work. Oh, please . . ." She did not try to keep the yearning out of her voice.

They looked at each other in desperation, each seeking reassurance, each unable to give it. We're really sinking now, Dana thought frantically. The illusionary moment of salvation was passing; could nothing be done?

"I can't change either." When he spoke, his voice once again had the flat, impersonal tone which was his habitual camouflage for emotion, "I don't want a part-time wife."

"No. I know. You want a wife who is willing to devote all of her time and attention to you. To please and please and go on pleasing." Suddenly she felt tired and bitter.

Beneath the plumpness of his jaw, a muscle twitched.

"I'm sorry, Don," she said wearily. "I'm sorry you didn't know what kind of woman you were marrying. But then, how could you when I didn't know myself? Find yourself an Eve."

"Eve?"

"Remember the dinner party we had here the night I decided to go back to work? I've thought about it so many times. Vivian said there were two kinds of women—Eves and Liliths. The Eves are the ones who are willing to live for and through a man. That's what you need, Don. It takes a special kind of man to be married to Lilith. We're the difficult ones."

"Vivian's dead. Did you know that?"

"No!" She stared at him, too shocked to believe. "What happened?"

"She killed herself. In Mexico."

"Oh, my God." She felt herself go weak. "Why?"

"I don't know. I thought Beverly wrote you about it. She called and told me."

"I never heard from her."

"I thought she'd told you. Now that you mention it, I remember that story Vivian told." He puffed on the pipe. "Didn't she say God destroyed Lilith because she didn't work out?"

"Yes," Dana said in a low voice. "That's what she said."

The pipe would not stay lit. Snapping open the lighter, he tilted the flame into the bowl. With anguish, she saw that it shook in his steadying hand. "You haven't changed my intentions about Jeremy," he said. "I need my son. Do you want me to help you find an attorney? I already have one."

"I can manage. Thanks." An impulse she could barely resist made her want to walk, to run even, away from this man, this room, this period of her life. Tears stung her eyes, but she forced them back. This last time, at least, she would match his skill at withdrawal. After all, she was an actress, wasn't she?

She picked up the small bowl of dried desert flowers from the table beside her and blew the dust off. "What are we going to do about the house?" she said, when she could speak.

Dana and Beverly had lunch together the day that Dana saw an attorney about the divorce. They ate at Columbo's, always their meeting place for special occasions. The last time they had come here was for Vivian's birthday.

"It seems funny not to have her with us, doesn't it?" Beverly said in her direct way. She took out a cigarette, and a waiter appeared to light it for her.

"What happened? Did you ever find out?"

"I didn't even hear about it until I called the paper one day to ask her to have lunch. They told me she'd killed herself and turned me over to the city editor for details. Lou Adams, I think his name is."

"Yes, Adams," Dana said, remembering. "What did he tell you?"

"Not much. Just that she'd been overworking and decided to take her vacation early and go to Mexico. Then just a day or two after she got there . . ." She stopped. "I was going to write and tell you, but I'd been having so much trouble myself, and I know you have, that I just didn't have the heart."

The waiter brought their drinks, and they sipped

them without speaking. At the other tables in the cool, elegant room, silk-suited businessmen conferred, and society women laughed and chattered in their flowered dresses and beach-club tans.

"I never really understood Vivian, I guess," Beverly said. "She usually seemed so happy and lively, but it was kind of feverish sometimes. You know. All that dating."

"I know. I haven't understood her very well myself the past few years."

"Do you think it was because of Sid? She never said very much about that."

"Sid? Maybe. Or somebody. Oh, that's impossible. She couldn't still be thinking about Joe after all these years."

"What's going to happen to us, do you think?"

"I have Jeremy, and you have Belinda."

"Is that enough?" There were tears in Beverly's eyes now, and she got out a handkerchief and dabbed at them surreptitiously.

"Do you miss Bob so much?" Dana asked wonderingly.

Beverly nodded. She seemed unable to speak.

"But I thought—I honestly thought, and I know you did, too—that you'd be better off without him."

"I know. That's what I did think." She blew her nose. "I thought I was smarter than he was, and stronger, and more efficient. And I am. But I still need him. Anyway, I need somebody."

"You have a wonderful job, you have Belinda—"

"It isn't enough. Oh, Dana, you're going to find out it isn't enough. We all thought we were career women first and women second, but it's the other way around."

"But you weren't happy with Bob! I watched you for years, and you weren't happy with him. Sometimes I could have hit him myself for the way he carried on with other girls right under your nose. Vivian, for instance."

"I know. He was probably punishing me."

"Punishing you?"

"For not letting him stand on his own two feet."

"But you were always trying to get him to take responsibility, and he never would! You said so yourself!"

"That was later. After Belinda came along. If I'd started in the beginning when we were first married encouraging him to take over little by little, it might have worked. Anyway, I didn't. I got too much satisfaction out of running things myself. So he began resenting me, and then after Belinda arrived, I began to detest him for being weak, and the whole mess got worse and worse until . . ." Emotion made her break off.

"Beverly, have you told Bob all this?"

She shook her head. "I didn't get it figured out until after we were divorced, and I started dating somebody just like him. I even got engaged, would you believe it?"

"I hadn't heard."

Beverly told her about Steve Chapman. "He's a nice boy, but I must have been crazy to consider marrying him. Which everybody tried to tell me in one way or another. My sister Shirley. Miss Bigelow. Even when he started resenting me, I didn't catch on. But you know what finally happened? My other sister came over one Sunday afternoon—Sherry, the beautiful one—and Steve was there, and he and Belinda went out in the back yard while Sherry and I talked. Belinda was teaching him to play hopscotch. I was telling Sherry about wanting to raise another family, and all of a sudden, she laughed and said, 'God, can you really see him as the father of your children?' She laughed. And when I looked out the window, I could see exactly what she meant. Honestly, Belinda is more mature in a lot of ways than Steve, and suddenly I realized that he was just somebody else who needed a mother, and I broke it off." She paused. "Isn't it funny how blind you can be where your relationships with other people are concerned? Anyway, ever since I broke up with Steve, I've been thinking about Bob. Stupid, isn't it?"

"The divorce isn't final yet, is it?"

"What difference does that make. It's all over."

"But maybe he misses you, too. Maybe now that you understand the situation better, you could make a go of it."

"Dana, it's too late." Beverly hesitated. "He's found somebody else."

"That's quick. Rebound?"

"Who knows?"

"I wonder what she's like?"

"As a matter of fact, I know. He brought her by the house just last Sunday when he came to see Belinda." Beverly paused, and her eyes were very bright. "She's nothing like me."

"I see."

They finished their drinks without saying anything more, while Dana searched her mind for something optimistic to cheer her friend. "Of course, you can always marry some other type of man," she said at last.

Beverly shook her head. "Not till I've solved one other problem. Me. It wasn't until I finally understood Bob that I began to see that my own emotional needs were just as contradictory as his. The big sister, the mother hen in me wants a man weak enough to need a lot of love and protection and guidance. At the same time, the wife in me wants a man to care for and protect her. I guess the second side of me didn't really develop until after Belinda was born. That's when I started resenting Bob for not being a man. But you can't have a man and a little boy in the same package, can you? No. So until I can make up my mind which I want, I'm staying single. Not that I can't see the healthy choice," she went on, and Dana thought that she had never seen her look so unhappy. "But before I can honestly make it, I'm going to have to change a lot. And I'm not sure I can, Dana."

"You can if you really want to," Dana said in a rush of sympathy. "And listen. Why don't you at least call and talk to Bob?"

Beverly laughed shakily and put away her handkerchief. "What about you? Here you are talking me out of a divorce and getting one yourself."

Dana frowned. "The opposite thing happened with my marriage. Understanding myself better made me see how impossible it was to continue. It works that way too sometimes."

"Then find somebody else. Oh, Dana, I know you're getting to be a big success and all that, but you'll find out it isn't enough. It may be now, but when you get older, it's a different thing. I watched Miss Bigelow, all alone and dying, and even though she talked about her life with great bravery, I knew I didn't want to end up like that. All alone."

"How is Miss Bigelow?"

"She's gone. Practically the last conversation we had, she gave me some advice about living alone. But I don't want to take it unless I have to. And I want you to promise me you'll look for a man to love and keep you."

"I think I've already found one," Dana said slowly.

"Really?" Beverly brightened immediately with interest. "Well. Don't just sit there. Tell Old Aunt Bev all about it."

Dana told her. As she talked, she realized how close she felt to Dan after only six months. He might have been her childhood sweetheart, her lifelong friend, so intimately were they able to discuss the things that mattered most to them, so intimately were they able to discuss the things that mattered most to them, to sense each other's thoughts and feelings. There was an instinctive rapport between them, stronger and deeper than the bond produced by years of friendship between persons who did not share this intuitive understanding. It was rare, she acknowledged to herself, much rarer than the romantic passion she had felt for Don. She and Dan had helped each other to realize themselves, and yet . . .

When she had finished, Beverly looked at her intently. "This Dan. Does he know your career comes first?"

"Yes, he knows."

"And he doesn't mind?"

Dana smiled a little. "I think maybe he likes it."

"Then marry him, Dana. For heaven's sake, marry him and be a woman. You know what happens to women who live without men, who live only for their careers. You've seen them. They stop being female. They get brittle voices and mean little eyes and bludgeon-shaped personalities. They get withered and hard, no matter how successful they are. You don't want to turn into one of those, do you?"

"No," Dana said slowly, "but I don't want to hurt Dan, or anybody else, the way I've hurt Don. And I think that no matter what he says, a man always expects to be put first in the life of the woman he marries. It's been going on for too many centuries to be altered overnight. No, I'm the one who must stay single."

Beverly made a gesture of impatience. "Dana, you're not the type. If I'm meant to be married then you certainly are. You don't know yourself as well as you think you do if you imagine that you're going to be a content spinster from the age of thirty on."

"It's not a matter of being content. I'm not imagining I'll be fulfilled in every way. What I said was, I will not hurt another man, and how can I avoid it when I can never put him first in my life?"

"Can't you?" Beverly asked, suddenly quizzical. "I thought you just did."

"Whatever are you talking about?"

"In New York. When Dan was on that binge. Didn't you say you nearly wrecked your own opening by staying up with him three days and nights? Didn't you knock yourself out because he needed you?"

A strange expression came over Dana's face. "I never even thought about it," she murmured.

"You mean you did it instinctively? You didn't weigh the odds? You didn't coldly calculate just how much time you could give him without losing so much sleep you couldn't perform?"

"No," Dana said softly. She felt genuinely confused. "He needed me, and it never occurred to me to do anything but stay with him until he stopped needing me. I didn't even realize how tired I was getting until it was all over, and then I was scared to death I wouldn't get through opening night."

"But while it was going on, you didn't think about that. And if Jeremy were terribly sick, would you leave him to go off and stand on a stage somewhere?"

"Don't be silly."

"Precisely," Beverly said triumphantly. "Oh, you're not as cold-blooded as you think you are, my girl. The right man can still make demands on you."

"Demands," Dana said. Bemused though she was, the word caught her attention. "Demands? No, that Dan would never do."

When they went outside, it was hot and dry and smoggy. The air was acrid, hazy with exhaust fumes, and the traffic thundered along Wilshire toward downtown, toward the beach, under the tall necks of the palm trees and the broad glass sides of the skyscrapers.

"Home, sweet home," Dana said, getting out her dark glasses. "My eyes are smarting already."

"Are you coming back after the show closes?"

"I don't know. Maybe—well, I don't know yet for sure—but that might have something to do with Dan's plans. I don't know, Beverly. I still have a lot of things to settle in my own mind. I'm not even sure I love him, what I feel for him is so different than what I felt for Don, but maybe . . ."

"Good girl," Beverly said. She put her arm around

Dana's waist and gave her a quick hug. "Till we meet again. I wish you all the success in the world. And happiness. Particularly happiness."

"You, too," Dana said. "I'll phone you when I'm back in town."

She watched Beverly get into her car and guide it efficiently into the noisy, unending stream of traffic. Her profile, as she passed, looked as firm and determined as ever, but there had been a softness about her at lunch that Dana had never noticed before. Maybe after we prove ourselves, we have more time to be feminine, she thought.

Slowly, with her mind not unpleasantly on the future, she began to stroll along Wilshire Boulevard.

Her loneliness vanished. And with wistful thoughts of Camelot and living happily ever after, Dana's lips curved into a smile.

FOR THE FINEST IN CONTEMPORARY WOMEN'S FICTION, FOLLOW LEISURE'S LEAD

2310-5	**PATTERNS**	$3.95 US, $4.50 Can
2304-0	**VENTURES**	$3.50 US, $3.95 Can
2291-5	**GIVERS AND TAKERS**	$3.25 US, $3.75 Can
2279-6	**MARGUERITE TANNER**	3.50 US, 3.95 Can
2268-0	**OPTIONS**	$3.75 US, $4.50 Can
2257-5	**TO LOVE A STRANGER**	$3.75 US, $4.50 Can
2250-8	**FRAGMENTS**	$3.25
2249-4	**THE LOVING SEASON**	$3.50
2230-3	**A PROMISE BROKEN**	$3.25
2227-3	**THE HEART FORGIVES**	$3.75 US, $4.50 Can
2217-6	**THE GLITTER GAME**	$3.75 US, $4.50 Can
2207-9	**PARTINGS**	$3.50 US, $4.25 Can
2196-x	**THE LOVE ARENA**	$3.75 US, $4.50 Can
2155-2	**TOMORROW AND FOREVER**	$2.75
2143-9	**AMERICAN BEAUTY**	$3.50 US, $3.95 Can